Danielle Ackley-McPhail

Today's Promise

Book Three in the Eternal Cycle Series

Pennsville, NJ

PUBLISHED BY
Paper Phoenix Press
A division of eSpec Books
PO Box 242
Pennsville, NJ 08070
www.especbooks.com

ISBN: 978-1-942990-59-8
ISBN (ebook): 978-1-942990-60-4

Originally published by Dark Quest Books (2012).

Interior Design: Danielle McPhail
www.Sidhenadaire.com

Interior Art: vector musical composition ©BuketGvozdey
http://www.shutterstock.com

Cover Art: L.W. Perkins and Christina Yoder
Cover Design: Christina Yoder

Copyediting: Wrenn Simms and Greg Schauer

PRAISE FOR THE ETERNAL CYCLE SERIES

ON YESTERDAY'S DREAMS

[Danielle Ackley-McPhail] certainly seems to know
her Celtic mythology…a solid story.
— Piers Anthony, bestselling author of the *Xanth* series

A powerful, poignant tale…a writer of talent, imagination,
and superb storytelling ability. — The Midwest Book Review

Yesterday's Dreams is an interesting mix of Celtic myth, women's
empowerment literature, and urban fantasy…The story, though set in a
modern period, is imbued with all the details and richness
that readers expect from Celtic lore.
— John Ottinger III, Grasping For The Wind Reviews

This novel will appeal to fans of Charles DeLint with its urban approach
to Irish mythology. At times I was mesmerized while at other times…
I had to get up and turn the lights on… — Bitten By Books Reviews

ON TOMORROW'S MEMORIES

The artist in me itches to have a crack at some of the vivid images that
are filling my brain after reading this book. I am eagerly awaiting another
installment. Please make it soon! — Helen Fleischer, artist

Danielle Ackley-McPhail seems to get better with every book…I didn't
want [*Tomorrow's Memories*] to end, and I'm looking forward to reading
the third novel of the trilogy. — Douglas Cobb, BookspotCentral

ON TODAY'S PROMISE

A solid end to the trilogy, well-paced and with a satisfying ending.
Everything came together nicely.
— Keith R.A. DeCandido, author of *Dragon Precinct*

Ackley-McPhail delivers the goods once again in the final book of
her Eternal Cycle series. [*Today's Promise*] is a must-read.
— Jan Nerenberg, Right, Write, and Word-Wright

Other titles by
Danielle Ackley-McPhail

THE ETERNAL CYCLE SERIES
Yesterday's Dreams
Tomorrow's Memories

THE ETERNAL WANDERINGS SERIES
Eternal Wanderings

THE BAD-ASS FAERIE TALE SERIES
The Halfling's Court
The Redcap's Queen

Baba Ali and the Clockwork Djinn
(with Day Al-Mohamed)

The Literary Handyman
The Literary Handyman: Build-A-Book-Workshop

The Ginger KICK! Cookbook

SHORT FICTION
A Legacy of Stars
Transcendence
Consigned to the Sea
Flash in the Can
The Die Is Cast
(with Mike McPhail)

Dedicated to my friend, Bill Hicks (a k.a. NOVLShadow),
and the rest of the crew formerly of the Alphabet Soup
Board on AOL's Amazing Instant Novelist, without
whom this book and series would never have been
conceived, let alone finished.

Also In Loving Memory
of my most rabid fan, Badger.

A Note of Thanks

This would not be the book it is today without the selfless, dedicated efforts of Helen "Halla" Fleischer, David Goldstein, Jeffrey Lyman, Keith DeCandido, and my husband, Mike McPhail. All sacrificed their time and effort to the cause.

I have the best friends in the world!

Thank you,
Danielle

PRELUDE

THE HOPE AND DREAD ON BARBARA'S FACE WAS HEART-WRENCHING TO BEHOLD.
Conall O'Keefe entered the box-strewn kitchen looking for his wife.
Instead, he found his daughter-in-law clutching the countertop on either side
of the sink. Her thin cotton shirt clung to her, and she was as covered in dirt as
the worn linoleum beneath her feet. Perhaps it was the moonlight streaming in
the window, or perhaps merely the strain of a day much longer than any of
them had anticipated, but poor Barbara looked paler than skimmed milk. A
single teardrop mingled with the dirt and the sweat beaded upon her face.

"Oh, darlin', a bit much for ye, is it?" he asked softly. "Ready to call it a
night?"

Her eyes drifted closed, and her head fell back. Conall did not miss the
reflexive gulp that rippled across her outstretched throat. *Oh, damn!* Within
seconds Barbara started trembling, and it occurred to Conall that what he'd
happened upon was more than utter exhaustion.

"Paddy! Paddy, get yer arse in here!" Conall bellowed as he quickly crossed
the room to Barbara's side. Before he reached her, she jerked with a growing
spasm until she bent over the sink and heaved. The sickly sweet smell of bile
drifted toward him. He hurried forward to catch his son's wife as her knees
buckled, and she lost her grip on the Formica countertop.

"Sweet Lord! Patrick! Where are ye?! Moira?" He cradled Barbara against
his chest with one arm and reached for the spigot with the other. As he opened
the tap, a spurt of rusty water poured from the rarely used pipes before the
flow ran clear, rinsing the bile and sick down the drain.

Grabbing at the roll of paper towels on the counter he gave a quick, sharp
jerk to tear off a sheet without the whole of it unwinding. Wetting it in the
running water, he gently wiped off Barbara's face. He tossed the soiled towel
aside and turned off the water, before he called out again, "Can I get a hand
down here, or na? Barbara's ill."

He could hear the others hurry across the floor upstairs, apparently bumping into packing crates and stumbling over items already removed from
the boxes. Satisfied they would be there in a moment, Conall peered around the

kitchen. He needed to sit down, but cartons covered every surface, including the mismatched, straight-backed chairs he and Moira had given the children until they could get a kitchen set of their own. A glance in the open box on the closest chair confirmed that it held nothing more than kitchen towels and other linens. A quick shove with his foot and the box hit the floor, freeing up the seat. Conall nudged the chair around until he could settle into it without disturbing his daughter-in-law. He focused all his attention on Barbara, seating her more securely in his lap and pushing back the sweat-darkened blonde curls from her face. He did not miss the quick flutter of her eyes or her quavering breath, evidence she was conscious, though she remained limp in his arms. And then he noticed something else more disturbing.

"Come now, Bobbi-lass, look at me," he murmured gently. "How long have ye been hiding this?"

Tears streamed from beneath her lowered eyelids, and her delicate hand came up to clutch the front of his green cardigan as she buried her face against his shoulder. He heard a gasp from across the room. A moment later, his son knelt beside him, panic glistening in his deep brown eyes. Conall's wife, Moira, stood quietly in the doorway, her sturdy frame leaning against the jamb out of necessity, as there was no more room in the kitchen. Something in her gaze told him that she already suspected what he had just discovered: Barbara was again with child.

The hope and dread now made complete sense.

Barbara O'Keefe hunched on her own chair at the care-worn table, trying to pretend that three sets of eyes weren't riveted on her. She didn't like being the center of such intense scrutiny. This was why she had kept her suspicions to herself. The heartache was bad enough, endured so many times before, without their fears amplifying her own.

This was not her first pregnancy; it was her fourth. In two years…and she had yet to give Patrick O'Keefe a child. Each of her previous pregnancies had been difficult, all ending in miscarriages. She was not supposed to have gotten pregnant again so soon…if ever, at all. Dr. Cohen cautioned that another miscarriage might kill her.

"Why, Bobbi?" her husband spoke in hushed, fearful tones. "Why didn't ye take the wee pills the doctor gave ye?"

Why indeed? She was not so good a Catholic that the Church's prohibition against birth control caused an issue for her. That element of matters had been more of an issue for Patrick himself. Then the doctor had outlined the risks of another pregnancy. Her husband's objections had quickly fallen away.

The medication was not a problem. In fact, in the short time she had taken it, she experienced none of the adverse side effects her doctor warned were possible. No, she had simply woken one day and reached for her packet, only to find herself overwhelmed by a sensation of wrongness and frustration. A sensation that she stood in the way of something meant to be. From that point forward, she could not bring herself to take the pills. But she had not been able to confess so to her husband.

"I don't know," she whispered. Guilt crept over her, and she could not look any of them in the eye.

"Ye don' know? Ye don' know!?" Patrick's voice cracked, and Barbara could feel fresh tears slide down her cheeks. He was frightened, not angry, and that alone kept her from breaking down completely. Her in-laws said nothing, though she knew they too questioned the wisdom of her actions.

"I'm sorry," she said. "I'm so sorry…" No other words would come, and these were less than adequate. Her gaze darted up to look into Patrick's face. He was barely twenty-four. Right now, he looked at least ten years older, his face gaunt with worry, and his eyes burning with fear.

What had she done?

Conall woke to the familiar sound of retching coming from the bathroom down the hall. His heart went out to his daughter-in-law as he lay beside his wife, staring at the still-unfamiliar walls of their room. They had not intended to move into their son's new home, but given Barbara's unexpected condition, they had all had agreed it would be for the best. Two months had passed since that fateful night of discovery. It had not been easy on any of them since. The elder O'Keefes helped their son shoulder the burden of settling in and running the new household, but Barbara grew increasingly wan, and her morning sickness lasted nearly all day.

Conall suspected that, by this point, tension and fear more than anything else caused Barbara's rough term, but they were long past the time of re-assuring words. The first failed pregnancy had been taken in stride, but by the second miscarriage, late in the fifth month, the sense of doom had begun to take hold. The third pregnancy had not gone for even two months. Now they all fought to hold onto hope.

"We hardly need bother with an alarm, now, do we?" Conall's harmless jest earned him a smack from his still-sleepy wife. He knew the comment had been in poor taste, but he scarcely knew how else to vent his frustration, other than the occasional snarky remark. There was no doubt their presence made a significant difference but was it enough? The fear of losing another grandchild was pure, protracted hell, yet it was nothing compared to the torment faced by Patrick and Barbara. What Conall wouldn't give to magically make things right…but no…he had already made a trip down to Yesterday's Dreams, the pawnshop owned by Maggie McCormick, only to be told there was nothing more she could do. Even had her skill lay within the realm of healing, which it did not, every bit of magic they had tried to safeguard the two previous pregnancies had failed. No, there would be no instant fix; only their prayers and diligence could make a difference now.

Again, the sound of retching and Conall glanced over at the little travel clock across the room; Patrick was long gone on his way to work. It was time for them to offer what comfort they could.

He looked at Moira. "Ye know I don't mean a thing by it. Hand me the crackers an' I'll go see to her."

Barbara heard Conall humming in the hallway, the sound joyous and lively. It woke her to a hunger she hadn't realized was there. He used to bring out his violin nightly, but for months they had all been too tired for such things. She missed it fiercely.

"Da?" Even to her own ears, the call was weak.

Patrick's father leaned into the doorway, his expression kind and patient, his arms filled with a basket of her dirty laundry that he must be carrying downstairs for Mathair. Barbara was overcome with guilt. At a time when they should be planning retirement cruises and shopping for that sailboat they had always wanted, her in-laws were instead taking over all the duties she no longer had the energy to do. He and Mathair O'Keefe were working so hard because she had selfishly allowed herself to get pregnant. And now she would add to this loving man's burden, and for what? Because she was music-starved and lonely…

"What is it, Bobbi-lass?"

She wanted to tell him never mind…that she was sorry to have interrupted, but she couldn't. Tears made her eyes glisten as she pressed her lips tightly closed against one of the uncontrollable emotional tempests that tore at her with increasing frequency.

Conall made soothing sounds and set his basket down, moving to sit beside her on the edge of the bed. With a gentle touch, he wiped away an escaped teardrop. "Come now…ye've had yer shower already, have ye na?"

Barbara laughed and twined her fingers with his as he reached down and took up her hand. She gave a little squeeze and leaned against his shoulder. "Would you play for me, Da?"

"Why, what a marvelous idea, Bobbi-lass!" His voice tender and loving as he released her hand and instead slipped his arm around her, giving her a gentle hug. "Shall I play for ye here, or do ye feel a mite adventurous? The day's glorious, and Mathair has taken her lunch in the garden. Let's just get you settled with her. Then I'll fetch Quicksilver."

Without waiting for an answer, he scooped Barbara up. He had her established on the padded lounger in the backyard before she knew what happened. Basking in the warmth of the sun, she could not protest. Barbara relaxed, embraced by a sense of pervading peace, as Conall bounded back into the house to fetch his fiddle, Quicksilver. Moira, her mother-in-law, followed him into the kitchen, emerging almost immediately with a second lunch plate, setting it beside Barbara with a contented smile. Conall quickly returned with the instrument. He began to play, kicking off an afternoon of laughing and singing in the sunshine.

For the first time in months, Barbara's fear lost some of its hold on her.

The release proved a balm to her soul as she felt energy flow into her on the melody, revitalizing every cell. Greedily she reached out to claim the unfamiliar strength…only to find her way blocked.

She would have nothing of that. Her spirit pushed and shoved until the barrier gave way, allowing her to claim that sense of power and potential she sensed around her, leaving her with the conviction that her future and that of her unborn child were no longer in doubt.

If her in-laws wondered at the serene smile gracing her lips, they did not question it aloud; they were too intent on watching as she lifted the sandwich from the table beside her, and with obvious enjoyment, devoured it.

Life was good, and Barbara marveled at her renewed sense of well-being as the music continued to weave its loving spell about her.

Conall was hard-pressed to understand what had begun that day. He well knew the level of his own mage talent, but what he could accomplish with his meager skill could hardly account for what he watched take place before him. He could feel a stirring in the currents surrounding the small gathering. Nothing malicious or harmful, but definitely bearing the aura of the fae. More: it was connected in some way to Quicksilver.

He nearly stopped playing. He had always known of the fiddle's nature, but what he sensed today was much more powerful than anything he'd noted in the past. It was as if some elemental force had slumbered unnoticed, deep in the grain of the instrument. That force woke now and with it a maelstrom of emotions: curiosity, sorrow, and an intense feeling of fierce, somehow maternal, love. The last spread with each note. He felt it wrap fleetingly about his own shoulders, emanating contentment and pride before moving on. The awareness barely brushed against Moira, showing only mild interest and acceptance, before enfolding Barbara in a shimmering, attentive envelope. The emotions spiked, darkening and deepening too quickly for him to gauge them. Barbara didn't seem to notice, but Conall took no chances. He didn't sense any malevolence, but that didn't mean there was no danger.

Conall O'Keefe mustered his ability and moved to warn off the magical presence he'd unleashed. Focusing his will through his music, he slipped his awareness past the fae force, interposing himself between it and Barbara. His fiddle transitioned into a battle anthem, leaving behind the softer melody of moments ago.

With a gentleness he would not have expected, the fae emanation reached out tendrils to extract him, gently removing the obstacle to its objective. Even now, he could sense no malice, but it was fae and foreign, and he did not understand. Conall dug in his psychic heels and leaned back into his position, doing battle with his bow…only to have an equally determined awareness reach out to shove him away…from Barbara behind him. Confused and not a little disgruntled, Conall struggled to hold his ground, but even without Barbara's unexpected efforts on behalf of the intruder, Conall could not withstand the fae. His mage skills dimmed, if only momentarily, almost taking his vision with them.

As he conceded, something astounding happened: the force he had foolhardily pitted himself against engulfed him and just as quickly released him. His bow faltered on the strings, and he trembled in the wake of the experience, but no longer did he doubt the benevolence of this entity; every whiff of energy he had expended in attempting to protect Barbara had been categorically replaced. So deep and all-encompassing had that brief connection been, that he would ever recognize, on an intimate level, the angelic being who had subdued him. He had no name for her, but he no longer questioned her intent: to love and protect his own family. The intensity of that love nearly floored him as he thought of the coming child.

His fae opponent seized upon his thoughts and once again reached for Barbara. Surprisingly, his daughter-in-law reached back, somehow bridging the gap between her ungifted self and the emanation.

Astounded, Conall watched with his second sight as the entity residing in Quicksilver galvanized and strengthened Barbara in every way possible. Gone were the doubts, gone were the fears, gone were the debilitating bouts of nausea and the air of frailty. The change was abrupt and astounding. He no longer had any doubts that in less than two months he would cradle his healthy grandchild.

A scream shattered the peaceful evening. Conall's heart took off like a trip hammer as he ran panicked out of the basement and up the stairs, the broken chair he'd been fixing completely forgotten. The kitchen stood empty, as did the living room, and he had cause to curse the fact that Moira had finally broken down and gone grocery shopping despite her fear of being away so close to Barbara's time. Even worse, Patrick had gone to work and wasn't due home for another two hours.

"Bobbi-lass…" Conall struggled to keep his voice calm and soothing as he took the stairs to the second floor two at a time. "Where are ye, love?" Another cry rang out, this time clearly coming from the upstairs bathroom. "Dear Lord…" he murmured, then louder: "I'm comin', Barbara!" He wanted to curse as he threw himself at the door, only to find it locked. "Unlock the door, sweetheart. Ye have to let me in."

"I c-can't get up!"

Damn! What had gone wrong? Conall wondered as he considered how to get the door open. Things had been going so well; Barbara was healthy and happy, with no further signs of the difficulties that had plagued her previous pregnancies. Now his past fears rallied from wherever they'd been hiding all these months. What was going on beyond this blasted door? If there was a key, no one knew where it was, and he couldn't break through it for fear of hurting Barbara, but maybe he could pop the lock; it was the safety kind with a small hole in the center to allow just that. He had to find something that would reach in far enough to trip the tumblers. A wire hanger should do it if he could find one. "Okay, love, I'll be right back an' see if I can't help ye up, ye just sit tight."

She didn't answer. Frantic, he ran into his bedroom and yanked open the closet door. All he found were those cheap, thick plastic hangers that used to be soda bottles in a past life. Blasted recycling!

What else? What else could he use? He looked around the room and spied Moira's bag of knitting. All the needles poking out were thick and nubby, but Conall seemed to remember a rather thin, fine one he'd had the misfortune to sit on some time ago. Pawing through her bag, he found one. Without a second thought, he slid off Moira's stitches and ran back to the bathroom door, praying that the needle was thin enough.

In seconds he had the door unlocked. Carefully he pushed it open, fearful that Barbara might be in the way. She wasn't, but he didn't know whether or not to be grateful. The tub was behind the door. In the mirror's reflection, he could see the shower curtain half pulled down. He struggled not to moan. Whatever happened, he could not add to the fear she must be feeling, not if he wanted to help her.

"Da!" Barbara cried out as he moved further into the room. He could hear the terror in her voice and her breathing was erratic.

"Shhh…shhh…I'm here, Bobbi, I'm here." He closed the door behind him so he could reach her. The sight that met his eyes drained the color from his face; Barbara lay in the tub, her face pale and clammy and her distended belly rippling all too regularly. A trickle of blood crept down the side of her face and her pale blue eyes were dazed. Only the curtain protected her modesty. "Dear *Jea*-us! Barbara, what happened?"

"I don't know…I don't know!" Barbara sobbed weakly, and he could see the terror return to her eyes for the first time in months.

Dear God…let everything be okay. He doubted any of them would ever be the same if things went badly. Conall pushed the thought away as he reached over and turned off the shower, noting as he did so that his daughter-in-law had remembered to use the traction mat. Not a slip, then. Most likely, dizziness or the onset of her obvious contractions had caused her fall. He reached out with the wet washcloth he found lying in the tub and gently wiped the blood from her face. "Are ye hurt anywhere else?"

Barbara shook her head but said nothing as another contraction took her. She hissed and clutched at her belly, her eyes pleading. To himself, Conall cursed. The contractions were coming too quickly…there was little chance of getting her to a hospital in time to deliver with all the conveniences and safeguards of modern medicine. In fact, if he didn't hurry, his grandchild would be born in a worn-out cast-iron tub.

Conall tried to smile reassuringly as he reached to pull the curtain out of the way, talking all the while to keep her mind off her nudity, if nothing else. "Good…Very good. Okay, now…Let's get ye out o' there. Just hold me tight 'round the neck."

He braced himself as he slid his arms under her and lifted. She'd always been delicate; pregnancy had not done much to change that fact, but her bulk was awkward. He carried her carefully into her bedroom. Laying her down, he grabbed her nightgown and covered her. Only then did he take a quick moment to make her comfortable before circling the bed to the phone. His first call was to 911, his second to the docks where Patrick worked. Both the ambulance and his son were soon on the way. There was little else Conall could do but pray.

No, that wasn't true…he could take Barbara's mind off her worry. "Hey, love, help will be here soon…"

"Patrick!"

"Shhh…I've already called him," Conall murmured as he brushed back her tangled wet hair. "Just give me a moment, an' I'll be right back."

"No, don't…*augh!*" Barbara spasmed again as she grabbed for his hand.

"Barbara, relax. It'll be all right, just hold on an' ride it through." He continued to soothe her as he carefully loosened her grip. "I'm going to get a few things we'll need until the ambulance gets here…I'll be but a minute. Okay?"

Fresh tears ran down her cheeks, but she nodded. Conall hurried back into the bathroom for water and as many towels as he could manage. He wet a washcloth and draped that over his arm. Back in the bedroom, he arranged the towels into a thick pad on the bed and shifted Barbara on top of them before using the washcloth to wipe the sweat from her skin. What she bore overwhelmed him. He couldn't imagine the strength it took to endure it.

"Ye're going to be fine, Bobbi-lass, everything's going to be fine." The words sounded empty, powerless, even to his ears. Would fate be so cruel to let them come all this way, only to lose another one? "Shhh…ye just hang on, darlin'…Da's here."

Barbara managed a weak smile and took a sip from the cup he held to her lips. She looked like spun glass ready to shatter. "God! Why aren't they here?!" she cried through clenched teeth as her abdomen again contracted. "Talk to me…Do something, please?"

The moment the words left her mouth, Conall remembered that day four months ago when something fae had emerged from Quicksilver. It had touched Barbara; changed her. He was confident that was the reason this child was so close to being born, instead of going the way of the other babes. From that afternoon on, he had not let a day go past without fiddling some for Barbara. The violin, or whatever resided within it, called to him now and had been since he'd heard the first scream, though he hadn't realized it.

"Music, love," he was quick to suggest. "How about I play ye some music?" He barely waited for her nod before he dashed down the hall for Quicksilver. The case was propped in the window seat of the room he shared with Moira. He could feel the charge in the air as the fae spirit within waited for him impatiently. Without even stopping, Conall grabbed the case and hurried back to Barbara.

He had never unpacked Quicksilver with such haste before. Settling her beneath his chin, he immediately tuned her and drew his bow across the strings. The change was astounding. Before the first notes faded, peace permeated the room, banishing the fear, stress, and doubt that had hung in the air like a *Bean Sidhe's* wail. The atmosphere took on a fae glow; the notes fell off his strings in perfection though he played no composed work, just what flowed from his heart. He put all his love and hopes and dreams into the music, his eyes drifting closed as he focused on the magic he could feel unfolding. At once, he prayed both to the God of his childhood and to the Mother Goddess of his otherworldly heritage…he prayed without end as the fae presence drifted toward Barbara, caressing her with pure energy, embracing her with intimate awareness.

With his mage sight, it was as if another woman had settled on the bed beside his son's wife and gathered her into insubstantial arms. There was a sensation that Conall had noticed each time he'd played for Barbara, but he was aware there was something wrong: it wasn't enough. Whatever watched over Barbara—angel or fae—it could not give enough without giving totally, and his daughter-in-law on some level resisted an absolute melding.

The fear came back, thick and heavy and oppressive.

"My baby! No! My baby!" Barbara screamed again, and suddenly Conall knew the problem: as Barbara's doubts grew, her uncomprehending mind interpreted what was happening as a threat…as some force coming to steal or harm her baby. But that was wrong; he knew it deep inside. And yet Barbara fought the spirit with everything within her until Conall could see her fading even with his normal sight.

No! They had come so far; too far to lose the little one now!

Instinctively, desperately, Conall started to sing. He sang from the heart…not in English or Irish, but what he recognized as the ancient *Sidhe* tongue, which he had no cause to know. He sang of love and hope and unity against the darkness, and suddenly he did not sing alone. First one voice joined him, and he knew it for Moira…then a second voice, and it was Patrick…and a third, more ancient and awesome than anything he had ever encountered; the thought of putting a name to it was too terrifying to contemplate, though the knowledge hovered on the edge of his perception. That was the Fae One.

And magic blanketed the room. He scarcely knew how he managed to keep standing…let alone play. But continue he did, for the life of his grand-child…and surely all the rest of them…depended on it.

He could feel the moment the struggle ended. There were grunts and deep groans, during which Conall could not help but squeeze his eyes closed tighter. He was startled when Barbara's weak voice joined the chorus. Joy soared in a dazzling crescendo, and like the sweet song of an angel, a babe's high, disgruntled wail rose from the bed.

Conall's eyes flew open, and Quicksilver nearly fell from his grasp. Two gasps from the doorway were proof he hadn't imagined the arrival of his family, but in this moment out of time, he could spare no thought for them. Every ounce of his attention was riveted on the woman propped up in the bed before him. She wore Barbara O'Keefe's face, but the eyes that stared back at him were an unearthly green. The Fae One watched him with a calm serenity the likes of which Barbara had never shown. Conall's heart threatened to stop as he questioned if he might have been wrong. The woman in the bed smiled reassuringly as if his soul lay open to her—as well it may. Behind him, Patrick and Moira gasped again and he suspected they witnessed some glimmer of the ethereal beauty that smile unleashed.

Love infused the face that was both Barbara and not-Barbara, and Conall heard again the newborn wail that drew him back from the mists of magic. The child! Irrationally, doubt supplanted his conviction; all the tales he'd ever heard of changelings and the faeries stealing children flooded his thoughts. The child!

Immortal eyes now chided him, again from Barbara's face, and Conall knew shame. There was no deception in the melding that had taken place. As elf-kin, Conall knew better.

The Fae One's smile returned, and love saturated the room; along with it came an influx of mage energy converging upon the bed. It gently en-compassed mother and babe like a cloud until both glowed with it. Graceful arms cradled the perfect little creature and soft, borrowed lips leaned forward to plant a kiss on the little pink head with its faerie puff of dark curls. The child's whimpers and wails faded away and all were enchanted by its coos. Conall nearly fell to his knees in awe as the little one reached out a finger, and with a pleased little gurgle drew the cloud of mage energy in like it was mother's milk. Satisfaction wreathed Barbara's face as the Fae One looked up and caught Conall's eye. He trembled beneath that regard, knowing, though no words passed between them, that there would be a day of reckoning somewhere down the line. They owed the spirit a boon for the miracle of this birth. As he nodded his head, green eyes lightened to blue, and time came rushing back around them. In that instant, his right wrist burned as if wound by hot wire. Just briefly, then the sensation was gone. Conall swayed and trembled as Patrick forced his way past. Only the support of Moira coming up beside him kept Conall on his feet as they all welcomed wee Kara into the world.

Chapter I

Kara O'Keefe stood between two worlds, separate from both in more ways than one.

Part of her longed to remain in this faerie ring where she need not face mortal or fae. At her back stood twenty-first-century Ireland. Before her stood the gate to *Tír na nÓg*…the Land of Youth. She did not belong in either place. And yet she had no choice but to walk through the portal before her. She needed to return Lugh's sword…the Godslayer. The one the *Sidhe* lord Bran had wielded, intent on slaying Goibhniu, the Smithgod and current ruler of *Tír na nÓg*. He would have succeeded, if not for her interference.

A fine tremor rippled through her. She forced her muscles still and straightened her shoulders. She'd faced down many enemies this night: Olcas and Dubh, the sons of the dark goddess Carmán; Bran, also called the Bone Raven… She could face the disapproval of the *Sidhe* after her seeming disobedience.

It didn't matter what anyone else believed, responsibility, not dis-obedience, had sent her through the faerie gate, despite their orders to stay put.

The grass rustled behind her. Kara grimaced. Aí, Goibhniu's messenger, waited impatiently. At his side stood the old Romani woman who had stopped her from slaying Olcas, a being of pure evil from the annals of *Sidhe* history, who had captured, tortured, and cursed her.

She sensed Aí reach for her before his hand came to rest upon her shoulder, and tried not to flinch as his essence unwittingly crept past her guard. He immediately drew his hand away as an uncontrollable shudder rippled through her. The recent battle had left her so drained she was unable to block the intrusion. It was not enough that he no longer touched her. She was too raw, and he was closer than she liked. True, the curse was broken — she would no longer look upon a man or feel one's touch and perceive him as Olcas — but that didn't matter. Even though Aí now wore his own face, and had touched her with his own hand, it was still too much for her.

Turning, she captured his eye, staring hard in warning.

"Yer pardon, Kara," he said softly, stepping several lengths back from her. He nodded toward the clearing they'd just left then forward to the path that led to where the *Sidhe* and Romani forces gathered. "Shall we go home then? I'm thinking they could use our help...."

Kara grimaced. He was right. There were wounded to tend...and an immortal "god" to face. He was also wrong. The fae lands were not her home. But she didn't have the energy to argue the point. Slinging the case holding Quicksilver over her shoulder by its strap, she accepted the sword Aí held out to her.

With an unvoiced sigh tightening her throat, she stepped into *Tír na nÓg.*

Her first deep breath of air in the fae realm sent energy flowing through her, easing the hurt, soothing the raw edges. She closed her eyes to savor the peace a moment. Instantly, a faeling swarm descended upon Kara and her companions. Magic tingled across her skin and down her veins, further revitalizing her. Diminutive hands fluttered across her body and tissue-thin wings swept against her face, banishing the remaining tension. For a fleeting moment, a sleek, sinewy tail twined gently around her wrist. Contentment and joy filled the air around her like a perfumed cloud, infused her soul like a balm.

Kara's eyes drifted open and widened in awe. Anu's children — the faelings — were everywhere. Sprites and boggans, sylphs and faeries. More kin-cousins than she could name. Kara didn't know why they were drawn to her, but they followed her like tiny, star-struck groupies. Right now, they filled the air and the surrounding landscape. Many darted forward to steal a touch, adoration free and open upon their faces. Others hovered close or shyly hid behind nearby foliage, their expressions both hopeful and hungry. Doubt kept them from coming closer. Many of the *Sidhe* saw them as vermin, refusing to acknowledge their shared nature. Kara had no such prejudice. She smiled at the kin-cousins, exchanging caresses with those that darted close, projecting loving thoughts to those too timid to do so. And then she laughed as a familiar trill tickled her ear. She tilted her head to discover Beag Scath, perched boldly upon her shoulder. He had been companion to Maggie McCormick, also known as Cliodna — guardian of Clan O'Keefe. Beag Scath was also the first sprite Kara had ever met, only weeks ago in New York at the pawnshop, Yesterday's Dreams. As was usual for him, the sprite artfully draped himself among Kara's shocking, deep red locks .

Will I ever get used to this? Kara wondered. She found the casual presence of the brazen faeling jarring enough, but her hair...Once a rich chestnut brown, the strands were now a shocking deep red, transformed by magic. That had not been very long ago. Just before the recent battle, Kara had instinctively channeled all of the magic of the faelings to cleanse an ancient evil from the shrine of Anu at the heart of *Tír na nÓg.* Little had they known the cause of that evil was closing in on them; predators from the very beginning of *Sidhe* history, magical beings called the *Namhaid,* part spirit, part physical, completely lethal. Invisible and deadly, only those with the Sight could see them.

Kara shuddered in atavistic response.

Beag Scath trilled again in protest. He instigated a game of peek-a-boo through the curtain of her hair, diverting Kara from her darker thoughts.

Grinning, she nuzzled him.

"Hello, my friend," she murmured. "Will you take me to Maggie?"

The sprite laughed as if amused she had to ask, though it wasn't really an answer.

Beag Scath could talk—she'd heard him do so—but he rarely uttered a word unless he was singing. Unable to read his mind, she accepted the laugh as agreement and, after gently but insistently shooing the rest away, she headed off down the path to find her family.

"Let's go," she called over her shoulder to Aí and the Romani woman. "They'll need our hands as much as they need to hear what we know."

There was no sign of Maggie, nor of Kara's parents, as the three of them made their way through the triage area. Kara paused a moment, looking around with a slight frown on her lips. There were rows of silken sheets laid out on the ground, the wounded stretched out on top of them. She'd expected the blood and pain, but the serenity, the relaxed pace of those tending the casualties, puzzled her. The rustic setting more so, particularly when they weren't so far from shelter. Aí stopped beside her, his head cocked and one brow lifted in silent question.

"Why?" she asked, her free hand gesturing to the sheet-strewn field. "Why here and not inside with beds and comfort and…" And she didn't know what else. Why did they even need anything as mundane as a triage?

"We're creatures o' nature, Kara," he answered, a slight, sad smile on his lips. "Those injured…those mournin', 'tis better they're tended here than inside. They find more comfort beneath the sky, among their Kin, than they would alone in a bed, closed within stone walls, even as familiar as these."

She turned and looked toward *Mór Halla,* Goibhniu's seat in *Tír na nÓg.* Though the marble walls were thin and cut in delicate filigree that would have been impossible in the mortal world, it was still a massive, closed-in building. No matter that it arose from the forest as if it grew from roots right along with the trees, it was still, presumably, a built structure.

Briefly closing her eyes, Kara exercised her senses, reached past the moans and blood and pain to the *susurrus* of the tree boughs, the scent released by the dewed grass, and the brush of a warm breeze over her face. She understood why the people of this Land would have a need to be as close to nature and its healing energy as possible. And yet, though she understood, an automatic thought escaped her lips before she could restrain it: "But it's so unsanitary!"

For a moment, Ai's face contorted, his lips flexing and his brow twitching, and then the laughter came forth. She scowled at him, only to laugh herself a moment later. This wasn't her world. Disease and corruption—physical, anyway—had no place here.

Kara quirked her lips at him in a good-natured grimace. "Come on, quit slacking. We need to return Goibhniu's sword…and find Maggie."

The others spread out to offer aid among the wounded, Aí in the glade among the *Sidhe*, and the old woman by the Rom caravans, which had been drawn into the safety of the protected realm. Each race took care of its own as Kara continued on with guidance from Beag Scath, searching the orderly rows of sheets for a familiar head of red-gold curls.

She watched a moment, as Miach, the most powerful of the *Sidhe* healers, worked to mend one of those worst wounded by the *Namhaid* and the demigods that ruled them. The wounds were brutal, senseless, clearly inflicted out of sadistic desire to disfigure and torment rather than in honest combat. And those responsible had gotten away. A powerless rage rose up in Kara at the sight.

If that was not enough to shore up her resolve, she turned to move on, only to note a couple of flower-draped bodies off to the side. She noticed these were laid out on sheets of black velvet, rather than brightly colored silk. The faces of the fallen were serene, but lifeless. She was surprised there were still bodies. Those that fell during the battle at Yesterday's Dreams had turned to dust.

By her ear, Aí spoke softly. "In your realm, the Eternal Flame comes to consume the bodies at death, unbidden, out of necessity. Here, those lost remain as you see them that their loved ones may say farewell before the Flame takes the fallen."

More than ever, Kara was driven to find Maggie. She had an overwhelming need to ensure her friend was well. She had even more of a need to resume her mage training. The recent battle had shown her she had much to learn if she were to stand against their enemies.

Reaching up, she gave Beag Scath's small leg a shake. "Find her," she murmured.

At some point, Aí fell away, caught up in the care of his people. Kara moved on with purposeful strides, unbothered that she went alone, eyes scanning foremost for Maggie, but also for the Smithgod, quite aware she still had the sword to return. No one chastised her or lectured—they were too busy—but occasionally, she caught a disapproving gaze on familiar faces. She sighed but did not look away. Although she had broken her promise, she could not regret what she'd done, particularly when she finally found Goibhniu healing the mortally wounded. The breeze tugged at his onyx-dark curls, and concern shadowed his soot-grey eyes even darker. He lacked the lean, slender build of many of the *Sidhe*. True to his calling as a smith, his muscles bulged, even when relaxed, and he was the apex of perfect proportion. Next to him, not one weightlifter in the human realm would look anything but grotesque.

The Smithgod merely gave her an assessing look before brushing his hand across her brow. At his touch, the small hurts she was just beginning to notice vanished. She nodded her thanks and presented the stolen sword. His expression grim, he magicked the blade away.

Relieved of that burden, Kara continued her search, helping out as she went along. She wiped brows and cleaned away blood, bandaged the simple hurts too slight to need magical healing, part of her looking among patients and caregivers alike, both hoping and dreading that she would come across Maggie.

"Good Lord, bless us an' keep us! Ye'd scarce know 'twas us as won." Seeing the aftermath of the battle before him, Patrick O'Keefe understood firsthand that there was no victor in war. Many *Sidhe* were wounded, a few slain. Himself, he had been lucky this time to come away with but a few scratches, easily bound up and quick to heal. It could be said they'd taken the day, but for how long? Their victory felt like no more than a standoff between themselves and these…Children of Carmán.

He bent a moment to adjust the soft sheet covering a fellow *Fianna*—*Sidhe* warriors newly formed in the tradition of those ancient Celts who had followed the legendary Fionn Mac Cumhail in the service of Ireland's High Kings. It bemused Patrick to be counted among their number, mortal though he was. This one's face was familiar, though it wasn't one of the men Patrick could remember speaking to. That didn't matter, though. He felt more of a connection with this *Sidhe*, whose name he could not even remember, than he had ever felt for those mortal men he'd spent nearly twenty-five years with on the New York docks and at one time had considered the next thing to family.

Without realizing it, Patrick reached out to smooth back hair the very shade of a deep, velvety red rose. The man stirred but did not wake. Patrick released a taut breath. He'd feared that the warrior had died in the battle.

Patrick turned to scan the clearing being used for triage. Where would he be of the most use? An agonized moan decided for him; hurrying toward the sound, he wended his way around others intent on their own tasks. He stopped short at the sight that greeted him once he was past the intervening obstructions. There on the ground before him, laid out upon a sheet of rich, black velvet, was an unfamiliar *Sidhe* woman. At first, Patrick was captivated by her glowing beauty. Though ghastly wounds marred her body, caked with blackening blood, her face had been tenderly cleaned of any sign of battle, as attested by the stained and crumpled cloth in the hand of the woman cradling the wounded one's head.

He couldn't help but wonder: Friend? Lover? Kin? No matter; the suffering in the caretaker's face would have struck at the soul of the most dedicated misanthrope, which Patrick most definitely was not. Even as he watched, an eldritch flame engulfed the body of the fallen, leaving in its spent trail a mound of glittery ash upon the bloodied cloth and the other woman's lap. He hurried forward to kneel behind the survivor as she swayed. No fool, he did not speak or try to pull her away, but only lent her comfort and support that she might fully mourn.

"It does my heart good to see ye well, my friend."

Patrick slowly glanced around in the direction of the familiar voice. Miach—the *Sidhe* healer he'd first met in New York—stood behind him, just off to the side. The healer looked on with compassion.

"Aye, 'tis hard to kill, I am, though the world certainly does seem to keep tryin'." Patrick allowed himself a rueful grin as he continued to smooth back the *Sidhe* woman's metallic gold hair in what he hoped was a comforting caress. Her lips moved, but Patrick heard no sound. She seemed altogether oblivious to his presence. He watched as she drew the velvet close—without disturbing the ashes—and folded the edges over until she had a small, flat bundle clutched to her chest. With unearthly grace, she climbed to her feet and drifted away, her words coming at last, barely heard, alien to him, and yet they slashed his mortal heart with their grief, a dirge sung to an unheard melody.

Patrick would have followed, if not for the healer's restraining grip on his shoulder. He looked up at Miach and considered him more closely. The tall elf looked solid yet ethereal, his face paler than the iridescent braid draped over his shoulder, and his eyes, normally lavender, a deep bruised shade of violet. The hand on Patrick's shoulder gave the faintest of tremors. He quickly pushed it away before the healer's natural inclination sought to mend the small hurts Patrick had taken in battle.

"Ah! There'll be none o' that now. Save it for them as need it, or better yet, for yerself. Yer transparent, ye've spent so much in healing."

Miach laughed softly, his eyes warming from their dim weariness. "Bloody stubborn Celt."

"Don' go flattering me, now, ye hear?"

The healer laughed louder, color seeping back into his pallid face, but he sobered quickly as he glanced over his shoulder and back again. Something flickered behind his eyes, something that made Patrick very uneasy.

"What? What's wrong?" Patrick scrambled to his feet, dire visions of his family as crusted and lifeless as the *Sidhe* woman left him pale and trembling. He stared off in the direction from which Miach had come. "What's going on?"

Patrick was ready to rush away in search of his own loved ones. They were to have been safe here, left behind in *Tír na nÓg*.

"'Tis a friend o' yers, Arnold Barnert." Compassion brimmed Miach's eyes as he continued. "I'm sorry. He was felled in the battle an' is nigh a step away from crossing the Veil, 'twere it not for the fact that death has no place in *Tír na nÓg*."

This wasn't the revelation Patrick had been expecting. How the hell had Arn ended up in the middle of a supernatural battlefield? He was a doctor…in Queens! What did he know of magic and battle? "Ye must be mistaken, 'tis'nt possible."

"There is no doubt. I heard him mutter yer name myself. He came from America to warn ye…*us*, o' the return o' Olcas."

This is getting more and more surreal, Patrick thought numbly.

"Patrick," Miach continued, his gaze both shadowed and intent, "I need ye to calm him. He can't die here, but he's already done himself more harm."

"Dear God…" What was Arn, his best friend, doing in *Tír na nÓg*, a world away from his normal life, in more regards than one? His normal life where he saw patients and played pool, where he made a mean barbeque and had a sweet, lovely wife? Lynn…oh, Lord…what could Patrick possibly say to her? How could he explain? Visions of the battle they'd just survived, the forces they fought, the scene he'd just witnessed, and the one left to mourn, flooded Patrick's mind. Lynn's world was hospital association benefits and volunteering twice a week at the local animal shelter. She would never understand her husband getting caught amid an immortal battle. She was a gentle soul who needed taking care of. She'd never survive Arn's death.

"Where is he?"

Miach led him to the next glade, where yet more sheets were laid upon the ground in disheartening number. Patrick's jaw clenched, and he sped his steps, leaving the healer in his wake. He didn't need a guide. Patrick headed for the oddest looking *Sidhe* he'd yet to encounter, decked out in punk gear with a metallic blue mohawk, sitting solemnly with Arn's head in his lap. The *Sidhe* was familiar, though the memory hazed. Patrick suspected he'd fought beside him atop the pawnshop roof. Which meant the *Sidhe* was likely responsible for Arn being here at all.

Patrick ground his teeth together at the thought, but pushed down his anger. Now was not the time. He had a more pressing concern: blood, bright as fresh paint on hands and faces, both fae and mortal. Bright enough that Patrick could almost believe it was paint, if not for the bitter bite in the air. The scent overpowered him even from yards away. And if the odor wasn't proof enough, fresh blood, dark and deep as the grave, soaked Arn's shirt down his left side until it nearly glistened. A second odor mingled with the first, subtle but more foul. Patrick could not identify the source, but his gut clenched in reaction. He could almost envision Death pacing in frustration just beyond Arn and his attendant.

In defiance, Arn's chest rose and fell in a strong, regular rhythm.

Patrick barely noticed the bustle of those tending other wounded in the clearing. He wove his way past the obstacles until he reached his goal, dropping to his knees beside the incongruous pair. Not until he was close did he notice the stranger placed steady pressure upon Arn's shoulders, gently, but firmly keeping the wounded man in place.

Arn's gaze was both feverish and determined, his skin taut and glistening as he strained to rise.

"Arnold Barnert! Ye damn well stay where ye are, do ye hear me?"

At Patrick's voice, Arn stilled, and his head came around. The breath rushed out of him and his obvious tension lost just a fraction of its hold. Their eyes locked, and Patrick saw his friend's frantic gaze, though he did not understand.

"They have her," Arn ground out. "Those bastards have my Lynn."

How did we end up here? Jacko Mack wondered. *How has the Rom again become entwined in a conflict not their own?* He suspected only Granddame Rose could satisfy his curiosity…which meant it would go unsatisfied. He would likely never know what had sent the caravan fleeing Wicklow Cottage in the middle of the night without a thought for their friend and hostess, Agnieszka Michaels. She must have wondered why they left so abruptly, without even goodbye, or thank you. Jacko wondered that himself.

He would have gladly stayed to protect her, had he been given the chance. Only, his sister, Sveta, had stolen him away as he slept, knowing he would have resisted otherwise. Even now, he needed to be on the road away from this place and headed back to Agnieszka, to make sure she was safe and well, to explain himself. For her heart and hand, Jacko would gladly give up the tinker's life.

But not yet. The Clan would need him once they took to the road, at least until the wounded had healed. After? Well, they would come to that when it was time. For now he would do best to focus on things other than what he could not change.

With the injured Rom tended to, Jacko turned his attention to what lay beyond their wagons. Slowly turning, he took in the disturbing wonder surrounding him. He had not been able to fully appreciate the landscape earlier when there were wounds to tend. Their camp was in a clearing surrounded by ancient trees bearing the weight of ages on their unbowed limbs: rowan and oak, yew and hawthorn. Other trees that he couldn't name, and suspected even a botanist would be challenged by, ringed a second clearing. Blossoms and herbs filled in the gaps, as well as strange, tall grasses, each tasseled in a small purple frond. Brilliant sunlight filtered through the leaves, filled with motes of glimmering gold. The land was glorious, and yet it was nothing compared to those that called it home. Even bloodied, as many of them were, the *Sidhe* were magnificent.

Jacko crossed over to the other clearing. The Clan had no need of him for now; the wounded rested, their loved ones hovering. Camp had been set, and what livestock they had was tended. As the least of those injured, he was at loose ends. He would repay their hosts' hospitality by aiding their healers in what little ways he could.

In transit from the Rom camp, he grabbed a waterskin, a wineskin, and a long-strapped bucket with clean rags draped over the lip. He hung the skins from one shoulder and slung the bucket strap over the other to hang by his waist. Filling the bucket from a nearby spring, he worked his way among the *Sidhe* wounded, offering drink and washing away blood, both to comfort those injured and to aid the healers in seeing what they dealt with. Of those casualties who were aware, most of them smiled in thanks, while some few others refused his aid, sneering at his seemingly uninjured state and drawing away from his mortal touch. Jacko kept both his gaze and distance from the still forms lain upon black velvet, sensing the Good Folk would want to care for their own deceased.

When his skins were near empty, and his bucket had been refilled with fresh water several times, there seemed no more that he could do. The few remaining injured were already being tended and many of those already seen to had risen and left the glade. Sensing it was time to return to his own camp, Jacko started back, only to stop abruptly to peer at one of the *Sidhe* men assisting the healer, Miach, who had visited the Rom camp earlier to heal their worst wounded. The stranger caught Jacko's eye, not for his coloring or features, which bordered on the mundane in comparison to those around him, but because of the cat coiling around his feet.

Jacko knew that cat. There was no mistaking Rex's trill or regal manner, the enigmatic gaze that transcended feline nature. The last time he had seen it was far away, in England, at Wicklow Cottage. Having a soft spot for strays, Agnieszka had taken the feline in, though it was unusual for her to do more than feed them on the stoop. Any doubt Jacko had evaporated when Rex spied him and came loping over, tail flagged, and purring sufficient to rattle the leaves overhead.

Stunned, Jacko nonetheless knelt down to scratch that large, upturned head and lost himself a moment in a kindred sense of longing. How did the little one get here? Why? And then he had to brace himself, arm to the ground. What of Agnieszka? Was she here? Or worse, once more all alone at her cottage, bereft and abandoned by yet another special friend? Vulnerable to the evil that Granddame Rose had sensed lurking?

He looked up as the *Sidhe* came to stand before him. Jacko vaguely recognized him from the battle. His hair seemed a normal chestnut brown until struck by the light, which released glimpses of deep green highlights, and his eyes were electric blue, like something out of a movie. There was no recognition in that gaze.

With a final scratch, Jacko pushed to his feet, uncomfortable with the implications of their relative positions. He glowered at the *Sidhe*, concern for Agnieszka overriding any sense of gratitude he'd felt earlier. "I'd like to know how this one came to be here, instead of where he belongs."

Both the *Sidhe*'s brows went up, and he seemed taken aback by Jacko's aggressive tone. "An' where is it ye feel he belongs?"

There was no animosity in the question. In fact, his manner was no more than curious. The *Sidhe* glanced down to the cat and reached out his hand. Jacko's gaze automatically followed.

He was floored when Rex shimmered and shifted into a perfect little man, only the eyes unchanged in their unfathomable intensity. Stunned, as the creature gripped the offered hand and scaled to the *Sidhe*'s shoulder, Jacko realized that whatever he thought, Rex was clearly where he belonged already.

"What of Agnieszka Michaels, who took that little one in, all the way in England? What of my little mother?" Meeting Rex's gaze, he now understood the look of longing there, though not the precise cause. "Where is she?" Jacko demanded, his voice rumbling. "And what have you to do with her?"

The *Sidhe*'s gaze darkened. "I am called Aí. Will ye come an' speak awhile with me?"

"I'm Jacko," the Rom answered, "and damned straight I will."

As they turned to leave the clearing side by side, in silence, Rex stepped to Ai's shoulder closest to Jacko then leapt the gap between them. Jacko stiffened only briefly, still stunned by the true nature of the creature. There was some satisfaction, though, as Rex twined Jacko's neck and buried his head among the Rom's curls for comfort. With the sound of the faerie creature muttering in his ear, echoing Jacko's agitation, the three of them left the busy clearing for an easy path through the trees.

Was it wise to follow an unknown fae into the forest? Not hardly. But frankly, Jacko didn't care. He'd been uneasy from the moment he'd woken up on the ferry to Dublin to discover his sister had whisked him away. To be truthful, he'd been worried well before then, at Agnieszka's, when it became evident something evil stalked her.

As though the memory summoned it, Jacko caught the barest, most fleeting hint of musk when Aí led him to a quiet, empty glade. Before he could wonder at it, at the center of the clearing, he saw the most amazing statue of a woman, clearly of the *Tuatha de Danaan*.

"Who is she?"

"Anu, sister to the Mother Goddess, and the reason your Agnieszka came to be where she was."

Jacko whipped his head toward Aí.

"At the dawn of our race Anu was lost to us, and nearly all the People with her, but for Danu, the Mother Goddess. To safeguard our existence, some number of our young were sent away from the *Sidhe* Lands to live among Men. As…insurance. While they were hidden in the mortal realm, unaware of their true nature, none could banish the *Daoine Maithé* from the earth by slaughter, for there would always be a vessel to bear us back again. These Hidden Ones were called *Cosaints*."

Jacko frowned at Aí and in frustration kicked at the deadfall at his feet. Again the memory of a scent wafted up, disturbing and familiar. Then Jacko truly noticed the leaves and realized they were the first such he had seen since crossing the faerie gate. They reminded him of another leaf-strewn ground and Agnieszka in his arm as they hurried to the safety of her cottage, surrounded by the musk of unseen predators. Predators that had recently attacked them on the threshold of the *Sidhe* Lands.

"The spirit women…they were after *her*!" Jacko growled, getting into Ai's face. "And what do you mean by *were*?" Aí took a step back, but he did not flinch or look away. His expression was perplexing: bleak with guilt, taut with anger, but not at Jacko. It was too distant.

The *Sidhe* nodded, then lowered his gaze before going on. "Agnieszka was a *Cosaint*…" Aí said, hurrying on before Jacko could jump on that tense again. "The Hidden Ones have been brought home again."

Jacko swayed with relief. "Where is she?"

The *Sidhe* visibly braced himself, causing Jacko to tense once more.

"Where is she?" he growled again.

"Taken by another, one following dark paths…Bran has stolen her away."

Jacko barely heard another word as Aí recounted the details.

Chapter 2

The walls shook, and crates shattered from the impact of raw energy bolts. Those remaining toppled from where they were stacked three stories high. The warehouse shuddered as the heavy goods crashed to the ground. Dubh and Olcas each flew backward through the air from the collision, both physical and otherworldly. Only through the furious application of mage power did they avoid damaging impacts, coming to rest some distance away from each other, battered but still able to right themselves. They squared off from opposing ends of the wide aisle, arcanely armed and cloaked with shields of pure energy. Dubh sneered. He hated Olcas as much as his brother hated him.

Really, Mother should have stopped at two, Dubh thought. *And been satisfied with perfection.*

For a moment, all was still and silent as dust settled to the concrete slab flooring the warehouse. The atmosphere crackled with unleashed power. Loathing and deep, barely controlled fury flavored the air with harsh, bitter tones. The mingled scents of blood—both old and new—and charred flesh permeated the warehouse.

"You dim-witted, magically stunted idiot!"

"You short-sighted, heavy-handed oaf!"

Tendrils of power tore through another mountain of packing crates while crowbars and wedging spikes torpedoed across the intervening space, flung by mental force.

"We had them!" Dubh's blackened form blended with the shadows behind him.

"She was in my grasp," Olcas snapped back, staring out from ice-blue eyes in a Romani-featured face.

"We weren't there for you to procure another plaything." Dubh's tone was sharp. "Vengeance was laid out before us like a banquet, and you went haring off after some mundane morsel like the petty little rodent you have always been! Calma and I were constantly making up for *your* shortcomings!" The final words were punctuated by snapping, whip-like tendrils of green-tinged energy that split the air with a crack as they lashed against Olcas's shields and chewed into the tempered concrete at his feet.

Dubh wished his older brother had been with him this time. The battle's outcome would have played out much differently. But no, it had been Olcas instead. Another whip lashed out. It was unacceptable that the *Sidhe* had barely suffered in this encounter. Scathed or unscathed, not a one of them should have been able to walk from the battleground. The *Bás*—deadly spirit women the *Sidhe* knew as the *Namhaid*, the scourge of the so-called *Daoine Maithé*—should have claimed victory and made victims of them, every one. Dubh growled at the failure and continued to lash out at his brother. The air sparked as if a dozen downed electrical wires repeatedly crossed connections.

"If you weren't such a blind fool, you would see the weapon that 'morsel' could be shaped into," Olcas countered, the words steeped in contempt. From his fingers shot bolts of red-toned energy.

With a sweep of his hand, Dubh deflected the bolts, but not the words. The surface of Dubh's burnt skin fissured anew as his stolen muscles tensed in response to his brother's taunt, revealing the tortured, angry flesh weeping beneath. He remembered the girl, her potential, and the somehow-familiar essence of her soul. Yes, she was tempting, but not worth casting aside over two millennia worth of pending retribution. After all, what was she to the hated *Tuatha de Danaan*? Nothing more than a quaint curiosity, surely. A short-lived mortal unworthy of anything more than a momentary diversion—for the enemy, as for him. How much potential could she truly hold in that finite form, anyway? Surely just a sip, a swiftly exhausted puddle of potential.

Dubh would not be distracted. Centering himself by sheer will, he stilled his rapid breath and forced calm into his muscles, shrugging off the influence of his brother's undisciplined outburst. Locking gazes with Olcas, Dubh took slow, measured steps forward, his shield a crackling nimbus surrounding him. He could see that his brother's resources were barely depleted, tied as they were to this place, which was his ground, drawing off links to the surrounding magics.

Dubh's energies—already low both from the battle just past and their escape through the ether—ebbed more swiftly with each strike. It was time to withdraw, before Olcas realized this. Though, given how inept his brother was with anything but mundane magic, it was quite likely Olcas could not tell Dubh's depleted state. It was wisest to regroup, to replenish his resources, perhaps to track down Calma. After all, there would be another day to destroy his baby brother…and not too far in the future, either, if Dubh could find the elder one.

Finding satisfaction in that thought, Dubh swelled his aura with what un-fettered energy he could gather and stopped inches from Olcas's protections.

Behind his glittering shroud, he honed a thin tendril of magic into a lancing point, holding it ready.

"If I ever see you again, I will slaughter you and whatever form cloaks you," Dubh warned his inferior. "I will cleave your very atoms one from the other until there is not even a single small piece for anyone to find and make a relic of." He thrust the hardened strand forward with a sudden and steady force, both physically and mentally, until it pierced his brother's shield. Olcas paled and flinched as the attack held together long enough to score his cheek, the bolt sizzling the flesh before being absorbed by the shield. "I will fry your essence until there is not enough spirit left to inhabit a thimble!"

While the sting of the strike distracted his brother, Dubh focused his remaining energy and tore his way out through the ether. With a thought, he arrowed away to where the *Bás* awaited him.

Swiping the back of his hand across his damaged cheek, Olcas indulged his rage, screaming as he sent more splinters of wood flying about the warehouse. Tendrils of energy whipped through the crates. Shards of shattered concrete *ping*ed off the walls. Olcas's efforts only increased his anger. He stood and seethed that his brother had fled his reach. When a final bolt shattered one of the high windows, Olcas quickly cut off the indulgence. There was no point in wasting more power, or losing more profit, which was power of another sort. Even so, neon red sparks tinged black at the edges continued to leap from his fingertips as he strode through the wreckage, heading for the sublevel where he'd set up his new lair.

He had to admit, after so many years of crippled ability—first through a lack of physical form to focus the energy, and then through the regrettable choice of the psychically blind Lucien Blank as a vessel—it was beyond gratifying to possess a tool with so much arcane potential, even though completely untrained. Olcas savored stretching his mage skills after so long without them.

Standing just within the entrance to his stronghold, he drew on knowledge gained from the grimoires and spellbooks he'd studied in his time as Lucien. He centered. He focused his will. With one hand, he gathered the native magics, feral and earth-based, with the other he drew on his restored god powers. A mental twist locked the two together, freeing him to draw a third strand from the ether, the power of chaos. Weaving all three into one rope of transcendent energy, he drew on the unique properties of each individual strand to create a complex barrier against all senses, arcane and otherwise.

The entrance to his warren now suitably safeguarded, he descended below.

"And how are my darlings doing today?" he purred, as he moved through the room to where the insipid mortal woman attempted to mother the demon-child. The prisoner looked up, her blue eyes dully lit with fear. The demon, however, was in raptures. Reflexively, Lynn Barnert tightened her thin arms around his creature, completely unaware of the fiend's true nature. Moving one hand up to stroke those golden little-girl curls, she pressed the "child's" face to her shoulder in a protective gesture, unwittingly feeding it richer fare as her anxiety ramped up.

Olcas was not there to torment her, though, as amusing as that might be.

In fact, it occurred to him that she currently held little value but for providing ready sustenance for the demon. Yes, she had been the lure that drew her husband across the ocean, and her husband, in turn, flushed out the *Sidhe*, but the man had not proven the key to sliding past their blasted gate into the fae lands, as intended. The memory of that recent thwarting kindled Olcas's anger. The link between Olcas and Arnold Barnert had been severed by some Romani hag, along with the curse that bound him to Kara O'Keefe.

A growl rumbled through his chest. No more back door into the fae realm; no more energizing terror from the girl. Olcas raged at this unanticipated change in his fortune. What gave everyone the impression they could take what was his? His brothers, the *Sidhe*, even mortals. It was an insult not to be borne. He *would* rectify the situation, though for now, both the man and the girl were free of his influence.

It was time for a new plan. *Perhaps there* is *a use the woman might be put to*, he thought as a cruel smile curved his lips and glee kindled his blood. *I must consider the matter…This could be…fun.*

Striding forward, he moved to the next chamber. Securing the door behind him, Olcas settled upon the opulent pillows topping his favored lounge. Relaxing into the hedonistic luxury, as his body recharged, he set his mind against the task of constructing a new path to bring him to the power and satisfaction his nature demanded.

While this mortal world was rife with life—and death—energy, it was nothing compared to the rich depth of power garnered from one sip of near-immortal force. Just as all life forms shed skin cells, causing common house dust, there was a corollary in terms of magic, the fact behind the fanciful accounts of pixie dust. Those versed in the arcane referred to the accumulation of this cast-off energy as ley lines. That energy was nothing in comparison to the direct source. In the mortal realm, it was like imbibing watered wine. On the ethereal plane…there was a reason the food of the gods was called ambrosia. Olcas could recall with stunning clarity that long-ago sip of not-quite-mortal essence that had heralded his own demise, and that of his family. They had not been slaughtered to avenge the mortals they had toyed with…or even the death of the unborn halfblood…but to safeguard the fae, who knew they had become preferred prey with that one savory taste, however unintended.

That was why Olcas would find a way past those gates, to claim both the power and long-due vengeance for himself. He even had the barest glimmer of a plan. Rising from his pillows, he moved to the door between the rooms. Opening it, he stared speculatively at woman and child, considering how deceptive that tableau was: how wholesome on the surface, how rotten beneath. Nodding slowly with satisfaction, he closed the door and returned to his rest. As he recharged his body, he allowed his mind to give the strategy shape.

Dubh stepped out of nowhere onto the shoulder of a far-away cliff well north of Ireland. Above him, lightning split the sky to the accompaniment of cracking thunder. Below, the wind shrieked through the honeycomb of caves that made up the cliff face. At the base, the waves raged with a mighty voice. The symphony kept discordant harmony with his mood.

In ironic mimicry of their first encounter, the *Bás* came to him from beneath the cover of the distant forest. He watched in grim satisfaction as they loped effortlessly across the intervening plain. Aloud he could hear their hissing growls as they drew closer. In his head, they seethed with incoherent anger. His ears and his head both recoiled from sudden raging screams heard at once on both planes of perception. In reaction, Dubh promptly shielded, waiting for them in a bubble of silence. His scowl deepened as his allies — or, as he thought of them, minions — drew closer. Of the forty-nine he'd managed to build up from the gaunt and wasted seven he'd initially discovered, a mere twenty-three remained.

Olcas will pay for this, Dubh thought, reactive magic swirling in sullen green ribbons around his hands. He quickly cut off the display before the *Bás* drew close enough to perceive his diminished state.

Forcing calm upon himself, he watched in appreciation as lightning flashes limned velvet pelts sheathing lean muscle. From the females, the wind lashed long hair that was the deep, almost red-black of heart's blood. The males' locks were shorter and a black darker than pitch, as were their eyes. Rather than run straight, they wove over and across one another's paths in a dizzying dance that made them seem more than their decreased number, several of them breaking away periodically to serve as outriders, guarding against unforeseen attack.

They stopped in a semicircle before him. He said nothing as he waited for them to settle. When all eyes were upon him — seven sets of black, sixteen red — Dubh spoke into their minds rather than lose dignity in yelling above the wind.

How many are sown?

They did not think in numbers but envisioned ten of the enemy subsumed. A paltry number, but they would build upon it. After waiting millennia,

Dubh was hardly inclined to be impatient with his revenge — with the Danaan, anyway. His brother was another matter.

And how many near to whelp?

This time, when they imagined only three, the demigod discovered a bit of impatience within after all. There was no reason for such slow progress. If the *Bás* were not so selfish with the power they glommed from around them, they could have trebled their number just on what had already been spawned. True, the whelps would mature on the energy inherent in the host body, but how much quicker they would mature with their progenitors' aid.

Go! Feed the others up. Pour your magic into them until they burst forth. You must swell your numbers more swiftly than that if we are to bring the Daoine Maithé down.

Grumbling and hissing, the *Bás* nonetheless did as he ordered, enticed by the thought of obliterating their ancient enemy. In this, Dubh was a kindred spirit.

Feeling drained himself, he opened a path through the ether and returned to the pub where he'd set up operations.

Chapter 3

PATRICK COULD DO NOTHING BUT WATCH AS THE *Sidhe* HEALER TENDED TO HIS friend. His thoughts were torn between the sight before him and the knowledge that his best friend's wife was in the hands of fiends. Patrick had seen what at least one of those monsters was capable of. Such atrocities visited upon his daughter. Cruelty and brutality did not even begin to describe what had been done to Kara. She had been in their hands less than a day; Lynn…it had been several. Such a gentle woman, an innocent at the mercy of this insanity…

And again, Patrick could do nothing.

Growling in frustration, he pushed his concerns aside. He watched as Miach gently pulled away shredded cloth from equally shredded skin. The blood was too thick to have caked just yet; it was a viscous gel clinging to both flesh and fabric. Underneath, there was the faint gleam of bone, and dark glistening shapes Patrick's mind balked at identifying. A groan ripped through the air, and he was hard-pressed to tell if it was Arn's or his own. His friend's hand reached up and grabbed Miach's in what seemed a purely reflexive action.

"What, you don't think it hurts enough already?" Arn's voice was lucid for the moment, and sounding so much like normal that Patrick nearly laughed. Only the look on his friend's face shut down the impulse. Death might not have a place in the Land of Youth, but that said nothing about pain.

"Hush yerself now, Arn. Let him clean ye up an' see to yer wounds."

"What…no, 'poof' and it's all better? I guess I don't have to worry about being out of a job, do I."

Patrick heard the strain underlying Arn's lighthearted joking.

Miach actually laughed. It was gentle, soft, and brief, but a laugh nonetheless. The sound was at odds with his solemn gaze. "My power's too spent to make ye as new. Why don't ye rest? One will be here soon to take care o' ye."

An unconscious shiver sped down Patrick's back at Miach's words. He barely noticed. All his attention was on his friend. The nod was shallow, but there as Arn closed his eyes, his chest barely moving as he breathed. Pain lined his face, despite that care, nearly the only sign he still lived. Choking back a groan, Patrick reminded himself there was no way for Arn to die in this place. Though it went against his own faith, Patrick had to believe that, or else Arn would have already been both stiff and cold.

Only…was that such a blessing, with a body so torn? Patrick looked up at the healer, eyes glaring. He shook with the effort to hold back the demand that his friend be helped *now.* Yet, all he needed to do was glance around to know healing must be a rare gift. Many even among the *Sidhe* bore the signs of mundane treatment. And Miach, though he could heal with a touch, was nearly spent beyond redemption from the looks of him—as Patrick had admonished him earlier before he'd known Arn was among the wounded.

Blushing, he looked away, nearly jerking back as the elven hand came to rest on his own.

"I'll be right back with help for yer friend," Miach told him, his tone low and soothing. The *Sidhe* was gone before Patrick realized, he must indeed be in a grave state to have to physically fetch help, rather than summon it with a thought.

Barely daring to touch, Patrick reached out to rest his fingers on Arn's shoulder—one of the few spots free of the blood and shallow cuts covering the rest of him—and sat down to wait. As Patrick looked down at his friend, his gaze locked on his own hand. He nearly flinched away at the sight of it, the sixth digit restored as if he'd never been free of that curse. Tension flowed through him until he had to draw away or risk disturbing Arn's uneasy rest.

A shadow fell across his face, and Patrick lifted his gaze.

He jerked back in shock. Both hands fisted as he came to his feet. In his heart, doubt and hope warred with one another.

"No," he said, his voice edged in panic as he looked past the Smithgod to where Miach stood. "Ye can't let him."

There were startled glances from those nearby, and down at his feet, Arn twitched as if attempting to rise. Goibhniu merely stood there, hands relaxed on his hips, his expression patient. Patrick scowled, but did not yield.

"Why?" Miach asked, exhaustion and confusion threading his words. "Ye were eager enough to have me heal him, but I have no energy left. Of all o' us blessed with the gift, there is none better able to…"

A bitter laugh raked Patrick's throat as his hands raised and unfurled, all twelve fingers flexing. "Believe me…I know how *able* he is. Yer magic heals the damage…*his* restores what's long been gone. What's to stop him from doing this to Arn an' then handing us some tripe that *he's* yer Miller's Son, all because I'll have no part o' yer faerie tales?"

Those gathered around him were stunned into silence as he ranted, waving about the extra digits he had so recently been careful to keep out of sight. All except the figure at his feet. Arn propped himself up painfully, his bloodied hand slapping Patrick's leg.

"Don't be an idiot, Pat," he said through gritted teeth. "I never cared either way how many fingers I had. That was all my parents. Now get out of the man's way before I embarrass myself from the pain."

Patrick's gaze darted from his friend to the Smithgod. It was a struggle. No matter how much he wanted Arn whole and free of suffering, no matter that none had threatened Patrick harm since his own hands were restored, the fear reared up just at the thought of what was to come. Long-ago memories of persecution and even violence, brutal enough to near kill him when he was just a young boy, froze Patrick where he stood. If not for those times, his parents wouldn't have moved him to America. He and Arn would have never met.

Long ago, they'd been introduced just before Patrick had the surgery to remove his extra digits. Arn had already had the procedure himself and the doctor and Patrick's parents figured the American boy might help calm his fears. That was the only good thing Patrick could say his mutation had brought him, not counting his wife Bobbi, and daughter Kara, who came later in his life, well after the surgery. But still…those fingers haunted him. Bad enough he had to deal with them again; he couldn't stand by and let the same thing happen to Arn, could he? And yet…his friend asked it of him. Shudders shook his body, growing in intensity, until Miach laid a gentle hand on his shoulder, and drew him aside to allow Goibhniu to pass.

"Ye need to set the demons to rest, Patrick," he murmured, low enough no one else could hear.

Shame burned through Patrick, and his head dropped forward in acceptance, though how he was to manage that, he hadn't a clue. Even now, he could not help himself; panic shoved at him, ordering him to yank his friend away despite all reason and Arn's own wishes. With Miach's help, he resisted the urge, but light tremors still ran up and down his limbs, and he nearly sobbed moments later as a blood-spattered set of six-fingered hands gripped his own. Arn's voice rumbled by his ear, "Come on, doofus, let's go find somewhere to talk."

Arn had no idea where he was going. He led Patrick through the grim rows. How ironic that Arn served four years in the Army without seeing any more excitement than an unexpected drill, only to land in the middle of a supernatural battlefield decades later. He'd like to think he'd represented himself well, but he was too honest for that. He'd needed rescuing almost from minute one.

But it was over now, and except for the bloody remains of the clothes he still wore, the only proof of the encounter was the triage they passed through.

Arn knew he would have to deal with this at some point, but he didn't kid himself that it was going to be now. When they reached the edge of the clearing, Arn continued a little distance into the trees. Not too far; he didn't want to offend. If he remembered anything from the stories Patrick's father used to tell, it was that you never wanted to offend the fae. When they were out of sight but not out of earshot, Arn sat down on the first boulder he came to and stared hard at his friend.

"Sit."

Patrick was clearly agitated as he parked his ass on another boulder. Other than his obvious stress, he looked good. He looked really good. Then again, so did Arn himself, so he couldn't dispute the honest-to-god healing involved. That wasn't why they were there, though.

"What's up with you, Paddy? What has you so spastic?"

"First I can't provide for my family, then I can't protect them. It's driving me nuts! They took Kara, Arn. They hurt her, hurt her bad…The same ones who tried to grab her in Queens."

Arn raised his eyebrows at that. This was news to him, the specifics anyway. He'd seen the news report of their disappearance on TV, and he'd seen the damage to the O'Keefes' home in person, but the details leading up to that were a mystery. He'd hear that story at some point if Patrick wanted to tell it, but right now, only one thing concerned him: "Are they connected to the ones who took my Lynn?"

Patrick looked guilty, though none of the blame was his. "I hope na. An' yet, the same time I do. I wouldn't want anyone in their hands, but I also hate to think there's someone else out there to worry about."

His gaze intent, Arn leaned toward Patrick. "How'd you get her back?"

"There's this *Sidhe* woman called Brid…she's a seer…she used her Sight to look for Kara until she found her." Patrick's voice grew hard. "Not her fault, but it took too long. Something blocked her an' she couldn't lock in until that was gone. Demigod or no, if I ever get my hands on this Olcas, there won't even be a bloody pulp left."

His friend fell quiet and would say no more. Arn was relieved at that. He didn't need the specifics twisting him up inside when he had to focus on getting Lynn back. At least he had a direction. Some potential for finding her.

Content with that for now, he turned the pressure back on Patrick. "Come on…purge the rest. You know cancer feeds on negative emotions."

Patrick looked belligerent. "I haven't got it anymore."

"Good, keep it that way. Spill."

"Fer God's Sake! They were supposed to be safe here! My Bobbi, one of the fae spelled her to sleep so the bastard could steal some other woman. What's to stop any o' that from happening again? And then this," Patrick said, his hands thrust up. "On top o' it all, *this*. I have my life back, clean bill o' health an' everything, but I have no friggin' control over it anymore."

That got a laugh out of Arn. A bitter one, but a laugh just the same. "I have news for you, Patrick. None of us have the control we think we do. We hold on and pray, and when that doesn't work, we curse and we grab onto something else."

They stared a moment into each other's eyes, a quiet, honest look. They recognized their kindred pains and fears, founded and unfounded, changeable or not. They each nodded, understanding that whatever came next, they stood by one another.

"You know," Arn finally spoke up again, raising his own hands. "This isn't a big deal to anyone but you, those who matter couldn't care less."

Patrick grimaced but nodded. "Aye, easy enough to say, but look…"

Familiar with the old diatribe, Arn cut him off: "…look at all the wonderful things that have come into your life because of it…your wife, your daughter…Me! I'd have to say you made out pretty darn good on that score."

It worked. Patrick laughed and gave him a shove.

"Just, don't let this twist you up," Arn added. "You can't be anything for anyone if you're locked in your own little dark place inside."

"Shut up, already." Patrick groused back, but his spirit visibly lightened. "I'm trying to find a pixie. Ye might turn that sharp eye o' yers to the task as well."

Arn chuckled and let his eyes scan the trees like a great big natural seek-and-find. Once or thrice, he thought he might have actually spied something, but it was hard to say, having never seen an actual pixie before.

"So…what does a pixie look like?"

"Shh. Ye'll know when ye see one."

Grinning and shaking his head, Arn went back to searching. It was good to have his friend as he used to be and hadn't been since long before this crazy business. Things were back on a comfortable plane now that they were confronting things together. They sat there and relaxed a while, sometimes talking, sometimes not. They never did find a pixie, though Arn couldn't swear any hadn't found them. When the sounds from the glade started to die down, they stood and returned to see how they could help.

"So, what's this Miller's Son you were going on about?" Arn asked as they wended their way through the trees.

"Huh." Patrick frowned and pursed his lips. For a moment, it seemed he would not speak. But then he tilted his head as he used to when they'd listen to his father tell a tale. "There's a legend of a warrior, Earl Gerald, the Wizard Earl, one o' the great protectors. 'Tis said that he and his warriors sleep in a long cavern under the Rath o' Mullaghmast. Every seven years the Earl wakes. He rides around the Curragh of Kildare on a steed with silver hooves. When they're worn thin as a cat's ear, the miller's son with six fingers to each hand will blow his trumpet to wake the warriors, an' *Gearoidh Iarla*, as he's called in Irish, will return to the land o' the living to defend Ireland."

Arn nodded, thinking of what his friend had told him. It was pretty amazing. Not that he believed in legends. But still…any chance to give Paddy a poke, right? "You do know my mother's maiden name was Miller, right?" Arn raised his hands to his mouth and mimed the motions of tooting a horn like he was Louis Armstrong.

Patrick laughed. "Ye can be such an ass."

Chapter 4

Kara dreamt longingly of disappearing into the forests of Tír na *nÓg*…and leaving behind the senseless debate going on around her, as many of the *Sidhe* waited for the rulers of the Lands to come out and make their decree in the matter of the one known as Bran. It was clear that most of them would have stormed the chamber by now if it weren't for the shimmering curtain of energy shielding the doors and the lace-like walls from both entry and view. She watched the goings-on from the other side of the clearing that led to the doors of Goibhniu's rath, too hypersensitive at the moment to get any closer to the emotional maelstrom. (Besides which, she had no intention of making herself a target for the disgruntled crowd.) Things were tense enough.

She turned away from the Court. Their intensity only agitated her more. Breathing deeply, she tried for a bit of Zen herself. The battle…the healing…the arguing…most of it was over for now. Even if they couldn't, she needed to let it go, so she'd be able to act rather than react. There were, after all, several enemies still out there somewhere.

Suddenly, the barrier dropped, and the doors to *Mór Halla* flew open. Within, attendants stepped back sharply and there was a whirl of activity in the entranceway.

*Oh no, not again…*Kara closed her eyes a moment, willing herself calm as she gathered her strength for whatever was about to hit. Meeting with some success, she slowly opened her eyes. Goibhniu strided forward like an angry Titan, the rulers of the other *Sidhe* Lands close behind him.

By now, Kara thought she was familiar with rage and anger, that she knew the feel of fury intimately. But anything she had experienced paled in comparison to the emotions radiating beneath the surface of Goibhniu's controlled expression.

"We have long overlooked the Bone Raven's dark ways. They were aspects o' his nature that he seemingly kept in check." Even Goibhniu's tone remained controlled and neutral, his voice like steel, regret and anger tempered with resolve. "But there are boundaries that must never be breached. In his actions today, he violated them. From this moment forth, Bran is no longer of the

Tuatha de Danaan, he is cast out from the *Daoine Maithé*. Let it be as if he never was. His spirit forfeits the right to mingle with the Kin."

It seemed to Kara that that final bit echoed both in her mind and her ears as if broadcast far and wide. By the gasps that escaped the group as Goibhniu spoke, and the horror and sorrow shadowing every eye in the Court when he was done, Kara gathered that this was the worst proclamation he could have made. There was movement all around as those who had remained away or had left the vicinity of *Mór Halla* returned.

Kara felt like a rock in the river, with immortals streaming past her on either side. Something within her urged her forward. Unsure of what it was or why, she hesitated.

A shuddering breath sounded by her shoulder, and Kara looked up to find Maggie beside her. The *Sidhe*'s expression was veiled, and her arms wrapped tightly, almost protectively about her stomach, as if she might be ill.

"What does he mean?" Kara asked after a moment. The *Sidhe* did not seem to hear. Trying to be patient, Kara rested her arm across Maggie's shoulders, offering comfort. She asked again, "Please, Maggie, what does it mean?"

Maggie swallowed hard and seemed to pale, her jaw flexing as she struggled to voice the words. "What it means is all places o' the *Sidhe* are closed to him. He will never be recognized again as a *Tuatha de Danaan*, an' his very pattern will be excised from the Great Wall as if he never existed. Bran not only is no more in the eyes o' his Kin, he never was. We don't kill our own kind in the name o' justice, but many would claim this even worse. It hasn't been done in living memory, excepting perhaps that o' the rulers o' the Lands."

"If thine eye offends thee, pluck it out," Kara could not help but murmur in response. She regretted the words the moment they left her lips, but Maggie merely quirked her mouth in a brief, grim smile. The reality of what the banishment represented settled in. Kara drew a sharp breath and hugged Maggie closer as the *Sidhe* trembled and shook, still clutching her belly protectively.

"Thank ye, love." Maggie managed before she continued. "What is worse, 'tis forever. Should he die, his soul will never rejoin the *Daoine Maithé*. With his evil act, he has diminished us all in a way that can't be repaired."

Kara felt Maggie shudder one last time before getting herself back under control. Breathing deep and regaining her composure, she offered Kara an apologetic smile. "Excuse me, love, I must leave ye for now. The Kin are summoned to take part in the ritual striking the abomination from the Wall."

All of pure *blood you mean*, Kara thought, though she herself felt something tugging her back to the Court. She followed though she knew many there would protest her presence.

In seemingly endless numbers, they streamed through the archways, their features as distinct as the lands they hailed from. By description alone, Jacko thought he recognized the Alvar of the Norse lands, thanks to their Scandinavian features and their appearance of elongated grace. For the rest, he had to dig through his smattering of world mythology to put a name to the fae creatures. He knew the Fossegrim of Norway by their mist-shrouded feet and the Devas of Persia by their angelic air. In their native dress, the Menehunas of Polynesia were easy to identify, while he would never have guessed the Rusalki of Russia, if not for being brushed by one of the women's cool, wet, and decidedly green tresses. He did not have names for them all.

On and on they came, from every country and land, every culture and corner of the world. They mingled with their Kin, the *Sidhe*, who called this land their home. Most were beautiful, or quite emphatically *not*; no in-between. All were terrifying and immortal, with eyes heavy with the weight of the ages. Jacko felt at once ancient and infantile in their midst. Every ache and wrinkle, every moment of weariness and grey hair threaded through his unruly curls, all of it came into abrupt focus against the glowing perfection, the eternal youth filling the hall around him. But as he looked into their timeless eyes, he truly understood how callow and untried he was.

He could not restrain his impulse to back away. The grief and torment around him felt intensely private, his own presence an intrusion. So focused on Agnieszka's plight, he had not considered this was not the time or place; he'd only seen opportunity.

Suddenly frantic to be away, he struggled to back out of the Hall, his progress impeded by the continued influx of immortals. It was a horrible parody of a salmon failing to swim upstream.

No matter how he tried, he could not make his way out past the influx. At last, he reached the protected vantage point of a massive pillar, one of a score that ran the length of the chamber down both sides. From his perch, his gaze locked on one other seemingly out of place. The girl, Kara, the unwitting cause of the battle just fought. There was something familiar about her.

The weight of the tension in the hall hung oppressive, hushed and packed, with no unnecessary movement. Every member of the elven race the world over had been compelled here. Kara swept along, driven to follow by an impulse deep within. Though not precisely included in the charge, her way had not been barred. More, she figured, because she'd gone unnoticed, than for any other reason. She made her way to where Maggie stood, careful not to draw attention to herself. Not that that was likely as the *Sidhe* all stood bound together by tension, every eye drawn to the Great Wall. More than architecture, more than art, that one wall represented the experiences of every *Sidhe* ever born. The intricate knotwork went beyond decoration; in color and shape, it grew and changed as the *Tuatha de Danaan* did. Smaller, isolated patterns she hadn't noticed before bracketed the main pattern.

Curious… She would have to ask Maggie about those later. For now, her eyes continued to take in the Great Wall, in awe of what it represented. For Bran to be stricken from this living history of the *Sidhe* race for all time was testament to the severity of his offenses. The grave nature of what she was about to witness floored her.

On the dais in front of the Wall, Goibhniu's massive throne was gone from its usual place. Where it had rested, an enormous forged-steel anvil stood; ancient, dark, and unyielding, like the Smith that worked upon its surface. Here was a stark reminder that the *Sidhe* had absolutely no problem handling cold iron or its derivatives. Before them stood the epitome of all blacksmiths, workers of iron. Goibhniu's expression remained completely neutral, as did his voice when he finally spoke.

Kara did not find that reassuring.

"Two things the *Daoine Maithé* honor above all else: kin an' oath. To betray either is to be banned from the Land. To betray both is to be banished from all Lands. The Cursed One has added treachery beyond measure to his crime, betraying not one o' us, but all o' us. As ruler o' this Land an' first betrayed, I invoke the Unraveling."

The pronouncement was a part of the ritual. Though it was no surprise, another collective gasp sounded through the Hall.

"Who bears witness to this betrayal?" The words broke over the Court like a tsunami upon the rocky cliffs. They were echoed by others, each voice terrible in its own right. Kara could not blame them; if one of them could be banished, any of them could. It was natural that they would need justification.

The collective rulers of the *Sidhe* Lands spoke.

Kara came forward in an unthinking haze, her feet compelled, and her eyes on those now arrayed upon the dais. Some instinct told her to level her eyes down; to bow her head to these who the native people called gods, but they were not her gods and she fought the impulse. If they were offended, it did not show, and Kara continued on with respect and dignity.

As she crossed the Court, hands reached out to hold her back. She felt their outrage, but it did not stop her. There were whispered hisses of "human" and "waterkin" from the crowd, and, in front of her, bodies moved to block the way. She lifted her chin and gave them a look completely foreign to the deferential girl she'd once been. For a moment, her obstructers glared back, and tension of another sort filled the crowd.

The sound of shifting came from behind her as gasps and grumbles peppered the air. Kara did not look away from those at the fore, but she felt the restraining hands drop off, and others replace them with the briefest touches of solidarity. She did not need to look to know the *Sidhe Fianna* had her back. The tension compounded until the air itself trembled.

Then Kara had to swallow a startled laugh. A trill rose from around her feet as a brush of fur against her ankles heralded a flood of kin-cousins invading the hall. They chuckled and cooed and brayed until the chamber echoed with an astounding ruckus. Each would-be adversary was beset by the faelings until they fell back in disgust. When the way was clear, the kin-cousins faded into the background.

From the dais, the voices repeated once more, "Who bears witness to this betrayal?"

Kara met their gazes with a respectful nod as she stepped down the path grudgingly opened before her. The *Sidhe* gods nodded, and Kara continued forward of her own will with confidence and dignity.

"I, Kara O'Keefe, bear witness." Her voice was clear and strong and no louder than conversation. It echoed righteously through the Hall. "I watched as Bran raised the god-killing sword to strike down Goibhniu. With my own magic, I yanked the blade from his grip before he could thrust it through Goibhniu's back."

The uproar was deafening. Kara blocked it out. She breathed steady and deep, her eyes focused unwaveringly upon the dais. Over the raging of the Court, another voice rose clear and unyielding, "I bear witness," Aí said. "From the battlefield, I watched this take place."

On the tail of his words, ten others moved forward, the woman at their fore small and delicate, even by *Sidhe* standards. "The Seers bear witness, all graced with visions o' these deeds."

The crowd went hushed on an indrawn breath. Outrage faded, re-placed by awe. Whoever this petite woman was, her word had consider-ably more weight than Kara's. It shouldn't matter, but Kara stiffened with resentment.

As one, those on the dais nodded. "By the word o' all these trusted witnesses," Goibhniu's voice rang out, "an' by the visions o' the Seers, judgment is called upon the Cursed One: the Unraveling."

The occupants of the dais echoed the last two words, as did the Court. Kara found herself mouthing them as well. She watched in fascination as the Smithgod picked up his hammer and a bar of cold, hard steel. After moments in his bare hand, the bar stock glowed the cherry red of metal pulled fresh from the forge, though none was in sight. Stock was laid to anvil and hammer to stock. Over and over, Goibhniu brought down his hammer; *tap tap tap* as sparks flew from the god-heated metal. It was not long before the blade of a dagger took shape. The raw end of the bar became a crude hilt bearing the impression of Goibhniu's fist clenched around it.

The hammer made one final *tap,* and Goibhniu plunged the completed blade into the bucket beside him. The Court hissed along with the doused blade. Goibhniu whipped the dagger through the air, held aloft for all to see, and, though it hardly seemed possible, the silence deepened with a roar that told Kara what it would sound like for bare steel to split an atom. It was almost easy to believe the fury of a god was in that sound—felt more than heard.

Kara jerked in reaction, but her gaze remained fixed on the dagger. Though she stood no closer than halfway to the dais, she sensed a presence in that weapon. Somehow it was familiar to her. Before Kara could puzzle out why, she was distracted. Her attention—along with that of every being in the Court—held captive by Goibhniu's movements.

Still holding the new-forged blade high, he turned and set the point upon a section of the massive knotwork engraving the Great Wall. Kara's chest tightened as she watched, and unexpected pity dulled the edges of her satisfaction. That knotwork was more than pretty decoration, certainly more than symbolic. The intricate engraving linked directly to the life-force of every *Sidhe*, from the womb to the grave and back again. It documented each lifetime, for good or ill. Bran's was twisted and colored in sullen and malevolent shades, but still beautiful. Goibhniu traced the section with the blade tip, taking meticulous care, not missing one line, and never straying beyond where he intended. Kara felt a faint tingle as color leached from the pattern. When he completed the circuit, the blade was passed to the next upon the dais. Each of the rulers followed suit as the dagger moved from one to the other's hand. Gradually, Kara noticed all the fae move forward to form something of a queue. Some moved with conviction, others grudgingly.

Her body buzzed as each *Sidhe* took their turn. She felt the urge to either flee altogether or fall in line. Her choice was to step forward, but once more, a hand restrained her. She jerked away and her head snapped around, heated gaze locking with regretful.

"'Tisn't yer place, love," Maggie murmured as the rest of the *Sidhe* steadily streamed by. "Only the *Daoine Maithé* may take part in the ritual. Only kin can banish kin."

But not waterkin. Kara's heart added into the uncomfortable pause; a seed of bitterness was planted.

This was wrong. Kara wanted to argue. Soul-deep, something told her Maggie was wrong. She couldn't even say which part of the statement was flawed, but the realization came with an edge of panic. Then her friend let go, moving past to join the procession herself. Kara's teeth ached as her tension grew. The urge to step forward was beyond a compulsion; it had the solid edge of conviction. There was something they had missed.

But no…she was not permitted. Again she was left out, yet she was as much a part of this as any of them.

Though her nerves continued to scream in protest, she kept her place.

When the need to take part grew overwhelming, Kara glanced away, her gaze wandering the Hall. She was somewhat startled to note that she was not alone in her exclusion; scattered about the Court were a double handful of men and women with the features and essence of *Sidhe*, but something more of her world about them. All of them, including her, wore flowing tunic and loose, silken pants, with long, wide sashes crossing one shoulder before circling their waists; the only variance in the outfits was color. The style was not dissimilar to what many of the Court wore, lacking only the embellishment that set apart those in personal garb. None of them looked particularly comfortable in what to her most resembled pajamas. Kara imagined her expression closely resembled theirs.

After a bit of thought, she realized who they were: the *Cosaint*s. The Hidden Ones, the *Sidhe* raised as human, who were not a part of the main pattern on the Wall, making them full blood-kin, but not Kin. Likely, if she were to count the smaller patterns she noticed earlier, they would pair with each of these people, with one left over for the kidnapped Agnieszka.

There was one other outsider among the gathered. Perched on the tall base of a far column was one of the Rom. A faeling sat at his feet, a dark fellow wearing the form of a mostly black tabby. Kara shivered at the look on the Romani's face, the intent way he watched her. He made her nerves twitch even more. Kara looked away, back to the Unraveling.

She shivered again, and this time, it had nothing to do with the Romani man. More akin to how she imagined a spider felt when something tangled in its web.

Her gaze focused on the Great Wall. The more *Sidhe* that traced Bran's pattern, the more Kara noticed that the colors drained away. It was nearly solid black now, as if he'd died, and as would be the case if he had, it would grow smaller over time until the two adjoining patterns came together. No new pattern would form at the open end of the spiral, and the *Tuatha de Danaan* would be diminished. Kara felt the sorrow of that; no matter Bran's actions, the *Sidhe* would mourn his soul's loss.

But Bran had misused his magic, kidnapped a *Sidhe*, and attempted to murder the ruler of *Tír na nÓg*. This Unraveling excised a cancer.

Her fingers itched as she watched, but she stood firm, Maggie's admonition still whispered in her ear.

Finally, after what felt like the better part of a day, they were almost done. The fae each accepted the blade gingerly as if they themselves would vanish at its touch. Most traced the pattern, passed the dagger on, and in grim haste departed out one of the many arches leading from the Hall. No few shot glowering looks toward Kara, as if she were actually to blame for the acts that called down the judgment upon Bran. She met their gazes with one of her own, though she could not say what it spoke to them. Kara looked away first, not because she felt shame, but because they weren't worth it.

And because despite those casting hateful looks—or more likely due to them—several of the *Sidhe* stayed, forming ranks around her. Not all of them were of the *Fianna*, the warriors who had rescued her, those hand-selected by Goibhniu to battle the threat of Olcas and his brothers, Dubh and Calma. Officially, she was not one of the *Fianna*; in fact, she was much more akin to them than she was to the rest of the *Sidhe*, her experience with the enemy having strengthened that bond.

Hands reached out to clasp her shoulder, to brush her back, to squeeze her fingers, but no one said a word as they all watched the final few sever Bran's existence from the *Sidhe* race. Maggie was the last. Her expression fierce as she drew the blade swift and sure along the blackened pattern. She then lowered her gaze and presented the blade to Goibhniu, who waited beside his anvil, hammer in his grip, eyes blazing and muscles taut and hard like carved marble. Kara flinched from the gaze he swept across the now near-empty Hall. His fury remained palpable as he laid the dagger's edge against the anvil and raised his hammer high.

Kara wanted to cry out, to stop him; at the last, she did lunge forward, though the *Fianna* held her back. There was no stopping the Smithgod as he shattered the dagger with one blow. Kara swore and ducked away as metal shards flew. By the time she looked back, Goibhniu had dropped the hilt upon the anvil and walked away, the crash of steel on steel loud in everyone's ears.

"It isn't done," she yelled after him. "It isn't done!" He did not slow or turn. She felt the truth of her words, though all around her, the *Sidhe* murmured assurance that Bran was banished. But no. It did not feel complete, the compulsion had not faded. She looked up to meet Maggie's gaze and all Kara could do was shake her head. There was understanding in the *Sidhe* woman's expression, but not of the truth Kara was at a loss to convey.

Kara sighed, and her eyes drifted closed as she bowed her head in resignation. She heard the others move off, felt a few hands reach out in passing, but she was too weary to move, drained dry by the judgment ruled and executed. She told herself they had to be right and it was done, but her heart did not believe it. There was something overlooked. But what could be done now?

A quiet murmur rose from around her feet. Still bowed, she opened up her eyes. Beag Scath crouched there, chin on his tiny knees staring at the near-perfect tip of the dagger resting close in front of him. With a soft, in-drawn breath, Kara reached down to claim it and knew what she must do.

"Come, love." Maggie's tone was weary, and her hand trembled as she tugged Kara's shoulder.

"Please…" Kara looked up at her friend and fought the urge to cry out at what she saw. She didn't know what was worse: having to watch the Unraveling, or participate, but Maggie looked paler than moonbeams on snow. "Please," Kara repeated, her voice calmer than she would expect. "I need a moment."

It looked as if Maggie would refuse, or worse yet, wait with her, but the *Sidhe* let out a long breath and nodded. "Come to Goibhniu's chambers when yer done, if ye would."

Kara offered a faint smile of thanks and agreed.

She waited a long time: Waited for Maggie to be gone. Waited for her soul to steady. Waited until the only sound she heard was Beag Scath's muttering. Waited for those gentle threads that always searched for her.

Come, she sent the summons as they brushed her thoughts. *Come.*

The kin-cousins crept from the hidden corners of the Court; Faelings of all types and sizes, on the wind and wing and little fae feet. Kara stood and watched, waiting as they thronged about her.

She smiled and let them feel her love, her thanks. "Please," she murmured, for they didn't really need the words. "Find these…" Kara held up the dagger point, and before she finished, the faelings scattered about the Court in a frenzy grabbing up the jagged shards. "Oh! Careful! Careful!" she cried out, louder than before.

As they scampered about the Hall, Kara stared at the point in her hand and had a thought. Perhaps the whole was not required…perhaps it would be enough… With desperate hope, she stepped forward and placed the dagger point to the blackened pattern. Slow at first, then with more desperation, she traced the lines as the others had, straining with her senses to capture some small sign the deed was done. She scarcely noticed the jagged edges cutting her flesh as she clutched the point tighter. The hall echoed with her frustrated groan as her hand dropped away, the ghosting of color upon the spiral taunting her with her failure. *Because, of course, it could not be as simple as that.*

Her only hope lay in reforging the blade. She suspected only once it was whole again could she hope to finish what had been begun in the Unraveling. How she would manage it, she had no clue.

Kara turned her back on her failed effort to discover a pile of shards already at her feet. A little of her heartache eased, though an edge of fear still wrapped about her. "Thank you, my little ones." Quickly, she stripped off the wide sash at her waist. Dropping to her knees, she gathered every shard and speck, wrapping them secure. And then she looked up. A large, rough hand dangled the bladeless hilt before her.

"They missed one."

The voice was smooth, lilting, but different from the prevalent Irish brogue characteristic of most of the company she'd lately kept. The tone it held was calm and non-threatening. Kara scrambled back anyway, heat fleeing her body as fast as the faelings fled the Hall. She suppressed a shiver before it could escape as well.

Looking up, she met the fathomless gaze of the Romani man. He was older than she'd thought, with threads of silver through his deep, dark hair and a tracing of lines about his eyes and mouth, evidence he had a habit of smiling, under other circumstances.

She'd thought he'd gone!

Slowly he knelt, eyes never leaving hers, and laid the bladeless hilt upon her dropped bundle. Apparently, the faelings had followed her request literally, bringing her only the blade shards. Settling back on his heels, The Romani locked his fingers together across his belly and tilted his head, just so to look at her with shrewd eyes, moving from her face to her bloodied hands and on down to the pile of shattered metal.

"Why are you staring at me?" Kara's former softness forged into a challenge.

He returned the ghost of a smile and gave a bit of a shrug as he handed her the kerchief from his neck to clean up her hands. Without conscious thought, she accepted. "You remind me of someone, is all," the Romani answered. "And my friend really likes you." Kara looked down to spy the dark sprite at her feet, still cloaked in regal cat pose and leaning until he just barely touched her leg. The little one's posture was subservient, and he would not meet her gaze. The hall rumbled with his purr as she looked down at him. "What do you intend to do with them?" the Romani man asked.

For a moment, Kara was confused until she looked up to see he pointed at the shards. She considered them a moment hoping for some inspiration beyond the impulse that drove her to gather them up. None came. Sighing, she folded the sash into a bundle, which she then knotted securely. Looking up at the Rom, she met him eye to eye. "I'll let you know once they tell me," she muttered wryly as she rose with her burden and went her way.

Behind her, the Rom laughed.

Chapter 5

Hidden deep in the bogs of Ireland where the ground was scarcely less treacherous than he, Bran the betrayer could not believe that he had been condemned to the Unraveling. That every one of his own kind would turn against him so. *Inconceivable!*

And yet, with every stroke of Goibhniu's blade, Bran felt the casting out as if it sliced through his very flesh. He cursed the *Tuatha de Danaan* from the moment the ritual began. He screamed and clutched himself tightly into a ball as they carved away at his soul's anchor. The agony long outlasted his voice. Screams diminished to howls, howls to moans. Moans did not make it to whimpers only but for Bran's pride. In agony, he lay there, surrounded by the opulence of his secret bower, conscious of the sole witness to his weakness. Was Agnieszka aware in her bespelled slumber? He had thought her human, or at best, waterkin, only to discover that she was full Kin. If he could have moved, he would have slaughtered her in his rage. But he could not. Instead, with each thread of his soul they severed, he made a fresh vow of vengeance against his entire race that they would suffer worse than even this.

He lay there waiting for the final thread to be severed.

He lay there for a very long time.

"Finish it!" he screamed, surprised that he was able.

It was a while longer before he grew enough accustomed to the agony to rise despite it, but with each move he made that final thread tugged. Each tug sent a shaft of fresh torment rippling through him. It ate at him as he wondered and worried at it. Why was it still there? To taunt him? To prolong his torment? Or was it a sign that at least one stood by him, faking the cuts of the Unraveling to leave him that tenuous hold, that one remaining link? It wasn't much. As thin as spider silk, as strong as well. Even if meant as a blessing, it was a curse.

Still, it was something. A weapon he would use against the *Tuatha de Danaan* at his first opportunity. He was still linked to the *Sidhe* Lands. Could still enter at will. He staggered across his bower, leaning heavily against the silk-draped wall woven of willow branches and magic. Trembling, fighting through the pain for his next breath, Bran lowered himself to his knees beside the "human" *Sidhe.*

"Not much longer, my prize, not long at all." Bran ran a hand along the woman's unlined face and up through her pure white hair. His touch was gentle at first, then with a vicious tug, he fisted his hand among the thick locks. He examined her features with cold hatred. A snarl twisted his lips, and only extreme restraint held him back from doing Aí's precious Agnieszka harm. It would be so wasteful to vent his anger on her now…the ritual would be soon enough, mere hours away. She represented a major victory over Aí and his blasted "god," Goibhniu. That one had given more care to her than he ever had to Bran, despite their ties. Stolen from beneath their very hands, she was both a blow to their puffed-up pride and the key to the willful destruction of Bran's former people.

Without sparing a second thought for the woman, he turned away, leaving her in her spell-induced slumber from whence she could not awake until Goibhniu released her. The condition suited Bran quite well; he couldn't ask for an easier prisoner to maintain, and unless Goibhniu knew where she was, she would remain that way for as long as such things mattered.

Clawing his way to his private chamber, its luxury at striking odds with the dank dreariness of the surrounding bog, he collapsed across a slowly-moldering, velvet-clad chaise lounge. Before this moment, his revenge had been well begun. Now this unexpected blow left him weak, unable to keep the nature of the bog from encroaching. He seethed at the need to recover before executing the next step.

First, through sheer brute force of will, Bran internalized the pain, deadening his senses to allow him to move in a normal manner despite his agony.

Hours. Days. Centuries. Bran had no concept of how much time passed before he had full control of himself. Once he did, he went to gather the woman and the other components needed to summon a demigod.

That was when he noticed the bog was in bloom. Unnaturally so, out of season, with a lushness the wilds of Ireland rarely saw. Not just his bower, which he'd crafted to be most pleasant, but the surrounding muck that was meant to mask their presence. Instead, it flourished like a beacon. Dying willows found new life, and the marsh flora ran as wild as a botanist's dream of heaven. Even the deadfall began to take root.

Bran glared across his chamber at the cause. Already, the depression the spell-locked sleeper rested in more resembled a true bower than the simple woven cot he'd magicked out of willow fronds. Even in her slumber, he could feel this aberration's magic altering their surroundings, fostering new life where before there had been but decay. The Unraveling had crippled his own magic, slow to recover, and lacking the strength it had before. Bran seethed as her effortless transformations mocked him.

"That is enough!" Bran hissed as if she could hear him. "Shall I show you what this feels like?" His pale eyes glowed with malice, his face taut with intense agony as he dragged his open hand across his chest in a clawing gesture. "It is worse than fingernails slowly peeled away one by one, more intense than skin flayed from flesh, millimeter by millimeter, and seawater used to bathe the blood away."

As he spoke in low, intense tones rife with rage and torment, Bran reached for the woman's hand. "Shall I show you?"

Abruptly, he curled his hand back to his side. She was destined for sacrifice. But would the offering suffice if it was marred? He could not say. What he little he knew of the god he summoned was vague: a hatred for the *Tuatha de Danaan* (Bran no longer considered himself such, despite that one last soul-thread), a need for a host, and a sacrifice required for the merging. Bran dared not risk damaging her.

The urge was overwhelming, though.

It was time. He could wait no longer. The strength of the sacrifice's mage potential would more than make up for any deficit in his own. And once Calma was summoned…surely, a god could do away with this crippling pain; vengeance could come later.

The air thickened. Bran imagined a sense of awareness blanketing all, curious, intrigued, ready. He ignored the sensation as he crossed his chamber to the pagan blade hanging on his wall. It glimmered in the sultry air, poised provocatively, as if waiting to descend. Bran claimed the athame from its mount, and gathered rope and ritual candles, placing everything in a simple rucksack. He then slung it over his shoulder until the weight of it lay across his back. Thus prepared, he slid his arms beneath the woman and hefted her up.

Just past the walls of his hiding place, a wind came from out of nowhere. It was an unnatural current, blowing first from one direction and next from another, wrapping close about him, plucking as if it tasted of him as one would sample the air or fine wine. Then it was gone, just as suddenly. Bran grimaced at the agony the buffeting enflamed. Snarling, he pushed through in the direction of his goal, following the scents of ancient spilt blood mingled with suffering. His pulse quickened at the aroma, and his steps grew steadier, despite his pain. Then, in the dying light, he saw it, an altar jutting out of the gorse, the ancient grey granite even now stained deep rust in a telling pattern at one end.

The Bone Raven smiled a nasty smile, eyes bright and eager for the first time since the Unraveling.

❋

Like turbulence whipping the waves before a storm, the darker muses bestirred Calma—son of the goddess Carmán, brother to Dubh and Olcas, darkest of demigods—rousing him from his more-than-two-millennia-long sleep. He felt their electrified caress glide over his dormant consciousness. Cool, liquid fire ignited his thoughts, flooding it with knowledge of the intervening centuries. His personal age of enlightenment transpired in a microsecond.

What remained of him now rose to shadow the cursed, barren earth where he and his brothers had fallen. A worthless tract of land yet abandoned by the sons of Eire though none alive remembered why. He knew this because he had made it his resting place the moment his spirit unhinged from his body. Across the intervening years, his slumbering soul had drawn off the life force of aught that attempted an existence below or above the soil that was long ago soaked in his blood.

Calma had grown strong on the stolen energy while at rest, but now it was time to awaken. The world reformed around him once more, not as sight or sound or touch, but in the ever-expressive and unavoidable sense of smell. Above all else, Calma savored the bittersweet tang of ambition mingled with the stench of moral decay; he lost himself in the miasma of betrayal and thrilled in the clinging, musty aroma of hopelessness. Society's bouquet had ripened in his absence. Underlying it all was one perfume that drew him more than any other. He allowed his senses to steep in the warm, revitalizing musk of mage energy. Like a moth-eaten blanket, it covered all, thick but for the occasional hole left by the rare magic-user left in the world. These were much fewer than they were long ago when he'd worn his own form. And still, he resented them, even as he coveted their potential.

An impatient tug on his awareness interrupted those bitter thoughts.

His muses.

Scrios…Togail…Díoltas… One by one, he drew their fitting names from his quickened thoughts: Havoc, Destruction, Revenge. *Hello children, has the time for vengeance come?*

They swirled about him. They appeared one moment as youths on the cusp of becoming men, eyes dark and fierce, bodies strong. The next, they seemed as sinister winds, crackling with energy, swift, cunning, and destructive. He found their manner invigorating, fraught with potential. Let mankind recall only the soft, creative muses of his mother's homeland; for Calma, those were of no import beside these instruments of disorder.

The more he roused, the more his intellect assumed control, his thoughts questioned. What had triggered the awakening? His wards had been carefully wrought; certain very specific triggers were required to bring them down. Only the most optimal conditions were to herald his return: his brothers must both have awakened, there must be a ripe opportunity for vengeance, and there must be a powerful and willing host.

A tendril of thought quested the mortal world for confirmation, finding first one brother, then the other. With that fleeting touch, Calma learned that Dubh's cruelty had fermented over the centuries, and Olcas had grown stronger beyond the bounds of any potential his former self had possessed. Neither had transcended the petty torments or the drunken response to the power that had brought them all down more than two millennia ago. Neither had used the centuries to garner strength or mature in their goals.

Calma's awareness writhed with annoyance. Shielding his thoughts from his own blood, he sifted through his brothers' memories, sneering at the wasted efforts, the grasping for petty power, the centuries of floundering without focus or progress. He learned of the *Bás* and the Danaans and the multitude of ineffectual harassments waged against their ancient enemy, not to mention his brothers' poor showing along the way, culminating in the recent loss of the battle atop the faerie mound. Clearly, they needed his guidance if their plotting was to come to aught.

Well, that served the first two requirements. But of the third?

Díoltas… he murmured soundlessly. *What of my host?*

Summoned, the muse drew closer, holding his mortal seeming, beautiful and ruthless, slyly cunning. *Díoltas* tilted his head and narrowed his gaze, his lips pursing in satisfaction of whatever thoughts roiled behind those eyes. Drifting closer, the muse paused and lifted his brow in unvoiced question.

Now, Díoltas!

The muse's head dipped in acquiescence, his eyes shrouded as he darted amidst the cloud that was Calma's current form and drew a seemingly un-ending breath until all the demigod was drawn into his being.

If not for knowing the muse was incapable of containing him long, Calma would have been enraged. Unless he cared to destroy his favorite servant, his ability to act was crippled, bound tightly within the constraints of the muse. A temporary state, for such was his power that *Díoltas* would shred into a billion unrelated bits if he attempted to claim Calma's energy for his own, but vexing, nonetheless. Yet, this was the most expedient way of going to where the host waited.

Once taken into *Díoltas*'s self, Calma was held firm even after the muse let go of his corporeal form to take on his wind aspect. In the dark of a moonless night, the two of them whipped the heather and rattled the windows of the mortal world as they howled over the land to an ancient stone altar, half-buried in bog and gorse. It reeked of blood and magic and the dark old ways. The memories it held were of stolen life force, not willing sacrifice. In the vein of that tradition, two of the hated enemy formed a tableau echoing those quaint, long-ago rites. Bound upon the stone was a *Sidhe* woman crowned by glowing white tresses, whose personal scent spoke of heartache, loneliness, loss, and betrayal, bound by a cloyingly sweet ribbon of hope, strong beyond imagining, for all that it was slight. Her body was bare, and unlit black candles stood ready at her head and feet. Standing over her was a man of her kind with hair the color of ancient gold. His scent was overpoweringly of bitterness threaded through with pain, sharp and biting like yarrow condensed a thousandfold. His pale ivory eyes would have been cold and dead but for the rage burning deep within them. Such hatred Calma had never seen, even before his body was destroyed, though he had intimate knowledge of it. Eagerness surged. Either would do, but the man would be preferred.

Calma had not anticipated his vessel might be of the *Tuatha de Danaan*. Shocking, but ideal. Not only would his power flow unhindered through such a magical body, but it brought him particular satisfaction to use a member of the ancient enemy race to thwart the "justice" they'd brutally imposed upon him and his family. There was no sweeter revenge.

Which has Díoltas brought me here to see? Calma wondered.

Both beings had the wherewithal to wield awesome power, but were either of them his willing host? While he could take such a one by force, it would reduce the effectiveness of the vessel. Calma would not handicap himself so. With a willing host, he would have full access to the body's potential without resistance. Not to mention the knowledge of the being with which he shared occupancy.

Below, the stillness broke as the elven man slowly raised his hands from his sides. As he did so, he spoke harsh, guttural words in a ritual summoning. With a gesture from one hand, the candles flared to life, their light reflecting off the gleaming blade of the ancient athame clutched in the other.

If Calma could have sneered at the pompous display, he would have. As if any of that were necessary. And yet his attention was caught, focusing more on the participants than the ritual itself, primarily the man.

What would it be like to be housed in such a creature? While Calma found it gratifying to use one of the hated *Sidhe* against them, what he sensed of the man's nature reminded him all too much of his brothers. Plundering of the man's thoughts confirmed this. This…Bran…was pretentious, arrogant, shortsighted, and likely to be difficult. Without a doubt, he would wrestle for control. Still such potential, such hunger…

Yet Calma could not discount the woman. He found her tempting on several levels. He was not so foolish to think she would be any more malleable than a man just by the nature of her sex, but he had no doubt she would be easier to seduce. On the surface, her potential seemed virtually untapped. Intrigued by the prospect more with each passing moment, he reached out his awareness to learn more of her.

Her thoughts named her Agnieszka, which was puzzling. That was not a *Sidhe* name. The anomaly did not hold his attention long, however. What he encountered beyond her surface identity sent a surge of triumph through every particle of his being, a sensation jolting and electric enough to draw a grunt of protest from *Díoltas*. Immediately, Calma began to form plans, grand and glorious and much more satisfying than simple revenge.

He now looked down upon the doom of the *Tuatha de Danaan*, their very demise incarnate.

The woman was with child…a pure immortal child with the inherent mage potential capable of containing the power of a deity, its soul as yet unawake. Never before now had it occurred to him there might be a means to resurrect the goddess Carmán, yet here he found that exact potential. And most fortuitous, the woman was bound in slumber beneath a spell, unable to hinder his intentions.

So, for him, the man…willing or no. For though it galled Calma, he sensed he could not break the enchantment. And for his mother…the child. Mother dear would be furious, but the unborn one bore the seed of potential greater than either the man or its mother, making it the better vessel to contain her divine force. And best yet, it was a spirit yet developed.

As this magnificent plan formed, the *Sidhe* completed the complex gestures of whatever ritual he thought he performed. Calma, not paying attention to the man's actual words, was startled to hear his own name uttered, but had no time to consider the relevance as the man stilled, arms upraised and hand clasped over hand on the hilt of the athame, the blade poised above the now-precious woman's breast.

Horror engulfed Calma. The fool thought spilt blood would mean more than the victim's potential…the dizzying potential that would be squandered in that foolish and unnecessary act. In an instant, Calma's perfect vengeance would be in ruin.

*No! In the name of my Mother, No!** Calma raged, broadcasting the thought across the land indiscriminately. The *Sidhe*'s head reared up in confusion, the blade canting out defensively as he scowled at his surroundings, clearly searching for the source of the outcry.

A mere thought from Calma tore the dagger from Bran's grasp, the threat to the woman definitively removed. Even so, outrage and an unprecedented sense of panic sent Calma's spirit thrashing against the bounds of the muse containing him until his servant cried out with a wind's tortured cry. Only the value of the muse as a servant preserved him.

*Díoltas, release me!**

Those below were whipped mercilessly by the current as *Díoltas* spewed out Calma's essence, releasing on the moor an unnatural whirlwind. The muse then fled to heal, his essence in tatters.

Calma took no notice. He billowed above the altar, unconsciously sending sparks into the air like miniature lightning bolts. The *Sidhe* straightened, triumph animating his gaze an instant before he veiled it. He stared into the cloud that was Calma as if he saw him for what he was. When he spread his arms in invitation, there was no doubt.

The demigod swelled in a triumph of his own, then drew himself into a tight, dark funnel, the tail hovering steadily above the vessel. *Breath of me, Bran, become my willing avatar,* Calma murmured, reasonable and lulling, into that receptive mind, the words establishing the demigod in the position of power, ensuring his ability to act through the vessel would be unhindered. *Take all of me within, and I promise you, vengeance will be ours.*

"Will you take away my pain?" The *Sidhe* needlessly spoke aloud as he balled his fist and rubbed at his chest; the molten agony centered there loosed a scent savory to Calma.

No, Calma answered, the thought abrupt, contemptuous. Cold.

"Will you add to it?"

No. If Calma still had eyes, he would have glared. He offered this one power beyond any he could hope to wield alone, and yet Bran did nothing but question. Only the desire for a greater hold on this vessel prevented Calma from just taking possession.

"What will you do?"

Lead you to vengeance…and provide you the power to claim that prize. Calma allowed fervor to creep through his response in sly tendrils, echoing Bran's own, setting the lure. *You will be above all that call themselves Tuatha de Danaan…above all the world, and every realm.*

The fool did not think to question what would be asked of *him*. Poised, Calma followed his victim's thoughts and knew he had him. The *Sidhe* was not blind to the threat lurking behind the promise. He saw the threat as empty — *what more could be done to one whose soul had all but been cut away from its core? What could go beyond eternal agony?* Calma would enlighten him someday, once their joint vengeance was secured.

Without further hesitation, Bran breathed him in.

Chapter 6

Despite Maggie's request, Kara did not go straight to Goibhniu's chambers. She felt it unwise to bring the shards there with her. Stopping in her own chamber—a small room amidst those housing the *Sidhe Fianna*—she first transferred the fragments to a leather pouch and then hid it away in the wooden chest holding her things. After the strain of the Unraveling, she also took the time to run a brush through her hair and rinse her face with cool water from a spring-filled basin in the corner. Feeling restored, she hurried from the room and headed for Goibhniu's chambers before someone was sent to fetch her.

There was no need to knock; the door had been left open. In the room beyond, Kara saw her parents and Maggie sitting on silk-clad couches, refreshments laid out before them. Goibhniu was just entering from his private grotto, his dark hair slicked back, and his face moist, as if he also had needed restoring. Nodding with a slight smile, he gestured her toward the food the others had been nibbling on. It smelled wonderful, the aromas savory and spicy, crisp and fresh. There were platters of meats and cheeses, and bowls of fruit and fresh greens, all of it the sort to be eaten with fingers. Beside that was a porcelain ewer cool enough to appear frosted on its outer surface, without any condensation to mar the texture. Kara's stomach rumbled at the invitation, but she could not bring herself to sample what was offered.

The truth was she didn't have a clear idea of why she was there. Though she thought it unlikely she was to be chastised—given the lack of tension in the room and the offer of food—Kara still felt unsettled. Not wanting to appear ungrateful, she poured herself a glass of what proved to be nectar and sat beside her mother. Beyond the first sip, she did no more than hold the drink, waiting to learn the purpose of this summons.

Goibhniu moved across the room, and by the time he settled in his more formal chair, his hair was dry, the black curls just brushing his nape. She could not decipher the look on his face.

Calm yerself, child. Naught is wrong.

Kara jerked as Goibhniu soulspoke in her thoughts, her drink sloshing over the rim. Would she ever get used to that? Grimacing at the Smithgod, she set her glass down and watched him pointedly. He laughed in her head, bowing as if he conceded.

He stood, and the quiet conversation between her parents and Maggie stopped. They straightened in their seats and turned expectantly in Goibhniu's direction. Though it was not asked of her, Kara stood as well and faced him.

"Kara O'Keefe," Goibhniu addressed her with formality, "ye have done me a great service. In recognition o' the personal risk ye braved during the battle, I grant ye a boon. Whatever ye wish—for yerself or another—an it be in my power, 'tis yers."

Kara did not miss how his eyes turned toward her father as he spoke that last, and she was reminded of Maggie's original plea on the first occasion they had all gathered in these chambers. The *Fleadh Ghoibhnenn*…the feast where the very food and drink was supposed to bestow immortality, Goibhniu would grant her even that. While she didn't quite accept he had that kind of power, not personally believing in the divinity of any but the God of her Christian faith, part of her could not help but consider the possibility. Willing to try near anything to ensure her father's survival, Kara opened her mouth to accept. She did not get the chance.

"If ye don' mind, lass," Papa spoke before she could voice the request. "A word, please." Kara was quite aware he wasn't actually *asking*. Standing, he gestured her toward the privacy of the grotto.

She didn't know what to do. What was the etiquette when offered a boon by a pagan god? Uncertain, she looked to those around the room for guidance, settling last on Goibhniu. He didn't seem upset, or even concerned, as he nodded in agreement. As she went to follow, Goibhniu spoke aloud: "Whatever ye choose, apart from yer boon, ye will always have a place among the *Tuatha de Danaan*."

Kara nodded in acknowledgment and turned to join her father.

Papa stood on the far side of the grotto, by an arch of filigreed marble leading to the outside garden. "No," he said the moment she was beside him, hard and fast and with no room for discussion.

"Please, Papa, won't you even consider it? We need you with us…we need to know you're going to be okay."

"Ye'll not ask it."

"But…"

"I'm a *man*, Kara," Patrick said, the words gentle, but abrupt. "Men die. As God is my witness, I've no longing to live forever, just the time I'm due. Do not doubt me."

"What is the harm?" On the surface, there didn't seem to be any, to her, but her heart knew, and she lowered her eyes before she was even done speaking.

"I can't begin to imagine. Excepting at the very least, what about twenty…fifty years down the road, an' those I love have spent their time an' gone?

"Kara, I can't stop ye from asking it if ye wish, but do ye really want to waste yer boon? Ye can request the *Fleadh Ghoibhnenn* for me if yer set on it, and I'll even be there if ye ask me to go, but I tell ye…I will *not* eat. The only eternal life I seek will come to me after the Judgment Day."

Kara blinked hard and lowered her head, her next breath quavering. She did not try to argue further, though she wanted to. In her heart, she agreed, but the thought of a world without her Papa…well, she would rather not think on such a thing at all. Ever. She could feel a scowl forming, fueled by frustration. It was a struggle to smooth it away as fingers bearing the memory of callous gently raised her chin.

"An' haven't I already been gifted even more than that?" her father asked, his tone much softened.

Kara sighed, conceding defeat. "I love you."

His smile was just a little sad as he hugged her. "I love ye as well, an' will for a good many years yet, so don't ye worry."

Smiling back, Kara nodded.

"So, go back with ye and let Himself know ye need to give it a bit o' thought, why don't ye? I'm sure something will come to mind."

He said that like she was going back alone. "What about you?" she asked. Noticing the strain in his expression, she stepped back toward him.

"No…" He held up his hand between them. "I'm fine. I'm just thinking I could use a bit o' a walk…fresh air and all that."

As if the air anywhere in *Tír na nÓg* was anything but fresh; still, she could understand his need for a bit of space. "I'll let Mathair know."

Her heart ached as she watched him walk away.

Returning to Goibhniu's chamber was difficult. Kara lingered a while in the grotto, rinsing her face in a warm spring, giving some attention to several brave faelings who crept in from the garden to splash around themselves. She actually laughed when she discovered in one deep pool something that resembled a narwhal, only delicate. It was beautiful, with a long golden horn spiraling gracefully from its head and a pearly cream-colored hide that looked like wet velvet. With its eyes—a startling, vibrant blue—it begged to be caressed. Kara knelt beside the rim and ran her fingers over the smooth brow, encountering fine iridescent tendrils that weren't quite hair, but not fins either. She sighed, wondering at the Old Norse legends that claimed this creature as the true unicorn.

Have we been looking in the wrong place? she wondered. *Were the Vikings right, or just sly?* How many of these creatures—or mundane ones like this one—had been slaughtered for the "magic" of their horn?

She was overwhelmed by a desire to climb into the pool and frolic. As if knowing she felt the impulse, the faeling flicked its tail like a graceful wave, sprinkling her with a gentle spray of water, then pirouetted away, weaving and dancing through the water enticingly, before disappearing deep below. Kara laughed again, then jumped, nearly tumbling in after all as someone placed a hand on her shoulder. Bracing herself with her arms, she turned and looked up to see her mother, her lips gently curved in a smile. Kara grinned back and pushed to her feet.

"Where's your father?" Mathair asked, and Kara's grin faded. She'd almost forgotten why she'd been out here. Kara sighed and her mother's eyes darkened. Her smile took on a desperate edge. "Is something wrong?"

"No...no," Kara said quickly, "nothing's wrong. He just needed a walk, some air..."

Mathair looked down at her hands, which were fidgeting. "He told you not to ask, didn't he?" She didn't specify, but of course, she was talking about the Feast. "Don't be upset, honey. I knew he would. It's okay." Then she laughed. "Better than okay! He's healed, he's well...and I don't have to worry about him looking for a hot, young trophy wife when I'm eighty years old. Just think...to achieve immortality only to be killed by a thrown-over wife...is that really what you want for Papa?"

Kara laughed and pulled her mother into a hug. "I get it, just part of me doesn't want to. I thought Mamó and Grandda were going to be around forever, and then they weren't...all of a sudden and all at once. I didn't even have a chance to say goodbye. To think of facing that with Papa...with you...Some really, *really* immature part of me wants to have a good, old-fashioned kick-and-scream at the thought."

Mathair leveled a stern frown at her, the expression at odds with her soft and loving gaze.

"Okay! Okay...I get it, no trying to engineer a miracle, and no temper tantrums."

But that still didn't stop Kara from wishing for forever. Not for herself, but those she loved.

"Well! Now that we've established that I'll behave like an adult and Papa's okay, what about you?"

"Oh...absolutely not," Mathair answered, her expression solemn. "I categorically refuse to behave like an adult."

"Quite the comedian now, aren't you?" Kara said, playfully swatting her arm. But Mathair sighed.

"I have to be."

"A comedian?"

This time it was Mathair that swatted.

"Okay," she answered. "I have to be okay. You all have too much else to deal with. You don't need me adding to that worry."

Kara frowned. Taking Mathair's arms in a firm grip, she pinned her with a dead-serious look. "It doesn't work that way, Mom."

It was rare for her to address her mother as "Mom." For Kara, that was the equivalent of the triple-name-threat parents throughout time used against their children.

Mathair knew it too.

She brought her hands up and rested them on Kara's shoulder.

"Really, I'm not just blowing smoke," she answered, using a phrase that was more likely to come from Kara as if to coax another smile from her. "I'm either mad, in which case none of this is real and there's nothing to worry about, or I'm sane, it's real, and I have a kick-ass daughter and her magical friends looking out for me, in which case, what's there to worry about?"

Kara wasn't going to argue. What was there for her to say, after all? Mathair had found her stride, it seemed. This wasn't the first time Kara realized how amazing her mother was, just the most profound. Barbara O'Keefe had faced—*still* faced—fear, danger, and loss, and it didn't faze her nearly as much as it would have before. She was stronger, more confident, no longer needing so much to be taken care of.

"I won't tell you I'm not scared," Mathair went on. "Then I'd just be a fool. But I won't be freaking out on you the way I did before…at least, I don't think I will," she added with a grin.

Her expression quickly sobered once more. "I am so proud of you, more than I ever have been before, which is saying a lot. But more than that, I believe in you, so don't you let anything get in the way of you proving me right. Please…"

Kara heard a faint whisper of that fear Mathair mentioned. She pulled her mother close and hugged her tight. No other answer would serve. No other answer was needed.

Chapter 7

If he ever got back home, Arn Barnert was swearing off Tim Burton films for the rest of his life.

Really, it was like he'd been picked up by the hand of God from Monty Python and dropped in the middle of one of the director's sets. Crack dream meets daydream with no hope of waking up to something normal. This wonderland kept his nerves on edge as he waited for the darker side to strike again. He'd been doing okay at first when he'd gone into the forest to talk with Patrick. There he could almost pretend his world hadn't changed. But when they came out of the trees to a swarm of little…creatures, he'd lost some of the composure he'd held on to. They'd all returned to some fantastical palace in the middle of all that green, and Arn hadn't had a chance to rebalance since.

Bombarded with the details of the battle, and what led up to it, he was even more frantic to rescue Lynn than he'd been. The more time he had to himself, the more agitated he grew. *There's nothing I hate more than twiddling my thumbs. Or any other digits,* he thought wryly as he slowly flexed his hands and felt the peculiar sensation of his sixth finger curling against his palms a little off from the uniform way in which the other five lay flush. He hadn't felt that in over forty years. Performing surgery was going to be a bitch…

A scoffing laugh broke from his lips at such a mundane thought.

He couldn't actually imagine settling back into his old life. So much was uncertain. His fate…Lynn's…The strangled sound he made this time wasn't even close to a laugh. But that was why he was here. Didn't matter how much his pragmatic mind told him he was nuts, Patrick said the elven woman behind the door in front of him was…what was it?…a seer. If Arn could work up the guts to believe his friend, there might be some hope. All he needed was to know *something* was being done. Taking a deep breath, he reached out and landed one firm knock. The door opened before he managed another.

"Hello." The speaker was short and delicate to the point of being frail, or that was what his experienced eye told him, the assessment automatic from years of practice. Despite that, she radiated peace and wellbeing. "Would you like to come in?"

"Um..." Arn didn't know how to say what he needed too. The words stuck before they even reached his throat. "You see..."

"Yes," she answered, the faintest of smiles flitting about her lips as she looked first down one end of the corridor then pointedly down the other. "Come on, you'll feel more comfortable inside."

He sputtered as she drew him in, rearing back and away though he'd come here by choice for this very purpose. Now that he was faced with her and what she represented, all manner of emotions bombarded him, foremost being doubt, followed by embarrassment. His eyes burned with the former, his neck and face with the latter. But ultimately, he followed, finding himself on a mound of cushions with a goblet of the freshest water he could imagine cradled in his hands. "I need to find her," he said, his voice strained.

The woman gestured to the cup.

He took a sip then set the water down. "Please, will you help me?"

She watched him patiently with eyes like two deep blue star sapphires, a stunning contrast to her hair, which was the pale yellow-white of some daffodil trumpets. When he just stared back, she dipped her head and raised her brows, as if encouraging him to continue.

"Um...Patrick, he says you...see things."

She nodded. "Sometimes."

"I need ya to see my wife," A bit of his native Brooklyn showed through as Arn rushed the words like they had to be said quickly before someone noticed his folly. "Now, please." He fumbled for his pocket, his restored fingers getting in the way. When he finally got them sorted, he drew out a battered Polaroid. The picture was creased, part of the image smudged where his blood had coated it, but clearly visible in the unmarked portion was a woman's terror-filled face. Lynn. His wife. It was the Polaroid her kidnapper had left behind for him to find. The hand holding the photograph shook and Arn had to gulp back his reactive cry. Was it only a week ago when lost sleep and mounds of new insurance forms were his worst concerns?

The Seer didn't even look at the picture. Her gaze darkened and her expression changed from serene to solemn. She opened her mouth to speak but Arn already shook his head in denial of what she hadn't said. More forcefully, he pushed the photograph into her hands.

"Arnold Barnert," she chastised him lightly. He jerked at her use of his name, eyes narrowing as he considered how she'd come by it. "My gift doesn't work that way, no matter how we will it too." As she spoke, she smoothed out the edges he had crumpled getting her to take it. When it was as flat as she could make it she pressed it to her chest as if imprinting it to memory though she had yet to even look the image. Her eyes closed briefly and opened slowly. "My name...it's Brid, and I vow that *should* I see your Lynn, I will come tell you before the vision has even a moment to fade. That is the best that I can offer." There was sorrow in her gaze as she handed back the picture. "I promise you this."

It was an effort not to snarl, not to protest. He locked his jaw and forced both his fears and anger deep. This changed nothing. Lynn needed him, and he'd find her. With or without this woman's help. Nodding in acknowledgment, he extracted himself from the cushions and shoved the hated image back into his pocket, jamming his blasted sixth finger in the process.

Without another word, he gave Brid as respectful a bow as he could manage, and moved swiftly from the room before he disgraced himself one way or the other.

✵

That night, a feast was laid out in one of the lesser Halls branching off Goibhniu's Court. A feast, not *the* Feast. The second since they'd journeyed to *Tír na nÓg*. The fare was normal, though exceptional, accompanied by fine wine, offered up on a low, Asian-style table draped in silk and satin and cloth of gold in some whimsical arrangement Kara could not fathom. The guests were likewise dressed both elegantly and fancifully, in everything from a Bob Mackey gown to elaborately enameled battle garb that had Kara wondering how that particular *Fianna* managed to sit down at all, let alone eat. Not to mention why he would even want to, wearing that. There had to be something more comfortable in whatever served to hold his clothes. Even Kara and her family had been polished up and made pretty, though in simpler attire, completely by choice. She and Mathair were dressed in something akin to a sari, without the Eastern flare, and Papa wore a rich, embroidered tunic over simple black trews. The shirt's tawny thread on deep rust silk drew blazing highlights from his deep red hair. The effect made Kara smile to see him looking so well.

Around the table—on an odd, legless combination of pillow and formal chair that reminded Kara of the upper half a sleigh bed if it were for a baby doll—sat the warriors who participated in what was being called the Battle of the Knock. Included in their number were her father and Uncle Arn, both seated next to one of the *Sidhe* Kara recognized from New York. Also seated at the table, though they had not fought, were Mathair, a seer named Brid, and two unfamiliar *Sidhe*. And Kara herself, of course, though she fell somewhere between the warriors and the non-participants.

All in all, she was having flashbacks to some of the elaborate productions she'd been a part of when she'd still performed.

The meal was over, and everyone's goblets had been refilled. Not one for more than a single glass of wine, Kara accepted fruit juice the second time around. She was glad she did. The name of it was something she couldn't pronounce and likely wouldn't remember, not that it mattered. She'd hardly find it on the shelves at Key Food if she ever made it back to Queens. All the more reason to savor it now. The color was light gold; the flavor, like honey-glazed oranges, with notes of both lemon and bittersweet chocolate. She was so busy analyzing the tart, sweet beverage she lost track of the conversation going on around her. One phrase snagged her attention, though.

"…called the Children of Danu?"

Her head came up, her drink forgotten in her hand. The speaker was Uncle Arn.

The guests quieted as Goibhniu sat forward, his head tilted consideringly, his eyes gleaming. "Would ye like the simple answer, or would ye hear the whole o' the tale, sir?"

The other guests laughed as Uncle Arn flushed, first seeming embarrassed, then annoyed. Before he could respond, Goibhniu spoke: "Forgive me, Dr. Barnert, 'twas not unkindly meant. Ye'll excuse me an I give ye both.

"First an' foremost, we *are* the *Tuatha de Danaan*…the Children o' Danu. Literally. Born o' her flesh, in a manner, the tale o' which I'll share with ye now if ye'll indulge me?"

Still a bit disgruntled, Uncle Arn nodded briefly, settling back in his chair to listen.

Goibhniu waited for him to get comfortable and then sat forward to tell the story. The *Sidhe* in the room surely already knew it, probably word for word, from practically before they'd left the womb. That did not seem to matter. They appeared as eager for the telling as the humans, to whom the story was new and enthralling, told as it was by a master storyteller. Or maybe Kara projected her own excitement, having been told tales by the Smithgod before. From the first word, Goibhniu echoed memories of her years of classical training at the prestigious Julliard School. Voice, Oration, Dramatic presentation. Her professors were a pale shadow of his rich, perfectly modulated voice.

"In the time before time, at the rebirth o' our race, when the way to *Tír na nÓg* was first opened to our people…" Goibhniu's deep, rumbling voice filled the Hall, pulsing and throbbing and flowing like honey. It soothed those listening until no murmur or movement was heard as the Smithgod told his tale.

🜂

The First Mother, Danu, fled a deadly enemy. Her escape bought at the cost of her twin Anu's life, freely given…reluctantly accepted. The last of her kind, Danu was forced to run from the Homeland in the North and the four great cities of Falias, Finias, Gorias, and Murias, as she remained the sole hope of the Daoine Maithé, the Good People.

In her survival, she saw only unending heartache…all those she had loved having crossed the Veil. Only the oath to her beloved sister and the quickening she sensed in her own womb drove her on. She had to survive if the Daoine Maithé were to lift their eyes once more to the sun and wind and moon. Her only hope lay in a sanctuary where the Namhaid could not pursue her...her only hope lay in the safe haven of the sea.

Drawing on the awesome power of her grief, channeling the raw, untapped currents of the elven power, and transmuting the feral earth magics surrounding her, she drew all of it in and made it her own, forced it to her will.

With all the energy trapped, throbbing beneath her skin, Danu marched gracefully to the water's edge. The sand crept over her feet, and the wind tugged at her tattered travel robes, running itself through her unruly braids and curls, but only as Father Sun closed his eye on another day did she enter the cold embrace of the waves. As they welcomed her, drawing her down to their hidden depths, she unleashed the awesome power that threatened to split her skin. Dancing through currents, both aquatic and magical, she wrapped her thoughts about her like a cloak. As her lungs threatened to burst, her braids whipped frantically about her head, her mouth opened wide to gulp at air that was not there, only then did the sea take her into its bosom. The transformation began as masses of floating hair gave way to close, glittering scales and did not end until Danu wore the form of a mighty salmon, great in size, wise and swift and hidden by the sea.

Bereft and alone, the goddess called up every memory she had of her people, and as each one faded, the young within her grew and ripened and strained against her womb to be released, until, in the cradle of the sea, Danu bore her many children in their true form. The race of the Daoine Maithé rose up from the waves, fully formed, returning to once more walk the earth.

❀

"And then what happened to Danu?" Kara asked. Though barely louder than a breath, her words echoed through the chamber. If any of the guests had spoken in even normal tones she would not have been heard. Goibhniu had told her this tale once before, but Kara needed that ending. Needed the reminder of something that nagged at her mind.

Goibhniu's expression was solemn, yet his lips tilted up the barest degree in a smile that spoke of fondness. For herself? For Danu? The latter was more likely, but either way, Kara would only be guessing.

He finally answered, "Transformation is not something our kind does easily or lightly. The Great Mother drew on all her will an' every stream an' pool o' energy she could access to safeguard her children. By the time she was done, she had contained the sum total o' the *Daoine Maithé*'s magic, an' more beyond that. None could do this thing an' not be forever changed.

"Danu is with us to this day, everywhere an' nowhere at once, in whatever form suits her, though rarely the one she once wore as a woman. I have seen her thus but once, and I was born o' her."

Everywhere and nowhere. Kara latched on to those words. Not intentionally, but they grabbed her and would not let go. *Forever changed and whatever form*...those held her tight as well, teasing at her thoughts. Her mind dipped in to churn things about, pulling fragments of memory to the surface, only to let go as they swirled back down.

Frustrating. So frustrating. There was something important there, but Kara couldn't get a grip on it before it was gone again, taunting and teasing. Somewhere in her memories lay all the little bits she needed to make sense of this surreal trip her life had taken.

The next day, Kara woke feeling as much in the dark as before. She growled and thudded her head back down on the pillow, disturbing Beag Scath and her cat, Pixie, both of whom had settled in while she slept though she had closed the door the night before. Climbing from her bed, she dressed quickly. Breakfast was some fresh fruit grabbed as she passed through the common room on her way to Maggie's chambers. It was time to get educated, and she was going to need Maggie's help with that.

Through all of this she had done little more than react, stumbling from one crisis to another. She bore the scars from that. Time to learn from those mistakes.

"Does *Mór Halla* have a library?" Kara asked the moment Maggie opened the door.

"Hello and good morning to ye."

"Morning…" Kara responded, chagrined. Civilities observed, she asked again, "Does it? Have a library?"

Maggie yielded with grace. Considering the question, she looked perplexed, as if the need for one had never occurred to her. "Not as such," she finally answered. "Ours has ever been an oral tradition. One o' the druids or bards can tell ye near anything. We aren't big on killing trees or sheep to record our history when there's always someone around to remember."

Kara grimaced at Maggie's answer. She hadn't thought of it that way, but it was true. Be it tree or plant or animal, something died to create many of the materials mankind wrote on, short of mud tablets or modern synthetics. Certainly not something the *Sidhe* would endorse, as linked as they were to nature. Anyway, that was beside her current point. To which the heart of Maggie's answer left her stymied.

Not that Kara wanted to keep her research secret or anything, but she didn't have time to sit and listen to stories when books could be skimmed. Still, if there was anyone she could talk to, it was Maggie. She would understand. She might even know the information Kara was after. "I know almost nothing about Carmán and her children…is there anything more you can tell me?"

"'Twas a bit before my time, love," Maggie answered her eyes completely serious, though her lips quirked a slight smile. "By about a few thousand years. I know they were evil and destructive and would not stop until they were destroyed…and clearly not even then, though that we couldn't have known."

It was an effort, but Kara managed not to growl in frustration. There had to be something more. There always was with legends. Some kernel of fact documented. Different regional variations…the stuff scholars scoured for dissertations. Probably not anything that could be used against the *Tuatha de Carmán*—after all, the good guys weren't exactly tripping over luck—but maybe they could learn something that would leave Kara and the *Fianna* better prepared to engage the enemy. She was determined to try, and her thought about scholars gave her an idea.

"Come on," Kara said, resolve tightening the lines of her face, "and grab your torc."

Hardly necessary, considering she already wore it. Maggie stepped back, her arms crossed and one brow raised. "And why would I be doing that?"

"We're going to Dublin to find a library. Trinity College to start, maybe some of the specialty book stores in that neighborhood."

The *Sidhe* stood unmoving, her gaze searching. It was enough to make Kara want to twitch. She needed to do something proactive, something beyond this pocket out of time. To be around people and to gather intelligence, if nothing else. And a hamburger. She realized she *really* wanted a hamburger. Something simple and unhealthy. With a week's worth of fat. A reminder that everyday life was still there, waiting, blissfully unaware of Impending Doom II.

After what seemed like a discouragingly long time, Maggie nodded slowly. "Aye, perhaps 'tisn't a bad idea after all. We'll go…but not alone."

Not the answer Kara'd expected, though she was grateful. Of course, the thought of going on the expedition with a bunch of *Fianna* in tow hadn't occurred to her either. Kara opened her mouth to negotiate when Maggie's eyes got that far-away look that said she was soulspeaking. Before Kara could regroup, Maggie reached out and tugged her into the room. "Come on," the *Sidhe* said. "I'd like to finish my breakfast while we're waitin'."

The public space in Maggie's chamber was decorated simply, with a carved table and chairs in one corner, similar to those used at last night's banquet, and a lounging area more central to the room featuring a couple of low couches and something resembling a more modern coffee table. That was where Maggie's meal waited.

"Would ye like some?"

Thinking of the hamburger she craved, Kara declined, her eye wandering the room. On the far wall, something caught her eye: a series of three shelves built into the stone wall. There was an odd mix of items arrayed there, distinctly out of place in *Tír na nÓg*. In fact, much of it she recognized from Yesterday's Dreams. That was like a kick in the gut. Uncle Arn told them what had happened, how the pawnshop had burned to the ground with all the treasures it contained. These items were all that were saved in the end, removed from the premises when Maggie took them away to Ireland on a cloud.

Kara must have sniffed or something because when she looked up she encountered Maggie's sympathetic gaze. "I know, love. I know. My heart aches, as well."

"We have to stop them. Now," Kara said. "There are more than enough predators in the world already without letting them back in."

As if there was any letting involved. Nor was the matter as simple as one—or three—more evils in a world full of them. They had to stop Carmán's children because if they didn't, the world likely would not survive the aftermath.

A knock on the door pushed that line of thinking back a bit. Kara and Maggie both turned as the door opened and Urias and three other members of the *Fianna* came in. All of them looked like they'd be right at home among the college crowd…age-wise, anyway. Urias had too much of the rebel image to pull off being a student. Not that he couldn't hide that behind a glamour as Kara assumed they would do with the swords and daggers they carried.

Maggie introduced the newcomers. "Áedán," she said as she pointed at the one with soot grey hair and umber eyes, "an' Éibhir," she gestured at the other, a man more slender than the others, with simple brown hair, but with eyes like sun-lit crystal. The effect was dazzling. Enough so that Kara was startled as Maggie continued.

"An' ye know this scamp already."

Putting on his best punk 'tude and a wicked grin, Urias busted out with an irreverent "Road trip!" His gaze, though, was all serious.

Maggie stood, her hand drawing the torc from around her throat. Kara flinched away from the memories associated with that particular adornment. The torc wasn't just fancy jewelry. The neckwear was the anchor for a magic portal, which was how the *Fianna* had rescued her when she'd been…taken by Olcas. With effort, she steadied herself and watched as Maggie held it up in the air, letting go as the ring expanded, fixed in place by the magic activating it. They each stepped carefully through once it was of a size to let them past.

The portal opened out to a deserted section of what was clearly a massive library.

Kara turned a confused gaze on Maggie.

"Trinity ye said, aye?"

Grinning, and still a bit nervous, Kara nodded. "Of course, I expected to come in through the front door…you know, like normal people. Anyone know the way to the research desk?"

No one did, though they found it easily enough, thanks to the location maps throughout the building. Not that it did them any good. Kara and Éibhir went to the desk together to ask for reference material that might contain information on Carmán and her children. The few books they were pointed toward had barely more information than they already knew: brief footnote-type entries referencing a feast day celebrated in Wexford, Ireland, and several conflicting accounts of the names of her three sons. That and a year of death cited as 600 BC were the only new facts they uncovered.

While they pored over their research, Kara's neck and shoulder muscles tightened and twitched, as if the barest touch brushed her skin. Or like she was being watched… She frowned and looked up, scanning the hall where they shared a table.

Feeling just a little embarrassed, Kara smiled. The librarian, a British transplant, must have noticed their underwhelmed reaction to the content in the books. At a quiet, dignified pace, she came over to the table where they had settled to scour the musty pages.

"So sorry there wasn't more," she said, keeping her voice hushed. "It's a bit of a specialized topic I'm afraid. Not much call for it. There were a few scholarly papers a while back. I've already checked, and regretfully, we don't stock the journals they were featured in…budget cuts, you understand."

She handed Kara an index card with an address and name written in a precise hand.

"You may have better luck at Arwyn's Attic, dear," the librarian told her. "It's something of a private library mingled with a curio shop. Wynnie has more of an eclectic selection: books and journals, obscure references that have fallen out of favor with the academic community. She specializes in the older myth cycles and comparative religions. Her place is very popular with the students."

Kara thanked her as they gathered up their things, leaving the books in her care. Again a sensation rippled across her shoulders. Frowning, she looked around. There was no one in sight. She remained alert as she followed the others out the main entrance. Like normal people.

Arwyn's Attic really wasn't far. They chose to walk there, enjoying the bustle of the city and the brisk autumn weather. When Kara stared long-ingly at the McDonald's as they walked past, Maggie took pity on her. They went in, ordered eight Big Macs to go and a drink each. By the time Kara and Maggie had finished their burgers, the guys had each devoured both of theirs.

"That's just wrong." Kara shook her head slowly from side to side as she savored her last bite of bona fide Micky D's sesame seed bun. "I thought you guys were all into natural goodness…these things barely even qualify as real food."

Urias held his hands palm up to either side of him, raising one higher, then the other. "Hmmm….real….or tasty….real…or tasty… O' course, have ye seen what real cows eat these days? I don't think ye can make much o' an argument pro or con on the weight o' that. Besides," he said with a wink, "Sometimes ye need the comfort o' tasty."

She had to laugh. Urias was right, though. As much as they joked, she had to agree that the burger was a touchstone to the world she'd grown up in. Right now, that meant a heck of a lot more than eating healthy.

Everyone was finished eating and in slightly better spirits as the quirky little shop came into sight. Arwyn's Attic looked like it came right off a witchy movie set, outside and in. The exterior was dark green and black, with a bright golden yellow door, a bit care-worn, with old, intricate architecture. Inside was shelf after shelf crammed with books, odd objects, jars full of powders and teas, and candles. Lots of candles.

While Kara moved to the counter, the others started browsing. The woman behind the old-fashioned register had more white than grey in her hair, and her cornflower blue eyes sparkled with a great deal of joy. They out and out ignited with passion as Kara told her why they were there. Research was clearly her life.

When they mentioned Carmán and her sons, Wynnie's expression turned down. "That one's a proper nasty piece, her an' her brats. Did ye know she used her magic to curse the land? Destroyed all the crops worse than any potato famine…They call Carmán the goddess o' black magic, an' to hear it, she could unmake anything just by saying its name three times. Took the Good Folk to end the terror, way back before the Good Lord were even born." She shook her head disapprovingly. "Some fools down in Wexford still celebrate her day…more like 'tis excuse for a party, an ye ask me. 'Tweren't any o' them anything to rejoice over."

If she expected an argument, she didn't get one. Kara asked a few more questions, but sadly there wasn't much more to say. Still, since going to the source wasn't an option, she was glad for all they'd learned in the two hours spent in the shop.

Before they left, Arwyn did push photocopies of several articles into Kara's hands. "Take them, child. Much better than depending on notes. Who knows what little bit ye might have left out just to find ye needed it later?"

The papers rustled in Kara's hands as she flipped through them. She was startled to see half of them bore Arwyn's name. Her gaze jerked up to look at the woman, who winked at her, the twinkle back in her eye and a saucy smile on her lips. Kara grinned back as she folded the papers and tucked them in her back pocket. They thanked the woman and went to leave.

All but Maggie and Kara were out the door when Wynnie put her hand out and stopped them. "A moment, an ye will, m'ladies…" Her eyes were knowing and somber. Kara held her breath until Maggie nodded, unsure of how her mentor wanted to handle this. Kara's shoulders twitched again, unexpectedly, as she stood by the front door. She was careful to keep her expression pleasant, almost neutral.

"Yes, Arwyn?"

The woman looked intently from one of them to the other before breathing deep and saying what she had to say. "The rare few claim Carmán'll return one day, an' Eire itself will be undone starting with her first breath. Best perhaps for all o' us an ye block that day ever comin'."

Kara was floored. She sensed nothing *other* about the woman, no magic, no mixed blood, but clearly something about them had clued her to the nature of her guests.

There was no need for direction from Maggie on this one. "To my last breath," Kara promised Arwyn. "To my very last breath."

Chapter 8

Olcas awoke abruptly to a pinch-like sensation. He extended his senses to investigate as he gathered mage energy to him, ready to attack. The sensation happened again and he relaxed. It was the tracking spell he'd placed on Kara using the scarf he'd taken from the ruins of her house back in Queens. He had all but forgotten about it. Digging the scrap of cloth from beneath the cushions of his bed, Olcas used it as a focus as he shaped the mage energy into a spell to transport him to where the girl had foolishly returned to the mortal realm.

As he stepped through the portal, the stench endemic to alleys everywhere assailed his nose: rotting garbage, fetid water, the odor of human waste, though that was notably faint. This was a "decent" part of town, then. He looked around, annoyed to find the girl nowhere in sight. The spell should have brought him reasonably close to her, but something held him at bay. She was close, though. He felt it. Moving to the mouth of the alley, Olcas peered out. It was afternoon, and the streets and sidewalks were packed. Certainly, there was no picking her out in this crush. Olcas closed his eyes and extended his *other* senses, seeking out Kara's essence.

He snarled.

Close though she may be, something continued to interfere with the link between her and the scarf (and thus his spell). Other than a vague direction, he could not get a sense of her location, only that she was not moving. Settling in, he waited. When she did move, he would follow.

Olcas continued to wait, his temper festering, as minutes turned into an hour. Several rats lay upon the ground close by, or what remained of them. No more than piles of cinders, after he'd vented his pique upon them.

Finally, she stirred. Back at his vantage point, Olcas spied her coming his way among a group of four others, all *Sidhe*, all armed…physically and magically. Other than Kara, the only one he recognized was the bitch from the pawnshop.

The brick wall beside him crumbled beneath his grip. That one needed to die already, violently but quickly, to ensure she never interfered again. As he watched, they ducked into a fast-food place. When they came out, distracted and occupied, joking among themselves, he followed them down the street. More bricks crumbled as he left the alley.

Unless she was extremely foolish—or he quite lucky—he would not claim his prize today. Still, there was a chance, so he persisted. Besides, he was beyond curious about what had drawn his little rabbit from the safety of her warren.

The group stopped at a tiny shop whose shelves were covered in a mix of cheap books, aged tomes, and odd items. Some seemed like they might have been of interest to him, were he still Lucien. As Tony, he barely glanced at them as he continued by, no longer needing the crutch of questionable arcane grimoires. Crossing the street, he tucked himself behind the corner of another building. His quarry, however, lingered in this shop even longer than before. Olcas snarled in frustration, no longer thinking this effort might be worthwhile. To satisfy his curiosity, he extended a bit of will and magic to siphon their conversation so that it sounded as a whisper in his ear. He jerked to hear his mother's name, then his own and his brothers, then details of their time before, accompanied by an odd jumble of fact and supposition.

He laughed. It wasn't pleasant.

It amused him that they tried to learn details mostly lost to time. It would do them no good, in the end. Let them waste their effort. Olcas was done doing so.

Turning to walk deeper in the shadows, he summoned a portal to return to his lair.

The night was nothing to them. The dark had no meaning. The *Bás* existed in the grey space between planes, the threshold betwixt the void and the physical realm, touching both but of neither. In their shadow realm, energy had a luscious, heady scent, unique to the source. It defined their world.

They hunted, navigated, existed by those scents, though their eyes perceived the energy as well, the color of the glow augmenting what the aromas told them. They perceived everything as energy of one sort or another. If it did not feed the *Bás*, it was beneath their notice. If it did…it best beware. Some were savory above all others, such as the effervescent musk of the ancient enemy. That is what the *Bás* sought this night, rich sup they could pass on to their young.

They yipped and howled and sucked the wind through open mouths, picking through its medley of scents for the bouquet they tracked. Beneath the mortal moon, their pelts glowed as they drank in the pallid radiance like children catching raindrops on their tongue. Dancing through the shadows, they skirted the realms, riding the cusp of the mortal world where men drudged and labored and forgot the thrill of the hunt they were meant for. Where the *Daoine Maithé* hid in the glimmers, spawning their young on mayflies. The mortals were insipid fare, enough to sustain the *Bás*, but not to flourish them. Yet mingled among their near-tasteless scent the *Bás* occasionally found a waft of something more; like watered wine among pitchers of swill, the half-bloods were more savory than their mundane parent, less so than the magical one.

Tonight the *Bás* hunted half-bloods because the full hid like cowards in their pockets of reality. As well they should, for the *Bás* would devour their souls soon enough. But first, the *Bás* must increase and avenge their fallen. To that end, they chose to follow the bidding of the one scented of sulfur and smoke and dark, rich energy. For now, they worked to a common goal. Later…well, they would see.

The *Bás* hissed as one and stalked the mortal village, claiming prey. A child from an isolated barn, a grown man leaving the pub, a wife from a quiet kitchen preparing a meal, suddenly became one. All three held a glint of power from their *Sidhe* parent. The *Bás* took them up and drained them to bare husks, then fed their bodies to the void.

Full to brimming, the spirit women went to feed their young.

❧

Olcas formed a simple plan in the end, requiring nothing more than the resources already at his disposal…a redistribution of assets, as it were, to borrow a phrase from his time as Lucien Blank. Distracting the demon-child with a tasty treat procured from among the street people, Olcas gathered the ritual elements he needed and entered the room where Lynn Barnert was imprisoned. He stopped before her, pinning her with an assessing gaze. Beyond her fear, she possessed, to her detriment, a spirit completely without guile. That would be a potent weapon against her man and his allies, not to mention a tempting lure for the demon, which had begun to erode the bindings on its current vessel.

"I know how hard this must be for you, dear, waiting here for so long, with nothing to do," Olcas addressed his victim, his tone anything but sincere. He reached out as he spoke, resting the tips of his fingers on her jaw. Beneath his touch, she trembled, and he smiled a smile that was anything but reassuring.

"People—" His lip curled in distaste at the word, despite the false commiseration in his voice. "—need to feel useful." He caressed her cheek, delighting in the terror brightening her eyes and quaking through her limbs. "Am I right?" he asked, sensing the depth of torment his attention caused, prolonging it.

She nodded though he doubted it was out of any sense of agreement. The aroma of her terror wafted up, heady, but not yet fully ripe. She still clung to hope, despite her imprisonment. He wished he could take his time and season her fear properly, but he needed her visibly unharmed. Instead, he snaked his hand up around her neck in a swift move, gripping her tight where her skull met her spine, locking her head in place. Her eyes went wide, and he focused his mental force, pinning her gaze before she could look away. That was all it took to mesmerize her, her spirit trapped beneath his will. He dropped his grip and stepped back. Her body went limp and pliable. Only her eyes remained animated. They held a surprising touch of wrath, courageous, if too late.

Olcas ignored it.

With gentleness, he stripped the woman bare, his actions cold, unmoved as he set her clothing aside until it was again needed. His motions were precise as he laid out the ritual: oils and blades, incense and herbs. Though he was no longer limited to the power of spells learned by rote during his hindered years, it was what he was most familiar with, which made it comfortable, reliable. His weakness had become his strength. He prepared the mortal woman with the ritual runes, then bound her body, mind, and spirit with sigils that the vessel could not become a weapon against him. He built the coercions to remain latent until needed, invisible to all senses but his own.

When he was done, he allowed his hands to roam over his victim, fondling and bruising, stroking and pinching, more to ignite the panic and hatred in her gaze than out of any carnal desire. He watched her closely as he withdrew his hands. Something within her snapped, leaving her gaze intent and fractured even before he offered her to his demon. In calculation, he turned his back on her, even as he released her from his will. Behind him, the woman's demented scream slid into an anguished cry as she rushed to attack him, triggering the binding sigils. He glanced over his shoulder. The woman had collapsed to the ground, her limbs twitching in agony. Contempt shaped Olcas's expression. "Thank you, my dear, for establishing everything is in order."

The woman sobbed with despair as he left the room.

In the next chamber, the demon had grown finicky, refusing to eat what Olcas had provided. Currently, it played with its food…quite inventively, by the sound of the whimpers. "Enough," Olcas said as he came through the door, sending a tendril of energy to clean away the remains of the victim. The smell of charred flesh reminded him of his treacherous brother. With a forceful breath, he shunted his displeasure aside and focused on the task at hand.

"Perhaps something sweeter would be to your taste?"

The demon-child looked up, its face bright and eager beneath its film of blood.

"I wish to give you the woman's form. It will serve us to better purpose than the one you wear."

The creature clapped and squealed with glee, altogether too influenced by its current host, but not much longer.

"We need her a sound vessel, sweetling," Olcas instructed the demon, "body, not soul. Break her gently, and both are yours, and then, we play havoc with the *Sidhe* and their pitiful human allies."

The child responded with an angel's smile nested beneath a demon's leer, clearly delighting in his promises of corruption and chaos. The demon-child turned from him and skipped from the room. A whimper rose from the woman's cell, followed by a tormented moan. Olcas smiled. With a gesture and a phrase murmured in ancient Greek, he triggered the binding spells, ensuring neither woman nor demon could resist.

Moving to the door between the chambers, he watched through half-masted eyes as the demon stood in the center of the space, swaying until its blood-spattered little-girl dress swished, bell-like and enchanting. Evil peered out from that innocent-seeming shell. Infernal desires, perverse thoughts, voracious hunger. The demon giggled as it moved forward until a high-pitched cry rose from the far corner of the room. Olcas laughed as he spied the woman crouched there, still naked, wedged in among stored boxes. Her hands wiped at the runes he'd etched upon her skin in preparation for this moment, to no effect.

What was she thinking to corner herself so conveniently? he wondered as he leaned against the door frame to watch the fun. *Some people deserved to be victims.*

The minion's eyes glowed, transitioning from toxic green to purest black to fiery red and back again. Its giggles blended into something more sinister, something with a mad edge that would have sent a psychopath screaming. Jarring in tempo and key, the sound spoke of all that was unhinged. Olcas leaned forward for a better view as Lynn whined and crushed herself deeper into the corner, not that there was anywhere to go. The woman tensed and arched. Her jaw stretched in a soundless scream as small, delicate hands locked onto her temples. Exuding an air of satisfaction, the wholesome-seeming demon-child bared its teeth in a monstrous smile before leaning forward in a perversion of a kiss, probing and sucking until the light left the mortal woman's tragic, weak blue eyes.

When the body went limp and the eyes nearly lifeless, the little one drew back, its head tilting in consideration of its handiwork. It looked back at Olcas, oddly as if seeking approval. He nodded and offered the creature a small, cold smile. It darted forward and locked its jaw completely over its victim's slack mouth, blowing in a twisted parody of resuscitation. Within seconds, the child-body blackened and flaked. Then, as if strafed by an infernal wind, the form disintegrated into pale gray ash, swirling through the chamber on a sulfur-scented current. As it did so, the crumpled form in the corner straightened in a slow, sensuous motion surely foreign to its former owner. The head rose last as the modest chest swelled with a deep breath, the nipples peaking enticingly, seduction outright promised by the sinister spirit staring out of blue eyes transmuted to a deep violet by the smoldering red glow at their core.

Olcas gave a hard laugh as his creature offered him a wanton smile from lips newly corrupted. "Restrain yourself, minion," he ordered, his gaze cold.

"Nothing has changed but your form. In fact, you will want to keep aside a morsel of that soul for those times when you must mimic her demeanor."

The lips pouted, and the chin dropped until the demon looked up at him in an artful and sullen invitation from beneath that delicate brow. Olcas merely stared the creature down, letting his own brow arch with disdain, not relinquishing one single thread of control. Sketching a seemingly casual gesture, Olcas set burning bands of energy through the sinister beast, reminding the demon who was the master in control of its current vessel. Fury leached the body's gaze of surface blue, leaving the eyes burning the dark demonic red of the truly damned. The creature's hand reached out. Talons formed that had never before graced that mortal flesh and shredded the wall in frustration.

Does it visualize me beneath its clawed hand? Olcas wondered, almost amused. He turned and walked away, the demon once more securely bound, forged into a weapon capable of delivering up the *Tuatha de Danaan* for destruction.

🌀

Calma turned a slow circle, his brow drawn down low and his lip curled tight in a sneer as he assessed Bran's lair. Nature ran rampant over it. Not because it was the season for it, but because of the *Sidhe* woman. His prize had verdant magic. How ironic. The child she contained would wield the most destructive force known to man and god. It would be amusing to keep the mother around to witness the undoing.

But not yet, and not here. Calma required somewhere more suitable to plot the end of the world.

We are leaving, he told his host as he turned and catalogued anything important enough to transport with them. Save for the woman, there was nothing worth taking.

Calma smirked as Bran bristled, taking offense at his thought. The sensation was odd. The body made equal effort to convey both their reactions, creating a discordant frisson. Calma found it rousing, but hardly productive. Before the *Sidhe* could protest or argue, Calma exerted control.

As if anything is to be accomplished here in the middle of nowhere. All you do is make it simple for them to come upon you as they will, using whatever means required to overcome your defenses. He allowed his disgust to color his thoughts. *There is nothing here to temper their efforts, no incidental population to force them to caution. It's like you* invite *them to come depose you and reclaim your prize.*

Where do you propose we go? The center of Dublin? Bran co-opted Calma's sneer.

Don't be a fool. We want potential witnesses to hinder them, not a constant audience to complicate our own actions.

Calma thought on it, considering their options. A wicked smile displaced both their sneers.

Menapia…we go to Menapia, he decreed, naming the ancient city that was now known as Wexford. He would destroy the de Danaans on the very land where his own lifeblood had been spilt. And destroy them he would, down to the last one. But first to gather his brothers and resurrect Mother, heralding the downfall of their enemy.

Chapter 9

As Kara understood it, the enemy engaged in a war of attrition. In the manner of a siege, they blocked all routes of transport, attacking both trade and travelers without warning. No one traveled alone or much at all unless protected by the *Fianna*. Too many had already been lost in the battle and through random attacks. True, most of those lost had begun their soul's journey back, but not all. They could not risk losing more.

Even the void was not safe.

Those only in *Tír na nÓg* for the Unraveling sought to leave as the threat increased. *Sidhe* with the ability to travel through the ether volunteered to shepherd the visitors to their own Lands. They had been certain they could not be touched as they slipped through the ether. They had been wrong. Several had nearly been taken while in the space between the planes, sustaining injuries to both body and soul that were slow to recover and could not be magically healed.

The *Fianna* gathered to plan in the public space of their quarters. Papa irreverently dubbed it the war room. Though not completely applicable, it had stuck. In truth, it was more like a living room…only with more stone than one would expect. It was a large open area with a sunken ring edged with cushions. The center of that ring formed a natural table, around which they all currently gathered. There wasn't much else to the room. The rest of their quarters, accessed from hallways extending from either side, were like a cross between a barracks and a dorm, with a customary arch leading to the ever-present garden outside. Most of those around the table resided here, even Kara, more at ease among them than in the company of the more elitist *Sidhe* that hid from the world in *Tír na nÓg*. Only Maggie, and of course Goibhniu, kept rooms elsewhere.

As the details were recapped, Goibhniu stood from his seat across the table. "We can't battle these threats if we can't move from place to place." From a pouch at his side, he drew six torcs similar to the one Maggie already wore around her neck.

Goibhniu placed them on the table and pushed them toward Maggie. "Divide yer warriors in six groups, one torc to each leader. They are spelled to open a gate to wherever the wielder visualizes, whether they have mage talent or not. With but a bit o' will and a clear mental image, no way is closed."

"Isn't that kinda dangerous?" Arn interrupted, a curious, intent look on his face. "What if someone else gets their hands on them?"

His gaze assessing, Goibhniu answered him. "They are keyed to the *Fianna*. To anyone else, they'll be no more than pretty metal."

Arn nodded, and Kara couldn't tell if that was doubt or disappointment she saw in his gaze.

"First," Goibhniu continued, "we need to get the rest o' our visitors safely away." He didn't look at Arn, but to everyone there his gist was clear. Frankly, Kara wondered if Goibhniu understood the fight the man was prepared to put up. There was no way he would leave without his wife, not even with the promise that the *Sidhe* would rescue her and return her to him safe.

Before that battle could ensue, Kara stood and faced the Smithgod, squaring her shoulders. "Please…has there been any word of…the Cursed One?" she asked, relieved she had remembered not to speak his name.

Inside, she quailed as Goibhniu's face contorted; the change was swift and harsh as he locked her in his gaze. This wasn't the first time she'd broached this topic since the ritual. "That one is o' no further concern to us."

"But…" she started, her voice trailing off as Goibhniu's brow lowered.

"But?" he prompted, his glower fierce. "Why do ye persist?"

"The Unraveling," she said. "It's not complete…if you look…"

"What do ye ken o' this?" he interrupted, his voice and his expression swirling with both pain and annoyance. He was not unkind, just unyielding, like bar stock before it's been heated in the forge. "It is done, Kara."

"But…" she tried again, getting no further as the Smithgod's hand slashed the air in front of him.

"Do not mention it again."

And he was gone. Just gone, no door required…conversation over.

Tears stung Kara's eyes but did not fall. It was a toss-up if her cheeks burned from embarrassment or anger.

"Why? Why is he so unreasonable? Why won't he listen?" Kara asked the universe at large, since she scarcely expected an answer from anyone in the room. They just stared at her, varying expressions on their faces…not all of them favorable, or even sympathetic. She barely held in a growl as she paced the chamber. "You would think someone his age would have more sense, but no…he has his head up his ass just like anyone else."

"Kara," Papa interrupted her ranting. He didn't raise his voice, but with one gruff word he made his displeasure clear. "Respect, young woman. I don't care if 'tis one year or several millennia, he's yer elder and yer his guest. Stop disrespecting the…man in his own place. I'll not have ye acting the spoiled brat because yer not getting yer own way. And I don't care for yer language much either, miss."

She stopped stalking across the floor, her head lowered as she ground her teeth in frustration. Her father's words stung. She wasn't some petty little fool pouting because she wasn't getting attention.

Still, he was right about one thing: it was wrong of her to bad-mouth Goibhniu. She just wished *someone* would understand. If she were wrong, she'd gladly bear the ridicule…but if she was right? God help them if they found out after it was too late, after Bran had slipped back in and made good on his threats…or worse. Until the Unraveling was complete, he still had access to the *Sidhe* Lands.

However, giving in to her frustration wasn't helping her cause. Several deep breaths later, she looked up to meet her father's eye. "I'm sorry. I am. I should have chosen my words better, but this isn't me being childish because he's ignoring me. I'm frustrated and tense and more afraid every moment that goes by because *this is important!* It is *so* important that I almost don't care that you're upset with me because finally *someone* is *listening,* instead of letting me talk without hearing a word I'm saying then telling me I can't possibly understand and not to worry because it's been handled!" By the time Kara was done, she nearly yelled the final word. Her body shook, and her hands fisted. Inwardly, she groaned. *So much for being reasonable.* She looked around the room, struck by the utter silence. Not one person would meet her eye.

Except for her father.

I've done it again, she thought, as she flinched away from his disapproving gaze.

"This is not the way to get anyone to listen," he told her, a frown deepening the lines on his face. "Ye've shamed me and insulted those who have given ye shelter…those who fought for ye. Get yer head on straight and apologize. When ye've done that, we can talk, and maybe see what's to be done." He turned and walked out the door. With a sympathetic look, Arn followed him.

Sighing, Kara turned to those still in the room. Maggie looked worried; Urias confused. The rest, well, she couldn't exactly read them.

"What you must think of me," she said, focusing on the rest of the *Fianna,* rather than her friends. Hopelessness weighed on her as she took note of their unfathomable expressions. "I do apologize…both for what I said, and for being rude in front of you. Please forgive me." They didn't speak, but each of them nodded their acceptance of her apology, at least. Kara nodded back. Then, with a sad smile edging up the corner of her lips, she left the chamber in search of her father.

"Kara…"

She turned and saw Maggie coming toward her.

The *Sidhe* stopped less than a foot away. "*Leanbh*, I don't know if ye're right to be concerned, but ye need to know…Goibhniu won't hear a word on this."

"Why?" Kara asked her, confused by the shortsighted attitude.

"I'm sorry, love," Maggie said, her expression haunted. "Ye couldn't know…Br…" She caught herself, then started again. "The Cursed One, 'twas Goibhniu's son."

By the time Kara sought out her father, she was much subdued, trying to come to terms with what Maggie had revealed to her. At first, she'd been confused. How could Goibhniu father a son? From what had been explained to her, the *Sidhe* did not couple to produce children. However, they did bind themselves as man and wife. Realizing that, it made sense to her. Just as in the human world there were fathers with children they had no blood tie to, and they counted them no less their children for that fact. Understanding that gave Kara more of a sense of connection to these People than she'd had before. Both somber and more at peace, she renewed her search.

She found Papa in the gardens surrounding *Mór Halla*, near the Court. Behind him, a spring burbled up over rocks that may or may not have been artfully arranged—it was hard to tell what occurred naturally in the *Sidhe* Lands. The sound transcended peaceful. He sat on a moss-covered rock as if it were a park bench, back straight, hands folded on his knees, and his eyes closed. Kara watched his lips move and knew he was in prayer.

Not wanting to disturb him, she almost turned and walked away. Her own eyes closed a moment as she tried to capture a small piece of the tranquility her father enjoyed before she left. Though she was brief, by the time she opened her eyes she found him watching her. His brow lifted, but he said no word.

Her gaze dropped, and she let out a sigh. "I am so sorry."

"Aye, well, ye could have handled that a mite better."

Kara nodded. "True."

"Ye ready to talk a bit more reasonable?"

Could she? Maybe. Maybe not; all she knew for sure was she had to try. "Yes, please."

Patrick O'Keefe pushed himself up to his feet and offered Kara his arm.

She smiled as she slipped her hand into the crook of his elbow, then briefly laid her head against his shoulder. "I love you, Papa."

He reached up and patted her hand. "O' course ye do. And I love you. Come, let's go for a walk."

Despite the differences in their height, they matched their strides with practiced ease. They said nothing, needing the time to restore the harmony between them. As they walked, they listened to the music of the civilized wilderness that was *Tír na nÓg*. One or the other of them pointed out wonders as they went, like the beauty of a blossom or the particular antics of the lesser creatures that called this place home. In their wake followed a timid procession of faelings.

They had wandered quite a while when the most amazing sound beguiled them. In unspoken agreement, they headed toward it. Pushing through the brush, they came upon an awe-inspiring sight: a waterfall that surpassed any in their own world in height and beauty. It sang with its own voice, accompanied by the tokens of the reverent. An air of peace settled over Kara greater than the one that had eluded her in the garden where she'd found her father. She let her head fall back as she breathed in the cleansing air. When she lowered it, she found her father had sat down beside the pool at the base of the waterfall, heedless of the spray spangling his hair. He patted the ground beside him.

"Set yerself down, lass."

Kara complied, shedding her slippers and dipping her feet into the cool waters. She let the sensation lull her as the cascade of water caressed her feet like a fine massage.

Papa cleared his throat. "Here's where ye talk."

His words called a brief grin to Kara's face, but it fell quickly. She drew her feet from the water and tucked them beneath her. "It didn't go right, Papa. It isn't finished, no matter what Goibhniu and the others believe."

His brow wrinkled as he considered her words. "What are ye saying, Kara? I need ye to be a bit more clear."

Quietly, calmly, Kara recounted all of what had happened at the Unraveling, filling in the details her father had not been there to see. She even told him of the dagger shards hidden in her chamber.

He listened patiently, nodding from time to time, or interrupting to ask her to clarify a point or two, but mostly, he just listened, and because he did—regardless of whether or not he was able to help her in any other way—some small measure of Kara's fears lifted. Someone else knew. Someone else *listened*.

When she was done, they rested there, absorbing the calm inherent in that place. As the light faded, and they lay back in the twilight, the waterfall softly singing to them, Kara admitted her greatest fear. "Papa, if I'm right…if I can't convince any of them this is not finished…" Her voice cracked in dissonance to the cascade's symphony. "If I fail and something horrible happens, it will be because of me. It will be my fault." She whispered that last.

Her father nodded, his lips slightly pursed. "As long as ye do yer best, none can ask any more o' ye," Papa told her as stood and pulled her to her feet. "An ye do that there is no fault or failing." It was the exact sentiment she needed to hear. Not comfort, not denial, just sense, bald and honest and common as the man himself. "But…what do I do?"

He remained silent a long moment, and then he answered her, as honest as before. "That, I'm afraid, will take a bit more thinking on. I suggest ye start off by resting yer head on it."

They turned to go back, once more arm in arm.

✸

When Aí answered Goibhniu's summons, the Court was dark, unlit but for the natural radiance coming from the Great Wall. The edges of the room were lost in shadow, the dais only as bright as early twilight. Uncommon for the *Sidhe* Lands, the air held a chill enough to draw a small shiver from him. The constant glow from the Wall drew his eye. The Smithgod waited there, silhouetted by the energy emanating from the knotwork. Aí could not tell which direction his liege faced, but the Smithgod stood before the blackened remains of the Cursed One's pattern.

The dark segments in the pattern still shocked Aí every time he saw them. Each one represented a lost life. One of the *Daoine Maithé* beginning a fresh round of the eternal cycle. As their ended pattern faded, a new one would take form on the tail of the spiral. In one sense, it brought joy, the promise of *Sidhe* children. In a deeper sense, it fostered outrage.

With the *Sidhe*, there was no such thing as death by natural causes.

Aí frowned and looked away a moment to compose himself. With his ability to project emotions, he could not afford to lose control of his own.

However, he must have made a sound. Goibhniu whipped a glance over his shoulder.

Aí went still, eyes wide and his throat bobbing instinctively. Reason told him to get out of there, to flee danger, which Goibhniu radiated as the wall radiated light. Honor and faith held Aí in place. First, he'd been summoned here. Second, Goibhniu was his laird, sworn to Aí's protection even as he was sworn to Goibhniu's service.

Still, in the glare on the Smithgod's face and the tension bulking those unrivaled muscles, there lay a warning to proceed with care. As he sensed the riotous emotions in Goibhniu's heart, Aí shielded, before they overwhelmed his empathy, making it impossible to function. Goibhniu looked back to the pattern, before turning and moving to his formal chair. A weary sigh echoed through the Hall as he lowered himself to the seat. With an exasperated twist of his lips, he motioned Aí forward.

"I have another task for ye," Goibhniu said, his expression growing more grim. "There is great risk."

"Aye, isn't there always?" Aí answered with a grin as he extended a bit of his gift, trying to ease some of the tension.

Goibhniu's frown merely deepened, and Aí immediately sobered, not that he'd been feeling much levity to begin with, and ceased his efforts. It had been worth a try. Goibhniu was an ember ready to flare. Who knew what fires would be sparked...

His liege looked away, as if aware how tenuous his hold on his temper was, and how misplaced an outburst would be. Aí breathed a little easier as the Smithgod spoke: "I've much to prepare before ye go. Meet me tomorrow morning at the Temple o' the Fallen. We'll discuss the matter then."

It seemed as if he was done, except there was a charged air about him, a tension that spoke of internal struggles. There was something more the Smithgod wanted.

Aí waited, his expression neutral, his body trying to relax. Perhaps he could influence Goibhniu more subtly by example.

Or maybe not. The Smithgod growled and pushed to his feet, fresh waves of tension radiating off of him.

"She is a puzzle I'd sooner not deal with," he said, leaving the dais to closer.

Confused as to which "she" he meant, Aí held steady, though his impulse was to step back.

"I'll leave that task to ye. Watch, pay attention when ye've the opportunity, there's something more to her than elf-kin. Ye figure Kara out."

"Are ye afraid she's a danger?" Aí asked, though he could not believe it.

"No! No...just a mystery. There's something I can't place. Perhaps I'm too close. But now isn't the time for the unexpected, so ye pay attention and suss out the answer."

Aí nodded. As if it would be a hardship to have to watch that one.

Goibhniu again turned away, his eyes trailing the Wall once more. "Remember, tomorrow, the Temple."

"Aye," he responded, then, recognizing a dismissal, Aí went away.

Chapter 10

Confused…conflicted…angry one moment, horrified the next…Kara haunted the passages of the *Sidhe* stronghold, avoiding any and all as best she could manage. Bad enough she doubted her purpose and her ability to meet whatever responsibility awaited her. The possibility of seeing that doubt reflected in the eyes of others was too much for her. She still had not figured out what to do with the shattered dagger or the role she was meant to play in the coming days. The pieces were in a pouch hanging from her belt, a constant reminder that Bran was still out there, as were Olcas and Dubh and the *Namhaid*…and who knew what other forces aligned against the *Sidhe* and their allies.

They seemed more adept at acquiring foes than banishing them.

Already, several chances had been squandered. A sense of personal failure weighed on her. She could not forget that one stroke of a sword would have removed any threat the *Tuatha de Carmán* posed, had she been allowed to make it. But would she have been able to? The sick, tormented feeling she'd had back in New York still crept over her from time to time, the one she'd had when she'd stared down at Lucien Blank after their battle. There was no doubt she'd willfully shattered his mind when she'd still been unaware he was merely a vessel. The reality of that had made her ill. By no means would anyone have described her as ruthless.

But then, that was before…before she'd fallen into Olcas's hands. A violent shudder ripped through her at the memory. Things had been different since then; Kara could no longer deny she had the will to end a life, but did she have the courage to act on that will? And would it be right to do so?

The demigods wore the bodies of mortals. Unwilling mortals. Olcas possessed Tony, a punk from New York. He seemed okay physically, though she couldn't speak for his mental torment. The other victim, however… Whoever he was, Dubh seemed to have taken him over in the aftermath of a blaze. The body was so burnt she could not imagine how it still moved, let alone breathed. If the stranger's soul was still aware, he must be in constant agony.

It would be a mercy to end that one. Only the Romani woman had stayed Kara's hand. Had insisted the vessels should not pay for evil they had no choice in. The evil ones escaped, still wearing their victims.

Could Kara have done it? Should she have? The demigods would resurface, and who knew what evil they would perpetrate before then. But did Tony or the burned man deserve to pay for the demigods' sins. Would she have chosen to stay her hand herself if she had known the truth of her opponents' dual nature? Worse yet, would she be able to strike next time now that she did?

Twice, Olcas had lost control. Both times Tony stared out of his own brown eyes in horror and confusion for mere moments before the demigod re-exerted control.

Kara still wasn't sure what she would have done. She had a hard time thinking of herself as a hero…but was she a coward? Why else would she have been so easily swayed by the Romani when she could have slain the evil one for all time? Was she up to this? Did she have a choice? No end of doubts assaulted her.

"A moment, if you please?" The old Romani woman asked, coming seemingly out of nowhere and placing herself squarely in Kara's path. If that timing wasn't creepy…

Kara stopped short, her head jerking up. A curse slipped past her lips. If she'd been avoiding anyone specific, this was the one. She wanted to be furious at this woman who had stopped her from banishing her arch-enemy, and yet how could she hold anything against the one who freed her from Tony's…no, *Olcas's* curse? How had the woman even found her, anyway?

A soft trill drew Kara's gaze downward as something soft brushed against her. At the woman's feet sat a familiar dark sprite. He had been with Aí, and before that with the Romani man at the Unraveling.

"I need you to know I didn't understand," the woman said. "I did not know what was happening, not until it was too late."

Frankly, Kara didn't care what the woman thought she had to confess, but they faced off in a narrow entranceway, so there was no going around her. Kara tried to keep her resentment and confusion from her face. "Excuse me?"

"I was too late to stop it, and you have suffered because of my blind, stubborn pride. I had imagined it could not be, that I had protected him and raised him well. You can see how wrong I was."

"What do you want?" Kara's jaw flexed and she drew herself up, tense and full of wrath she fought to contain.

"I wish to say I am sorry…I had no choice. My grandson has fallen, his soul captured by this Evil One. I allowed that to happen, did not take sufficient action to prevent him from becoming as he is, and for that, I owe you a debt of honor.

"Whenever you call on me, I shall stand by your side, no matter what, until I have paid my penance. And should you need a safe haven, you have a place among the Rom. I will leave you now and only hope you will consider talking to me more at another time."

Kara drew a startled breath, her hand clutching her shirt above her breastbone where the knife scar had been. She remembered what the woman had said as she stood between Tony and Kara: *Family before all others*. Suddenly the cryptic comment made sense.

This woman was Tony's grandmother.

The realization was most unsettling. Before, Kara had been content to picture Tony as some beast, some monster. It had not occurred to her he was a normal, if ill-fated young man, somewhere about her own age, with a family who cared for him deeply. Not perfect, but perhaps also not evil.

What had happened to him was a mystery, but the Romani woman implied that he was as much victim as Kara was…well, not quite, but surely far from the monster she envisioned. Once again, memories surfaced from more than one occasion, the image of cold, hateful blue eyes that suddenly darkened to brown, filled with confusion…and fear.

"Thank you," Kara answered, trying to be gracious. In truth, she was relieved. She still had doubts, but understanding brought some peace to her mind. She glanced down, where the sprite now crouched at her feet, staring up at her with bright eyes. Shaking her head, she smiled softly at him. "It's okay, little one." She dangled down a hand, which he quickly grasped, using it to pull himself up to her shoulder. For some reason, he made anxious little sounds by her ear, where he'd tucked his head beneath her hair, his arm curled about her neck, as if for comfort rather than stability.

Nodding, the woman drew something from her pocket, then took Kara's hand in her own. "This isn't much, but I would provide what protection I may to you." She sighed. "Anthony has one as well. They are linked; this one meant for me, the other for him. I never had a chance to see if the link would work, but if you hold this in your grip, it should trigger the shields on the other, freeing my grandson from the hold of the monster within him, for a time, anyway. I'm afraid you must be close for that aspect to work. If not…well, it will still protect you."

Kara's brow drew down as she accepted the token, a rune-covered copper medallion on a leather thong, twin to the one she'd seen around Tony's neck. She flinched, remembering the last time she had his in her hand. "Why doesn't it work while he's wearing it?"

The Romani grimaced. "The beast is within him, thus within the shields. The most the charm can do now is give Anthony temporary control of himself. Maybe it will be enough to help him, should you figure a way to banish the evil one." Sorrow deepened the wrinkles in her ancient face. "I would like my grandson back if you can manage it, please."

Kara's breath caught in her chest, and her hand tightened over the medallion. Again she saw Tony's tormented eyes, this time in his grandmother's face, deep brown, sharp and fearful, as no one's eyes should have cause to be. "I'll do everything I possibly can. I promise."

The woman dipped her head respectfully and turned to shuffle away.

"Wait…" Kara called out, and then realized she didn't know what she intended to say.

Stopping, the woman glanced over her shoulder. "The caravan leaves tomorrow. I and a few others will remain behind—I won't leave until we've won Anthony free. But for those departing tonight, we celebrate to wish them safe journey. You are welcome if you'd care to join us…"

Kara started to answer, but paused, flustered as she realized she had no idea of this woman's name. That seemed wrong somehow, with all that had passed between them, however briefly. The Romani laughed, not unkind, but full-bodied and strong. The woman was so vibrant and alive for one who was clearly very old.

"They call me Rose, Gypsy Rose. It's a name as good as any other, though it isn't mine. You're free to use it. Though I think I'd rather you call me Granddame Rose, as those more familiar do." Her head cocked a jaunty angle, and she smiled, clearly confident in Kara's answer. "Look for us just beyond the magic gate, but still among the trees…the Good Folk pushed the protections further out after the battle, to keep the threshold clear."

Kara actually laughed, her negative mood temporarily banished. "I would like that. Thank you…"

✺

Jacko dropped a final load of deadfall beside the nearest bonfire and looked around him. Everything was almost ready, the celebration poised to begin. Out of deference to their hosts, the fires had been laid in braziers, rather than the usual firepits, as this was the threshold to the *Sidhe* Land. Though in the mortal realm, the wold was ancient, and none among them was willing to put it at risk, not just from fear of offending their hosts. Such locations were rare and revered by the Rom, symbols of the roots they had lost long ago when the first of their blood was cursed to roam.

Moving toward the main circle, which consisted of logs, low folding chairs, and assorted benches surrounding their largest brazier, Jacko smiled at those already gathering. Some of the younger folk danced lazily off to the side, more out of boredom from waiting than anything else, their energy still leashed as the musicians sat the circle tuning their instruments and warming up their fingers. His sister sang quietly by the cook fires as she tended the pots. Jacko changed his course to join her. As he drew closer, the spiced scent of warming cider struck him hard, and he felt cold despite the nearness of the fire. The last time he'd smelled that aroma had been at Wicklow Cottage. The sudden memory of Agnieszka in her neat, tiny kitchen, struggling with a pot of cider bigger than she was, nearly staggered him.

He must have made a sound. Sveta turned from the stew she stirred. "What's wrong?"

Jacko gritted his teeth and looked down a moment, schooling his expression. "Nothing," he lied, not wanting to ruin the evening for anyone, even her. Sveta was the reason he wasn't with Agnieszka now, protecting her. His sister had slipped him a sleep draught when they'd been at the cottage so that he couldn't protest when the caravan left with him as so much baggage. Sveta still wouldn't explain what had frightened her enough to betray him that way. The memory roused his anger even yet, particularly now that he knew what had befallen the woman he cared for deeply enough to call her love, though Agnieszka refused to hear such talk from him.

The fire popped as his sister returned to her stirring. She gave him a sideways glance, her brow furrowed. Jacko's heart softened. Yes, he was angry at her, but he knew, whatever her reasons, she'd acted on them out of love and concern for his well-being. He could not fault her for that.

"Smells good," he told her as he came closer, wrapping his arm around her in a hug without disturbing her efforts. She smiled but shooed him away when he made a grab for her spoon.

"Off! You'll eat with everyone else."

He considered pursuing the matter in the name of good-natured teasing. Before he acted on that thought, a series of high-pitched squeals had him whirling around. The sight of a half-dozen children running pell-mell across the clearing, tumbling and leaping over obstacles like the performers they often were, was enough for anyone to quail at. Jacko, however, was used to it. Shifting away from his sister, he braced himself for the impact as his nephews and young cousins launched themselves at his legs.

"Umph!" he exaggerated the sound as he allowed his body to stagger and sway, then tumble to the ground well away from the fires. The laughter rose joyously as wrestling ensued until the youngest bumped a nearby table and was almost crowned by a toppled jug, were it not for Jacko's reflexes.

"Enough! Away from the tables," Sveta called out, her voice firm, but not unkind. "Or none of you will eat tonight."

The eyes of the boys grew wide at the threat, and their swarthy skin went several shades pale. "Even Uncle Jacko?" asked Marco, the youngest of his sister's sons.

"*Especially* Uncle Jacko," she answered, a mock fierce expression briefly twisting her features before she gave in to the laughter bubbling beneath her words. "Away! Before Baba Yaga comes for you and puts you in her pot!"

Shrieks and laughter pelted the night, mingling in surprising harmony with the murmur of the trees and the music being played. Jacko sprawled a moment on the ground, lying flat and relaxed, his eyes closed, and his spirit soothed by the sounds of life and youth and joy. Contentment settled over his soul as he slowly sat up, braced by his arms, and watched the celebration taking form around him. "Is it so bad, this?" his sister asked softly, the faintest bit of strain behind the question telling Jacko he hadn't fooled her earlier.

"No," Jacko answered truthfully, though his heart was troubled and his thoughts would not please Sveta if she could have read them. He had learned things this day, things he struggled not to hold against her. Later, when he told her he was staying here, she would not understand, but neither would she change his mind. Perhaps he would have been able to affect things, had he remained with Agnieszka before, perhaps not, but he could not take to the road knowing she was out there somewhere, prisoner to one capable of crimes dire enough to be banished as Bran had been. By staying here, Jacko gained the chance to help in finding her…freeing her, even. At the very least, he would hear word much sooner when she was rescued, and be here waiting for her return—he would not allow himself to think of any other possible outcome. Besides, there was Granddame Rose to consider.

As if summoned by his thoughts, the woman herself slowly took shape as she walked from beneath the shadow of the trees. She stopped before him and looked down. "I wish to join the singing," she told him, then waited expectantly.

Jacko quirked a smile up at her, not bothering to point out that she had only to walk over and sit down in the circle. Climbing to his feet, he offered her his arm. As if a queen and not a Romani crone, she placed her hand on his forearm and allowed him to lead her to the fire.

They were almost there when another stepped out of the shadows into the light of the dancing fire. She was dressed in a simple, unembellished version of the tunic and trews worn by the *Sidhe*, the color indeterminate in the dark. For the briefest moment, Jacko thought it was Agnieszka, but the coloring was wrong, and the way the girl moved was less than British proper, though the tension hanging off her shoulders somewhat mimicked the effect.

Not girl, he thought, as his gaze settled on her familiar eyes. *Young woman…old soul.* "Kara," he said aloud in both recognition and greeting. She gave a start as he called out to her. He offered her a half bow and waved her forward with his free hand. "Come, we celebrate."

She looked uncertain, as if she would fade back beneath the trees the moment he looked away. Something in her gaze told Jacko it was he who made her uncomfortable…and perhaps the secret they shared from the ritual, rather than the gathering itself. He gave her a reassuring smile, and inclined his head again, willing her to come forward. He liked this girl…her spirit, though her faint resemblance to his love called forth a fresh ache. It would be nice to have a chance to talk to her in less-than-tense circumstances.

Beside him, Granddame Rose shifted impatiently.

"Well…come on, girl," she called out brusquely. "There is no place for wallflowers here."

That startled a laugh from Kara, who shook her head at the old woman's manner but still came forward as bid, and they all moved to the circle around the fire, where space was made for them. Somehow Granddame Rose maneuvered matters so that Kara ended up between them. Jacko hadn't noticed at first, but Kara had a fiddle slung across her back. She drew it off and propped it beside her against the bench they shared. Within moments of her sitting, all manner of creatures crept from the forest. Most kept to the fringes, beneath the boughs of the trees or within them, but some few found sheltered spaces around the Romani camp from which to watch. Three came forward boldly to drape themselves around the girl's feet. They all had the look of catlings, but only one stared up with feline eyes. That one—a marmalade tabby—meowed, somewhat plaintively. Jacko hoped none of the others realized it was an actual cat, and not one of the faelings glamored to look so. The Rom considered both cats and dogs unclean. He had been around Agnieszka and her clowder too long to hold such prejudices.

"Pixie!" Kara bent to scoop up the petite cat. The little one snuggled into the girl's arms to nap. Its angular head rearing up to bump Kara's chin before the cat settled. The purring commenced.

Jacko laughed low and deep, not wanting to disturb the cat's contentment. Perhaps it would rub off on them all. His hand reached out to ruffle her fur. One eye opened indignantly, only to close again in pleasure as his fingers scritched gently.

"She won't let you stop now." Kara leaned toward him slightly as she spoke. The cat grumbled, and Kara straightened again.

Chuckling, Jacko looked up to meet her gaze. "There are worse things that could happen."

He meant it to be lighthearted, but Kara's expression dimmed. Her smile lost most of its curve. "I know," she murmured, her hand coming up to cradle the cat more firmly.

They said nothing else to one another for a long while, though Kara occasionally asked Rose to translate the words of the traditional songs the Rom sang. Surprisingly, the elder complied, softly, as to not disturb the singers.

Gradually, the tension of recent days fled the circle, banished by the ebullience of the celebration. There was singing and dancing, impromptu performing and constant music, all engaged in with the passion and energy of a people who worshipped life and all the joy it held, no matter how fleeting, precisely because it did not often last. Kara found herself swept up with them, easing some of the tension across her shoulders as the evening progressed.

The circle eventually broke into scattered groups, some still singing, others holding quiet conversation. Mulled wine had joined the scent of spiced cider, along with the slight smell of charring from stewpots nearly bare but for the scrapings. Jacko still sat where he had been around the main fire. He had ended up with Pixie curled in his lap, while his other companions had moved off or been drawn away. Pleased, he watched as the younger set slowly showed Kara the steps of a Romani dance. Though she moved with an inherent grace, the intricate steps caused her to stumble. Even so, she showed no sign of frustration; she merely laughed and tried again, lightheartedly shoving at her "tormenters" when the lesson devolved into a parody of her efforts. Despite that, she caught on quickly enough, given that she was new to the movements.

Jacko marveled as he watched her, trying to isolate what of her features had called to mind his love. Other than her general build, it was nothing physical that he could pinpoint. It was more a sense of bearing. Despite her relaxed posture (compared to Agnieszka, anyway), the girl carried herself with dignity not often found in modern-day youth. Given that, it was nice to see she knew how to let go even this much. He watched the group as they started to wind down, his hand still idly caressing the cat.

As the energy went out of their horseplay, there was a soft thud at Jacko's feet. He glanced down to spy the two other cats—both tabbies, one brown, the other shaded more in black—bumping the fiddle case with their heads. Neither made a sound, but their unnatural eyes compelled him. Reaching out, Jacko took up the instrument. In that fleeting instant, he was swept by a feeling of awe in the truest sense of the word, and yet there was no threat in the sensation. Jacko swiftly released his hold, not dropping the fiddle, but with haste setting it away from him. He was a simple man and knew such was not for him.

Now the felines sat before him yowling imperiously. At the sound, Kara turned, a question in her eyes as she sought the creatures at his feet.

"Beag Scath?"

The little brute, the one mostly brown, purred and sauntered close to her. The one remaining leaned in heavy against Jacko's calf. Looking back down, he realized with a shock that it was Rex, Agnieszka's adopted stray. In the dark, he had not recognized the wee one. "Humph," was all the acknowledgment the Romani made as his spare hand trailed down to scratch Rex's scruff. *How did I not realize this one was familiar?* Looking into those fae eyes, it struck him how apt—and ironic—that thought was.

Rex stood and paced a step away to lean now against the fiddle, looking patiently back at him.

"Humph," again.

Jacko finally realized what the beasties were after, if not why. Being curious himself, he complied. "Lass," he called to Kara. "Will you play for us?"

She looked…not quite nervous but uncomfortable. And yet she nodded and stepped away from the circle she'd formed with the younger folk.

Slowly, the Rom gathered back around. Among them were one or two *Sidhe* who had been invited to the celebration. Rex chirped at Jacko's feet and darted away, his long, thick tail curling in a high wave as he bounded toward one of them. It was Aí, the Danaan who'd told him of Agnieszka's fate.

A deep frown came to Jacko's face. It bothered him that Agnieszka's special little friend had only come to her because of this elf. Was their interference the cause of her plight, or truly an attempt to protect, as Aí claimed? Jacko would have pursued the matter, but then he heard the sweet notes of classical violin weave through the circle and among the trees. For a moment, it faltered, beautiful but somehow wrong, not meant for this place. Apparently, Kara agreed. She abandoned the air and let her bow dance where it would.

Jacko was delighted to catch whispers of the Romani songs from earlier threaded through the playing as if Kara had glommed on to the spirit of his people that quickly. She seemed particularly taken with the Tale of Tam Lin and his lover, Janet. There wasn't much. Just a measure here and there among what was clearly inspired rambling. Kara swayed and dipped and brandished her bow with passion and energy. The people were entranced; the lurking creatures lured closer. Rex and his *Sidhe* companion came forward, a look of stunned wonder on the immortal's face.

The legends of the region spoke of the magical skill of Bards. Kara cast those legends into a dim light. She was music and magic, and there was not a being listening that she did not move, body and soul. Above her, a swirling haze took loose shape. There was something of the *other* about it, though Jacko could not put a name to what he sensed. Threads of it trailed from her strings and from her bow like dancing ribbons drawn off from a rainbow. They sparkled like a loved one's smile until a sense of peace and contentment settled over all.

No one clapped, or whooped, or stomped their feet. By the time Kara lowered her bow, all had sunk down, sitting or reclining against any surface available, doing nothing but listen in abject wonder. None spoke as she packed her instrument away and set it aside.

She stood there before them within the circle, seeming almost dazed.

Jacko was struck again by awe. There was not a one who witnessed that performance that would not gladly follow anywhere she led.

From the threshold of the faerie ring, Kara watched the Rom depart. Last night they had invited her to join them. Made it clear she would be welcome among their clan. There seemed to be a lot of that going around. It surprised her how disappointed she had been to tell them she was not free to follow where they went. Someday, perhaps, but not now. So she watched with an aching heart as, like an anachronism rolling out from the mystical, magical past, the caravan of brightly painted, intricately carved vardos wove its way across the Irish countryside toward Dublin. At nearly every window perched dusky little faces with bright, bottomless dark eyes avidly staring out. Here and there, a giggle rose from amid the children or a pair of hazel eyes glimmered among their dark-eyed kin. Kara felt an unexpected longing for the carefree, mobile life of these people. She was sure they had most of the same concerns as everyone else, and certainly a few all to themselves, but to have such freedom…

As the caravan passed, Kara was moved by a haunting, familiar melody played by a young Romani boy in the last wagon, exhibiting casual mastery on the reed pipes. He perched on the ledge of an open window on the rear of the wagon, dangling one leg out of the vehicle with complete confidence in his safety, his eyes busy gazing at the fading stars, unconcerned with the asphalt road passing below him.

Kara longed for even a glimmer of his security in her own heart. At the moment, she was all too aware of her own precarious position dangling between two worlds, if not more. She wanted to justify Maggie's faith in her ability, to exceed the expectations of the *Sidhe* and humans alike, to remove the burden of worry from her parents' shoulders.

Still, she was tempted to turn away from those responsibilities…formal or informal as they were. Only it wasn't just that she hadn't been raised that way. No, it was a matter of who Kara was at her very core, instilled before she'd even drawn her first breath. Whatever other doubts she had about her abilities, one thing she knew with unwavering conviction: she could no more turn her back than she could kick a kitten. It wasn't a matter of being able to do what needed to be done; it was being incapable of not trying with everything she had. It was not in her to give up. She came from a fine tradition of stubborn Celts, after all.

Kara had no choice but to accept that, as much as a part of her wanted to take what the Rom offered, now was not the time. Acceptance settled on her heart as the caravan disappeared into the darkened countryside. Then, not quite ready to leave this world for the other, she stepped across the ring boundary and made her way down the knock and across the rocky meadow, toward granite cliffs Maggie had shown her beyond the rocks. Kara followed the barest hint of a path through monolithic boulders to the cliff's edge beyond. The shoulder was a muted grey in the moonlight, the edge limned silver against the blue-black sky. She should have been uneasy at the way the brisk wind tugged at her loose elven clothes, as it if would pluck her off her perch, whipping her hair about until she looked like the Medusa. Instead, she savored the salty tang of the ocean carried on the pre-dawn air, thrilled in the autumn chill that invigorated her as she stared out across the water.

As if she were surrounded by the bright light of day and her person caressed by only a gentle breeze, Kara sat on the ancient outcrop. She had the passing thought that these same rocks may have once bore the weight of the legendary Brian Boru, the last High King of Ireland, or Fionn MacCumhaill himself, never once considering that in some distant future someone might wonder the same of Kara O'Keefe.

Though she did not realize it, her expression echoed the serenity of the Romani lad she'd watched play, her confidence shored up. His enthralling melody echoed in the corners of her mind. It took another moment for her to realize the gift he had given her. The song he'd been playing was no ancient melody...it had been Lynyrd Skynyrd's "Free Bird."

It was this detail that convinced Kara that it did not matter how many worlds her feet straddled; if she could find the balance within herself, she could not fall. If a Romani boy could play rock tunes on a reed pipe while traveling in a traditional vardo, then Kara could find unity in those parts of herself that were *Sidhe* and human. Many worlds met within her, making her neither one thing nor another but uniquely Kara.

She slowly climbed to her feet and wended her way back toward the gate to *Tír na nÓg*. Whatever else she was called to face in the days to come, she no longer felt as if the only ground she had to stand on was shifting sand. And when those days were done, maybe not too very long from now, she and that Romani lad would play a duet from his open window as the wheels of the wagon they traveled in measured the road.

Chapter II

Calma had forgotten how pathetic mortal man could be. It took no effort at all to take over the owners of the McCorry Inn and their family, who served as workers there. Far enough from town to make casual traffic unlikely, close enough to be convenient in sensing any disruption that might impinge on Calma's plans, the place was perfect.

The humans remained enthralled in a backroom sustained by the merest thread of Calma's power, in case he had need of them. Unlikely — unless he needed a snack — but always a possibility. Outside, a NO VACANCY sign had been hung, and neighbors had been told some vague excuse of fumigation to keep them at a distance. There was always the potential of the unwitting showing up, or someone on official business, but nothing a bit of vigilance could not circumvent.

In the meantime, Calma settled into a necessary period of waiting as he adjusted to both the modern world and his host. He must have full understanding and physical command before approaching his brothers. They were each of a kind and might do something brash if they thought him weakened. Such an ill-advised act would finish the destruction of all three of them. Unlike his brothers, Calma had pondered their state for over two thousand years and was quite aware that they were linked by more than familial bonds. When Carmán had shrewdly sacrificed her power to sustain their spirits, it had forged an even deeper link. None of them would survive the death of even one of them…not the brothers, not Carmán. Vexing, true, particularly as his family — much like any group in nature — would benefit from the culling of its weaker members. That was no longer an option. Thus Calma must ensure he remained in the position of power in relation to his brothers.

He was nearly ready, just a bit more "juice," as they said in these perplexing times, and he would have more than enough strength to withstand even a combined assault, should they be foolish enough to attack him. Not that it was likely they would reconcile enough to join forces, but still, Calma was not foolish. He would prepare for even the impossible to the best of his ability. No sense in encouraging bad behavior.

Just a bit more mage power and Calma would be ready. And so he came to the other reason Wexford was so ideal a place to fortify his position. The population of the town and surrounding region was unsurprisingly comprised of mixed stock. Clearly, the de Danaans were not above taking advantage of the locals' gratitude. They hadn't been long ago when they'd destroyed Calma and his family, and they remained thus, given the undiluted strength of mage energy bound to some of those mixed-bloods he sensed within the boundaries of his territory. The demigod snarled. It was time to wreak some vengeance and recharge his resources in the process.

He summoned his favored muse. *Díoltas.* Revenge.

The others, *Scrios* and Togail — Havoc and Destruction — grumbled and fretted at their exclusion. Calma ignored them. Very soon, all his darker muses would have their roles to play, but not now. For this, he needed only the one.

Bran intruded, his tone both wary and suspicious. *What are you about?*

"We are going hunting," Calma answered aloud, a satisfied smile on their lips. Before Bran could press for further answers, Calma shoved his host's awareness back into the depths of their being as a whirlwind swept the room. Some things the demigod did not intend to share, this knowledge, in particular.

The air grew dry and hot, infernal and wild, as *Díoltas* arrived. Knick-knacks and bric-a-brac crashed to the floor. Draperies were disheveled and torn. Calma was annoyed by the disruption. Now one of the thralls would have to be brought out to straighten the mess, lest any outsiders did come by and discover the truth of the matter at the Inn.

Enough, Calma said, his voice brimming with impatience. *We have business to be about.*

Díoltas settled and took his human form. These muses had no voice beyond the screams of their battle cries, so he waited, a look of query on his face.

The blood of our enemy populates the veins of many in this region. I can sense them, but I need your finer senses to suss them out. Lead me to the richest source of power that I may sup.

With those instructions, the muse took his natural form once more and was away, the wind of his passing leaving more debris in its wake. Calma waited, not moving. His servant would not be long at his task.

And what are we hunting? Bran forced his awareness back to the fore. His mental voice sounded winded. Good, he wouldn't have the strength to struggle back a second time.

"Power," Calma answered, and pushed Bran back into the dark depths until Calma's business with *Díoltas* was done.

There was a knock at the door. Before he could react, it swung open. Instantly, Calma went taut and crouched at the ready, tearing a bolt of power from his resources to blast the unexpected intruder. Instead, *Díoltas* stood in the doorway smirking, a bit more malice than mischief in his eyes.

Separating out a thread from the bolt in less time than it took the muse to blink, Calma exacted retribution. The smell of scorched ozone filled the room, and *Díoltas*'s smirk vanished as the bolt connected with his physical form. If not for the warning in Calma's expression, likewise, the muse would have fled as well. As it was, he only rubbed at his shoulder and turned to mist, hovering between the door and the stair as he waited for Calma to follow.

They left the cottage and trekked across the countryside on foot. Though the sun beat down in pleasant warmth and the smell of barley scented the air, Calma ignored it all. He proceeded with long, impatient strides over the green, gently sloping hills, taking note of the landscape only enough to avoid the sheep droppings. He kept his features harsh to dissuade any who might notice him along the way from attempting a friendly conversation. *Díoltas*, much diffused but still quite obvious to Calma, was a faint mist moving on before him. One patch stayed tinged a faint purplish-grey, unlike the rest of the muse, which was virtually colorless.

Now it was Calma who smirked.

After a while, they came upon a farmhouse not too far from the inn. Spending another whisper of power, Calma hid his form from view. He could sense the intoxicating energy ahead, taste it like ambrosia on his tongue, only faintly bitter with mortal taint. Restraining the impulse to breathe deep like some common fool who thought to draw the power in like smoke, Calma moved closer to what appeared to be a barn. A child played there among stacks of straw, a little girl luring kittens with a piece of twine. She nearly glowed with mage potential. Surely, here was one more than half *Sidhe*. Hunger seized Calma hard, the magical equivalent of salivating. The child was his.

Moving forward, he was about to enter the building when an unexpected jolt rippled the surrounding energies. A scream came from the barn. High pitched in agony, it abruptly cut off. From the doorway, Calma spied six women slinking about, clawed and fanged, white as death and red as blood…fitting, for he was sure he looked upon Dubh's minions, the *Bás*…or in the Irish tongue: Death. Rage boiled in his blood as they toyed with the child's corpse like the kittens had the string, tossing and tearing, with sometimes a pounce just for the joy of it. When they were done, they opened a pathway through the nothing and disappeared with the remains.

In their wake, not an ounce of power remained.

Calma snarled as he wheeled away. Impressive hunters to be sure, but these creatures had stolen his prey. That was more than enough to pit him against them, but deeper still was the sense that they were a danger. Nothing to be tamed or allied with. Beings who fed on magic could be but two things to him: competition or threat. If bringing Mother back were not so vital, requiring all his resources, Calma would bend all the power in his control to eradicating the *Bás* from the world.

Of course, there was always later…

Kara found herself standing before the monument known as the Temple of the Fallen. It was simple and quite similar to any number of monuments in the world Kara grew up in. At one end rose a detailed statue of a woman, young and beautiful. Stretched before that lay a long slab about a foot and a half off the ground. Both were of creamy pristine marble and held a constant, subtle glow Kara was told she was responsible for. There was engraving on the side of the slab.

In contrast to the glow, it blazed as if lit from within:

> TO THE VALIANT SOUL OF ANU, CHERISHED SISTER AND SAVIOR,
> TORN FOREVER FROM THE HEART OF THE *Daoine Maithé*
> STOLEN FROM US, BY THE *Namhaid*,
> DENIED THE PURITY OF THE ETERNAL FLAME.
> ALL HONOR AND LOVE TO YOUR MEMORY.

She avoided looking closely at the statue. Something about it made her uncomfortable. On the surface of the slab lay all manner of tributes: fruit, blossoms, goblets of mead, savories, even trinkets. The muscles in her gut tensed as she realized what it reminded her of: the site of an accident on the highway. Sad recognition of something precious lost—a rare thing for the *Tuatha de Danaan*. Though there was precedence for banishments—uncommon, but there had been cases, as Maggie had explained—and, of course, the recent Unraveling, Anu was the only soul lost to the *Sidhe* in a manner that could not be explained.

Overhead the tree boughs rustled, echoing Kara's sigh. She could not explain the heaviness in her heart or her growing irascible mood. But as peaceful as this place was, Kara had no doubt something about it contributed to her state. Anu's story weighed on her.

She remembered the sight of Murna: a fallen *Sidhe* at one time lain in state upon the marble slab, a sight the unknowing would have thought inconsequential. Only there was no such thing as a *Sidhe* corpse, not for long, anyway. Soon after a normal death, the Eternal Flame came upon the body until all that remained was a kind of glittery ash. *Hmm,* Kara thought wryly, *that explains where someone got the idea of pixie dust.*

Murna's had not been a normal death. She had been all but slain by the *Namhaid*, though none recognized this at first. The memory of their ways lost to time, even for a race as old as the Danaans. Still, the effect of the evil nested within Murna had been felt, if not seen. None of the *Sidhe* understood what had happened because they could not conceive of such a thing. How Kara knew what must be done, she could not explain. That she'd been capable of acting at all—new to magic as she was—astounded her. In either case, she did not know, nor did it matter to her. As long as the evil had been banished, she was content to let things lie.

Despite the darker memories, Kara felt a kinship here. She found peace beneath these boughs. It somehow felt like *her* place. Perhaps because of her part in the cleansing; perhaps for some reason beyond her understanding. It didn't matter in the end. She found herself repeatedly drawn to the monument, particularly after the tension of the Unraveling and her recent conflicts with Goibhniu and her father. Kara lowered herself to sit alongside the marker stone, the shards of the dagger in the pouch at her side, twice hidden from sight in leather and the shadow she cast.

For the moment, she tried once more to clear her thoughts. The murmuring of the tree boughs and the serenity of the glade combined to calm her spirit. She allowed herself this pocket of peace, to absorb the love enshrined in the monument. Her eyes drifted closed, and she let her awareness float to the faint murmuring of the faelings spying on her from the foliage. They had their own connection with this place. When she'd freed Murna's soul the faelings shielded her against interruption. They were as much a balm to her as the shrine itself, and she willed them to banish the last of the tension plaguing her.

As she regained her composure, the bravest of the kin cousins ventured forth to cuddle among the loose folds of her tunic. Beag Scath was the first, naturally, claiming place of pride in the cradle of her crossed legs. Nearly as bold was the sprite she had seen in the Court with the Rom. She almost tensed at the sight of him, only he *chirled* at her with such longing that she instead drew him close by her side, beneath the protective shelter of her arm. He remained there a moment, clutching her sleeve, then he clambered up to her shoulder. Suddenly, his little body tensed and his grip on her shirt tightened, binding her uncomfortably. He gave a low *chuff* and was gone before she could even wonder or lift her head to see why. By the time she noticed him twined about Aí's ankles, most of the timid faelings had scattered. She had half a moment to compose her face.

"*Lhiannon*, are you well?"

Sighing, Kara slowly looked up into Aí's open gaze. Some tension crept back into her limbs. Almost automatically, she brought up the shields Maggie had taught her, keeping her thoughts private. Even with the curse gone, this man made her uncomfortable. It was like his eyes asked her for things she could not bear to give…did not want to give? Or maybe they just hoped for more than she was comfortable with. She couldn't say which. Not that it mattered when they all amounted to the same thing.

Rather than invite concern, she bent her lips into a semblance of a slight smile. "What does that word mean…what you called me?"

There was something jarring about seeing a *Sidhe* blush. He looked down a moment then back up again to meet her eye. "Lhiannon? It means… sweetheart."

Kara lost the smile, though she did manage not to scowl. Who was he? She barely knew, but one thing was certain: she was *not* his sweetheart. She was not anyone's sweetheart, and she was fine with that.

Aí recoiled as if he heard her thoughts or something, though she was shielded.

Before she could say a word, he continued, "Sorry, no disrespect meant."

"I'm fine, just needed some quiet time alone after all that's happened." No need to explain further. The *Sidhe*'s eyes darkened with understanding. All were still unsettled by the Unraveling.

As if sensing how she felt, instead of lowering himself to the ground beside her, Aí moved about the clearing. His hand reached out to rub the bright green leaves of an oak between his fingers, to caress the silvery bark of an ancient birch, bending to gather up the deadfall that carpeted this ground for the first time in known memory (or so Maggie had told her).

Events must have prevented anyone from coming to clear things out. Why else had the signs of death and decay remained there? Kara would have thought the *Sidhe* would have swiftly removed any reminder of the evil they'd unwittingly harbored. To leave it in this place was like sacrilege.

Aí appeared to feel the same if his expression was any gauge. In fact, as he pulled an empty canvas sack from his belt, it appeared that was the reason he'd come. Blushing, Kara felt foolish thinking he'd been seeking her out. She watched as he worked a while gathering up the debris that resulted from the brief time the *Namhaid*-infected corpse had brought corruption to this place. She shuddered, remembering the battle, where the spirit-women had maimed and slaughtered with such brutality.

Kara was almost glad of the distraction when Aí turned to speak to her.

"Did you see this place…before you cleansed it?"

Ah…of course…the other topic she most decidedly did not want to discuss.

Kara rose to her feet, dislodging those faelings that had not already fled at the *Sidhe*'s arrival. Only Beag Scath still clung to her, hissing quietly from where he gripped her tunic across her chest, upset at almost being deposed himself. She reached up to give him a brief caress in the hopes of calming him.

Aí stood there, waiting for a response. The sound of him idly shifting his stance plucked at her nerves. She was extremely aware of the pouch hanging against her hip; every instinct told her to hide it. There was no way, of course, without Aí seeing. Even more questions would follow. Resisting the urge to brush off her fae-woven pants—they seemed impervious to dirt and debris anyway—she shook her head without looking him in the eye. "I don't remember much past getting here. I was unconscious by the time they carried me back to the Hall. Maggie thinks whatever I did scrambled my memories a bit while I was at it.

"Listen," she went on, trying to sound casual and failing miserably, "no sense you doing this when I need some time to myself, right? I'd be glad to finish…"

He did not seem to hear her as he went on, his voice a bit far off. "Ironic, we brought the corruption here, thinking to honor…when we were but fostering the very evil set to destroy us; that took away our homeland, to begin with." His eyes drifted up the length of the statue. "The very evil that cost us Anu herself…"

Time slowed, and Kara watched his hand rise as if he would caress that marble face. Something about that possibility disturbed her more than his presence or even the topic of conversation. Before he could connect, she interposed herself before the statue. As his fingers brushed her cheek, she flinched back. Frustrated with both him and herself, she spoke again, more brusque than she'd intended. "I said I've got this, okay?"

He blinked rapidly and barely seemed to breathe as he searched her face. If she had to describe his expression, she would have called it sucker-punched, though she couldn't imagine why he would look that way. She cleared her throat, and he drew a sharp breath before breaking his gaze, as if uncomfortable. When he glanced up again, his expression was rueful.

"I'm sorry, but I can't leave," he answered her. "I'm here to meet with Goibhniu."

Now she really felt the fool.

The flinch was more internal this time. Things were not altogether comfortable between her and the Smithgod, either. She was pretty certain she didn't want to stick around with the shards hanging on her belt. Call her crazy, but he might take exception to that.

She still did not know how to fix the blade. Could not even explain why it needed to be done. All she knew was she could not do it alone—a difficult admission for her. By fate or happenstance, for so long, it had fallen to her to make things happen, to make things right. She wouldn't call herself a control-freak…but then who would?

Aí lifted a hand toward her. She backed up, not sure why the prospect made her uneasy, yet certain the answer was nothing simple. Not ready to deal with either him or Goibhniu, Kara gave a sharp nod. Pivoting around, she hurried away.

"You should have said," she muttered to herself as the distance grew between them.

Maybe it was a bird…maybe it wasn't, but a chuckle-like sound followed her down the path.

Coming before Goibhniu was never a comfortable prospect. As his messenger, it generally involved gaining a new responsibility, rarely something pleasant or simple. This time, Aí had arrived at the Temple of the Fallen, as instructed, only to find Kara there and the Smithgod nowhere in sight.

Goibhniu?

I'm on my way, his liege answered.

Aí sighed inwardly. Kara was agitated and his presence only seemed to add to her troubled state. Even if his gift had allowed him to read thoughts, he feared he would not have made sense of the maelstrom surely spinning in her head. The emotional barrage was hard enough to decipher. His attempt to keep his distance was unsuccessful. For a moment, it seemed an argument would spark between them, but his mention of Goibhniu motivated her to leave. Though that had not been his intention, he was relieved she went away.

When she was well gone, a form stepped from the foliage, not far from the path. It was Goibhniu, a sword belt slung across his shoulder and a deep pouch hanging at his side.

"I didn't want to disturb her further," he explained, though he had no need to.

"She is burdened," Aí agreed. "By what, I can't say."

They moved toward the monument, standing several feet away, heads bowed respectfully. From the air and a wisp of magic, Goibhniu drew a smattering of snowflakes and cast them across the slab like a bejeweled blanket. Tribute observed, the Smithgod turned toward him, his features dark and fierce, eyes smoldering like the embers of his forge. "We cannot lose so many with no hope o' gaining them back. The *Namhaid* took five from the battle. We must find them before we are forever diminished, and the enemy built up."

Aí's expression went grim at the harsh facts. Thanks to Kara, they had learned that the *Namhaid* whelped their young in the carcasses of magical beings. Suspended a breath from dying, the victim cradled the monsters, who slowly devoured the soul, leaving nothing to return to the People. That very concept alone marked them as anathema. "What would ye have o' me?" Aí asked, knowing what he would hear, poised and ready for it, even eager.

"Will ye serve as Hound again?"

Dropping to one knee, Aí brought his right fist across his chest and bowed his head.

"Unleash me on the *Namhaid* and I'll tear their throats out with my teeth."

Aí remained where he was until the Smithgod drew him up. "'Aye' would have served just as well."

"Maybe," Aí said. "But it wouldn't have done justice to the oath."

With a nod, Goibhniu turned back to the monument before speaking. "Then 'tis time ye scented yer prey."

With a frown, Aí turned his gaze to his liege. "How?" He was not sure he wanted an answer. If they knew where to find them, the point would be moot. Besides, his brief experience with the *Namhaid* already filled him with distaste. Still…when needs must…

"Time has no place in *Tír na nÓg*. We are the masters here," Goibhniu answered. "So, come. Let's see what time would hide from us."

Aí laid his hand on Goibhniu's shoulder and followed as the Smithgod stepped between the layers of memory to the point before the now when the monument had yet to be cleansed. The first thing to strike Aí was the stench of decay: rotting leaves, rotting flesh, mildew and mold and the earthy scent of suffering. Blanketing it all was a heavy, sickly sweet musk, unfamiliar and cloying. Despite his disgust, Aí drew the scent in, imprinting it in his mind.

Through his empathic gift, he felt Murna's soul in frantic torment nearly overwhelmed by an alien hunger. His heart shredded in that brief moment of immersion. His fingers tightened on Goibhniu's shoulder in reaction. The sensory impact threatened to leave his legs weak with the force of it all. He stored this sensation as well until he could stand no more.

Enough, he begged unabashedly, soul to soul.

The Smithgod stepped back, and layers of insulating memory rose between Aí and the horror Kara had cleansed. His awe of her trebled in that instant.

When the sound of faelings rustling the glade mingled with his own chuckle as Kara went away, Aí knew they were leaving the folds of memory for the now. He let his hand drop away and did not even try to brace his legs, still weak with the intensity of what he'd just re-experienced. He landed in a pile of deadfall he'd yet to clear away and let his head fall forward on his knees, tempering the memory with the scents of clean air and rich, dark loam.

Goibhniu squatted down beside him. "Was it?" he asked.

Aí lifted his head. "Enough?"

The Smithgod nodded.

"Yes…With this memory, I will track the *Namhaid*'s victims…and the creatures themselves." Aí shuddered with the need to be away, to assume his task. A flex of his neck did little to relieve the tension gathered there. He was still at a loss for how to proceed. Expectantly, he turned to Goibhniu.

"Aye, ye could say I came prepared," the Smithgod said. "The Seers advised me to see ye armed proper." Unslinging the sword belt, he held it out toward Aí, who accepted it with a frisson of unease. The weight was familiar. This was something other than one of Goibhniu's usual blades. Something more. Before Aí could look closer, the Smithgod drew two things from the pouch at his side: a dagger and an ornate torc. He held those out as well. "Every

Hound needs both tooth an' claw, use them well." From the other side of his belt, Goibhniu removed a little leather box about the size of a narrow brick, a hand-span wide. Opening the tight-fitted flap, he revealed an insulated chamber cradling five tiny coals, glowing red and strong with magic. "These are embers imbued with the Eternal Flame. 'Tis the best way to deal with what yer setting out to find. Slay the vessel and bless it to the Flame. An if these are not enough—blessed Mother forbid—I'll have more for ye when ye next return."

With reverence, Aí accepted the tools he would need to carry out his charge. He held up the torc questioningly.

"'Tis akin to Cliodna's…Maggie's." Goibhniu clarified, using the name Aí was more familiar with for the leader of the *Fianna*. "Wherever ye will, it'll see ye safely from here to there."

"When shall I head out?" Aí asked, his thoughts drifting to Maggie's student, Kara.

"A day or two, no later. The other Hounds will be selected by then. Prepare…make a plan for yerself an' the others. They'll answer to ye for this hunt."

"As ye will it," Aí responded. Nice to know he wasn't alone in this responsibility. Daunting to know he would lead the effort.

Girding his hips with the sword belt, sword sheathed on one side, the dagger on the other, he slid the torc around his neck and bowed once more to his liege, before returning to *Mór Halla* to prepare.

Chapter 12

The sheer emotive power hidden beneath the surface of mortal society stirred Olcas's hunger. He wasn't interested in the anguish or concerns of humanity, though he delighted in it and drank in the savory vapors of those emotions. No, what really drew him were the threads of barely masked rapture slowly wafting from those who secretly thrilled in the carnage and destruction, those who would feed on it even as he himself did, if only they were able. He pitied them. Blessed with the souls of devourers, yet shackled in weak, human shells very much in the way he had been shackled to Lucien. But that was past, and his situation with Tony was so much more satisfying.

Or it would be if the boy's spirit weren't rearing up at the most inopportune moments to throw off Olcas's timing. He had been so certain that the loathsome punk would be forever lost in mage-blasted oblivion, leaving this eminently suitable body for Olcas's sole use. For a while, that was so, but something had drawn the boy's spirit back to awareness, and Olcas grew fed up with the ongoing struggle for control.

The boy had always been a little too soft, not ruthless enough. Olcas would have to do something about the matter soon. But for now, it had been a while since either Olcas or his pet demon had been out to play. And if he combined some fun with the next step in his plan against the enemy…so much the better.

Olcas snagged the leather jacket draped over the back of his chair and shrugged into it, making sure his switchblade was in the pocket. It was a modern affectation, completing the image. Olcas knew that appearances created expectations in others, which meant less effort on his part. Humans, after all, were sheep. Easily fooled, easily slaughtered.

That made the final conception of his plan ideal. He moved through the chambers of his lair, searching for the demon. Ever since the change, it was acting more erratic. Time to make it someone else's problem. He found it lurking among the stacks of crated merchandise. It had shoved at the lower section of one stack until a hidey-hole had been created.

Holding out his hand, he impatiently waved the creature forward. "Come…we're going out." It hissed and drew back into the shadows. Growling back, Olcas carved a sigil in the air and snatched his hand close to his body, jerking the demon from its lair with a howl and a whimper. Teeth gnashed the air but could not come near to Olcas's skin thanks to the compulsions built into the bindings. He turned his back on the sulking demon.

"Get dressed," he ordered. The demon grudgingly complied.

Smiling, Olcas led "her" out of the sublevel and through the warehouse. The steady drip of condensation from the pipes followed him through from zone to zone until he reached the security door beside the massive roll-gates to the loading dock. Reaching out with his awareness, he encountered no other consciousness within the security fence or beyond, though a few cars went by on the nearby service road. No one close enough to take notice, though. A gesture brought down the wards safeguarding this area and triggered the automatic gate on the fence outside. Opening the door, he stepped through, the demon close behind.

Olcas scowled. Their best opportunity for fun was in Dublin, not out here in the industrial park. It would be so much quicker to simply tear a pathway through the void. Unfortunately, that was unwise. Not only did he need to conserve his energy, but somewhere out there, his brother lurked. There was no telling when the crispy bastard would lash out, and the void was Dubh's particular turf. Snarling with frustration, Olcas hopped down from the loading platform and stalked out onto the macadam surrounding the warehouse.

"Follow me," he ordered his creature as he moved out into the night; without the words, the demon would not have been able to leave. To one side of the loading area sat a blood-red Kawasaki Ninja he'd appropriated for more mundane transport.

Swinging onto the cycle, Olcas gestured for his minion to get on behind him. He gunned the engine and roared through the opening gate and onto the road.

The drive to Phoenix Park was uneventful. Olcas moved them deep within, where there was some seclusion, but not too much. He dismounted, drawing the demon with him, then reached out with his senses until he brushed a hunger similar to his own, constant, aching, dark, with just enough mage potential to damn the target. Close enough, surely, to be tempted.

"Let's make this convincing, shall we?" Olcas told the demon. "We must mask my presence, or the ruse may fail. The blows that mark your skin must come from another." He slapped one hand against the other in mimicry of a true blow. Obedient, the demon cried out. A firm yank from its own hands tore open the blouse. The buttons pelted the nearby foliage but otherwise made no sound. Olcas nodded, pleased, then used his magic to shake the host until the demon screamed and fought convincingly, as much as the bindings would allow. The dull thud of footsteps drew near. Olcas "released" his hold, and the demon fell to the ground as a human predator parted the bushes.

With a sharp-toothed grin, Olcas tilted his head toward the cowering woman.

"Have some fun," he said.

The stupid human thought Olcas was talking to him. To be fair, he was supposed to. The demon knew, though. It toyed with the man, scrambling away to lure him, then lashing out with claw tips and teeth. Their victim got in his fair share of blows, but in the end, he was doomed. As the demon sat atop his chest, duly battered but savoring the blood on her fingers, Olcas reached down and drew her off. While she snarled and paced behind him, he drew the man to his feet, mimed a kiss, and drew a faint glimmer of mage potential from him, savoring the fear of a failed predator before carving a slit into the ether and shoving their victim through. That should confuse his brother.

The man already forgotten, Olcas turned to consider the results of their play. *Very nice...* Colorful bruises mottled her skin, here and there was a speckling of blood from an abrasion, or a thin runnel trailing from a split in the skin. Her clothing was torn and disheveled, and her hair as snarled as the sounds still coming from her lips.

"Enough. Play is over, it is time to do my bidding."

Olcas took the knife from his pocket and hit the button releasing the blade. Placing the tip against the host's flesh, Olcas traced delicate mystic patterns into her skin. One to allow him access to the creature's senses. Another to shackle the demon's usual impulses. A third to make a natural seeming for the beast from the remaining fragment of the woman's soul. The last to shield the demon from detection beneath that seeming. Each sigil disappeared from sight as it was completed. Olcas instructed his minion as he finished his work.

"You will observe them, nothing more. You will do no harm to the *Tuatha de Danaan* or those under their protection...until the time is right. When Kara O'Keefe is firmly within your reach, you will capture her. Bring her to me...unharmed...undrained...unwilling." His pulse sped up in anticipation with that last. He quelled the reaction until it could properly be savored, fed with plans of all he intended for the blasted girl. After completing the final sigil, Olcas absently licked the blood from the blade before retracting it and returning it to his pocket. He stepped back and considered his efforts.

A deep, cold smile graced his lips, followed by a satisfied sigh. An inspection with his otherly senses showed the governors firmly in place. The demon would to all effects be Lynn Barnert until the ideal opportunity to capture Kara presented itself. Well pleased with the arcane preparations, Olcas quickly took care of the physical. The demon burned with hatred, but did not evade or strike back as Olcas attacked with a blast of the energy he'd torn from the thug; bound, as the creature was, behind those insipid blue eyes.

When he left, the demon's host lay unconscious on the ground, clothes torn and body bruised, but mostly unharmed, the fragment of her soul dusted off and at the forefront, waiting to be "found" by her loved ones…and their allies. Drawing off the shields that had prevented the *Sidhe* from locating the woman previously, Olcas returned to his cycle, mounted, and sped away.

CHAPTER 13

DISTURBED BY RECENT REPORTS FROM BOTH THE MORTAL REALM AND THE *Sidhe* Lands, the *Fianna* gathered in the war room to plan their strategy. Though not formally *Fianna*, Kara was among them, as were Goibhniu, Urias, and Doctor Barnert, who sat next to her father. Worried about his wife, the doctor refused to be excluded. All of the warriors were there except Aí, who was sent away on some mission by Goibhniu. They all sat comfortably in the public chamber, leaning back against their cushions. The center of the table held the remnants of refreshments, carefully arranged, so they did not endanger the various notes being spread out across the surface. With the meal done, it was time to settle to the task.

Kara, who had been playing softly in an attempt to lessen the tension in the room, lowered Quicksilver from beneath her chin. Rising, she picked up the violin case and headed down the corridor to her room to put the instrument away.

When she returned, the discussion had already begun. She frowned as her sense of belonging fled. It stung that they had not waited for her. It was an effort to keep the hurt out of her expression as she settled back down in her seat. "What did I miss?" she asked.

Papa looked over at her, but with half his attention still focused on the one speaking. "There've been more attacks. Some by these *Namhaid*, some not. No more o' the *Sidhe* have been taken so far."

Kara nodded. More talk of the *Tuatha de Carmán*, more accounts of sudden attacks by the spirit women. In the time since the battle on the knock, life had begun to take the feel of being on the front lines, only without the bombs exploding…yet. Tempers were stretched taut.

Into that tension, a quiet voice rose. It cut across the discussion and the side conversations both. The speaker was one of the warrior women seated across the table from Kara. Her name was Mabh.

"There's been another strike," the *Bean Fianna*—woman warrior—said. Her eyes were solemn, and her mouth set in a tight, grim line. "Someone's taking our children from Clan O'Shaughnessy."

Many of the *Fianna* came to their feet, their expressions fierce, and the color drained from their already fair faces. Those seated were no less furious for all their stillness. Kara looked from face to face trying to understand. She dare not ask — not when she sensed the roused ire sparking through the chamber — but she couldn't help wondering…what children? The only ones she knew of had not yet been born. She looked over at Maggie, one of those still sitting. The *Sidhe* had one hand protectively on her belly and the other around the warrior beside her. Part of Kara wondered at that. It was not the first time she'd seen her friend make such a gesture. She was distracted from that thought by the grief and torment shadowing the man's features. Kara finally realized which children.

While fae women only bore young when one of their number died, if a male of the race lay with a human woman, the coupling was always fertile. If it was a love match, mother and child lived among the *Sidhe*; if not, they remained in the mortal realm with whatever protections could be bestowed by the father. Demne had told her that…only a few short weeks ago.

The half-fae… Kara soulspoke to Maggie, not wanting to add to the torment of those more closely affected by speaking her realization aloud. *They've taken the children the Sidhe men have had by mortal women.*

Maggie gave a faint nod and 'spoke back, *Aye, they've taken the elf-kin.* The images she projected, though, were of people of all ages, not just the young, and Kara had to remember those before her measured their age in centuries more often than years. It made no difference, though, that some of the children were older than herself; Kara felt her own wrath rise on behalf of those taken and the families left to wonder. *She* didn't have to wonder. These warriors feared for their children with only an idea of what was possible. Kara had experienced what Olcas was capable of. True, there was a chance he wasn't specifically involved, but there was little doubt whoever was responsible was of a similar character. Evil was evil, and everything within Kara wanted to stand with the *Fianna* against such foulness. Here was a purpose she was suited to. Here was her chance to shake off the final vestiges of his hold over her, the lingering poison locked in her heart and soul.

"So," she said as she pushed to her feet, "what are we going to do about it?"

"*We,*" one of the *Sidhe*, answered, "are going to get our children back. *You* are going to stay here. There are too many already at risk." His words were not spoken unkindly, but Kara was fed up with being shoved back.

"I'm sorry, but you don't get to choose for me. None of you do. I am not a child. When there is a wrong to be righted, each of us has a responsibility to do everything in our power to see it done." Kara did not waver as she confronted those in the room, including her father. His feelings on the matter so were conflicted she could barely untangle them, as fear and anger and pride chased one another around his face. She had to look away.

Determined, she locked her gaze on the Smithgod. "You said it yourself, Goibhniu, there are others capable of taking up the tasks we seem destined for, we are each just one option. I am not indispensable. If I am going to be anything but a burden to those I care about, I have to do this. It is more than defending myself and others. It's even more than freeing myself from the harm done to me. It's conquering evil. It's making sure that evil doesn't get an opportunity to scar even one more person. I can only do that by standing up to the darkness.

"I am not helpless. I've taken plenty of self-defense classes. Hell, I've had *sword* training, and I'm damned good at it, even if I never did expect to need it outside of competition. I've even had some mage training, though I hope Maggie plans to continue that."

Mabh looked up at her, an oddly combined look on her face, both aghast and perplexed. "An' ye expect those little drabbles to serve ye well enough against a demigod?"

Willing patience into her words, Kara shook her head. "They're coming after me either way. Don't you think it's better if I try to prepare, or do you expect me to be a prisoner here forever? Because Olcas assaulted me right at the threshold of your Land. As far as they're concerned, if it weren't for the sword, they would have had me. Do you think they'll stop after that? Until I face my demons, I am useless to anyone who depends on me. Until they're gone for good, *none* of us are safe."

"You're the reason Neasa is dead," a woman's quiet, pained voice spoke from somewhere to Kara's left. Others muttered in response, but no one else spoke up loud…except for Goibhniu.

"No." His voice shut down the protests. "Kara is the reason I'm still alive. 'Tis Carmán's sons who are responsible for our losses." He stood, his eyes scoping the circle of warriors, holding each gaze briefly before moving to the next person. "Would *ye* be content for others to risk their lives for ye while ye remained safe in *Mór Halla*?"

Like a shared breath, all answered, "No."

"Would ye suffer dark forces to go unchecked?"

Again, "No."

Goibhniu nodded as if all were settled then. Kara went still, her muscles taut as he turned to her. "Ye argue with more skill than that trickster Abarta," he said, naming one ancient even for the *Sidhe*. Familiar with the man and his ways, Kara blushed as Goibhniu went on, "And to better purpose. To my eyes, ye bear as much o' the spirit o' the *Fianna* as any here. If ye will it and swear to the oath, I'd count ye one o' them from here forward. Ye may join us in whatever our plans."

She didn't know what to say. How had they transitioned from "Let me help you rescue your children" to "Welcome, new recruit"? She suspected she'd gone as pale as Papa had. And yet, after all that had just been said, she didn't feel she could really say "no thanks." Not that she wanted to, but it would have been a nice option.

That left only one thing for her to say: "Thank you." She wondered how long she would mean it.

Goibhniu then spoke the oath into her thoughts, and Kara repeated it aloud. Those in the room saluted her when she was done, some with more enthusiasm than others.

The Smithgod then soulspoke her directly. *That means ye listen now, and don't go making yer own plans. Yer bound by the oath that governs all the Fianna. Like any in yer human military, ye'll follow orders or face discipline. Understood?*

Yes, sir, Kara thought back at him, somber and not a little nervous.

Despite that, and even given what was being said, something about this intimate conversation set Kara at ease, eroding some of the awe that kept her from relaxing around him, and the unease that arose from their argument about the Unraveling. Even with all the magic and the power of his presence…even with the fact that he was talking directly into her head, she got the sense it was like talking to the President, a man due respect, but not worship. She was comfortable with that. It felt like the right perspective.

Of course, even the President could turn her world upside down with just one word to the right people.

Her eyes narrowed as that triggered a thought that had not occurred to her. *Deal fair…no ordering me to stay here and quietly behave.*

Goibhniu laughed aloud at that, to everyone's confusion, but did not bother to explain.

I don't suppose ye count this yer boon?

It was Kara's turn to laugh, with a bit more of an edge to it. *Nice try, but not hardly.*

She sat back and glanced at those waiting, reminding him there was another discussion pending.

"Shall we get back to it?" Goibhniu said as he sat back down and looked expectantly at those gathered.

Papa cleared his throat and, without looking at her, leaned forward to speak. "What about that lady who helped us find Kara?" His eyes darkened as they glanced in her direction now. He looked away quickly, his jaw tightening. She tensed herself at the memory of the time in question. Likely that had been her father's intent.

He went on. "The Seer…can she or one o' hers do anything to tell us where they are?"

Part of Kara listened closely to the resulting debate, another part worked on coming to grips with the sudden change in her circumstance. Though unexpected, she embraced her new status. It would take getting used to—and a serious training program ASAP—but that was a given. What clenched her gut was wondering what her father would say once he had her alone.

There was no use worrying about it now, though. Adults made hard decisions and lived with them, regardless of whether their parents were happy with the choices made.

Weary and worn, but no less driven, Aí continued the hunt. Swiftly he had tracked and freed one of those lost, the body liberated from its contagion and given to the Flame, the soul still intact. Better, perhaps, he had not had such immediate success, followed by fruitless search after fruitless search, broken by the occasional return to *Tír na nÓg* to report and regroup. The strain wore on him. With each day that passed, it was more likely he would be too late. And here was another trail. Was it false, or would he shake this frustration at last?

Drawn here by a particularly strong trail of the scent he'd imprinted, Aí cautiously entered the cave, sword drawn. Immediately, he was assaulted by the cold, bitter odor of spilt blood. It was most likely the leavings from an animal, but he had to check. Climbing nimbly over immense boulders and sliding through narrow crevices, he made his way deep into the hidden recesses of the cavern. The darkness was absolute, even to his fae eyes. The only sound was a steady drip as the cavern built upon itself in slow and steady measures, the pings echoing endlessly. Reaching for the shimmer of surrounding magics, he called a fraction of them to rest in his palm, casting the chamber with an eldritch glow.

Before him, laid out across a boulder, was a body. Bright copper hair draped to the ground, and slate-blue eyes stared sightless across the cavern. He knew him. A man of the *Daoine Maithé* long ago cast out from the Lands for his dark ways, but not cut loose from the People through the Unraveling. He'd moved on to Aberdeen and taken to calling himself Ewan, though his true name was Dulachan.

This was unexpected. He was not one of those taken at the battle. Both a good thing and a bad one. It meant Aí was not out of time to rescue those he'd been charged to find, but it also meant that there may be others needing rescuing. Or beyond hope.

It was too late for Dulachan. The flesh of his abdomen was peeled away like a fruit. The edges glistened black with blood and decay, the remaining skin mottled. Though the stench was fetid, the breach looked fresh, not crusted.

Aí had only that instant to take in the horror revealed by his mage light. A sudden impact low and hard brought him to his knees. He immediately scrambled back to his feet, crouching in a ready stance, searching the gloom beyond the mage light's glow.

His attackers squatted in a circle around the cavern, watching him from beneath lowered brows, eyes glowing an animalistic red, pelts gleaming white and sleek like satin, where in adult form it was like crushed velvet. The *Namhaid*, only tiny. He shuddered in automatic revulsion. This was how they whelped, then; and they were still here.

His heart seized in disbelief as his mage light dimmed; he knew it could not be, but it was as if they leached away his power, stealing it from his very grasp. Aí went cold at the realization. How could an animal possess such ability? For animal they were, no matter the manlike shape they would grow into. Even newly born, the pattern of bait and attack was too clear, speaking of racial instinct rather than reason. Unlike most young, they were born with functioning defenses, which he was unfortunate to learn as one darted forward in a blurred movement and claws bit into his flesh. The others acted in kind. Each slash took him no higher than two feet or so above the ground, not deep, but draining. It felt as if the attacks leached away both magic and soul.

An animal that drew mage energy…a more than chilling thought. Well, he would see how true their aim was without his powers to draw them. Suppressing every bit of his god-given ability, he crept with the stealth of a cat from the spot where they had struck him. Crouching atop a ledge he'd noticed earlier in the brief illumination, he carefully raised the sword Goibhniu had given him and watched as five sets of glowing, ruby-red points darted about the cavern, hissing in frustration. The sound of claws screeching along stone told him they lashed out blindly, and he breathed easier…easier, that is, until the sound of a sucking pant filled the darkness, like a hunting cat sampling the air, followed by a triumphant yowl. The ruby points converged. His own nostrils flared as theirs must have—the scent of his freshly drawn blood disappearing beneath the pong of the hell-spawned cubs. A sharper, more pungent version of the one he'd imprinted. Perhaps they learned to mask it as they grew older.

These here would not live to learn.

And that was when he heard it, a demanding yip from the far side of the cavern, and two more pinpoints in the darkness shimmered and glowed, this time like ebony velvet buttons. Six targets, then.

The ruby points drew nearer.

A predatory grin crept across his face, and Aí tensed, crouched ready. Soundlessly, he leapt down and swung his sword in a powerful arc a mere foot off the ground. Fierce satisfaction flooded him at the minute points of resistance that told him his blade had found its mark at least twice. Again he struck, lunging and slashing, barely noting the rare slice his opponents managed, not yet fully equipped to engage a mobile target with his reach. He did not slow until there were no more sets of glowering rubies stalking him. The black gaze simply watched on, mewing petulantly from the shadows.

With nary a qualm, Aí strode over and thrust the sword point through the final whelp.

When he walked away, the mouth of the cave glowed with cleansing fire.

Jacko could not take it. Ever since that blasted ceremony, he had been trying to get close to Goibhniu. Something always got in the way. A meeting, some crisis, a bloody useless bit of elven fluff who demanded her liege's attention to some senseless matter. Jacko would not give up, not after all Aí had told him. From what little else he had been able to learn—not much, given that few of the *Sidhe* had any desire to talk to a mortal—this Smithgod was his best chance at getting Agnieszka back. Not only did he truly care for each of his people, but her abduction was his fault to begin with.

Finally, Jacko's diligence paid off.

After stalking the corridors of *Mór Halla* for what seemed like days on end, he turned a corner to find the man…god?…himself standing in the middle of the corridor, clearly waiting. "I can't help ye, lad," Goibhniu said by way of greeting.

Jacko frowned, his brow drawn down in a stubborn scowl.

"Don't mistake me," Goibhniu continued. "I'd dearly love to be able to…"

"Then do it," Jacko cut in, not in any sense ready to accept excuses.

"Aye, and yer world 'tis as simple as that?" There was true heartache in the immortal's voice. "We've tried all we can since the end o' the battle to track Agnieszka and her abductor, but something blocks our seers and everything else we've tried so far. We're left to more mundane efforts now, and those have been just as fruitless."

"Tell me what you know, I'll find her myself. I'll get her back."

"Will ye now? I certainly wish ye well, but I can't say I have much faith in yer success, even with the bit we can tell ye to start ye off." There was no malice in the words, no scorn, just a simple resignation Jacko found odd in one hailed as a god.

"*I* will never give up." Jacko's eyes darkened, and his muscles drew tight from his forehead to his toes.

Rather than taking exception at the implied insult, Goibhniu chuckled. There was something of respect in the sound. "Far be it from me to stand in the way o' such determination. I certainly wish it were as simple as that in my case, but I must have a care for all o' my people, and so my efforts need go a bit more cautious. O' course, ye'll find it slow going yerself, I'm sure…"

"Damn it, you're a god, where are your powers? Where is the knowledge and insight that's supposed to make you better than us mere mortals?"

There was patience and resignation in Goibhniu's gaze. It made Jacko bristle even more in defiance of the dread seeping up from deep within him.

Then the Smithgod spoke. "I am not a god as ye mean the word, and truth be told, 'tisn't a title I claim for myself. I have abilities, I do things, I *make* things, but I do not create out o' nothing but thought and will. I'm not everywhere at once, I'm not all-knowing."

Jacko found his gaze locked with Goibhniu's as the weight of truth settled on his heart.

Goibhniu continued to speak. "I wield power, I forge steel, I've been gifted the ability to heal, but I am not the Creator. We all o' us have special gifts given us by Him, gifts we are meant to use to better His world. Some of us forget that. I'll not.

"What it comes down to in the end is that even I need help. An ye think ye can be patient awhile, ye might be what we need to find yer love much faster than either o' us alone."

That was unexpected. Yet the sincerity in the words was undeniable. This was no false modesty. Then the last sank in, and Jacko's face burned hot, his eyes fierce. He ignored his discomfort at such a private feeling brought into the open by another and focused instead on the chance offered. "How do you mean?"

"Bide a while here, work with our seers…ye ken Agnieszka better than any o' us. Might be that touchstone's what we need to break past whatever blocks us. Once that's done, we can act as swift as a thought."

There was no arguing with that. Alone, Jacko's resources were limited to the mundane, the physical, and a network of connections that would take time and effort to draw on. Jacko had no guarantee any of it would be of use against this magical foe, whom he knew only secondhand. Agnieszka's risk grew with each moment that passed. Worse, his efforts could prove useless, likely to place him far from being any use to his little mother, while her people rallied to the rescue.

The Romani had to be clever, astute…that was how they'd survived in a world that, for the most part, spent no love on them. Jacko could not deny the wisdom of Goibhniu's proposal. He held out his hand and braced himself as the Smithgod reached out to accept it. They stood there a moment, hands gripped to the other's forearm.

Goibhniu was the first to release, reaching into the pouch at his waist. From within, he drew a familiar vial. Jacko braced himself as Goibhniu wet his finger with the contents and swiped them across Jacko's right eye as he had when this had all begun, gifting him with the Sight.

"The first bit was worn away," Goibhniu explained, referring to the salve he'd applied to Jacko's eye before the Battle of the Knock. "From what we know o' the enemy, ye'll need the advantage o' Sight."

Jacko noticed no difference. His brow wrinkled in confusion.

Goibhniu laughed. "What did ye expect? Ye're in the middle o' *Tír na nÓg*. Nothing's hidden to yer sight here. Beyond our gates is when ye'll need to see the truth o' things seen and unseen."

A sobering reality…for both of them. The silence hung heavy as side by side they made their way back to the more populated areas of *Mór Halla*.

Chapter 14

In the end, the *Fianna* went nowhere. There was no need. Whatever had taken their half-blood children had left nothing to rescue...not even remains. One of Goibhniu's messengers brought the news. Patrick's heart tore at the grief-filled cries of those clearly related as the liveried woman came into the chamber in the midst of their planning, tears silvering her cheeks. All eyes locked on her, hope and despair wrestling in their expressions. She shook her head and, in a soft voice and brief detail, told them what they did not want to hear. What carnage the runners sent to investigate had found. Then, with a lowered gaze, she left the chamber.

The meeting ended immediately, the *Fianna* scattering to mourn as they would. Patrick looked for Kara, but she had already slipped away. He went hunting for her, gripped by a deep, heartrending need to see and feel that she was unharmed. There was no rational sense to it, being they had just been in the same room, and he knew without a doubt she was hale and whole, but parents weren't always rational. He would not be satisfied until his daughter was in his arms. Just one quick hug would rob his fears of their strength and quiet his heart.

After that, he intended to tell her just what he thought of her joining the *Fianna*. It made him ill that she deliberately risked harm, particularly after all that had happened. He knew what she had been through...nearly every detail. More than he wished and yet not enough at all.

Renewing his search, Patrick O'Keefe finally tracked his daughter down. He found her in a cozy room, the arrangement of which gave him a vague impression of a kitchen without the familiar appliances. She was reaching up to a head-high shelf where rows of mugs were lined up. They had the look of something hand-thrown on a potter's wheel, rather than factory-made. Each distinctly unique—like his daughter.

"Kara."

She turned to him, not looking too surprised, and reached up for a second mug, placing both on what could only be called a kitchen island surrounded by tall stools. The silence grew a little thick, and she turned and leaned her butt against the counter behind her, casually crossing her arms as she considered him closely. He felt his cheek twitch in response, as anger and fear and pride did a triple jig in his gut. Her expression remained neutral as she patiently observed him.

He glowered back and opened his mouth to set a few pertinent matters straight. Before he could speak, she lifted her chin slightly and stared him in the eye, a faint swirl of challenge in her gaze.

"Am I twenty-three, or three?" she asked, both reasonable and serene.

He'd expected heat. He'd expected temper or tears or even sullen pouting. He did not expect calm rationale. Breath left Patrick in a great gust. Shot down before he could raise one argument or vent a single concern. She'd lampooned his lecture with his own words, spoken back when this all began, not so very long ago, on the night she told him she'd pawned her grandfather's violin.

So much had changed since then.

Patrick's head dropped down, his chin resting briefly on his chest as he readjusted his mindset. Unhappy, but unable to deny the sense behind her simple question, Patrick quirked a wry smile at his daughter. "I could wish ye had not listened half so well. Ye got that trap o' a mind from yer Grandda."

"Och, and there ye go flattering me now," she quipped at him, putting on the brogue.

He grinned, as she'd intended, but it was fleeting. "Just be safe, lass. It doesn't matter how proud ye make me if we're putting ye beneath the sod."

She sobered just as much as he. "I couldn't agree with you more."

Again, she turned his words right back at him. He just stood there staring at her, not knowing what to say. While pointed, her response bore no heat or rebuke, and after making it, she puttered about the space at some task he couldn't fathom. Abruptly, he became painfully aware that his little girl really had grown up, and he'd no one to blame but himself.

"Sit, already," she ordered him, ushering him toward a high stool.

"What are ye doing?" he asked as she searched cupboards and cubbies, her hands running over crocks, tilting bins until she had what she was after. She turned with several containers in her arms and placed them on the table before him.

"I, with the help of a few friends," she said, gesturing behind her, "am making you a cup of cocoa."

Patrick quirked his lips at another parallel to that not-so-long-ago night, then frowned faintly as he peered across the room. "Friends?"

Kara just grinned and refrained from answering as she measured out the ingredients. His head swam with the mingled aroma as shaved chocolate, fresh cream, and the innards of a vanilla bean went into what would have been a pot, had it handles. The vessel then went on a counter that looked like a slab of metal over honeycombed rock.

"Ready," she murmured, and from the crannies and crevices flew tiny spurts of flame. They swirled and danced, up through the air and down again into their pockets of rock, flickering and flaring. The stretch of counter swiftly took on the appearance of a miniature lava flow: a dark slab on top, with fiery heat glowing below the surface. With care, Kara stood nearby, stirring gently with a long-handled spoon. When the scent rising from the pot developed into that of rich, dark cocoa, she drew away.

"Thank you," she said in the direction of the fae equivalent of a stovetop.

Dimmed, but no less excited, the tongues of flame rose up again. Patrick was startled to spy tiny faces in the fire. They cavorted before his daughter, darting close, then veering off. Her still-shocking red hair glimmered and glowed, reflecting the aspects of their flame, making her appear like one of them…only supersized.

She laughed and blew them kisses before she took up something that resembled a blacksmith's tongs and carried the pot to the table, where the two comfortable clay mugs waited. She poured the steaming drink and from another container drew out what looked like two homemade marshmallows. As she placed one atop each mug, a flame creature darted forward, settling on the table beside the drinks. The sprite's fire faded and went out, but for a banked glow at her lips. Patrick blushed at her bare feminine form, rather like a Barbie doll's, only proportionate. He watched in fascination as she breathed gently across the mugs until the marshmallow settled into a molten cap over the chocolate, lightly and pleasantly browned across the top.

His brow furrowed as he witnessed these preparations. The simple, homey act perplexed him, but not nearly as much as this evidence that someone actually cooked in faerie land. The furrow blossomed into a full-blown scowl, accompanied by a frown as a thought occurred to him, insidious and disturbing. He watched his daughter's face close as she pushed the mug toward him, and could not tell from her expression if he'd grounds for his suspicions. Try as he might, he could not forget the boon she would have asked for, had he not stopped her. Though he knew the words would hurt her, he had to ask. "'Tisn't a trick ye work on me, aye?"

The fire faeries flared like an angry blaze and disappeared within their honeycombed lair as Kara lost her smile. Picking up both mugs, she sipped from each and replaced his before him. With white froth on her lip and her mug still in her hand, she turned away. She finally spoke over her shoulder on her way through the arch leading from the room, "Nothing more than cocoa, Papa," she said with faint threads of sorrow. "A bit of 'I love you' in a cup. Your soul is safe from me."

"Kara, stop." He hurried to her, his thumb unconsciously wiping away the mallow out of habit. "I'm sorry, I shouldn't have thought it. Forgive a foolish man?"

His daughter ghosted him a smile and pushed up on her toes to kiss him. "Already done."

They sat back down and shared a space of quiet among the turmoil. Not speaking, not worrying—much—not hurrying through their mugs. When the cocoa was nothing more than a pleasant scent and a memory lingering on the tongue, Patrick stood and looked around for the equivalent of a sink, his brows raised in question when he spied nothing of the sort. Kara grinned at him, mischief in her eye. She took the mug from him and placed it back on the table among the supplies she'd neglected to put away. "No, really…it's okay," was all she said. Realization hit him at her words. He grinned back and shook his head, still not used to the surreal bend life had taken now that they lived among legends.

"Come on, then," he answered, careful to pay no mind to the impatient flickers he'd begun to notice in the shadows, from the corner of his eye. "Time for a bit o' rest, I'm thinking. Sure by now yer mathair's waiting to go to bed."

He offered Kara his arm, and they returned to what he thought of as the dorm. They entered the public room to find it deserted and the lights dimmed. When Kara would have hugged him and gone on to her own room, he stopped her.

"I have just one thing I must say to ye."

She nodded. He moved to stand in front of her and found it difficult to speak, his throat tight and himself not anxious to disrupt the peace. Kara widened her eyes expectantly and tilted her ear in his direction. He blew a hard breath and said what needed saying.

"I've only ever wanted three things for ye, lass," Patrick said as he took his daughter's hands in his, dipping his head to stare her in the eye. "Be happy, be well, and be safe. Ye'll forgive me if I revise my priorities and move that last to first."

"I know, Papa, and I'll do my best to meet your wishes…but consider this, how can any of us achieve those things if we step back and give evil free rein in the world?"

Before he could tense up, she moved in close to hug him. "I love you, Papa. Rest well, and try to leave the heavy thinking for tomorrow. We have training in the morning."

She gave him one last, tired grin and went off to her room, leaving Patrick's head spinning.

When had his daughter gotten so wise?

It was like flashbacks to basic training. They gathered at a large, flat field surrounded by trees that would have dwarfed the Redwood Forest. Patrick was there, and Kara, plus about forty or fifty of the faerie warriors his friend called the *Fianna*. The one named Aí showed Kara some pretty brutal moves: throws and defenses, stuff like that, with Jacko, one of the Rom, looking on. When they were done, they swapped with Patrick and the fae he was sparring with, Kara partnering with her father for some sword work, while the other warriors moved off, the Rom in tow.

Everyone paired up except Arn. He didn't have any magic. Most of his combat training was in small arms and squad tactics, not to mention learned over twenty years ago when he was earning money to put himself through medical school. Short of learning from scratch, there wasn't much he could do. Instead, Arn stood off to the side, just within the drip line of the trees, watching with growing frustration because it was better than stewing someplace else alone. His hand rested on the butt of his empty Ruger. One of the Rom had found it on the battlefield and later returned it to him. Without ammo, the gun was as useless as he felt, but the cool grip beneath his fingers at least held the comfort of the familiar. Precious little else did in this place.

He wanted out. He wanted to find his wife and kill the bastard who had taken her, who had put that unaccustomed look of terror on Lynn's face. Not long ago, the thought of killing was a dilemma for him. There was something seriously wrong when a healer had an unremorseful need to take another's life. That didn't change anything, though. Arn's body had healed, but inside… he was broken. Without Lynn, he was likely to stay that way.

Pushing those grim thoughts aside, Arn focused on Kara and Patrick. She was patiently showing her father how to wield a sword with more finesse, drawing on her experience as a competitive swordswoman, something she had taken up when her "Sword for the Stage" class had kindled her interest in the sport. Patrick wasn't doing too badly. This was a refresher for him since he'd been her sparring partner when she'd had time to practice. Arn used to watch them then as well, only with a beer in his hand and not a gun. Right now, Kara stayed plenty far back from Pat's practice lunges. Not that Arn could blame her, as Pat's foot slipped on the meadow grass, and his thrust went skewing wildly to the side. The two of them laughed as he scrambled for balance, then engaged one another, Kara adding playful slaps and flourishes with her blade. That spoke of her skill with the weapon even though Arn knew she'd given up her formal training when her father had first fallen ill.

Anger flooded through him as he watched the lighthearted moment between father and daughter. He'd always been a touch jealous that he would never have that; fresh resentment caused that darkness in him to flair uncontrollably now. Despite all that had happened, they had their family safe and complete; *because* of all that had happened, Arn had lost everything that defined his life. Loosing a snarl he could no longer suppress, he spun away to leave only to come face to face with a pair of serene, sapphire eyes.

Brid's serenity was an illusion.

He felt the tension strumming through her the instant she reached out to grip his hand. Arn looked over his shoulder and, without waiting for Brid to speak, bellowed: "Patrick!" His friend was at his side in no more than three long strides, his face somber, and his body poised to act. The others quickly followed until they all huddled beneath the edge of the towering trees. Personally, Arn didn't see them gather; he merely heard their arrival as his eyes locked on Brid's face.

He tried hard not to be too hopeful.

She nodded, and he nearly closed his eyes as relief made him sway. Yet he did not miss the absence of a smile on her face, or the darkening of her gaze. He took one step back as the *Sidhe* known as Maggie went to the Seer's side, slipping a supporting arm around her.

"What are you here to tell me, Brid?" Arn asked. It was odd to hear such a neutral tone come from his own mouth when inside was chaos.

Her brow drew together, and she pursed her lips ever so slightly, as if bewildered.

"We have seen her. Odd flashes, disjointed. I don't know…she is a stranger to me, but I see her face. If you go now, I can show you where." Arn had the sense she would have added more but hesitated.

Maggie frowned, clearly catching it as well, and Arn had the urge to pull Brid away from her. "What's wrong?" the *Sidhe* asked. The last thing Arn wanted to hear was talk of something being wrong. They shouldn't be talking; they should be rescuing his wife. He wanted to tell Maggie to shut up.

Brid wet her lips and dropped her gaze from his. "I don't know, but all of us are uneasy."

A weight came down on Arn's shoulder. He didn't flinch. It had the feel of Patrick's beefy hand pressing him in a show of support. Arn's gaze went to Maggie's and found her already staring at him. She was the leader of the *Fianna*. That meant Arn needed her cooperation. The muscles in his face twitched with the need to speak out, but he knew it was better to keep silent for now. He watched as Maggie thought things through; prayed she'd hurry up. She and Brid looked one another in the eye, and he suspected he'd missed something important.

Finally, Maggie nodded, her hand coming up to grip the torc around her neck. "Who?" she asked, and Arn frowned in confusion until Brid spoke five names, Arn's among them. Maggie scanned the rest of them and called out to one of the men: "Aí, if ye'll inform Goibhniu that we'll be back shortly." He nodded and jogged away down a worn path between the trees. Then Maggie turned back. "Well, come on…it's time to go save yer lady."

Those staying dropped back as Maggie drew the torc from around her throat. Before Arn's eyes, it expanded until it hung on the air large enough for the biggest of them to step through. Past the inner ring stood another wood, smaller…younger, with more manicured paths and enough litter for him to identify it as his world, if not enough to tell him where. Not that that mattered.

It could be Hell and he'd step through, to reach Lynn.

He would have done so now, only Maggie intercepted him. "Ye last, Arnold…ye have no weapon." Arn wanted to scream at her, but she was right. What did he expect to do? Club the bastards with his unloaded pistol? Heck, he was surprised he wasn't being told to stay behind. As patiently as he could, he waited beside Patrick and Kara.

"Steady, Arn," Patrick murmured. "Ye'll have her back soon." The words might have soothed if Arn hadn't done stints in the ER as an intern and then a resident. Too many times to count, he'd seen loved ones who would never make it home.

He immediately thrust that thought away hard…but it was still there. Arn took a step closer to the portal and out from beneath Patrick's reassuring hand. Three of the warriors had climbed through into a night-shrouded wood, and the last straddled the portal. Maggie turned from where she waited beside it, no longer holding the torc, which somehow hung in place. She dismissed the remaining *Fianna*, then turned to Arn and his friends. "Kara, Patrick…please find Miach."

They nodded and went the way Aí had earlier, after first sheathing their swords across their backs. Maggie then laid her gaze on Arn and reached for his arm. Something in her expression had him snarling as he backed away. Her lips turned down, and her brow wrinkled in a slight frown. "Anger won't change things, Arn," the *Sidhe* said. "I won't tell you she's fine, but she is alive and she needs ye. She won't let the others near."

Choking on a sob, Arn pushed past her through the portal, stumbling on the other side as his foot jammed on the rim of the torc. He caught himself, but still went to his knees at the sight of his wife, her back against a tree, hissing like a feral cat.

Bruises mottled her skin and there was dried blood speckled everywhere. Her eyes weren't right, what he could see of them, and she hardly seemed to recognize him.

"Lynn," he called to her, his voice breaking as he held out his arms. His stint at the hospital had taught him victims should always be invited, not approached, but waiting was agony. He groaned and leaned a little closer, barely aware that the warriors had formed a protective circle around them.

"Lynn…" he tried again. Desperate tears burned his eyes. He didn't care who saw them.

This time her gaze tracked to him and the change was jarring. She didn't say a word, but recognition lit her face up like a sunrise…colors and all. One second, she was plastered to the tree; the next, Arn had to drop back on his heels with his arms braced behind him, or they would have both sprawled on the ground. He was torn; needing to hold her tight to him, but knowing it was exactly the wrong thing to do. No matter that her arms…even her legs were wrapped around him tight enough to make him groan. That made no difference in cases of assault and abuse. Any seeming effort on his part to constrain her could trigger a damaging response.

His eyes closed hard on that thought, and his tears flowed more freely. It was no longer difficult to keep his hands where they were — supporting both of their weights — as he looked to Maggie for help. Though she made no sound, the warriors dropped their perimeter and helped him to his feet, Lynn still firmly entwined.

So great was his relief, Arn barely noticed he'd wrapped his arms around his wife as they passed through the portal. Without warning, she bit him hard on the shoulder, thrashing hard to get away. Her face was twisted in a soundless cry.

Only years of practice kept him from cursing, or dropping Lynn…maybe that wasn't such a good thing, he realized as he felt something tear, corresponding with an intense pain. He groaned through his teeth in spite of himself. "I could use some help here!"

"Let go…just let go." By the calm, familiar tone and unruffled manner, Arn recognized Miach, the *Sidhe* who'd been too spent to heal him after the battle. It was difficult to say who Miach spoke to, but given how insensible Lynn was at the moment, Arn would assume the words were for him. Trusting the fellow healer, he simply let go. His wife's legs dropped away, but her teeth weren't going anywhere. Arn let his upper body slump with her weight to keep his shoulder from further damage.

"Can I get that help now?" Arn snapped.

There was snarling and screaming and a sudden flurry as Lynn released him and dashed for the trees. The *Fianna* moved to block her flight. It was a delaying tactic; they did not reach for her. Her movements were frantic and her eyes crazed, all her focus pinned on the warriors in front of her while Miach slowly ambled up behind, murmuring soft sounds with no meaning. When he was close enough, he placed a flat palm against Lynn's back. Instantly, she slumped. The healer caught her before she reached the ground, sweeping her up into his arms.

Arn had to look away. He was too disturbed at the sight of his blood all over her mouth. He was aware, though, when Miach strode away, carrying Lynn off toward the fae stronghold.

Maggie was right: anger didn't change things…but it sure helped keep Arn going as he followed in the healer's wake.

Chapter 15

Tír na nÓg SEEMED TO TREMBLE IN AGITATION. THE FRAUGHT ATMOSPHERE WAS absorbed by every pore of the residents, drawn in on each breath until tempers spiked and faelings hid away from even Kara. Practically burnt out from the constant strain, she ventured past the faerie gate, still within the protections of the threshold, but outside the influence of the prevailing mood. She took herself to the cliff edge once more, drawn to the power of the ocean waves.

She found the crisp, clean scent rising on the wind familiar and soothing. The only sound was the seagulls crying, with the occasional crash of clams dropped to smash against the rocks. The only tension was the birds squabbling over the treasure among the fragments of shell. Kara laughed at their antics, reminiscent of the faelings.

As she sat there absorbing the tranquility, the sound of human squabbling reached her ears, halfhearted and strangely soothing in itself.

"Careful! Step careful, before you turn your ankle on the rocks."

"You've become a proper biddy, boy. Watch your own feet. Mine have been about their business a lot longer than those."

Jacko and Granddame Rose.

Kara smiled and had to force herself not to laugh, not wanting to offend the Rom as they drew closer. They stepped within the circle of boulders where she sat, still snipping and snapping as they went, all good-natured and without heat.

"Hello," she hailed them. "Come for a bit of fresh air?"

Rose gave her a look that said "don't be dim."

"As if the air isn't fresher there than anything here." The old woman gave Kara a snip of her own, one hand waving in the direction of the faerie gate, the other clutching a fringed shawl around her shoulders. "We're here to see you, girl. And to get out from under the weight of that place."

Kara did laugh then, particularly at the sympathetic look Jacko sent her way. "Come on then. Pull up a rock and join me."

Rose *harrumphed* and Jacko chuckled as he helped her settle. He then drew some chunks of peat from a sack slung around his back and kindled a small, comforting fire in the protection of the boulders. The rich, earthy aroma delighted Kara even more than the flickering flame. More comfortable—and skilled—with the concept of shielding after some pretty intense sessions with Maggie, Kara raised a simple barrier around them, protecting them from both sight and Sight.

They sat awhile in easy silence. All three rested on their boulders as if they were the most comfortable cushions, Rose upright and proper, as befit her dignity, and Kara and Jacko slumped against the support of higher stones, their bodies limp as if just released from a prolonged strain. The cool wind off the ocean would have chilled them without the snapping fire radiating its heat off the surrounding outcrop. Though there was no avoiding the burden of their worries, this field trip offered a break from the *Sidhe* and *Tír na nÓg*, particularly after the tension of Aunt Lynn's rescue and the events that followed. Kara needed to forget all that for a while. It felt good to touch a bit of normal life even if it was only through a bonfire on a crisp autumn night. Apparently, the Rom felt the same.

As if by common agreement, they sat without speaking, enjoying the real world, the sparks of a natural fire and the scent of burning peat mingled with that of salted air. After a time, though, Kara sat a bit straighter and shifted to watch Rose's face. There was sorrow there. The fear of losing a loved one.

Jacko bore the marks as well, but Kara felt more of a connection to Rose and her grandson. Despite their history, other than their brief and corrupted encounters, Tony…the true Tony…was completely unknown to Kara.

"Please," she said softly and quietly, respecting Rose's pensive mood, "will you tell me about him?"

Jacko straightened, watching them both through hooded eyes.

Rose did not speak at first. Her fingers plucked at the rough tassels on her woolen shawl, and her gaze remained distant, focused far from there. "Anthony DeLocosta is a good boy. He has always been a good boy…not an angel, but then who is?"

Kara relaxed fully, as she had been taught, closing her eyes and focusing on the woman's words. Her mind visualized the escapades of the younger version of Tony as a carefree Romani boy. His life on the caravan trail, performing before crowds by the age of three and loving every minute of it. Raised to be scrupulously honest among the Rom, but not above fleecing the *gorgio*…the non-Romani folk. Between the evening spent around the campfire with the Rom and what she'd seen of the children as they took to the road, Kara could well imagine how blithe and magical his early childhood had been, but was in the dark on what had altered his later years.

There was a pause in the telling as Rose's voice drifted off; fainter, more distant, caught up in some remembered pain. Kara came out from under the spell of the woman's words and turned to face her. The flicker of the flames reflected off the tears tracking Rose's cheeks. "When Anthony was eleven, there was an accident in the mountains of Virginia. A reckless driver ran his family's vardo off the road, sent them into a ravine."

Kara flinched, more than able to picture the heavy, colorful wagons, the painted carvings smashing against the rocks. Her imagination supplied graphic details of the likely result.

Rose continued: "His parents were crushed, the boy thrown free, seriously injured, but alive. His mother was my granddaughter. When the local doctors said he might not walk again, I refused to listen. I took the child to New York, where he could receive better care for his injuries. When he finally recovered, it had been so long we just never left. It was my fault he ran the streets, with no respect for anyone not Rom, with more than plentiful opportunities to be influenced by the wrong sort. Though I have something of the Sight, I was blind to the warnings the visions showed me.

"Until he met this devil, it had been nothing but petty thieving and the like. What you saw of my grandson was nothing from his nature. Tony is all I have left of close family. He has cared for me…stood by me…I failed him more than he ever failed me. He is a good boy, even yet."

Kara nodded. "I've already promised you to do what I can. I stand by that promise. Thank you for showing me what it is that needs saving." She paused a moment, her expression tightening. "I have to tell you, though…if he is as much a victim as I…there is no guarantee he'll come out of this the same Tony you remember so fondly."

"Free him. I'll take care of my own guarantees," the ancient woman said, her jaw set and her eyes blazing with conviction, much as they must have been that long-ago day some country doctor told her to give up hope.

Despite herself, Kara felt a connection to these nomads, a realization that followed her long after they left the cliff edge and returned to *Tír na nÓg.*

Talk of Tony stirred Jacko's restlessness, a reminder of what Goibhniu had asked of him. Rose's grandson was not the only victim needing to be freed. Nevertheless, Jacko had yet to seek out this seer, Brid. Part of him had wanted to track her down right away; another part let fear prevent him. What if it wasn't enough? What if his memories were not crisp? What if his emotions were too weak?

He told himself he loved her; Agnieszka told him more than once he merely played a game, with her a safe focus for his meaningless flirtation. God, he prayed her wrong. Her life might well depend on it.

Returning to *Mór Halla,* almost too warm after the brisk breeze at the cliff's edge, Jacko flagged the first *Sidhe* wearing what passed for Goibhniu's livery, a comfortable tunic and trews in iron-gray with an anvil in black and silver threads embroidered on the right sleeve.

"Please," Jacko asked the woman. "Where can I find Brid?"

"Come, I will show you."

They traversed the halls in silence, not uncomfortable, but inevitable. Jacko was preoccupied, and the *Sidhe*, well, they generally did not subscribe to small talk, that he had noticed. He thanked her as she brought him to a simple door, knocking lightly before she left.

Almost immediately, the door opened on the smallest elven woman he'd ever seen. Not quite on par with Hollywood's depiction of the North Pole's denizens, but were she even a bit age-worn—and the actress considerably less plain—Linda Hunt could have played her in the movies.

Brid smiled an amused smile, her deep blue eyes dancing as if she were well aware of his thoughts. All of them.

Jacko blushed.

"Hello, Jacko," she greeted him. "I was told you would be along."

He couldn't resist. "What, you didn't know already?"

Her eyes narrowed, and the smile thinned, but more as if she were calling him a wiseass rather than out of any ire. "Have you a preference where we speak?"

"I have a choice?"

"Here, if you like, or we could take a walk where things are more peaceful."

"A walk would be nice."

Again the trek was made in silence, Brid lost in her own serenity, Jacko in awe of the land they traveled. More beautiful yet than those parts of *Tír na nÓg* he'd already seen, wild and lush and undisturbed. From the dense brush, creatures peered out at him, timid, curious, occasionally malicious. All kept their distance, though, as if Brid were his safe passage through their territory.

At long last, they crested a rise, and even if Jacko had had anything to say, he would have been speechless. All his life, he'd been a nomad, having seen virtually all the world had to show of both nature and man. He had seen white sandy beaches, common tan, even black or pink shores in startling contrast to the sea.

He had never seen a beach that glittered with the iridescence of a pearl, or waves that were violet. And yet, he had to laugh. The palm trees were much the same as in the everyday world, making the whole of the view reminiscent of a rather gifted child's painting. The susurration of the waves drained the last of Jacko's stress away. He followed as Brid descended to the sand, smiling with delight at several faelings playing among the surf.

"Sit," she said as she lowered herself to the sand, her fingers running absently through the grains. "I am going to tell you something I have seldom told another."

Jacko complied, sitting cross-legged beside her, staring out at the surreal waves.

"I have the gift of seeing, as you know. For most, this means visions of the past or future in brief, frustrating glimpses. When I see, it is like one of your TV shows, not always complete, but likewise not piecemeal. When I am blocked, I see nothing, where others with my gift are tormented by disorienting glimpses, like a photograph taken out of focus." She glanced sideways at him, as if to see if he understood, so Jacko nodded, still not looking directly at her, his only means of granting her privacy as she revealed her secrets.

Taking a deep, steadying breath, she went on. "I am different in yet one other way, which is the reason Goibhniu has sent you to me. When someone thinks of the past, I can see their memories as clear as my visions, unblurred by time or the person's perception. Not as if I read your mind, but as if you were reminiscing with me over a photograph book. Only what you share with me, nothing more."

She waited for some response. He didn't know what one to give.

With a frustrated sigh, she tugged him around until they stared eye to eye. "Will you share your Agnieszka with me? Will you give me an anchor to find her by? Your memories can serve as a guide, leading me to what I otherwise might miss if the barrier goes down only to come up again quickly."

Jacko felt dense and could only suppose it was the lulling atmosphere of this faerie shore. "Of course! Of course, you could tell me you needed to pull my brain apart, and if it would find her, I'd tell you yes again. What do I do?"

Relief smoothed the lines of Brid's face. "For now, just talk to me. Tell me of her, and as you allow yourself to wander those memories, I will follow."

It sounded so easy, but Jacko felt his eyes tighten with the pain. For long moments he just sat there, focused on forcing the heartache back. It felt all too much like a wake, with the mourners sharing tales of the departed.

She's not dead, he snarled silently at himself, struggling to keep his expression calm. *Do not even think such thoughts.* He gulped a few breaths, each less frantic than the last until Brid brushed a hand along his shoulder. *It isn't like that,* he thought. *It isn't. It just hurts to know I let her down. To know that if she were, I'd bear some of the blame for not being there.*

"You're wrong," Brid murmured. "You hold no blame in any of this."

"No mind-reading, huh?"

"There's no need to read your mind when your guilt is stamped all over you."

His lips quirked in a wry smile. Though his last deep breath shuddered, his soul was calmer. Softly, he began to speak, his eyes locked on the horizon for a completely different reason now. "She was a friend to my grandfather, Mateó, long before I met her. He would visit this orphanage in Cornhill, England, where Agnieszka had lived since she was just a baby. St. Michael's it was called. He visited, but never often and never long, lest anyone get the wrong idea about an old tinker man visiting young girls." Jacko shared what his grandfather had told him of the sad little girl, unwanted, shunned, persecuted for her differences: pure white hair, amber eyes, a way of looking deep inside a person that made most nervous. Superficial, but all of it was so obvious as to be impossible to overlook for potential parents and bullies alike.

Jacko himself had not been born until much later, when the girl had been at least sixteen, by his grandfather's reckoning. "I did not know her well myself until well past Mateó's death, only seeing her in person a time or two when Grandfather allowed me to come with him to St. Michael's. He always told me he'd wished he could have brought that bonny girl home with him…only, tinkers were not on the list of acceptable adopters.

"For a while, I forgot about her, the memory of her face surfacing from time to time, but nothing more. Then one day, I stopped at the orphanage. I was thirty then and feeling nostalgic, missing my grandfather. I never expected to see her there, or anyone else I would recognize, I just wanted to leave some toys for the never-ending stream of children without much hope or joy in their lives. When I walked through the doors, she was standing in the foyer, preparing to leave for the day, and I felt like one of the caravan mules had kicked me in the shin. She was beauty and grace, and yet loneliness stared at me from beyond her eyes."

Jacko lost himself in the memory. He'd hailed her by name, that long-ago day. He looked enough like his grandfather that she knew him, even remembered his name. She told him she worked for St. Michael's now, and he was forced to tell her of Mateó's passing. They'd both wept, and in the end, they left together after a happy fifteen minutes distributing the toys. They shared a meal at a local pub, and in an uncharacteristic moment of forwardness, she offered her land as a resting ground for his caravan whenever their travels brought them to the region. She even extended the offer to other clans, as long as Jacko vouched for them, betraying the generous nature of her heart, which he learned she generally kept hidden from all but cats and children.

For fifteen years, Jacko had subsisted on this friendship. For fifteen years, he remained absolutely faithful, to his heart, if not to any vow between them. And he had failed her. His chest tightened, and he forced his way past the pain, sharing every memory within him, desperate to reinforce that anchor Brid had asked him to provide. And finally, the memories had been spent, from the most joyous to those wracked with pain.

"Grandfather Mateó would have been devastated to see her solitary life. I've tried my best to change that, making sure the caravan stops at her place regularly, taking care of what repairs I can while I'm there, showing her in a hundred ways my feelings for her, but even me she cannot trust." Jacko heard the sorrow in his own voice, and yet Brid did not interrupt as he continued.

"With her home and her strays and, on occasion, her secrets, but never her heart. She calls me a flirt, laughing about it one moment and scolding me the next, but never once believing I acted with honest affection. More than affection, which any man can have for a friend or a dog. I love her, and she will not hear it, though my heart cries each time she rebuffs me. And yet I must smile, and laugh, and pretend I am not wounded, lest she back away from even us and truly be alone."

Jacko finished, at last, his throat dry and his heart raw. Beside him, Brid was in tears. Neither of them said another word as they rose to their feet and returned to *Mór Halla*.

Before they went their ways, he had to ask, "Was it enough?"

Regret shadowed her gaze as she gave him an answer, both frank and honest. "We won't know until the moment's on us."

He turned and walked away before he embarrassed himself by crying.

The dream was like sunlight on water, glittering and magical. There were no shadows or deep dark pools waiting to drag her down, captive and helpless, only color and faerie lights, laughter and song. Kara looked around in wonder as the points of light resolved themselves into all types of creatures; some she had encountered since coming to *Tír na nÓg*, but others she could never have imagined, or they had only populated her childhood daydreams. Each point was a magical creature: faerie, deva, selkie, pixie, and any number of equally magical creatures whose names were just beyond her grasp. All of them were knots in a netting of iridescent, silk-like strands that were there and yet not, allowing all to move freely through the ether, though each was continually linked to the other.

Gently she reached out a fingertip and traced the air, feeling the power binding all these creatures; there was something familiar and heart-wrenching at the very core of this magic. She closed her eyes and drifted from point to point. It was like reacquainting herself with old friends only more intimate… something within her recognized each spark she touched. And wandering through their midst, viewed only as an evasive reflection upon polished surfaces, and in the eyes of the fae folk themselves, was the Lady, Kara's savior from her darkest hour after her torture at Olcas's hand.

There was a puzzle here. The key to resolving the turmoil in Kara's own heart. Lurking in the center of this web of power was something she must know to move on from here, one way or the other. Breathing deeply, she relaxed her hold on control. There was no guiding or choosing in this place, only letting go. Kara felt them reach out to her as she floated freely among the strands, their gentle caress drawing her along.

This was important…vital…so why then could she not unravel the mystery? Desperate to know the answers, Kara allowed herself to be guided until finally, they stopped and lowered her gently to what served for ground in this realm of mists. Before her rose a silvery surface, at once reflective and flowing, faceted and smooth. Surrounded by these ambassadors of the fae, she peered into that surface. Her ever-changing image dipped and dove and twisted about, revealing tantalizing bits of what she thought were her true self, only to whisk them away and interpose others. It was like a surreal rendition of a folk dance where the figures whirled too swiftly for the eye to catch the fine details, so only the grand pattern could be appreciated.

More and more, that was not enough to satisfy Kara.

Slowly turning, she looked across the mist. Beyond the netting of fae, more distant, less firmly bound to her was another weave: looser, sparser, the substance more like cobweb than silk. Tethered to each knotted strand was another essence, their fates loosely linked to hers. Not faeling, but human, mostly, with the piercing spark of a *Sidhe* soul interspersed among them like the bonus tiles in a board game. None were as vibrant as the Lady, none so firmly linked.

The faces she could not see clearly, though some souls she knew too well to be deceived by the shrouding mist. Kara strained to identify the others, to study the shadowed planes of their faces, and know the secret chambers of their hearts…To know herself more thoroughly through her reflection in their eyes. To know what linked her to them and what that meant for her future.

Her attempt ended abruptly in intense pain. Brutal, bursting shards of color punched through the mists, dispersing it in wisps of swirling strands. A firm grip yanked her back even as something else reached out to snatch at her, stinging and burning her soul's surface as it brushed against her. Kara's heart pounded, and her soul screamed. There was something familiar in that brief touch, still there but out of sight before the mystery could be discovered. Crumbling to her knees, cushioned and petted by hordes of faelings desperate to comfort her, Kara found herself once again planted before that smooth, reflective surface, looking up to find her own face staring back, crisp and clear and more knowing than Kara herself could claim. And then she noted the vibrant, startling green eyes, like grass in springtime. Ancient, framed by a thatch of long curls a deeper brown than hers had ever been, and weren't at all now.

"Who are you?"

"Ye aren't yet ready for this. 'Tisn't time. Heal…learn…grow, and then we'll talk o' this."

Kara ignored that. "You're my friend…my shadow lady. You saved me from…" She couldn't finish, even now the emotional wounds too raw to consider, barely scabbed over.

"Shh…I am the pulse o' yer heart the other half o' yer soul, but it can only hinder ye to ken so soon." There was sorrow in those eyes, and a yearning Kara did not understand. "But true enough, I'm also yer friend…'tis all ye need to ken for now. *Dearmad…*" *Forget.* The woman reached out a gentle, graceful hand from the mercurial mist, reminiscent of the one that drew her from the dark paths she'd nearly lost herself upon when she'd first been rescued from Olcas. The hand that comforted her when she'd fled the lingering pain of his torture and the agony of his curse. Now the fingers reached out to caress her tormented thoughts. To take them away, Kara realized, an instant too late. Before she could resist, they wiped clear both agony and memory from her bruised mind, leaving behind only a vague remembrance of swirling colors and a pleasant jaunt in faerie land. Kara's heart rebelled even as the healing touch mended, though it reduced the heart pains to a dull ache whose origins were hidden by swirling mists.

✦

Was he insane? Or was he in Hell? Tony couldn't say; all he knew was there were large spans of nothing taking over his life, missing time he could not explain. He was only aware of this because of the brief instances that were his own. Sometimes minutes, sometimes an hour, never more than that. They never matched up. It scared the piss out of him. There was no sense to what was happening to him. Nothing he could point at to say, "This is why." The only thing he knew was when it first happened: He'd found himself in the apartment with no recollection of getting there. He was alone, and the place was empty…completely bare, except for his room. His grandmother and all her things were gone, no note, no explanation, just one of her trinkets left behind for him to find, one of the nicer copper pendants. Tony went to leave, disheartened, and time ended.

The next time he returned to himself, there was blood in his mouth and the girl from the pawnshop — Kara — trapped beneath him, looking like she was ready to personally discover the color of his heart. That time was just a blip. A glimpse, then gone. Long enough for her to loathe him and no more. Tony couldn't imagine what all that was about. He was pretty sure he didn't want to be able to imagine, considering the next thing he knew they were in the middle of the woods, her with a friggin' sword pointed at him, and Gypsy Rose hauling back on her arm. He'd been ready to cry at the sight of his grandmother. Of course, before he could beg her help, the dark nothing had him again.

Tony refused to think of the bubbles of time where he came to himself amid some heinous act; couldn't think of them without doubt and despair drowning him. He'd rather have the nothing than claim those memories. There was no denying he wasn't a choirboy, but no matter what he'd done back in New York, he hadn't been a monster or a thug. A punk, maybe, if he were honest, but no worse than that…

God, let this be a nightmare, he thought desperately. It could be. Hell, he'd even take being insane, as long as the memories turned out not to be real.

While his thoughts thrashed about, Tony wandered a grey space, kind of misty and soft, with half-heard sounds. Ghost images flittered across it like a home movie played on a wall without the solid white of a sheet behind it. He was creeped out as all kinds of impressions brushed against his senses, but only faintly, like the memory of something that just happened instead of being in the here-and-now. A taste of chocolate. The lingering whiff of fire. The echo of a laugh. Tony tried to shrug it off as he continued through the grey.

He didn't understand anything but, if he focused, some things became sharper, like they happened seconds ago instead of minutes. A gentle, insistent murmur, like the echo of a conversation he couldn't quite hear. He needed to draw closer, to reach out and touch another soul.

As he tried, there was a gasp, and the black swarmed up again, leaving him with the afterimage of a confused amber gaze. Then the black nothing had him.

❦

Kara woke, gasping, the image of haunted, Romani-dark eyes fading in her mind, and the medallion clutched in a tight-gripped fist. Hardly surprising given she'd spent the evening listening to tales of Tony's misspent youth. Or was that what was going on here?

Forcing her rapid breath to slow, Kara unfurled her fingers and let the copper charm fall to her chest. She lay for a long time in the dark, wondering, had it been a dream, or had she shared headspace with the enemy?

Chapter 16

There was a claw-wound down Aí's side that wouldn't heal. Here in *Tír na nÓg*, he wasn't at risk, but it drained him. Bandaged tightly around his torso, he moved stiffly, cursing his slow progress—both moving down the hall and in his hunt in general. If he did not discover where they hid soon, he feared failure.

Of the five victims he searched for, he'd freed two souls, and found himself too late for two others, including the unexpected discovery of Dulachan. That left two unaccounted for of those taken at the Battle of the Knock. How many more were out there that they did not know of? How many would be lost forever to the *Daoine Maithé*? They knew some of the *Cosaints* and outcast *Sidhe* had been taken. Aí focused just on the five he had been charged with, those most likely to be reclaimed, if not restored. That had been the hardest part…slaying the victims found, but there was no other way. They were already dead, but for the dying, once the *Namhaid* implanted their spawn.

He shuddered a breath and made his way toward his chamber in the section dedicated to the *Fianna*. It was not far, but the trek took him a long time. Despair weighed heavy on him. He'd known the last victim well, and it did not ease his heartache to know she was one who would return to them. Or her soul, anyway.

Purposely blanking his mind as he entered the common room, his bleak expression likewise disappearing, Aí was relieved no one was there. Dropping his things in his room beside the door, he grabbed fresh clothing, a clean bandage, and a small green silk pouch about the size of an apple hanging beside his door, then left the room. He needed peace, and of all the places in *Tír na nÓg*, one place above all others meant that to him: the waterfall known as the Flow of Danu's Tears, mostly just called the Flow.

Ignoring the door back into *Mór Halla*, Aí left by the *Fianna's* private grotto, which led to a small garden. There was a path just past the garden wall that led to the falls. As he passed through, Aí barely noticed the splendor of the blossoms, or the soothing burble of the spring-fed pools, warm and steamy, fragrant with healing herbs that grew around the rim to one side. He hurried through on his way, encountering no one. That was a bit unusual, but barely feeling conscious, let alone social, he was glad.

The music of the falls greeted him well before the Flow was in sight. The cascading waters raised a distinct voice. More than just a simple drop from top to bottom, part of the Flow followed channels in the naturally honeycombed rock, producing a variety of tones. The rest danced down over boulders that broke its surface; from the initial descent, all the way to the immense and bottomless pool at its base in crashing accompaniment. Woven through this mighty song were those of the birds and faelings that flocked there, amazingly not drowned out by the falls. The sound was soothing and musical, a giant's lullaby constantly played. Over the millennia, Danu's Children had added to the song in tribute to their Mother Goddess. Crystal chimes and delicate bells shaped in every possible resonating substance dotted the expanse; Aí savored their sound as he approached.

Setting his change of clothes on a boulder well outside the reach of the mists, he moved closer with only the green silk pouch in his hands. From within, he took out a shiny brass bell with a simple handle. He then withdrew a braided cord of sky-blue satin and approached the towering falls. The spray wrapped around him like a caress. His eyes closed a moment, and he breathed a contented sigh, letting the Flow work its peaceful magic. He felt cleansed and caressed as if a soft hand soothed his brow and tried to brush away the heartache. Sadly, it wasn't enough. He opened his eyes and quickly hung his bell among the other tributes. Then, without care for seam or weave, he tore off his ruined clothes, letting the shreds fall away.

Bare and bloody, he dove into the depths of the pool. The cool, crisp currents wrapped him in a gentle embrace, sloughing off the dried blood in a faint cloud of brownish-red. Aí did not surface until his flesh was clean, and his wounds flushed, and even then, it was only to pillow his head and arms on the soft grasses edging the pool.

He seemed peaceful, at rest, but his heart remained in turmoil, haunted by the memory of his sword cleaving *Sidhe* flesh. Forewarned by the echoes of Kara's cleansing of the Temple, he'd readied a shield around the body first to ensnare the spirits of the *Namhaid* whelps, not lowering the wards until he'd unleashed the ember of Eternal Flame Goibhniu had given him before he began his hunt. The brand kindled and flared, leaving behind seven fading puffs of sullen smoke — all that remained of the unborn *Namhaid* — and a glittering pile of ash. Étaín. His friend. Ai's breath quavered as the memory of her joyous laugh haunted him, seemingly weaving itself into the strands of the Flow. A black velvet grave bag filled with her ash waited in his chambers.

It made little difference that he'd freed her soul. The wounds were too fresh, the frustration and doubt too deep. With his face hidden in his arms, he wept bitterly as the spray caressed his shoulders.

His heart lightened with each tear that fell, but there weren't enough in all the worlds combined to take the ache away.

The last thing Kara expected to see were bare, muscular shoulders draped in hair as dark and sleek as a seal's pelt. When she noticed that they shook, she nearly turned and left, not wanting to intrude. Something stayed her, though, like an encouraging murmur in her ear. Instead of leaving, she quietly settled on a mossy boulder with a depression ideal for sitting, taking care that she was beyond the reach of the spray.

She could sense the *Sidhe*'s weariness, his sorrow, not through any mystic gift, but because it was dreadfully familiar to her. When he'd been battling cancer, Papa had been bound by similar tension even on good days. It ran through every muscle like taut, burning wires. On bad days…even worse.

Now, as then, she tuned Quicksilver and drew her bow across the strings, softly, fiercely doing battle with the specter of melancholy. With a stubborn determination, she wielded music and magic both against the ruthless enemy attacking this beleaguered soul. She didn't know whose defense she came to. It did not matter. She, too, had felt the same assault not so long ago, nearly fell beneath the weight of it herself. But not him. Not here in this haven of all havens, where a *Sidhe* named Danu sought her own solace.

This place had seen enough of despair.

No longer gentle, no longer quiet…her bow flew in combative flourishes, sawing and drawing as her fingers held the chords. Fast and bold and relentless.

Joyous!

In helping this one, Kara found release she didn't know she sought, loosening the hold of her own persistent fears and doubts.

The *Sidhe*'s head rose, turned. Familiar, electric-blue eyes met hers.

"Sweet Danu…" Aí breathed.

Kara laughed, her breath coming fast, her chest heaving. "Not hardly."

He laughed back, fainter, but just as heartfelt. With the languor of exhaustion, he propped his head on his hand, still watching her over the curve of his shoulder. Astounded by everything that had just taken place, Kara dropped her gaze. On automatic, her hands expertly detuned the fiddle and put it away, setting the case aside. When she turned back, Aí knelt before her, naked and in no way wizened by the cold water. His skin gleamed, and his muscles were cut despite being relaxed. And he was completely naked. A man she only knew in passing. Her eyes widened, and she jerked back, nearly tumbling off her perch. She hadn't heard him over the sounds of the waterfall.

She wanted to close her eyes, or at least look away, but didn't dare.

For an instant, she saw Tony's face ghosting Aí's features, a product of fear, rather than of Olcas's broken curse. Before she could panic...okay, before she could panic any more, Aí laced his fingers together behind his back and leaned forward just enough to bring his lips in contact with hers; in his touch, respect, in his gaze, awe and reverence. Both confused her.

Thank you, he soulspoke to her, allowing her a glimpse of the healing she had aided. Her eyes widened, and she gasped. Her mouth tingled, not unpleasantly. It was almost enough to distract her from his nudity.

(Yeah...*right*. There was a reason the *Sidhe* were also called the Fair Ones.)

While she sat there, stunned, he pivoted and rose. Completely at ease, he moved, unhurried, toward a boulder on the other side of the clearing, stopping by the clothing piled there. When he turned, she gasped at the sight of a nasty wound she hadn't noticed before. She ached at seeing that damage on what she had to admit was a perfect form. The sight of it stirred guilt in her. He'd clearly been out there—with hope—accomplishing something, while she'd been here in *Tír na nÓg* acting the angst-ridden fool. Her hand came to rest on the shard-filled pouch that had become a permanent part of her attire. She knew what stood in the way of completing the Unraveling, as she was certain she needed to do: nothing more than this broken blade. There had to be a way to make it whole again. In fact, she admitted to herself the most obvious one...the one she'd been avoiding out of nerves, fear, doubt, all the negative emotions that had plagued her since life had taken this fantastic spin.

Grow up! She told herself, shamed by her own lack of effort. Others had clearly been doing something about the problem when she'd only been thinking about it. With new respect, she considered this man of the *Sidhe*. Perhaps he could help her convince Goibhniu.

But in the few minutes, she'd been lost in thought, Aí had bound up the nasty wound she almost hadn't noticed. As he dressed swiftly, her eyes locked on the firm, round curve of his cheeks.

Then he was gone, and Kara realized she'd missed her chance.

The sound of the waterfall, augmented by the music of the tribute adorning it, was suspiciously reminiscent of laughter. Against the dense spray at the base of the cascade, Kara could have sworn she saw the impression of a familiar face form among the rainbow shimmers. Then it too was gone.

Time to stop *acting* responsible and start *being* responsible!

❧

Kara again stalked the halls of *Tír na nÓg*, this time with purpose. Deep beneath these Halls was the Smithgod's forge. Deep enough to tap into the fires of the Earth. Deep enough that the hammer blows were like a heartbeat. That was what she sought: the heart of *Tír na nÓg*. She was wrapped in a robe, with her sash draped across her shoulder and circling her waist as usual. The shard-filled pouch hung from it as she headed for the nether regions of Goibhniu's domain.

She found him there, as she sensed she would. Unsurprisingly, he was not glad to see her.

"You promised me a boon."

Goibhniu scowled as he crossed his arms over his chest, hammer still in hand. "I did."

Kara held his gaze as she removed her pouch and poured out the shards. The bits made a pinging sound, the distinctive hilt, a thud. "This blade, I want you to remake it for me."

She nearly flinched as he answered her through gritted teeth, "I will give ye another."

Her jaw was just as set. "*This* one. It is my boon, and this is the one I would have."

"Ye bloody stubborn *waterkin*," he snapped at her. "It is done, why will ye not let it lie?"

If not for the pain in his voice, she would have wondered if he had meant it. But no. She knew what it was to lash out where you were hurting. Part of her wanted to snap back that she had his more-than-sufficient example to follow, but that would be counterproductive. Biting comments would not help her cause. The other part still staggered beneath the brutal and unexpected attack, but as in the ballad the Rom had sung of Janet and Tam Lin, she knew when dealing with the fae that to let go of what she wanted was to lose it forever.

"It is not done, and without this blade, it never will be," she spoke with deceptive calm.

"Ye know nothing of this."

"I know the shattering of that dagger was no more than symbolic. I know that even if I'm wrong, for you to make it whole again will not undo one moment of the Unraveling. And I know if I'm right and the ritual is not yet complete, the soul has not been severed, and we'll have left the door wide open for harm to come to us if *that* blade is *not* restored. I would have the dagger as my boon."

He roared in response, a sound filled with torment threaded through with doubt and pain and yes...love. The hammer slammed down on the anvil a hair from her hand. The shockwave sent a stinging throb through her flesh, but she didn't flinch away. "Ye were to ask for the *Fleadh Ghoibhnenn*...for yer *father*."

As if that guilt would sway her. She would have gladly asked that, if only it would have done any good. She said as much, still not looking away, though her hand trembled in reaction to the hammer's impact. "Please...have faith in me."

"Have it then, and leave me be." As he turned, he threw something on the anvil. She looked down, startled, to find the blade whole and unmarred, lying where the hammer had struck. Across it lay a simple leather scabbard that had not been there before. When she looked up, Goibhniu was gone.

She was astounded that even in his outrage, he'd had a care for her safety.

Taking up the restored blade, Kara sheathed it and headed for the Court. *'Twere best done quickly, to quote the Bard,* she couldn't help but think as she hurried down the corridor, then had to laugh at the grim parody her actions represented…dagger and all.

It was night, and though the Sidhe kept their own hours, the halls were empty of traffic for now. Uncertain of how long that would last, or of the response she would receive if anyone were to notice the dagger in her possession, Kara slipped it into her sash, grateful for the sheath Goibhniu had given her. The weapon's edge was blunt and unhoned—after all, it had been forged for a single task—but the tip was still capable of piercing flesh. Again, it said something that Goibhniu went to the effort to protect her, as angry as he was.

She did not like that she had upset him. Whatever else, he had already given her back her father, hale and whole and healed. That still amazed her. That gift alone was worth any amount of cooperation on Kara's part…if not for what was at risk.

After all she had experienced, there was nothing that could induce her to step back and allow anything with harmful intent the slightest potential access to those she cared for. Though she had known him briefly, Goibhniu numbered among them. *Tír na nÓg* and those who lingered there were not perfect, but they also were not evil. Sometimes petty, cruel, and shortsighted beyond a fault, but not evil. She knew evil intimately, and she had seen its reflection in Bran's eyes, Goibhniu's son or not. Everything within her demanded she make sure the Cursed One's ties were fully severed and the gates to the *Sidhe* Lands locked to him forever.

Ice formed along her spine at the thought of him loose, with free rein and no one but her guarding against him. It was time to cast out some demons. Though the halls echoed like any other, the sound had an otherworldly softness to it, rather than being harsh and disturbing. Finally on the way to right matters, much of Kara's tension had loosened its hold. She could draw a breath without tightness, and her shoulders were no longer a series of knots below her neck. As relieved as she was to finally act, it was sobering to know that she would soon complete a ritual casting out a soul.

She should have been paying attention. Nearly there, no more than fifty yards away from the Great Wall, a sound just ahead brought Kara out of musing. The rustle of harsh fabric at odds with what the *Sidhe* wore, the scrape of a foot against stone. Peering into an alcove off the hall, Kara was startled to see Uncle Arn's wife pressed against the intricately carved marble wall characteristic of *Mór Halla*.

"Aunt Lynn?" Kara greeted her softly, moving with careful steps toward the alcove. "Are you okay?"

There was no answer. Lynn hadn't spoken, or made any other sound since she'd been brought to *Tír na nÓg*. Though they had always gotten along well, Kara was uncomfortable now. This woman before her lacked some vital characteristic of the one Kara had grown up thinking of as family. It was hard to reconcile. That was Lynn Barnert's face, seen at least once a week for all of Kara's life. The features were there in their proper order without even a bruise thanks to Miach, but her essence, whatever combination had made her the kind, gentle Lynn, seemed no more than a thin skin stretched over the unfamiliar.

Perhaps it was the trauma of being brutalized, or maybe it was because Kara had a hard time separating her own experience from the equation. In either case, she found it difficult to be familiar with the woman. Heck, she was having trouble just drawing closer to confirm all was well. Stopping a few feet from the arched entrance, she tried again.

"Do you need help?"

Lynn did not even nod in response.

Kara could not bring herself to move to the woman's side. She stood there desperately wanting to continue to her goal but unable to do so, for the sense of responsibility holding her where she was. Though she didn't know the details, they were kindred in their trauma, and it was not right to leave the woman here alone. Sighing, Kara glanced toward either end of the corridor, looking for anyone to assume this burden. She thought she heard someone hurrying in her direction, but in the low light couldn't see who, or if they truly were coming this way. Given the peculiar echo, whoever it was could be in a completely different corridor.

Resigned, Kara turned back, ready to force past her own hang-ups and care for the immediate need. In the low light, Lynn's eyes had grown dark, giving the illusion of a reddish tint. The look within them now was more disturbing still: hate and hunger and some darker desire Kara immediately recoiled from, thrust back into the memory of her own ordeal.

Before she could put more distance between them, Lynn bared her teeth in an infernal smile, snapping them in Kara's face before grabbing her arm in a bruising hold and yanking her close. Kara must have made a noise of some sort, likely a yell from the feel of her clenched jaw and the anger rising in her.

Down the hall came the sound of running, but it was too late. Kara jerked her arm away only to find the other woman had an unnatural grip. Rather than pull free, all Kara managed was to pull Lynn toward her. Whoever ran down the hall called out. She thought it was Uncle Arn.

The older woman snarled, again silently, and her expression twisted into a brutal grimace as she wrapped both her arms tight around Kara. There was a high-pitched shriek from the air itself and reality tore, leaving a gaping hole beside them.

"Shit!" Kara cursed, trying to shrug her attacker off, but unable to dislodge the barnacle-like grip.

Lynn dragged both of them through the nothing. Shocked, all Kara could do was gasp before the chill of the void invaded her open mouth and froze her cry. Just minutes from her goal, and she'd managed to be stolen away from the stronghold of the *Tuatha de Danaan*. Even in the numbness of the swirling ether, she knew her face twisted in frustration. Something raked at her in this place that was not there, but the one who looked like Lynn threw her weight to one side, pivoting Kara out of reach. Then they were falling out of the void onto scarred concrete, and the doppelganger rolled away, leaving Kara gasping on the ground.

She scrambled to her feet, only to stumble hard against Olcas, pinned by his ice-blue eyes.

Chapter 17

THE DOOR TO MAGGIE'S CHAMBERS CRASHED OPEN, AND ARNOLD BARNERT stumbled in. His lips were blue, and his face pale. He shook so bad Maggie thought he was having a seizure.

"Lynn…" His jaw locked, and he shook all the harder. "Lynn…" he tried again but got no further. When a shattering sob broke loose, Maggie thought she understood. Sometimes the trauma of an ordeal was slow to manifest. The woman couldn't be dead—this was *Tír na nÓg* after all—but likely she'd done herself some serious harm.

Not much more than a stranger to this man, Maggie stood back as both Patrick and Barbara rushed to help their friend. With another wrenching sob and a lost look in his eyes, Arn flinched away from them. Jerking his gaze down, the man drew a few hard breaths, getting himself back under control. He was still noticeably shocky, but the tremors stopped, if nothing else. The lines of his face had deepened since this morning, Maggie noted, as he turned toward her rather than the O'Keefes. Another deep breath and the man's composure settled some more, though the stricken air did not lessen.

"Lynn…has kidnapped Kara."

Sweet Mother! How did I miss it? Maggie felt the blood drain from her own face as a memory that had been taunting her slammed into her with the force of a body check. Part of her had known, had made her uneasy in the woman's presence. There had been a faint dark tinge about Lynn's nature, which Maggie now realized was familiar. It echoed Olcas's attack on Miach's clinic in New York not so long ago. The dark god had taken over the homeless with his demons to get past the magical protections on the building, which he otherwise could not have breached. The shields, when fully activated, allowed those whom the *Sidhe* invited in to pass through, but otherwise blocked out anything of a magical nature. Fooled by the masked demons, one of the *Sidhe* brought the "innocents" into safety.

Tír na nÓg's protections were more rigid yet, but one thing was the same: The way was wide open to those invited in…even a demon cloaked in a loved one's form. Maggie should have paid attention. She knew Olcas's tricks yet did not think to guard against them.

This aftermath was her fault, but Arn suffered the guilt near as much as she.

Not wanting to upset him further when the fate of his Lynn was unknown, Maggie said nothing of her revelation. The strain he was under worried her. Much more and she feared he'd come to harm. Stepping closer, she laid her hand on his shoulder, all the while humming beneath her breath. The magic mingled unnoticed with the tension in the air. Maggie shaped it to bring him a moment of peace. The Sleep came down over the man with no resistance. She was ready and caught him easily before he could crumple to the floor.

"Well," she spoke over her shoulder without turning her head. "Come and help me then."

Patrick moved swiftly to her side, grim-faced, his arms ready to accept his friend despite the harsh and personal news the man had just delivered. Barbara followed him, surprisingly determined, if appearing a little lost about what she could do.

"Take him to Miach," Maggie instructed as she transferred her burden. "Then meet me at the *Fianna*'s chambers, Patrick. Barbara, if ye'd stay with Arn? He'll need someone familiar nearby when he wakes, and we'll need to know anything more he can tell us once his head is clear."

Though their fear was palpable, both nodded with conviction. When they were gone, Maggie soulspoke the rest of the *Fianna* as she hurried through the door. *Everyone, to the war room. Now.*

The council was short and hardly more productive than not meeting at all. Afterward, Maggie sat at the table with Patrick, Aí, and Goibhniu—who showed up with Beag Scath wrapped around his bicep, before anyone could be sent to inform him what happened. Both had been extremely agitated.

They still were. As was everyone seated at the table.

The rest of the *Fianna* had returned to their beds, or wherever else they'd been when summoned. No use having them add to the tension when there was nothing they could do. Those remaining dredged their vast collective memories for anything they had not tried. Maggie's link to Kara as *Bean Sidhe* of Clan O'Keefe could not pinpoint where she was. The seers were bombarded by roiling mists and a sense of dread, but no clear images. Scrying and dowsing had failed spectacularly, as had everything else attempted. Olcas was a master at deceptive magic, he had cloaked his location—and thus Kara's—to a fare-thee-well. It was as if they were removed from any plane or dimension known to man or *Sidhe*. As if they no longer existed in the known universe. Maggie restrained a shudder at the possible implications.

Beag Scath paced the room, hissing and spitting and lashing out at the air more vigorously than before. Maggie had never seen him in such a state. He had distracted them all evening, trying to draw them away from their discussion of Kara's rescue. Familiar with his single-minded focus when he fixated on some object he wanted, Maggie ignored his persistent efforts. Now he cast a disgusted scowl at them before disappearing down one of the hallways. Though Maggie had noted it, she did not give it any thought. He could do no harm. Out of necessity, all the private chambers were warded against the inquisitive and often mischievous faelings. Nothing harmful, but it prevented them from entering by magical means and discouraged them from the physical, somewhat like the electric pet fences in the mortal realm.

Already focused back on the discussion, Maggie was startled by a jolt to the magical ambiance. An unexpected frisson rippled the air, followed by an offended *Yipe!* echoing down the hall. Suddenly, Maggie felt a flood of magic flow through the room and down the way by which the sprite had vanished. She sensed it as the energy converged from every direction. Another determined growl corresponded with an abrupt *pop*, then everything went still.

Everyone at the table instantly fell silent, their gazes jumping to the arch Beag Scath had taken. Bangs and half-satisfied grumbles could be heard next, followed by the scraping of wood against stone.

All eyes widened in shock as the sprite stalked back down the hall, amazed when his unruly curls brushed the high arch as he passed beneath, they barely noticed his nakedness. His determined gaze was dark with intent, glittering with the accumulated sum of magic he'd absorbed. He thrust his arm forward toward Maggie, brandishing Quicksilver in his now-massive hand. Drawing a sharp breath, she looked to Goibhniu, uneasy with the instrument after what had happened the first time Kara had been rescued, when the girl had been lost in her torment and had nearly drawn all the *Sidhe* down into madness with her. The spirit residing in Quicksilver had averted that disaster, leaving Maggie in awe. Now that the violin was close, she sensed that some of the agitation she now felt came from that same soul.

"Why?" she asked, her gaze circling from Goibhniu to the violin to Beag Scath and back again, not sure where her answer would come from.

"Because I don't hear Danu the way you do."

The sprite spoke. He never spoke. She was startled by the full, rich tenor. She blinked, startled by his uncommon coherence. It should not have surprised her. Whatever seeming he took on had ever been seamless in both form and manner. Still, it shocked her. She had known him to be canny and sly, had never doubted his intelligence, but she had never seen him so focused. If he'd been human, she would have had him treated for ADHD well before now. Of course, at the moment, he was more focused than she was.

His gaze and his words revealed the truth Maggie could no longer deny, what her heart had told her from the beginning: the Mother Goddess's essence was ensconced within the violin. Maggie had already been weighed and judged by the goddess once, back at Yesterday's Dreams, when the *Sidhe* had sought to shield the instrument, before she'd completely understood its enchanted nature. She feared with her most recent mistake she would be judged once more…and this time found wanting.

"She'll tell you, and I will go."

"Why?" she asked again.

"*Mar aon ó thús, mar aon go deo,*" he answered. *As one from the beginning, as one forever.*

Maggie didn't quite understand what he was trying to say, but there was no arguing with his conviction. If he felt this was what needed doing to find Kara, there was little harm, though how the violin could help was a mystery. Still, just the chance that there was something they could actually do had her pulse quickening.

She reached out and wrapped her arms around the belly of the violin, ironically echoing Beag Scath's actions of many times past. Gently holding it to her chest, she closed her eyes and opened herself to what resided there. How could she not have realized before? Her body tensed as Danu's awareness joined with her, flooding her with more than she could comprehend, and yet she sensed it was but a fraction of the whole. If that wasn't sobering…

"How?" was all Maggie managed, suddenly feeling particularly dim, not even sure what she was really asking: How Danu came to be in a fiddle? How to rescue Kara? How to make up for her error in judgment? How? Or again, perhaps, the proper question was still "Why?" The scope of it all was dizzying.

As for him, the same for me, Danu herself answered in a soul-voice that made Maggie weep in wonder. *A good Mother always knows where her Children are, though they can't always say the same. It suits me.* This last was added in a touch of wry humor, very fleeting. *Give the wee one what he asks for and he will bring our* geal leanbh *home safe again. Only he and his can.*

*Geal leanbh…Cherished child…*Was that metaphorical? Somehow, Maggie didn't get that impression, though the spirit said nothing on the matter, despite being privy to Maggie's thoughts. And as for the rest…why Beag Scath? Why not Maggie and the *Fianna*? Why not Goibhniu?

They were back to "Why?" it seemed. It was like being two years old again, though that age was the vaguest of memories. No end of questions…precious little answers. Maggie gritted her teeth in frustration.

She felt a disorienting pressure between her eyes, like a kiss upon the brow, and then the spirit of Danu faded back to where she'd been, leaving behind the knowledge of where Kara would be found, but not how to get there.

"You can't, only we can. There is nothing he can do to block us," Beag Scath answered her aloud, biting off the words. By 'we,' she presumed he meant the faelings.

"*Mar aon ó thús, mar aon go deo,*" he repeated, and with a dangerous glint, he drew more magic about himself, closing his eyes in concentration. It settled on the surface of his form as if there was no room for it inward, and hardened into a dark blue, scintillating armor that reminded her vaguely of a scarab she'd once had, which his more spritely self had found fascinating.

He grinned at her, and she took a half step back, disturbed by the predatory cast of his expression. Before she could recover he was away, stepping through a fold in reality that hadn't been there the previous second.

"Bloody Hell!" Maggie said to the room at large, shaking her head slowly as she went to return Quicksilver to Kara's room.

Chapter 18

"Come back to play, little girl?" Olcas narrowed his eyes, pleasure and satisfaction causing them to glow. "Your timing is perfect. I grow bored without my usual diversions. Let's see…where were we?" He flicked his fingers toward her dramatically, a sick smile on his face, pulled a little out of line by a vivid scar on his cheek that had not been there at their last encounter.

Stinging pain ran down the center of Kara's chest, followed by a hard snap in her right hand, at the base of her thumb. A scream erupted from her, rising deep from her gut as Olcas induced the memory of the last time he'd tortured her. Kara shoved him away and yanked up the shields that still weren't instinctual for her. She was mostly in time to block the tearing pain at her breast, the nipple only stinging as it tightened involuntarily. Before she could control the impulse, Kara threw up.

Nasty laughter echoed from the bare walls of either a small warehouse or a large storage room. Kara glared at the sadist and swiped her arm across her mouth. The physical pain was gone the moment her shields were in place, but the torment and the horror of it was now as fresh as the day it was inflicted. She attempted to spit in his face, but she was shaking and had instinctively moved even further back. The bile landed on his shoe.

Olcas laughed harder, a contemptuous sneer twisting his stolen face. Then his expression changed into one of obscene anticipation. Kara had to fight the impulse to look away. She steadied herself, refusing to be ill again.

"That was nearly as enjoyable as the first time." The exhilaration in his expression was all too familiar.

Kara nearly went for him. Her fingers clawed, ready to do damage. Before she could leap at him, a hand came down on her shoulder in a grip as inescapable as a nightmare. It effortlessly held her back. Again instinct kicked in, augmented by the magical counterattack Aí had shown her during training. She reached back and grabbed the head of her assailant. Pushing her hips back, she angled her upper body, ducked her head, and drew her arms forward. Her magic worked in conjunction with her physical force to propel the enemy to the ground.

Echoes of her self-defense trainer's voice sounded in her head. *When someone threatens you harm, you run away. If that is not an option, you do not hold back, do not assume their intent is anything less than lethal.* In response, Kara twisted hard from her shoulders, her mass and magical energy both behind it, aided by the body's momentum.

There was an audible snap.

An infernal howl ripped simultaneously through the room and Kara's head. Though the body fell limp to the ground, something evil attempted to claw its way up her arms through her fingertips and the palms of her hands. It felt like the bite of acid eating away at her soul, desperate to latch on. Kara had no experience with demons, but Maggie had told her about the ones the *Sidhe* encountered in New York. No doubt that was what Kara wrestled with now. She panicked at the thought of such evil taking hold.

"God!" she cried out, overwhelmed; this was too much for anyone. Her walk was not all it should be, but her faith was there nonetheless. Calm settled over her, and a cleansing fire twined itself through the magic current already coursing down her arms. The howl briefly became a shriek before ending abruptly. The burning was gone, and for a moment, all was still.

Then Kara looked down into the sightless eyes of Lynn Barnert, an innocent in every way. She had not deserved this end or anything that had led to it. That would haunt Kara the rest of her days, however many that might be. One foot lifted to step over the fallen, and then the other. When she was clear of the body, Olcas's former victim raised her head to confront him, righteous wrath seething within her until she felt her skin twitch with it.

They held each other's gaze, then, as if by pre-arranged agreement, they both unleashed the whirlwind.

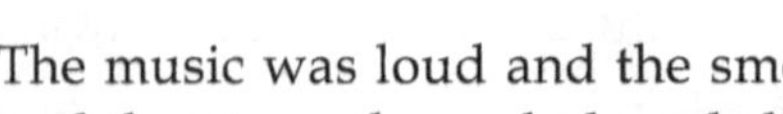

The music was loud and the smoke thick in McGarrity's Pub. Emotion charged the atmosphere, dark and sharp, as if a fight simmered but had not yet reached a boil. Dubh breathed it in with a satisfied sigh. The anticipation tightening his gut was not just for the pending blows, but savoring a more distant confrontation he could feel like a sharp jab against his spirit. The girl, Kara, had not proved the easy conquest Olcas had expected. Even now, they fought somewhere outside Dublin, the magical strikes lashing the night in a glorious display to any with the ability to see. Well…the fool had wanted her bad enough, and now he had her, to some extent. Perhaps if Olcas survived the encounter, Dubh would stop in again and allow his brother to rethink his role in the destruction of the Danaans.

And if he didn't survive…it was hardly a loss.

Dubh crossed his arms behind his head and savored the agony the motion tore from his seared limbs. To look at him, none would know the true state of his body, or of the soul trapped inside, with just enough awareness to suffer from each movement Dubh forced upon him. The man's agony satisfied the demigod's tastes more than any food or drink the world over, or in any other world. Waiting for the distant battle to play out, what better time to indulge? He was about to partake in a full stretch when the door of the pub slammed open. Something tugged at Dubh's spirit. He looked sharply toward the door.

A tall, pale man stood in the entrance, his essence shielded in a way that spoke of the *Sidhe*. His hair shone like antique gold, his eyes like old ivory. The face was unfamiliar, but the essence echoed oddly as if overlaid by something that Dubh should recognize. He frowned briefly. Letting it simmer at the back of his thoughts, he turned his focus on assessing this intruder. The cold rage in his gaze would have been bliss to sample if not for where it was aimed. Dubh pushed to his feet as his lip curled, magic gathering at his fingertips. A subtle nudge at the more aggressive mortals in the room would unleash the fight that had been pending all evening, masking their magical confrontation. Before he could act, the other cut the air with a hard slash of his hand. Conversations literally paused midsentence. The patrons went unnaturally still. Even the music pouring from the radio was arrested.

"Who the hell…?" Dubh started, only to trail off as his opponent strode deeper into the room and bared a glimpse of what before was hidden. A curse snarled from Dubh's charred lips.

"Calma." He spat the name of his eldest brother. In the recent conflict, Dubh might have wished his eldest brother by his side instead of the youngest, but he hadn't meant it. Even before their destruction, he had been too much in Calma's shadow, expected to be content with his elder brother's leavings. Now that Dubh had the opportunity to wreak vengeance on the enemy, of course, *he* would resurface. "It's been…a while. What, did you get lost?"

Ignoring the jibe, Calma asked, "What are you doing here when our brother is under attack?"

"Where were you when he was acting the imbecile…again?" Dubh shot back.

"You fool! You divine idiot! You don't get it, do you? Should anything happen to him, it happens to you…and *me*." Calma's words chilled Dubh to his scorched bones. "Can't you feel the pain?"

Dubh laughed — a nasty sound, dark and dire. "I always feel pain, if I can help it. What's a little more, except sauce?"

Rather than comment, Calma continued his tirade. "No longer bound by blood, we are linked infinitely tighter by spirit. That means should something happen to one of us, it happens to all three. Do you understand me?" Dubh's hands fist as Calma went on as if he were deficient. "There cannot be one without the other two. If one should be destroyed, whatever the cause, all of us perish."

If there was anything honest about Calma, it was his wrath. Dubh had forgotten how bound up his brother could be in that singular emotion. Amusing enough to see, when not on the receiving end; utterly infuriating, otherwise. Right now, Dubh was furious but too canny to invite a battle he had to admit he could not win.

A growl rose from his blackened throat, and his hand shot out, green sparks of magic arcing from his fingertips. Across the room, a man frozen in the act of lifting his pint went slamming into the wall behind the bar. For a few long moments, the only sound was that of falling glass as the smoky scent of whiskey rose from the shattered remains of a bottle knocked from its shelf.

Calma's brow rose in disdain. "Finished?"

Dubh answered in an abrupt nod.

"Then come," Calma ordered in a tone all too familiar, though Dubh had not heard it in over two thousand years. "We have a fight to stop, and once we rescue our brother, upon the ashes of our Mother, you *will* swear him no further harm. Now move!"

Again the magic kindled as Dubh glowered at his eldest brother. Before he could strike, Calma peeled open the ether and drew them both through. In an instant, they stood before the warehouse Olcas had claimed as his own domain. In the night, all seemed quiet and dark, but Dubh and Calma sensed the combat taking place within those walls.

"His private place is below the surface levels," Dubh informed his brother grudgingly. "He's warded them fairly solid. Olcas has become adept at mortal magic, the more ritual, the better."

"No matter," Calma replied. "We are linked…he cannot bar us access by any means, as long as he is within. Think of our brother…"

Dubh thought of him, alright. He thought of him flayed by a knife fine enough to carve his essence; he thought of him drained as dry as an Irishman's bottle of Jameson's by Saturday morning; he thought of him as no more than an unfond memory of the delightfully departed. And for his efforts, he gained a cuff to the side of his head as Calma eyed him sternly. Smirking, Dubh returned the glare before closing his eyes and visualizing the form Olcas now possessed.

Again the ether opened, this time the barest slit. They slipped through and came out in a chamber twice the size of the small pub they'd just left. Along the walls were stacked crates; the center of the room was clear except for the three forms occupying it before their arrival. All around them, the air hummed.

Across the room, Kara O'Keefe stood, the picture of outrage, her features fierce and her stance braced wide, balanced as if to leap or lunge as needed. On the ground behind her lay the crumpled form of a mortal woman with no essence of life about her, but the taint of the infernal on her flesh. It was impossible to tell who claimed that kill or why. Dubh focused once more on the girl.

Crude but powerful magic swirled about her. Olcas fairly frothed as she flaunted all he coveted. As untutored as she clearly was, the combat would have been over swift and sure if his brother weren't trying to ensnare rather than obliterate. For his folly, he bore the signs of her earlier attacks, damage both to the body he wore and to his spirit, proof of his obsession that he did not just strike her down and be done.

Kara, it would seem, had no such qualms. There was something of the cornered animal about her, her eyes glinted with a touch of the unhinged. As Dubh watched, she lashed out with the magical equivalent of napalm, disregarding the arcane wounds she rendered herself as she struck. Dubh did not know what impressed him more: that she was capable of such, or that she did not even seem to feel the effects. The energy arrowing away from her crackled and flashed with the strength of unmitigated fury. Had Calma not deflected it, the bolt would have burned through Olcas in an instant until not even a smudge marked the ground where he stood. What a pity. The remnants of the deflected attack zinged off everyone in the room like a static discharge.

Before she could strike again, Calma drew a common gun from beneath his coat and pulled the trigger. Dubh watched as the blunt-nosed round pierced her gut; he had to wonder why. If Calma wanted a long, lingering death for her, there were more interesting ways to play. Now, as ever, Dubh did not understand either of his brothers. He would not, however, let that prevent him from benefiting from their actions. The girl staggered and curled around the wound, but did not fall, lines of determination etching her face. She tried to ready another attack but seemed to have trouble getting past the pain. Imagine that. Closing his eyes briefly, he drew an appreciative breath, savoring the sudden agony peppering the air, feasting on its negative energy. When he opened them, it was to see her disbelieving expression mirrored on Olcas's face. The irony was too rich not to laugh…as if there was any reason not to anyway.

Dubh glanced at Calma, and his mirth died abruptly as he was struck by the depth of contempt and hatred in his brother's gaze as he stared at the girl. Somehow there was a history there. What had Dubh missed? He caught a flash of something that should prove an interesting tell. Leverage, perhaps, if handled subtly enough. Before Dubh could focus in and identify it, Olcas swayed, then dropped to one knee, his face pale despite the anger radiating from him. He swayed again and looked up in confusion from deep brown eyes that just a moment before had been blue.

"Grab him and let's go," Calma snapped, his gaze still locked with Kara's. He sent a spear of energy lancing into her, throwing her back. There was a loud pop like a joint forced from its socket, and the girl's right arm hung unnaturally. Blood soaked her from her waist down her thigh. A medallion she'd been clutching now swung free about her neck. Dubh liked the way her eyes rolled back into her head, though the pain wasn't as rich with her unconscious. Without a sound, she fell forward, landing face down, her dislocated shoulder bulging upward.

"What about her?"

"Dead bodies are of no concern to me," Calma answered. "Just make sure no one interferes with her becoming one."

There it was. A glimmer of that echo Dubh had noticed when he'd first seen this new Calma…almost as if…well, as if two spirits stared out of those bone-colored eyes. Interesting. When Dubh extended his will to end her himself, Calma reached out a hand to stop him.

"You'll not speed her along either…it suits me that she suffers a while." The words were steeped in malice.

Dubh narrowed his gaze but nodded. With a thought, he called out into the void, summoning the Bás. "Whatever you say," he answered as he ordered his pets to circle the lair both in the mortal realm and in the void. He then raised a shield around the warehouse, feeding it from Olcas's deep reservoir of resident magic, rather than his own. Between that and Olcas's existing wards, there should be no way that anyone could enter. The task done, he and Calma gathered up their brother and stepped with him through the ether.

After over two millennia apart, Carmán's children were united once more.

Chapter 19

Kara was dying. Blood, magic, and soul seeping from her broken body. A ragged sob raked over her throat, catching on her clenched teeth. A sound fueled more by frustration than pain, though there was enough of that in the mix as well. Once again, Olcas had been whisked away from her.

Her gut spasmed in reaction until unconsciousness drew near. She fought it off. It puzzled her briefly that she had been left alive …but Carmán's children were uniformly sadistic, as was Bran. They had left her just well enough to linger a while. After all, how else would she suffer sufficiently to satisfy them?

With a flinch, she abruptly shunted her thoughts away from the dark mound to her left. Lynn…or what had looked like her. It was difficult enough to breathe without the crushing weight of that guilt.

Not having arrived under her own power, Kara had no idea where she was. There wasn't a chance she could focus her will enough to slip away by magic or mundane means, assuming the way was even safe. But perhaps she could summon aid.

Lowering her head to the cool concrete, she squandered a bit of magic. She extended a weak tendril, probing beyond her immediate surroundings. For a moment, she encountered the faintest trace of deep relief, but it was distant and quickly drowned out as more intense feelings converged from closer by. Kara recoiled as she recognized grasping hunger and malice that was all too familiar. The *Namhaid*. They seemed to be everywhere, physically and through the ether.

Even as she considered her likely fate, the edges of the wards visibly thinned. Once the shield around the building fell, or they found a way through it, the spirit women would be upon her. She knew the results of a *Namhaid* attack, had personally cleansed Murna of the evil spirits nested within her…. Kara quaked at the thought of being subject to such invasion, to being forced to spawn pure evil into the world. She would rather die.

She felt a pop as if the pressure in her ear equalized, only nothing so physical, followed by a faint echo of satisfaction, quickly doused. Her heart fell, and her mind visualized the *Namhaid* swarming the building. To think after all she had been through it would come to this. Yet she still had one last say in her fate. It was difficult to reconcile herself to what she must do, but the alternative was not to be borne.

Not. Like. That, she thought fiercely. Determined, she focused her will on snaking her good arm beneath her, where the reformed blade remained hidden in her sash. To draw it free, she was forced to push her torso partway off the ground. Something in her gut tore further, and the flow down her belly increased.

Her scream echoed through the warehouse.

Now she trembled for a completely different reason, nearly done in with just the effort and the pain. For a moment, everything went dark grey again. Kara fought off unconsciousness, closing her hand on the rough hilt of Goibhniu's dagger, though she could barely force them to close in a tight enough grip.

The darkness nearly won. She staved off oblivion, breathing deep and walling off the pain. Slowly, carefully, she drew the dagger from its sheath and worked it to her side. It wasn't Lugh's sword, to slay with just a scratch, but Goibhniu's blades were special in their own right: they always struck true. It seemed to take an hour, maybe more to get the blade in place. In reality, it couldn't have been more than minutes. Edging the point beneath her arm, by feel alone, she found the gap between her ribs, using the pommel and her wrist to prop the blade off the ground. Exhaustion bled her strength more quickly. Letting her head drop, she rested a moment. She had no choice. The feel of steel piercing her shirt set her to shivering harder. Every instinct ordered her to roll away. Sheer will kept her in place. Evil would not be spawned from her. She would not allow it. The *Namhaid* could not whelp from a corpse. When they overran this place that was all they would find.

Rallying the strength to carry through her plan, Kara raised herself enough that dropping her shoulder would be enough to drive the propped blade straight into her heart. The tip already bit into her flesh. The steel was cold, and Kara's survival instincts raged against her intentions. Her determination remained steadfast. Now if only she could get them to work together and have done with the deed. As she gathered her resolve, there was a flutter beneath her skin, kind of like a breeze, only felt within, not on the surface. She shivered in reaction, and the point went a little deeper.

An enraged scream slammed into her, sudden and furious.

Startled, she jerked in response, and the dagger fell away. Kara fell to the ground, slamming into the concrete, landing against her dislocated shoulder.

Kara screamed, and her body wanted to arch away from the intense pain. She forced herself to remain still rather than add to her agony. The blade lay flat beneath her. Blood ran down her side in a thin stream, lost in the pool already formed around her. The scent from the fresh wound was lost amid the blood spoor already saturating the air, stirring within her a deeper sense of uselessness. She wanted to cry at the wasted effort, more so because she wasn't sure she had either the strength or the doggedness to start again.

She would never know.

Again, an incensed howl echoed from the walls. There was something familiar in the cry. The feel of it, if not the sound. She felt she should know what voiced that outcry. It didn't have the feel of the *Namhaid*. *What else is coming for me?* she wondered, ready to give in and let the darkness draw her down rather than face more brutality.

And then she saw him…a Shadow stalking out of the gloom.

Was she dreaming? She must have been, because though she could not make out the face, her mind told her she knew him and his tousled thatch of multi-hued hair, the locks reminded her of Maggie's sprite, only this one could never be called "Little." The man was massive, easily over seven feet tall. All of him perfectly formed and proportioned. No steroid enhancement there. She didn't have the strength to be afraid, though she knew she should. Maybe he wouldn't notice her…it was dark, after all. Or was it? The air itself started to take on a muted glow.

Kara blinked and shook her head before remembering why that was inadvisable. The sound she made was too faint to be called a gasp. Yet the vision homed in on her, looking pissed enough to shred bone if he got his hands on whoever he was after. If she'd had the strength, she would have quailed beneath that fierce glower. His orange eyes kindled like flame. Several long strides and the colossus stood over her. He was encased in what looked like iridescent armor, like the carapace of a beetle, only shaped to his form. It was scratched and gouged but otherwise appeared sound. He crouched down so swiftly her head spun.

The giant had Beag Scath's face.

I must be delirious, she thought. Then he quirked the ghost of a familiar impish smile, and reached a hand toward her, but did not touch. *Was it really him?* Kara did not even try to understand. She stared in wonder at her friend, glad for one last chance to see a loved one. For this *was* Beag Scath, despite the sudden upscaling. The eyes, though, were still uncharacteristically violent as his gaze ran across her then continued to scan their surroundings. She could feel his frustration that the foe had departed. Fine tremors of anger went through his body. Her heart told her it was on her behalf, not against her, but that was no comfort. It felt too much like another innocence lost.

Kara began to cry.

Before she could say a word, or even summon the energy to reach up a hand to make sure he was real, others crept from the depths of the shadows. How had she not sensed them? Being upon being, some identifiable only by remembered descriptions, some strange and wondrous and completely outside of her knowledge. All of them familiar in spirit, enough that if she tried, she realized she *could* name them all. There were more than a few sprites (of the more usual size), and boggans and domovoi and…oh, too many to single out. Yet all of them kin-cousins…faelings…and something more. There was a name her heart strained to lay upon them, only she could not focus, could not hold on to it, any more than she could stay fully conscious.

They circled her, their faces solemn, and heartache etched into their expressions. Some reached out, eyes full of longing, but did not touch, and she sensed they would not for fear of hurting her. There were coos and cries and odd little shrieks, grumbles and groans and somehow deep resounding silences. The creatures kept coming until the once-empty warehouse was packed, except for a space around her several feet deep. Only the supersized Scath remained close, protectively crouched over her.

Then the faelings parted, and a slow procession made its way into the open space. Kara's jaw dropped, and reflexively, her eyes blinked. She had never before seen anything of fae blood look ancient—their eyes excepted. That was not so for those gathered directly around her. They were all manner of creatures she had already seen, one representative of each…though some were oddly absent. Of those there, all of them *looked* older than forever. At their backs stood a gate like those to the fae lands, only leading to no destination she recognized. The feel of the place was intimate as if a part of her resided there. How or why she could not say, and that didn't matter, for some aspect of her awareness nodded sagely in the background, accepting and unconcerned. Anyway…they were here. Kara's question now: To what purpose?

"What…?" she managed, but nothing more.

Beag Scath shushed her gently, then pivoted and beckoned to the ancient at the forefront. It placed what could only be called a tendril in his hand. Looking back at her, the sprite offered her his other hand, lowering it within reach. It was a struggle, but she stretched across the concrete and took it. And questioned her sanity once more.

Beag Scath spoke, his voice oddly deep and lyrical: "The soul-born come to be rejoined. They return the life you gifted them long ago."

Kara's eyes went wide, and her hand trembled in his grip. She had only heard him speak once before, and that only four words. His voice had grown with the rest of him. Intimidatingly so. Where their skin touched, a fierce burning sensation rippled down her arm. As she watched he drew the willing creature closer. With a brilliant burst of energy, the aged faeling flared up like a brand, enshrouded in swirls of what she recognized as magic, threaded through with a ribbon of vivid white light. Her soul twitched in time with that luminance. As the energies increased, the being faded until there was nothing left of its physical form. Kara cried out in protest, trying to jerk her hand away as she watched Beag Scath absorb what remained. There was no getting free. Not because he gripped her tightly, but because it was as if their flesh was fused. Helpless to resist, Kara felt the other faeling's essence flow into her own through that bond.

The next to come forward she recognized as a redcap. He wore a look of devotion at odds with what she knew of his race's nature. Kara tensed and watched closely as he scurried forward, drawing an iron pike behind him. She jerked as the creature whipped off the namesake cap with his free hand and swiped it all around her. His black eyes gleamed as he plopped the sopping hat back atop his head and grinned at her. The sight of his sharp-pointed teeth unsettled her enough without the runnel of her blood snaking down his forehead. The concrete beneath her had been swept clean, and Kara had to wonder if this one had come in malice. The doubt lasted only a moment. He bowed low to her and placed his hand in Beag Scath's like his predecessor had. As he grew transparent, he closed his lips over those teeth, and suddenly, she saw the benevolence of his smile. She felt a pang as he faded, followed by a jolt as the essence of her blood returned to her.

And as each ancient kin-cousin offered itself up and was absorbed, all she could do was sob. With each sacrifice, she felt replenished. Her body healed, and her spirit more whole than it had ever been before, though she had not realized it until now. Each creature's spirit as it joined with her whispered one name: Anu.

Kara was startled as the truth of it echoed from her soul. She suddenly remembered her earlier dream, the web of connections, her lady…she could almost see it once more as her children returned to whence they began. Her heart knew each one for what it was, heard the echo of the names her other self had whispered into being so very, very long ago. As awareness flooded her mind, she realized not every type of faeling had come forth, not because others had held back, but because the part that had been those creatures was already inside her, unbound from the physical by natural attrition. The thought would have been sobering had the situation not already been grim.

And the procession went on.

When it was done, Kara—Anu—lay there, spent but complete in both body and spirit for the first time in near forever. Then she knew the how and the why of the connection that allowed Beag Scath and the others to link to this place. No shield raised would ever block its creator, and thanks to her bond with those ancient faelings, she'd shared oneness with them all…even before their sacrifice.

Kara was so spent she barely noticed that her hand was no longer locked in Beag Scath's grip. Yet the sprite still crouched at her side. Gently he slid his arms beneath her. She was jolted by the feral magics flooding his form, filling it fuller than it had ever been before, clearly the source of his sudden growth spurt. Standing, he hefted her up, cradling her against his chest as if she were all that was precious to him.

There was something she should say, something important she was forgetting, but the trauma and recovery were too harsh and swift. Her hand clutched reflexively at the empty air as if to grab an object where there was none. Fretful, but unable to focus, she let the worry go. She reeled from the extremes she'd just experienced and could barely lock on even the one thought she clung to, though she wanted it more than anything.

"Please…take us home," she murmured, the words barely spoken aloud, her hand gesturing toward Lynn. She wasn't even sure where home was…and scarcely cared as Beag Scath carried her into the void. The remaining faelings — those not the original soul-born — followed in their wake, Lynn's body hefted between them.

Like the aftermath of an earthquake, *Tír na nÓg* shuddered once, and again, and one time more as something blew through the added protections raised upon the discovery of Kara's abduction. They weren't shields so much as alerts, but they came down like shattering glass as the force punched through them.

From all across the Land, the *Fianna* converged, tracking the mystic trail to their own quarters. A handful of others followed them, the most sensitive, or the most curious. Those were repelled at the entrance. The *Fianna* made it through to the public chamber; some even made it down the corridor housing Kara's room. Maggie stood before the girl's door and nearly fell to her knees as anguish emanated from the chamber within. Urias and Miach caught her, despite not being much better off. The air crackled and flashed as she reached out a hand to the doorknob and could not even touch it for the shield raised around the entrance. Drawing the torc from around her neck, she tried to circumvent the barrier, but to no effect.

She did not realize tears veiled her eyes until a faint touch trembled against her ankle. Looking down, Maggie had a hard time making out Beag Scath's crumpled form. The sprite reached out to her but had no strength left to draw himself closer.

"Let me down," Maggie said to her companions, her voice tight and pained. Gently they lowered her beside the sprite. Feeling stupid not to have done so immediately, she raised a shield encapsulating the one already in place around the room, cutting off the emotional bombardment. Instantly, she steadied. Picking up her little friend, she drew on centuries of familiarity to link with him. They could not speak mind to mind, but she could and did get flashes of memory and emotion from the sprite enough to understand something of what transpired. Kara in a too-familiar warehouse, prone, bloodied. A rescue staged by the faelings. Any details were unclear beyond those simple facts. She also caught flashes of Lynn's dead body, which Maggie gathered the faelings had left at the Temple of the Fallen. There was a third-hand sense that Kara had something to do with that change in state.

Maggie understood the anguish now.

Behind the protection of her shields, Maggie ached for her friend. It was never easy to end a life; worse so when it was one you knew and cared about, no matter the circumstances. Concerned for Kara's physical and mental well-being, and not quite knowing what to do given the surprising strength of the shields, Maggie rose to her feet and turned back to the public chamber, Beag Scath cradled against her chest. The others trailed after her. Too tired to explain, she opened her thoughts to Miach, letting the healer glimpse the bare facts she had gleaned. Urias followed silently.

They found Goibhniu waiting for them. Maggie quickly explained.

"We can't get in," she ended.

"An' the wee one?"

Maggie looked down to where Beag Scath had curled tight, his body shaking with exhaustion. "There'll be no piggybacking across the shield through him. He's not harmed, but fair spent." There was nothing they could do for him but allow him time to rest. Sharing magic would do no good when he had no energy to make it his own, and there was nothing about his condition that required healing. All Maggie could offer was comfort, and so she continued to cradle him against her warmth.

The Smithgod nodded, his expression dark and brooding. "Something must be done. Not only do we not ken her condition, but she's projecting again." His brow drew deeper down, and a frown bowed his lips. Maggie felt her own mirror the expression.

Before she could respond, Goibhniu nodded again, sharply, and drew the torc from around his neck. "I'll be right back." And then he was gone.

It took Maggie a moment to realize she cradled empty air. She had no idea where either Goibhniu or Beag Scath had gone.

Goibhniu seldom left *Tír na nÓg*. A ruler must be available to his people, there when they needed ruling, judgment, defense…But there were, on occasion, things outside the realm that could not be dealt with by his messengers, Hounds, or *Fianna*. And so, the Smithgod left *Tír na nÓg*.

Stepping through a portal of his own making, Goibhniu stood in the center of a faerie ring near the ruins of Kilkea Castle, ancestral home to *Gearoidh Iarla*—Gerald, the eleventh Earl of Kildare, known as the Wizard Earl.

Goibhniu stared up briefly into the night sky, a faint echo of the splendor that arched over the Land of Youth. The heavens were less accessible here; they hid more of their glory, as did all nature. He gained a deeper sympathy for those afflicted with what the mortals termed a "cold." This dampening of senses seemed a close approximation to that suffered state.

In the distance, he heard the pounding of hoof beats that cracked like thunder. Among them, one set pealed with a sweet ring, like a giant's bell.

Though too far away to see, the Smithgod knew those silver shoes belonged to a blinding white steed bearing the Wizard Earl. The shoes were thinner than a dime, though not yet as thin as a cat's ear, as they would be when he returned to the land for good. By night's end, the Earl would slumber again beneath Mullaghmast to await the call raised by the Miller's Son of legend. *Whoever that turned out to be*, Goibhniu thought grimly.

It was not time for that particular summons, but while the Earl was occupied, Goibhniu was not above borrowing his steward — particularly given the situation back in *Tír na nÓg*.

"Conall O'Keefe, I summon ye."

The herald resisted the compulsion.

"Now, Conall O'Keefe." Goibhniu's tone dropped low and grew harsh. "Or would ye abandon yer granddaughter yet again? 'Tisn't the time to add to yer disgrace."

Instantly, a form took shape, seemingly from night-shadow and stardust. A horror from any man's nightmares, gaunt and pale with lips tinged faintly blue and down his front a blood-tinted froth, evidence of the offense that had drawn him this penance. The eyes — ever hovering on the cusp of death — deepened their haunted air. If not for the protection of the faerie ring, the man would have breathed one last breath and gone to dust.

Goibhniu shook his head at the sight. To the Sidhe, life and family were sacred. The one summoned had, in the end, shown irreverence for both, in the eyes of the *Daoine Maithé*. Not unforgivable, but given recent happenings, Goibhniu was particularly sensitive to the events that brought the elf-kin to his current state of existence.

"Kara?" Conall rasped, his voice forever marred by his body's attempt to reject his efforts to end his life.

"Here's where ye make up for not having enough o' a care for her then." Goibhniu gestured to Conall's state. The man looked down in shame. As well he should. Fifteen years before he'd attempted to take his own life, too heartsick to go on after the accidental death of his wife, Moira. None knew of his effort, beyond the Sidhe. They'd left a changeling in his place when they claimed him as their boon servant. A kindness to the family, really, to spare them the true state of his corpse had he been left to his dying.

"It was not to be like this. I was just to go to sleep, is all." Conall's eyes came up, begging forgiveness he'd learned not to ask for.

He met only disappointment in Goibhniu's gaze. "An' would that have been any better for those ye left behind? Does it justify the suffering, the pain? The horror o' the one to find ye? The doubts and regrets o' those wondering did they fail'd ye…when the opposite 'tis true?"

Conall flinched and squeezed his eyes shut as if he feared to see those images played out again, as he had when he was first claimed and put to service.

"Ye acted the selfish man, Conall. Ye thought only o' yerself and *yer* pain, instead o' waiting for it to fade, as it would have. Ye had obligations, and even if ye had not, ye threw away a gift…a life meant to be long and full. How many have that gift ripped away from them before 'tis time? And ye threw yer's away…or would have if not for the debt ye had forgotten."

The Smithgod reached out and took Conall's right hand in his, pushing back the man's sleeve. A mark glittered on the uncovered wrist, a twining knotwork symbol, perfect and beautiful in disturbing contrast to the pale flesh. Conall hadn't even known it was there until the instant before his death. It was a pledge mark. It indicated a boon owed to the *Tuatha de Danaan*, in this case for Kara's healthy birth, when as a babe, she'd been so close to lost. Before Conall could take his last breath, it warned them, and a *Sidhe* had been sent to call the marker in. Once his boon was met he would have the choice, to go on to the end he had chosen that ill-considered day, or to enter the *Sidhe* Lands and serve life. Until that day, he was theirs to command. "Ye cannot cheat the fae, man. We'll always have our due… ye know that now, aye?"

Conall nodded.

"Kara needs ye. We can't reach her, can't draw her out. We can't even physically get near," Goibhniu said. "The lass was forced to kill a demon wearing the form o' a dear friend. She's shielded herself in her room. We've no idea if she is well, body or soul; she's blocked herself in so tight."

"Oh, my Kara-lass…" Conall closed his eyes in pain as the words "kill" and "demon" were used in conjunction with his granddaughter.

"Being in between the planes, ye might manage to slip past," Goibhniu continued.

"But…how can I go to her?" the man's brow furrowed, knowing well he'd breathe his final breath the moment he entered the mortal realm any place not beneath *Sidhe* protections.

"She's in *Tír na nÓg*."

Conall's eyes snapped open at that. "Clearly, a lot's been happening."

"More than we have time to go into."

Kara's grandfather nodded, drew a deep breath…or tried to, his damaged lungs protesting with loud and violent coughs. Grimacing, Conall gestured down at the evidence of his weakness. "Please, will ye hide this? I'll not give her nightmares o' her Grandda on top o' it all."

With a touch, Goibhniu granted the request, restoring the appearance of health and vigor to the man. Still holding him firm, the Smithgod stepped them through the portal to *Tír na nÓg*.

The Hounds converged on *Mór Halla* from across the mortal world. Some with empty hands, or haunted eyes, some weighed down by the burden they bore. All with heavy hearts. Between them, they returned five black velvet grave bags and two of a deep, dark red—the latter the remains of those whose souls they had not saved. All those known to have been taken had been accounted for, along with several others the *Bás* had claimed without the knowledge of the *Tuatha de Danaan*.

Aí received the grave bags from the others, placing them in a larger sack slung around his shoulder. His free hand rested briefly, firmly on each of their shoulders in unspoken thanks for the grim task they'd carried through. He knew what some of them had been called to do and felt their anguish. Peace would soon be theirs.

Accepting the final bag, Aí turned and led the procession of Hounds through *Mór Halla*. They had discharged their duty, having found the victims or dispatched the enemy's young, those they were able to find. The trail had gone cold. Either they had found all there was, or they were too late, and the whelps had moved on from the places of their birth. The Hounds would perform one final task as honor guard, and then be released from obligation. Until the Welcoming, anyway, but to Aí's thinking, participating in that ceremony was anything but an obligation. The Hounds would have the joy of escorting the blessed—those whom Fate had selected to bear the returning *Sidhe* souls into their next childhood.

But for now, there was the grimmer task of returning the remains of the fallen.

They approached the Court, a solemn air preceding them in a gradual wave as those first to see them ceased their chatter, then all beyond joined suit. A path cleared to the dais. As the procession made its way forward, Aí could swear the cloying musk of the *Namhaid* wreathed the air even here, though it could only have been the product of his imagination. Reaching the dais, Aí and the Hounds arrayed at his back knelt before Goibhniu. Without raising his eyes, Aí unslung the pouch of remains and laid them before the Smithgod. A hand came to rest on Aí's shoulder in benediction. Only then did he speak. "Danu's Children have come home."

"Ye have our thanks," Goibhniu answered.

Formalities observed, they stood again, and the honor guard departed.

CHAPTER 20

KARA WOKE FEELING BOTH THE BEST AND WORST SHE HAD EVER FELT. EVERY CELL felt full and charged, but her mind staggered. What was real? What was dream? Part of her wanted to fly into a million pieces; the other part was afraid she would.

Memory told her she should be dead, on a cold and dirty slab....

....slab of concrete...like Aunt Lynn was.

Kara gasped and cried out. That bit of remembering had crept up on her and stomped her gut with hobnailed boots. Her closed eyes squeezed tighter as she fought her balled fists flat and pressed them against the bed, desperate to banish the sensation of a human head gripped between them.

She couldn't breathe. Her body shook, and her cries pierced the darkness of her room. Yet no one came to her. It was as if the air curled tight around her to block the world out. Did they know? Had they shunned her? The memory of Uncle Arn's desperate determination to save his wife slammed into her next. Bad enough to take a life, but someone you cared for? Someone who cared for you? And to have to then face those you denied the return of their loved one...

Any well-being Kara had felt on waking vanished.

How can I tell him? she wondered before the fear returned that perhaps he already knew. Again despair crushed her. She keened and rocked and hardly seemed to realize either until there was a sudden, familiar pop, more intense this time, like the pressure in a giant's ears equalizing. There was a faint light. There was a man-shaped silhouette near the door, shimmery through her cascading tears.

Slowly it walked toward her, leaning forward as if fighting a wind.

"Shut it down, Kara-lass, and let someone in, why don't ye, before ye do yerself harm."

Her body stiffened, and her eyes went wide.

"Am I dead then?" she breathed the words on what little air was left in her when her visitor triggered the mage light by her bed.

Conall O'Keefe laughed ruefully as he sat the edge of the bed and gathered her close.

"No, though ye have them all afeard ye might be yet." His hand cradled her head against his chest, running down the length of her hair. Again she wondered: real, or dream? "But yer not, lass, and ye won't be, so shake away this funk. Ye're fine and good and all without blame, my little love." His voice was gentle but forceful, echoing oddly against her ear pressed against him. "Ye hear me? Never ye doubt it."

Well, she no longer had to wonder if they knew.

She curled in tight against him as she hadn't in over fifteen years. But when that fact hit her, she pushed back.

"How could you, Grandda?" she demanded, anger and hurt threading tremors through her voice. She might not know the specifics, but she'd spent all this time thinking him dead when here he looked well enough for her to wonder what the hell was going on.

He did not pull her back, though she could see he wanted to desperately.

"I'm sorry. I can't explain meself, but I am sorry…Please, don't harden yer heart to me. We have but a little time to us."

It was too much. She threw herself against him and clung tighter. "No…" she cried. "No, no, no!"

Perhaps she was three, after all…but she didn't care.

He rocked her until her cries died away and her body relaxed against him. He sang to her in Irish. He sang to her in another tongue, familiar, though she could not name it. He murmured words of comfort she didn't hear and bawdy jokes she did.

By the time he was done, faelings crowded the room — Beag Scath notably absent.

"I see ye finally found them," Grandda chuckled, and Kara was reminded of a long-ago day in Central Park when they'd gone busking. Her younger self had squatted among the clover looking for pixies. The irony had not registered until now, what with everything else going on.

She chuckled to herself, surprised that she was able.

"More like they found me," she said. Drawing a deep breath, she sat back, more surprised by the depth of peace she now felt than she was by her mirth.

"Aye," he said, a knowing look in his eye. "Ye good now?"

Kara nodded and knew that she was. She'd lost it and lost it good. It was hardly a surprise. Too many things happening one after the other, with almost no relief between…The tension and the horror had overwhelmed her, but that was past, and she'd found her strength again. She had no idea how long she'd wallowed here, but there were things she needed to do. Demigods to trounce. Fae to banish. Maybe another batch of cocoa to make…this time for three. Her breath caught at that thought. Papa. Did he know? She looked at her grandfather but was afraid to ask. Scooting to the edge of the bed, she stood, turning toward him.

"Shall we?" she asked, telling herself she didn't already know the answer.

Sorrow blanketed his expression, falling heavy across his slumped shoulders. Grandda shook his head. "No, lass, it cannot be. I'm back to my duty and ye to yers. None must know that don't already ken I've been here. They would not have even fetched me if ye had not been in such a bad way."

Kara's head dropped a moment, but she would not add to his obvious heartache. She reached for his hand and drew him to his feet, first kissing his cheek, then hugging him tight. His shoulders shook as she did so, and his lips were wet when he pressed them to her forehead. When he folded her in his arms, she soaked up the memory, a gift she would cherish when he was again beyond her reach.

And then she had a thought. There was one thing she wanted most of all, other than to have him back forever…Turning to the chest holding her things, Kara drew out Quicksilver. Without a word, she held the violin out to him. There was still the briefest tinge of sorrow amidst his joy as he accepted the fiddle. He removed it from the case, and already Kara felt the magic hum in the air.

Grandda sat on the bed, and Kara sat at his feet with the faelings crowded around her.

They lost themselves a while in the memory of a simpler time; he playing their favorite songs, she singing as she rarely did anymore, until neither of them could go another note. Then Grandda handed Quicksilver back, bent to kiss Kara's head, and disappeared, dissolving like a mist before he'd even stepped across the room.

Kara sat there stunned, hardly noticing the crowd that gathered at her now-open door.

Brid found Arn on the practice field where he and Urias were sparring. He wasn't hiding from her, but he certainly wouldn't have sought her out either. She kept trying to tell him things he couldn't bear to hear. He knew it wasn't Kara's fault. That she'd only put down a shell holding….

He couldn't complete the thought.

The sword he wielded slashed down with the alarming scream of steel cutting through air. Fortunately, it wasn't one of the special blades that supposedly never missed—the ones made by that Smith guy—because Arn forgot to temper his swing. Urias met the attack with a calm block, but just barely. When the elf disengaged, he stepped back, lowering his own sword.

"I told ye, not angry," he said, his tone chiding and his expression both worried and resolute. "I'll not cross swords with ye when yer angry."

Gulping air, Arn let his sword tip lower to the ground. Damn, but he was out of shape. Even Patrick could kick his butt right now, and Kara…he forced his way past his automatic recoil…Kara would show him the door if he were ever dumb enough to cross swords with her.

He huffed and tried to shove down his aggression. Laying the blade on the ground safely to the side—avoiding where Brid stood watching—he placed himself squarely in front of Urias, feet spread, knees bent, and arms poised at his side.

"Sorry, didn't see it coming. How about we go at it without the pointy sticks for a while?"

Urias shook his head. "I'll not stand proxy for the personal demons ye're fighting, my friend."

Arn flinched at the use of the word "demon."

"Physician, heal thyself," Urias quipped, not unkindly. "Calm down, and I promise ye we'll train some more, but now? It will not help ye." Sheathing his sword, he clapped Arn's shoulder as he went past, grabbing up the discarded practice blade and heading down the path toward *Mór Halla*.

Arn dropped his head down and fought off a scream. His friend was right, but that didn't mean Arn wouldn't feel at least a little better for a good brawl. He huffed in frustration, his teeth grinding and his hands curling into fists. He almost didn't notice the shadow that fell across his feet.

"Well, come on, then…If you won't talk to me, we might as well fight."

Whether it was Brid's presence—which he'd forgotten—or her words— which he'd *never* expected—Arn almost fell back on his ass, he jerked upright so fast.

"Excuse me?!" He stared at her, aghast, taking in her waifish frame and delicate features, everything within him screaming "protect," except his inner doctor, which screamed "feed her, for God's sake"…which was likely why he never saw the punch that clocked him.

"Friggin' Hell!"

A whole other set of instincts kicked in. He forgot she was a woman (may his mother's soul forgive him); he forgot she was roughly the size of a rather small tweenie; he forgot she wasn't the one he was angry with. At first, his strikes were full of anger and lacking focus, wild and poorly aimed. Brid easily dodged them, her eyes serious, and her movement fluid as she lured him deeper into the clearing. He garnered more bruises from her effortless blocks than he did from any direct strikes, but as he calmed and became more centered, the fight transitioned from a mostly one-sided brawl to serious sparring. There were shockingly few occasions when his fists actually connected with her flesh. Hers landed all too frequently, despite his best efforts, though he suspected that was more due to his moving unexpectedly into them when she had intended to pull back. Gradually, their efforts to engage slowed, then stopped, until both of them stood there in a circle of flattened grass at least thirty feet across.

Who knew how long they went at it? Arn was a little ashamed to realize he didn't care. By unspoken agreement, they lowered themselves to the ground, sitting with their legs crossed and their elbows on their knees. Brid cupped her chin between battered hands and watched him with peaceful eyes. He noticed a bruise darkened her cheek, left by one of the few punches she hadn't managed to block or dodge.

He suspected she'd done it to make him feel better about getting trounced.

"Why'd you learn to fight like that?" Arn asked her as he fiddled with the tasseled top of a tall grass stem. He liked her serene voice, and it was one of the few in this place lacking a brogue. He wondered why. Not that it particularly mattered, as he found her lack of accent comforting. Almost like he could pretend he was home, chatting with a stranger in the park...though she was actually something more than a stranger to him now.

She smiled. "As many who revere me for what I can do, there are at least as many who curse me for it. None have offered harm as yet, but I thought it wise I be prepared for the day."

"Huh..." He didn't like the sound of that, though having just fought her, it kind of made him want to see the shocked look on the asshole's face who tried to hurt her.

Arn gave in to his curiosity again and asked, "So...why don't you sound like everyone else here?"

She cocked her head to the side and gave him a slight, sad smile. "This land is a part of us. The *Sidhe* are connected to Ireland at their very core. Even those that never leave the *Sidhe* Lands are touched, and so they speak with a common voice, as it were, with the humans that live there, unless the *Sidhe* in question makes a conscious choice to put aside that manner of speech, of course."

That didn't quite answer his question...or at least, he wasn't sure if it did. "Is that what you do?"

"No, I speak with my own voice because I must keep myself apart, tight behind shields unless a good reason brings me out from them. Otherwise, the world would destroy me."

A scoffing laugh broke away from him. "Yeah, right! You just handed me my ass...what do you have to be scared of?"

She was quiet a moment and lost her earlier peace. He could have kicked himself.

"Visions of a broken world," she answered in soft, sad tones. "There are so many, I would never be free of them until they broke me, body, mind, and soul." Her words were a jab to his gut, packing just as much punch as her fists had earlier. "It's not like this for all Seers, but my Gift is particularly strong."

They again lapsed into silence, if a little less easy than before.

The sky dimmed to twilight. The meadow rustled soothingly around them, what wasn't flattened, and tranquility wrapped them both again. Somewhat stiffly, and biting off a yawn, Arn laid back, hands beneath his head and knees in the air, watching the faerie lights—literally—dance through the air. He must have drifted a bit because he didn't realize they had company until he heard Brid's voice raised in welcome: "Kara…come, sit awhile."

Arn jerked upright at her words, fighting the tension that came rushing up from his gut. Brid's fingertips on his arm kept him in place.

"Stay, talk a bit…both of you."

He watched Kara fold herself down to the grass, her expression perplexed. She chewed her lip lightly but said nothing.

When she was settled, Brid pushed to her own feet. "Well! I've been away long enough. Best I go see if I've been needed."

"What?!" Arn almost stood as well, only the Seer pinned him with her gaze.

"Don't let the path remain broken between you, Arnold Barnert. Some things need saying. She's come to you herself, so say them. Now. Before they fester both your hearts."

Brid looked at Kara then, her features softening from the light scowl she'd given Arn. "If you need me, dear one, you've only to ask. Until then, let me tell you…you did your Aunt Lynn a mercy, or what was left of her. You freed the remaining fragment of her soul before it could be consumed. When you have the nightmares, remember that. I'll see you both later." With that, she left.

Talk about pole-axed.

Arn and Kara met each other's gaze. She just watched him, but Arn almost recoiled, and not because she technically killed his wife. Young Kara had grown up the hard way. There was a maturity in her gaze even beyond what she'd always had. Though she had no visible injuries, the tightness around her eyes and mouth spoke of pain. The eyes themselves held a disturbingly familiar look that shocked him more than anything else that had happened that day. He'd seen it immeasurable times at the VA hospital where he'd been stationed in the service.

"If I was still a corporal," he said to her, his voice low and his eyes never leaving hers, "and we weren't in faerie land, I'd take you to the Enlisted Club to drown that empty feeling you have inside."

She laughed, but it was an empty one.

"It's never going to be easy," he told her, affection and a kindred sense filling his quiet words, "for either one of us, but it does get easier."

"How?" she asked, frustration popping the word. "I was doing okay yesterday, then today…"

He nodded, finding a sympathy he never thought he would. "That's how it goes for a soldier, Kara. You let yourself enjoy the good times and you fight your way out of the dark ones, knowing they'll come back, but making damn sure they don't stay." Arn leaned forward and gripped her shoulder firmly but gently. "For God's sake, make sure they don't stay. Don't let what you had to do destroy you."

Her chin lifted. She closed her eyes briefly and took a deep breath.

"I'm sorry."

"I'm the one who's sorry, Kara. So sorry. I never thought having her back could be worse than not." Arn's voice sounded lost even to his own ears.

They both fell silent, the tension eased, if not gone, and the healing begun. They sat there for a long time.

Much about Kara had changed over the last few weeks. Changes that staggered her, left her weak and afraid, but also forged her into more than she had ever been, or ever thought she could be. Now that she had recovered her equilibrium, it was time to act. And if that required becoming confrontational, well…she was up to the task. Entering the Court with poise enough to rival the grandest *Sidhe*, and fortitude enough to carry her across any battlefield, Kara walked to the dais, mounted it, and passed by the Smithgod to the Great Wall. Those behind her murmured in speculation, but Goibhniu said nothing, not even in her head. She expected him to complain, to grouse, to grumble. To demand what she thought she was doing.

He did none of that.

Yet, the weight of his gaze remained constant and heavy as she went up on her toes and traced one hand in the air over a particular pattern, sullen and dark enough to be mistaken for pure black. Bran's pattern.

"Why is this still here? Have none of you wondered that?" Kara was frustrated that they would not see. True, few, if any of them had actually experienced an Unraveling to know what was proper and what wasn't, but instinct told Kara the pattern should have vanished with the end of the ritual. She had no way of knowing for certain. Maybe she was wrong. Apprehension crept along her gut, though, telling her she was not. "Banished means gone, doesn't it? Nothing should linger, right?"

Kara ignored the Court. All her focus was on Goibhniu.

He frowned, and his gaze rose to the offending pattern. "Ye will not let it go, then, will ye?"

With a sigh, she moved closer, knelt before him, and looked into his face. "I'm sorry. I would never choose to hurt you…but it *isn't* done. I *know* it isn't. I am pulled toward that wall every moment I'm awake. It haunts my sleep. My hand feels the hilt of the dagger no matter that I'm not holding it. He isn't banished…not yet, He can still return to *Tír na nÓg*. He can still hurt you, or others I care about. And if he does, it will be because I didn't do my part."

"What do ye need?"

"The dagger, please. My boon."

Goibhniu's brow twisted. "But, *leanbh*, I gave it ye already."

Kara breathed in sharp and found it hard to breathe out again. Any noise the Court made was lost in the white noise roaring in her ears. She settled back on her heels to support her body. They'd hardly take her seriously if she toppled over. "No…where did they put it? When they brought me back? It's not in my room…"

"Kara, breathe," Goibhniu commanded her. She tried to listen. "I'm sorry, lass," he went on as she focused on following orders like a good *Fianna*. "But as far as I ken, the dagger was not with ye when ye were brought back to us."

"Shit!" That came out louder than she'd intended. "Oh, my God." That was half swear and half prayer.

She'd foolishly assumed the faelings would bring back the knife. If it was still at the warehouse…Visions of the place overwhelmed her, cutting off her thoughts and plunging them into that dark hole within her. She remain conscious somehow, her breath shallow and sweat clinging to her skin, but her memories went a little erratic until Uncle Arn's advice cut through the panic. Kara looked up and met Goibhniu's eye, then looked beside her where Maggie now stood, her hand hovering over Kara's shoulder but hesitant to touch. The rest of the *Fianna* had circled protectively around them. Glancing past them to the Hall, Kara was startled to see that the rest of the Court had departed.

Managing another breath, Kara rose to her feet, forcing the tremors from her hands and ignoring her chilled skin. "Where's Beag Scath?"

Maggie frowned. "We haven't seen him since he brought ye back."

Kara reeled. "No…" She closed her eyes and cast her thoughts out wide and far.

In no more than an instant, she had a sense of the sprite, wan and weary, but unharmed, holed away in a grotto somewhere Kara had never been, but felt was only a wish away.

Drawing a deep, shaky breath, she let him be, marveling at the brush of other faeling thoughts as she withdrew. A bond had been forged in that dark place, one that could swiftly engulf her if she did not take care, her thoughts as swarmed as her person when the faelings converged in the physical world.

That was not for now, though.

"It's in the warehouse," she announced without hesitation. She had understandably not been herself when rescued—and never would be again, actually—but she couldn't believe she'd left the blade behind. "For the ritual, must it be the same dagger?" Again, she asked more for form's sake, her soul already told her the answer.

"No other will do," Goibhniu said. "Even were I to forge one anew in the very same manner, it would not serve."

The heart ached even when irrational hopes were dashed. Kara's nearly stopped. The answer was as expected as the solution none had yet voiced. Someone…*Kara* needed to return to the warehouse to retrieve the dagger. She forced the panic down. Not once had she been to the cursed place under her own mobility. Hell, she didn't even know if it was in Ireland or East Jabip. "How do I get back there?"

Maggie moved closer. "As one from the beginning, as one forever."

Goibhniu nodded, his expression pensive.

Kara's brow furrowed as she looked from one of them to the other. "What?"

"Ye left a bit o' yerself in that place," Maggie said. "Once something is a part o' ye, there is always a connection, unless ye take steps to break it. Some call it sympathetic magic…"

"Sorry…can I get the Cliff Notes?" Kara interrupted.

"Ye can get back there by following yer blood trail. It does not matter how long ago spilt, blood calls to blood. No shield can keep ye from yerself without serious intent and special effort. The bastards did not plan for keeping ye out."

"Just me?"

"Maybe one or two others, if they're close and holding ye tight."

Kara turned to Goibhniu. "Please, may two of the *Fianna* aid me?"

"Sure and ye'll go by yerself regardless, aye?"

"Aye," she answered the Smithgod, just a touch irreverent.

Goibhniu grimaced. "An they choose so, it'll be with my blessing." He glanced around the circle, waiting for a response from his warriors.

Though by no means the only ones to agree, Aí and Urias were the first. Kara blushed and looked away from the former; the latter surprised her. He was vaguely familiar, but she did not know him well. She drew her attention back to pertinent matters as the serious planning kicked in.

It was decided that they would depart within the hour, leaving just enough time for Kara to check on Beag Scath. Instinct told her to go to him, and not just to ensure he was okay. The entire time they had formulated a strategy, a part of her remained linked with the sprite. Even now, she felt his weariness, how utterly drained he was from wielding so much magic: first to grow himself so large, then to forge a path to her, and finally as the conduit for the soul-born. Kara now knew it had nearly been too much for him.

Somehow the thought of that almost-sacrifice was harder to take than the combined events she'd had to cope with since walking through the doors of Yesterday's Dreams to pawn Grandda's fiddle.

The memory of the pawnshop gave her an idea. Hurrying to her room, she scooped up the violin, which still lay across the bed where Grandda had set her down. The urge to go to Beag Scath grew stronger and stronger. It had to be possible. A persistent little voice…many, actually…fairly cheered in her head each time she thought of doing so, but they bloody well weren't offering any suggestions on how to get there. When she thought about how easily the faelings found her when they wanted to, appearing out of nowhere regardless of where she was, she growled in frustration that she couldn't figure out how to do the same.

She pictured him.

She said his name.

She told herself to go where he was.

None of it worked.

"Gah! I don't have time for this!" And yet, she felt strongly that until it was done, there was no moving forward with their plans. To do so would be foolish and dangerous. Not only was she distracted, but Beag Scath had knowledge of the place that she lacked. She'd never gotten there under her own power and knew virtually nothing about the warehouse other than she had hellish luck there.

The *Fianna* and other *Sidhe* couldn't help her, not even Goibhniu. Not with the warehouse and not with getting to Beag Scath. They had been unable to get through the shields surrounding Olcas's domain, and they didn't have the connection to the kin-cousins that she did. Hell, they didn't even *know* about the connection. (Now did not seem an appropriate time to rock the *Sidhe* world with news that she bore Anu's soul.)

Desperate and needing comfort, Kara placed Quicksilver across her lap. In the method called pizzicato, Kara used her fingers to pluck and strum her way through a simple folk song Grandda used to play for her when she was upset.

Maybe it was her imagination, but Grandda's lips brushed her forehead and his voice whispered to her, *Reach, lass. Reach for him.*

Kara couldn't bring herself to consider anything impossible anymore, not after all she'd seen and done. Closing her eyes and wrapping her fingers firmly around Quicksilver, she reached.

And her world spun.

When she came to her senses, Kara found herself curled in a comfortable grotto that reminded her of the shore of the New England coast where she and Grandda had once gone spelunking all summer, or at least what had passed for spelunking when she was five. They had wandered in and out of the caverns revealed at low tide, a cool breeze tugging at their sweaters and the waves outside swooshing their gentle melody. Grandda always seemed to find the most glorious caves. The ones with ceilings of glittering crystal lit up by sunlight lancing through crevices above, or with deep dark pools full of magical—to a five-year-old—creatures that glowed translucently in the beam from their flashlight. And always there had been a soft bed of moss or a tatty blanket they'd brought with them where they could sit and eat their snacks, making up stories well into the afternoon.

Where she sat now was not in the least rivaled by the wonder of those childhood explorations. Here, the ceiling glittered with faceted diamonds, emeralds, and rubies, and it was not sunlight that made them sparkle, but some inner glow. The moss she sat on cradled her like the finest velvet, and flitting past her were the most amazing creatures. Not faelings, interestingly enough—she could tell—but something other and delightful in their own right, with jewel-bright wings and doe-like eyes set in…flesh that almost appeared faceted. Their singing made her wonder, were the voices of angels any sweeter? The breeze that teased her curls was perfumed with amber and a lighter scent strangely reminiscent of cotton candy.

Distracted in equal parts by her senses and the creatures' antics, Kara almost didn't notice the slight weight cozied up against her thigh, between her body and where Quicksilver lay as if slipped from her hands.

Beag Scath had wedged between both of them, positioned as if he could not decide which to press against. Kara laughed, her body relaxed, and her nerves calm to the point of being officially laid back, a state foreign to her for much longer than the current chaos her life had become. Stroking the sprite's shoulder lightly with her finger to get his attention, she smiled down at him.

"Hello," Kara murmured, not wanting to disturb the tranquility of the grotto.

Sleepily, his head rolled until he looked up at her, eyes droopy, but a broad smile of contentment gracing his lips. Beag Scath's chest rose and fell in a satisfied sigh. Beyond his open joy, Kara could not help but notice the drawn lines of his face or the wire-thin scars across his limbs that had not quite faded. As he rolled his body to rest more fully against her, Kara winced to see the effort it took. When he reached to draw himself to his normal perch, only to end up stretched his length and no closer to where he wanted to be, Kara reached down to lift him up.

Apparently, even sprites had dignity capable of being offended. Beag Scath fussed and grumbled, but did not pull away.

He did not make it as far as to perch on her shoulder. With her arms to support him, he draped her chest, his tousled head pressed to her neck. Kara giggled as he managed a purr in rhythm to her heartbeat. It fluttered against her skin in a most peculiar way. She allowed herself this peaceful respite, her head carefully resting against Beag Scath's in a mother-and-child moment that almost jarred her right out of it again as she experienced a still-unexpected sense of rightness.

She could have stayed that way forever…or at least for much longer than she allowed herself, but urgency pressed her until her muscles twitched with the need to act. "I must go back," she spoke softly.

Beag Scath tensed where he lay, his essence too intertwined with hers for him not to know precisely where she meant, any more than she could miss his vehement rejection of the necessity.

"I must," she repeated. "We cannot do without the dagger, or the Cursed One may return." It was hard to say what he grasped of her words and what he didn't, but clearly, he did not miss the mental image of Bran that accompanied her words.

The sprite hissed and drew back, his small body twitching and his hands gripping her shoulders tightly as he searched her face, as any person would, hoping to have misunderstood. Even as he did so she sensed his attempt to draw magic into him, as well as the needle-like pains that wracked his body with the effort.

"No." Her tone stern as she frowned down at him. "Stop, now, before you hurt yourself."

He obediently settled, but still fussed, and she could feel his agitation. Not what she'd wanted to accomplish by coming here. Reaching over with one hand, she lifted Quicksilver to her lap and idly plucked at the strings. Somehow even that was musical, if not proper music, and for the most part tranquility returned to the grotto. The wee creatures flitting the air settled nearby to watch her, and Beag Scath relaxed once more. She felt his head pivot, and she had no doubt his hungry gaze locked on the instrument. Ever had he been drawn to the violin. One final pluck, and she laid her hands across the strings, stilling them.

"Will you do me a favor, Little One?" she asked.

With a bit more energy than he'd had before she'd taken up Quicksilver, the sprite clamored to her shoulder. Gently gripping her ear, he leaned around and met her eye to eye, some glimmer of the warrior sprite creeping past his normal puckish nature.

"Will you watch over Quicksilver for me while I'm gone?"

His expression was comical, a unique blend of avarice and astonishment threaded through with delight. When he nodded, it set his multihued curls bouncing.

As if he would have said no. If the sprite coveted anything, it was that violin. His eyes narrowed in concentration, and a neon green rose appeared in his free hand. He held it out to her. Kara shook her head, her expression stern. She remembered Maggie's account of Beag Scath trying to capture what he desired by gifting the one who possessed it. "Not a gift. You just watch it for me, or I take it away with me." Beag Scath frowned but nodded, the flower fading away.

Relieved, Kara set the instrument aside but restrained him when he would have tumbled down to wrap himself around the belly. "Watch, not keep," she reminded him more firmly. "And only until I return with the dagger."

Abruptly, Beag Scath stopped straining to get down. He dropped to her knee—which she allowed—and turned to stare up into her face. His stance was akin to when she'd seen him at the warehouse, battle-ready and poised. He held her gaze then suddenly hissed and howled and dropped into a half-familiar pose, his head cocking and darting as his arm lashed out, finger clawing the air a breath from her chest. Kara jerked upright at the startling behavior, wondering what possessed him…figuratively or literally. Before she could react in any other way, he dropped the pose and watched her with solemn eyes darkened to rust with worry. As if to make a final point, he hissed again, and images slipped into her thoughts. Pale white women with blood red hair, their movements a mirror of his, or more precisely, his earlier movements a mirror of theirs.

The *Namhaid*.

Though she had only seen them from a distance, the accounts of these infernal creatures were etched in her mind: their look…their behavior…their predatory nature…their parasitic spawning. And then she remembered her dying moments before the faelings worked their miracle. She'd been ready to take her own life rather than fall into the possession of the *Namhaid*, who had stalked the warehouse, barely kept at bay by Kara's waning shields.

Even now, her heart quailed the slightest bit before she shored it up. Last time she had been at risk through no fault of her own; now, she intended to walk into it open-eyed and willingly. She had no choice, though. The dagger was not optional. If any of them were to be safe—at least from Bran's particular malice—the Unraveling must be completed.

Touched by the depth of Beag Scath's concern, Kara leaned forward, meeting him eye to eye. "I have to go, but I'm not going alone. I will take every care."

Content, Beag Scath pivoted and leapt from her knee with a hint of his past energy.

By the time she reached her thoughts to *Tír na nÓg* and drew herself back, the sprite had already attached himself barnacle-like to the violin.

Chapter 21

On the outskirts of Wexford, reality tore in a jagged slash across the gloaming. Three men stepped through, two with certain steps, one stumbling. Once they were in the front garden of the McCorry Inn, the gash sealed.

Calma whirled on Olcas. "You truly are a complete fool!" he snarled as his hand lashed out, entwining in the lanyard strung about Olcas's neck. "Were you even aware of this? Did you, in any sense, realize the enemy had a link to you? A way to *control* you?"

Olcas did no more than blink. Between the battle and whatever effect the charm had had on him that allowed the host to surface to the fore, the idiot was still addled.

Calma shook his head in disgust. "Oblivious!" Yanking sharply, he snapped the leather. A few twists of his wrist and the medallion and cord disappeared into his fist. He focused his anger, his magic, all on that one point. A blue flash engulfed his hand. Black flakes of scorched copper fell to the ground as he opened his fingers. He then turned to Dubh. "Bring him inside."

Not waiting, Calma spun around and headed into the B&B he had taken over. He strode past the tableaus he had staged of the innkeeper at the front desk and three patrons artfully arranged in the parlor. All were abnormally stationary and would remain so unless someone other than him or his brothers entered the building.

Calma ignored all of them as he took the stairs to the third floor, where he had claimed the most opulent chamber as his own. He ignored that splendor, moving to stare out the window as he waited for his brothers. His eyes did not see the lush countryside, green and fertile though it was autumn. Calma saw a much different version of the landscape; ancient and wasted, sucked dry of its energy, fields and hills brown and brittle, trees withered, both fruit and limb. A crowd of human cattle circled the space in his memory, likewise sapped of strength, or at least the bulk of them, clothed in the rags of garments out of another era. In sharp contrast, the fae stood among them, protectively, vibrant and full of ageless life. Powerful.

In the center of that throng stood Carmán and her children, Calma himself upright and defiant, despite the iron chains binding them, his brothers at his back moaning and quivering against their bonds; Dubh in ecstasy and Olcas in pained desperation. They stood there until the de Danaans reclaimed the life force the brothers had taken from both the land and people in their conquest of Eire.

In the far-off age he was in now, Calma's ears still echoed with their agonized cries, even his own, as in the end, he could not stave off the anguish when their spirit and flesh were rent. Would that he were there again in that moment to make the mortals pay for their triumphant cries as Calma and his brothers fragmented, torn asunder by the fae and the wind. Bad enough, that, but fresh in his final memories as a corporeal being, Calma could still see their exuberant cheering as Carmán, through her gag, wailed her final breath at the death of her sons. Their remains were cast on a bonfire and spat upon as the flame reduced them to purified ash...or so the mortals thought.

Those humans were beyond Calma's vengeance...but their descendants weren't, and neither were the *Sidhe*. He chuckled deep and dark as visions of his new world supplanted those memories of the old.

But first...to make that come to pass they must unmake the *Sidhe* for all time. For that, Calma needed Mother. For some time now, he'd felt her awareness stirring, reaching out to him, demanding that he act. Calma was at least as eager as she to initiate the plan.

It will not work, Bran soulspoke, interrupting Calma's thoughts with his own. One of the drawbacks of a willing—thus unsubsumed—host. The demigod ignored him.

Calma had not anticipated this day before he saw the *Sidhe* woman on Bran's altar, but now that the idea had taken root, nothing would swerve him from this course. Now that he and his brothers were reunited and a vessel stood ready, it was time. Each of them bore a piece of Mother's essence, which had preserved them for millennia beyond the deaths of their bodies. Through that connection, they would summon her spirit and, with a bit of her ash from the soil where she died, seat her, body and soul, within Agnieszka's unborn child.

I tell you, it will not work...

Hush! As if I would trust a word from you, who would betray your own so casually, Calma 'spoke back.

As if you wouldn't...

Precisely how I know what you are capable of...

Before they could go any deeper into their argument, the door behind him opened.

Without turning around, Calma spoke. "Tonight…during the dark of the moon, we must summon Mother and teach our enemies what it feels like to be unmade."

For once, they were willingly silent as he shared his plan.

Gathering what they needed, they prepared themselves and met in the basement. As the three of them came down the stairs, Calma was more than aware of the hungry looks his brothers locked on Agnieszka. Her power spoke to them, as did her beauty, though for vastly different reasons. This was the first they had seen of her. In fact, until they'd arrived, neither of them had even known she'd existed.

Calma shielded the entrance behind them, then used a bit of power to cleanse the room of any lingering impressions, careful to remain between his brothers and Agnieszka at all times. She was a tempting lure, and he would not have them disrupt his plans out of self-centered impulses they could not resist. By the time he was done and turned to them once more, Olcas had taken out a thermos and poured them all steaming mugs of some brew he'd concocted.

"To heighten awareness," he explained.

Calma and Dubh both curled their lips at the mortal magic but drank all the same, once they had tested their cups to ensure they were safe. After all, they would be foolish to turn down a possible advantage.

When he drained his cup, Calma spat to clear his mouth of the bitter taste. He could sense no increase in clarity, but when he looked at Dubh and Olcas, their eyes were bright and intent. Perhaps it only affected those of human blood, as both his brothers' hosts were. Calma hardly cared. He set no store in alchemy or herbs, even less in his lack-witted brother, who could barely rouse a glimmer of the divine magic he was born to. Why should Olcas be any better at some foreign quackery?

Putting the matter from his thoughts, Calma stepped further into the room. Before him, at the center of the chamber, was the immortal beauty, Agnieszka. She lay on a narrow, discarded sideboard, apparently relegated to the basement due to a leg that wobbled. Walking around the makeshift altar, Calma waved his hands over her distended abdomen. Within her was the culmination of his plan: the babe that would house their mother's soul.

Bran remained a smug presence at the back of his mind.

Calma's eyes narrowed as he reached out to Dubh and Olcas, focusing on the goal rather than the doubtful voice sharing his head or the animosity he and his brothers held for one another. They stepped forward to the other side of the table from him. The three of them joined hands, the woman's belly centered between them.

"Carmán," he murmured, his brothers echoing him. "Carmán." Louder. "Carmán!"

The weight of the earth surrounding them pressed in, dark energy welling up from deep below. Something familiar pinched and plucked at Calma's awareness. By the way they fidgeted, his brothers were similarly beset. The musty scent of old earth grew stronger, though the basement was well finished, and a chill crept across their skin.

"Hello, Mother," Calma spoke to the air. He felt her approval as their intent came clear. Her slumbering power surged into full awareness.

As if they had coordinated the motion, he and his brothers released each other's hands and moved one grip up the arm to the shoulder of the brother to their right, so they remained connected. As one, they brought their sinister hands down to rest on the mound of the woman's womb. The *Sidhe*'s skin rippled and jumped as if to flinch away, but she remained trapped in her unnatural rest. Their mother's disembodied presence crackled around them, charged and eager.

The pressure grew to a point close to smothering, and still Carmán's soul remained unseated. The air thrummed as she grew impatient, and Calma could hear the cinderblock walls popping as tiny fissures crackled the surface.

Enough, already, accept it can't be done! Bran finally protested.

"Explain," Calma snarled aloud, to his brothers' confusion.

The soul, the one anchored to the babe in her womb, it has not yet been cleansed of its memories. Bran answered. *Until it is, the new identity cannot form…or be imprinted. This is why it is not further along on its journey back to life.*

Calma cursed, first in his native tongue, and then in Bran's, both silently and aloud, so wrought was he at being thwarted. *You did not think to mention this?*

Oh, but I did, Bran reminded him.

"What the hell is going on?" Olcas interrupted, though he hardly realized it. Beside him, Dubh wore a considering expression on his face. Calma's brothers were not his concern. Bran was. He ignored them and focused on his host.

How is this done?

Bran did not answer, exercising what petty power he could.

Tell me how the soul is cleansed, Calma 'spoke. *Now.*

Still, the host would not speak.

Calma reached a mental hand deep within their chest and lightly grasped the remaining strand of soul still anchored to the Sidhe race. He didn't yank, he didn't tighten his grip, he just held it lightly. The presence of Carmán noticeably swelled, as if looming at their back.

Bran finally replied. *There is a ceremony. Those to bear the young release the memories any and all have of the one passed. The more memories released, the quicker the child is born.*

Calma released his psychic grip. *Hardly an option, wouldn't you say?*

There are other ways, though none other would consider them.

Dubh and Olcas were becoming more obtrusive as Calma conversed with his host. To forestall any rash act on their part, Calma explained the problem, if not how he'd been enlightened.

"How do we circumvent the issue?" Dubh asked, echoing Calma's thoughts.

Bran?

Secure the remains of the one who last bore the soul. Steal them from the very halls of Tír na nÓg, then wipe the memories as if they'd never been.

He did not trust Bran. And yet he had to. It rankled that their revenge depended solely on his host's remaining link to the *Sidhe*. If anything happened to complete this "Unraveling", they would lose their best opportunity. They needed to act.

"We're going visiting," Calma told his brothers, then he filled them in.

This time Kara was conscious of the journey as she slid between the fabric of reality to *Tír na nÓg*. Her skin prickled, like walking through a curtain of minuscule beads, as she brushed against thousands of awarenesses as she passed. The contact was not at all intrusive, but just enough that she knew the others were there. She shivered at the intimacy, one-sided and fleeting, yet closer than she'd allowed herself to be with anyone, except for her recent encounter with Grandda.

So distracting was the sensation, she nearly forgot to "reach" for her chamber halfway there. She wasn't sure what impact that would have—figuratively or literally—and she wasn't anxious to find out. Refocusing her thoughts, she felt the slightest pressure as she transitioned from there to here, like passing through a bubble or a cobweb. And then she was home, or what passed for it now.

Her door stood open. The room empty. She noticed a man's silhouette in the doorway.

"Calm yerself, cara." It was Aí. By the inflection, she knew he used the Irish word for friend, rather than her name. Kara frowned at the informality, uncomfortable with the memory of his bare ass...not to mention other bits of anatomy. She tensed more despite knowing the identity of her unexpected visitor. She could also tell he wasn't so calm himself.

"Is it time to go?" she asked as she pushed past him, fleeing the confinement of her room for the public space. Aí followed. Now that his face was not in shadow, she could see the anxiety there. The muscles in his forehead bunched, and his head tilted slightly to the side. Almost absently, she noticed the crossed swords on his back, and several daggers sheathed about his person.

"It's as if ye had not taken a single harm," he said like she hadn't asked a question. Kara fidgeted and looked away, but not before she noticed his hand twitch, as if he would touch her to be sure. She sensed the effort it took him to resist. "I did not ken what happened when we were in the Hall, I'd just returned from Goibhniu's business. Maggie told me ye were taken, that it took the faelings to rescue ye…that yer clothes were stiff with blood and full o' holes when ye came back to us, yet yer body without a wound. Blessed Mother, am I glad ye're fine."

His fervency startled her, and she returned her gaze to him. If a *Sidhe* could look haggard, that was how he seemed. The skin around his eyes and mouth tightened, and his gaze traveled from one end of her to the other, repeatedly. Not in any lewd manner, but as if to confirm she was okay.

Again she fidgeted, twitching beneath his perusal.

"Where have ye been? I came for ye, standing and waiting in yer very door only to spy ye stepping out o' nowhere. What manner o' maid are ye?"

"An uncommon one. Is it time to go?" she repeated, somewhat impatient.

"I was worried for ye. I've come to ask ye not to go. Please, let me do this for ye…"

"You can't. You heard Goibhniu, no one else can get through the shields."

Aí grimaced. "Would ye be willing to let me try?"

She didn't like the implications of that. "Why does it matter if I am or not?"

"I'd need yer help," he said, drawing one of his knives from a sheath at his side. Kara backed away. "Just a touch to yer finger, enough for a spot o' blood."

Why not? she thought. *It's not like I actually want to go, right?* She didn't expect it to work, but it was worth the try. The faintest tremor betrayed her nerves as she held out her hand. It was quick, just a sting. Aí wiped the blade clean on his skin and sheathed it, then took her hand in his, giving a light squeeze to send a rivulet of blood over his fingers. When he seemed to be satisfied with the coverage, he raised her hand to his lips and licked the last bead of blood from the wound.

That gave her a whole other kind of jolt as she remembered the last time they touched. Such an innocent kiss to inspire such impure thoughts…He let go and vanished, only to return as quickly, flat on his ass, his hands unmarked by her blood.

She'd never heard him curse before.

He was good at it.

"So…I guess that's a no?" she couldn't help jibing, but beneath the light mockery lay an unspoken fear. If her blood wasn't enough to get Aí through the shields, what of her touch? She very well could find herself alone, encircled by the *Namhaid*.

"Aí…"

He looked up at her, a slightly sour look upon his face. Beyond it, she could see his worry. With a huff, he got to his feet. "Yes?"

"Is it possible to send something through a shield…to someone else?"

It took the look he gave her for Kara to realize it would not matter if she could or not, in this instance, anyway; if she didn't make it back herself, the matter was moot. "Aye, an the other is reaching for what ye send."

"Good to know," she said, striving to sound nonchalant. "Where's Urias? I'd kind of like to get this over with."

There was the sound of a throat clearing by the door. There stood the final member of their…away team. His metallic blue mohawk and biker leathers were a strange contrast to the architecture. And the masses of weaponry he likewise had positioned around his body.

Kara was glad to see none of them wore a red shirt.

"Shall we?"

The *Sidhe* men drew close. Kara took their hands in hers and brought them closer still until they were all pressed leg to shoulder. By chance, Aí gripped the hand he'd bloodied. She tried not to think about that. Closing her eyes, she visualized the warehouse and reached.

This wasn't like before. She felt jerked and pressed and buffeted around, right up until it seemed like she hit a concrete wall. It tried to block her. The resistance was agony. One arm jerked sharply, coming loose with a pop, the other felt like it was locked in a vise, held fast until she was afraid something other than air would pop. By the time she was done, it was quite likely she would be able to describe what it was like to be sieved through stone. The journey was so intense she barely registered her arrival, despite landing hard on concrete.

Kara lay there, waiting to die, too drained to defend herself. One arm burned as if wrenched, the other, she couldn't even feel. As for magic, it ebbed low enough she wondered if she had anything to fight with, let alone get home. After a while, it occurred to her that death was a long time coming.

Dragging her eyes open, she looked to her right. Nothing. To her left, she spied the back of a head draped in chestnut locks, not spiked metallic blue. She wasn't sure why Aí made it through and Urias hadn't, but she was glad not to be alone. Had Urias merely been left behind, or had he come to harm in the void? That thought reminded her of the *Namhaid*.

Urias! she called out with her mind.

For a long moment, there was silence, then a faint tickle in her brain. *I'm fine. Look to yerselves, aye? Be safe.*

Kara lifted a swift prayer of thanks and then brought her mind back to their circumstances. Groaning, she heaved herself off the floor, struggling to stand at first, but determined to face the enemy on her feet.

There were none.

The realization was not a comfort. Instincts Kara had learned to trust twitched.

"Aí…I think we have a problem." Echoing her groan, Goibhniu's servant rolled over and looked up at her.

"Just one?"

She ignored his sarcasm.

"If the *Namhaid* aren't here…where are they?"

Aí gained his feet in an instant. "Come on, we need to find that blade."

Chapter 22

Leaving was not as simple as deciding to go. Not with his brothers. Not now, and not ever. Calma and Bran both chafed as the minutes passed, waiting impatiently as Olcas—hide-bound to his ritual—prepared, and Dubh went off to summon his minions. The hard way. Because they wouldn't come to his call.

Pathetic.

To distract his host, not to mention vent his own frustration, Calma went out into the garden and stripped bare. He warmed up his muscles in preparation for the ancient forms of pankration, a martial art popular in his native Greece three thousand years prior (give or take a few hundred.) It was difficult without an opponent but familiar and comfortable. A combination of no-holds-barred wrestling and boxing, it suited his demeanor and nicely worked the total body. A useful diversion, presuming they actually managed to raid *Tír na nÓg*, as planned.

Calma threw a particularly vicious punch at the thought, then he settled into the discipline of the ancient art. Drops of sweat filled the air like mist as he whirled and kicked and ducked.

There was a flush of pleasure and satisfaction from his host as Calma went through his warm-up. Then, sudden and unexpected, the forms were no longer being run by rote. Counter, hold, strike…each was met by a corresponding move, not physically, but in Calma's head…or, more precisely, *Bran's* head. Calma closed their eyes and threw himself into the fight, their body moving at his command, but in reaction to Bran's responses to Calma's chosen moves. Apparently, the art of pankration was not unknown to his host. There was no physical resistance, as there would be with two bodies fighting, but this wasn't about exercise or combat, as much about learning how his new body moved and responded. Invaluable knowledge, given the potential conflict to come.

They were in their cool-down when the brothers returned.

"Done playing?" Dubh asked with a snarl.

Calma was a bit startled, though he was careful not to show it. Of all of them, Dubh was the only one that could be described as laid back. While by no means a pushover or easygoing, as the humans of this time thought of the phrase, Dubh was not known for his aggression…he preferred to strike covertly, with forethought…and against opponents he stood a chance of besting. Something must have gone wrong; in saner days, Dubh never would have challenged him in the slightest.

"Trouble with your friends?" Calma countered as he dressed, emphasizing his scorn.

"They've killed nearly all the young we fostered!" his brother screamed. "The *Bás* want blood, and so do I." Dubh never had liked it when anyone messed with his toys. Presumably, "they" referred to the de Danaans. Who else could have seen, let alone dispatched, such creatures?

In truth, Calma could not count it as a bad thing. He was pleased to know the spirit women were fully vested in the fight. At the same time, he had serious reservations against fostering a race as vicious as they, particularly when they fed off mage energy.

At some point, there was bound to be a conflict of interest.

"Good," Calma said. "You can't chain a tiger and expect it won't bite you someday. You would do to remember that."

Dubh went Spartan…nearly Viking, his eye wild and the lines of the tendons in his neck pressing hard against his charred skin, causing fissures. Pinning his brother with a stare from beneath half-lowered lids, Calma raised a bit of power in warning. As he did so, Bran readied their body to meet physical attack.

Into that fraught silence, Olcas spoke. "The girl is mine."

Both older brothers turned a look of disgust on the youngest.

"We have one goal." Calma's tone was bitter cold. "Once we achieve that, the world is ours."

"Unless all you want is one little bitch," Dubh added, his animosity in equal parts for both his brother and Kara O'Keefe.

Olcas ignored the wise-ass comment, all his attention on Calma. "Like I'm likely to get anything but the leavings."

He was right. Olcas had never been Mother's favorite. Too spoilt. Too weak.

"Jeopardize this, and that will no longer be a concern."

Before Olcas could counter his remark, Calma turned and headed inside. "We need to follow the soul link to the remains."

"How are you planning to get past the faerie gate?" Dubh called out.

Without turning, Calma snarled.

At first, he ignored the question, not about to tell his brothers of his unique partnership with his host. They would see it as a weakness to be exploited. It was getting harder to mask his agitation, but then Bran spoke, and Calma was reassured. *Tell them…there is no harm in them knowing my body is a natural key to let you pass through. Only partially correct, but enough to set the matter away from their thoughts and allow us to move on to more important things.*

Calma did so, turning to gauge their expressions. Olcas stared him up and down in a clearly covetous manner. As for Dubh, his gaze was a bit skeptical, but for now, he let the subject go.

Once inside, they descended to the basement where Agnieszka remained unmoving, but for the rise and fall of her chest. Calma went and stood as they had earlier.

"Come, let's be done with it."

His brothers took their places, watching intently as Calma pressed a hand against the woman's belly. After millennia as a disembodied soul, he was intimately aware of the spirit realm and quickly identified the sparkling thread that would lead the soul to the child's body when the time was ripe. Not that things would progress that far…for this particular soul. Calma tagged the trail and opened his eyes to find his brothers staring intently around the room. The air was rife with anticipation.

Mother was back.

He ignored her unspoken demands that he hurry. "I have it," he told his brothers.

"And?" Olcas asked, nearly as eager as Mother, if for different reasons.

"Now what?" Dubh raised his skeptic's voice.

Can you open a way direct, or must we take a faerie gate? Calma asked Bran while glaring at his brother.

If you touch, the three of you can infiltrate direct, anywhere in Tír na nÓg, save for Goibhniu's forge. But only you, not the Namhaid.

The word was not familiar, but Calma gathered from the *Sidhe*'s mental images Bran spoke of the *Bás*.

Once in place, you and the charred one can open the way for them, though.

Calma passed that knowledge to his brothers, adding, "Have your minions ready at the threshold. You must summon them the instant you are able."

"That's it?" Dubh looked disgusted, or as much as he was able to with skin like scorched leather. "We all rush in? I'm in awe of your brilliant strategy."

"This is not an invasion. We seek the ashes, nothing more," Calma said. "Your *Bás* distract them. We find the ash and get out. When Mother is back among us, there will be time enough to strip the *Sidhe* Lands bare."

Dubh spat. "You are less than you were. The Calma of old would not have been satisfied with petty thievery. He never would have skulked in behind a diversion."

"I have no death wish!" Calma roared at them. "We are not an army! By ourselves, we fall. With Mother restored, we can unmake them. Just one word. Just 'Danu' is all Carmán need utter thrice to undo all the *Tuatha de Danaan*. If their blessed Mother Goddess never existed, neither did they! And all we need to make it happen is a bit of ash…"

Even Bran went still at his words. There was a fleeting sense of something…denial…disbelief…protest…. It didn't matter; they weren't important. Only one person mattered—beyond himself.

And Carmán…she was proud.

Without speaking, they joined hands over Agnieszka's body while Calma followed the trail to *Tír na nÓg*.

The *Namhaid* were everywhere, it seemed, and this time they weren't holding back, as they had at the Battle of the Knock.

The dagger safely retrieved, Kara and Aí fought their way past Dubh's shields one final time to arrive in *Tír na nÓg* amid an attempt at wholesale slaughter. Strangely, Goibhniu was nowhere to be seen, and neither were the *Fianna*. It could only be that they fought on another front. There were plenty of others doing battle here, though. Kara gasped at the bodies strewn about, mangled and maimed, some all but unrecognizable as men and women. Others clearly were the enemy, gravely wounded and likewise trapped in limbo. All of them were still alive, bound to their agony. None knew death in *Tír na nÓg*.

These only wished they did.

Their cries wrenched her heart; the scent of blood, her stomach. For an instant, Kara froze. She could not bring things into focus or figure out what she should do next. Despite all that had happened, and her training aside, she was a complete amateur at war. She'd gladly act if only she knew what to do.

Aí turned to her, pressing the longer of his swords into her hand. The weight of it was strangely familiar enough so that for a moment, Kara did not move, turning the blade to the light to look at it closer. "Go! Take the dagger and get yerself to the Great Wall. Finish it and we will not have to worry about Bran adding to all this." He gestured with his other blade toward the chaos behind them.

She nodded, but before she could turn and hurry away, he grabbed her, kissing her fiercely.

"I couldn't have ye thinking that other was the best I could do," he murmured as he pushed her away, turning her in the correct direction for her objective.

Good thing he did, because she could have killed him for that distraction. Why now, when she needed her wits unscrambled? She growled and forcibly closed her mind to the scorching memory newly made. At her back, she heard Aí laugh. She'd almost swear she felt his fervor as he engaged the enemy.

Surprisingly, there was nothing to hinder her as she rushed to Goibhniu's Court. Perhaps she was oversensitive, or perhaps there were *Sidhe* out there hiding from the horror, but Kara could swear she heard shuffling footsteps in her wake. There was no time to stop and investigate. The Unraveling was her one and only goal. Until it was complete, there was no room for anything else in her focus. The hilt of the dagger burned in her grip. The Wall drew her unerringly toward it even without Aí's...*helpful* push.

Finally, she reached the doors to the Court. They were partly open. At her back, another scuffling step. Kara stepped into the Hall, her hand on the door; she couldn't resist looking back to see was the sound friend or foe.

Stupid! Granddame Rose skulked down the corridor, moving from shadow to shadow.

In that moment of distraction, Aí's sword was plucked from her hand, and a familiar chill crept over her.

"I see you brought your own toys this time, little girl. You don't mind if I use this one, do you?" Olcas's smile chilled her further, and she had to physically shake off the paralysis gripping her. "I don't have much time, so make it interesting. My brothers are on the way."

"How the hell did you get in here?" she asked, but his only answer was to raise Aí's sword and bring it down again, nearly in slow motion. She parried the blow with the dagger, letting his blade slide down the length of hers and away. Her arms jarred, and she was afraid the dagger would shatter from the impact.

He toyed with her. The son of a bitch toyed with her. For an instant, she was angry before common sense caught up with her.

Let him! He had no clue why she was here and so no reason to stop her. Thanks to the magic of *Tír na nÓg*, he could not kill her, and he had already taught her much about fighting her way past pain. Kara smiled as she realized there was nothing to fear.

Her opponent stumbled, and she had to laugh at the shocked expression on his face.

Kara actually began to enjoy herself. She forgot Rose, forgot the Wall, and the Unraveling and the *Namhaid*. Just for a second, she lost herself in the joy of a well-fought sword engagement. She barely remembered to direct the fight enough to bring her closer to her goal with each crossed blade. A part of her wondered why all his attacks were physical in nature.

"Having fun, little girl? Consider it foreplay," Olcas taunted her, lunging and nearly pricking her arm. Kara gave a vicious twist with the dagger, sending his sword skittering to the side, but not loosening his hold. Reversing her grip, she actually succeeded in catching the back of his hand with the sharp tip of her otherwise blunted dagger.

"You bitch!" His expression grew ugly, whereas before it'd just been nasty. The fight turned serious. She was at the dais, so she fought to hold her ground. Her hand itched with the frantic urge to turn and complete the tracing of Bran's pattern. And yet she fought on. She had no choice. Blow after blow rained down. His blade rang like the fine steel it was, hers clanged like raw iron in comparison. Neither one gave, though she expected it at any moment.

There was a commotion at the door. Kara barely ducked a serious blow, the sleeve of her tunic parting as the tip caught it. She felt the blade just miss her flesh.

"Kara! Don't let him hit you!" Rose cried out, her breath panting. She was closer than she was before. Much closer. Kara gritted her teeth and fought to hold her focus. She couldn't afford to let the old woman distract her. *Please,* she prayed silently, *Please, God, just don't let her get in the way.*

And then Olcas's blade came right for Kara, hard and fast and at an angle she could not hope to deflect. Where she was, positioned by the wall, there was nowhere to dodge. She raised her chin in defiance, waiting for the steel to pierce her chest. It never did.

Crying out in a language Kara didn't know, Granddame Rose took the blow. Olcas—or was it Tony—jerked in reaction, pulling the strike, but not enough. The tip of the blade slid through the elder woman's chest. Her head fell back with a soundless scream as blood welled from her mouth. Olcas dropped the blade as if it burned him, and for a moment, he froze as if his body recognized his victim, though his eyes did not. Snarling with outrage, Kara brought the pommel of the dagger down on the base of his skull. Soundlessly he dropped, unfortunately not falling on his own sword.

A cry choked Kara's throat as she knelt beside the Romani. "It's okay, it's okay. I know it hurts, but they can heal you," she stumbled over the words.

"Stupid girl," Rose moaned no breath behind her words. She shook her head and slapped at Kara's hand, the one still holding Goibhniu's dagger. "Lugh's sword...I'm already done and dying. Finish it, finish it now!"

Horrified, Kara thought Rose asked for the mercy cut, then she realized what the woman meant. *The Unraveling.* The Unraveling must be finished. She could not believe that she'd forgotten.

Briefly, Rose grabbed her hand, "I have seen it...I have seen you banish them for good. Kill one of them...kills them all."

She was fading, and Kara could barely make sense of what she said. Then suddenly, she was gone, her eyes flat and her chest still. Kara was stunned. None died in *Tír na nÓg.* They told her that! And then she realized what the woman had said, or at least one of the things she said: Lugh's sword...the god-killer. Apparently, that one could kill where it wanted, even in the Hall of the *Sidhe.* Standing, her heart heavy, Kara stumbled toward the Wall, dagger raised and ready. It was a reach, but she managed.

There was a sound at the doors behind her, but Kara dare not stop to look. She was nearly done; one final loop of the pattern and Bran was banished for good. *Magic. Here's where one of them strikes me down with magic,* she thought, her body tensing in expectation. The blow did not fall.

"Get your ass off the floor and stop her, you fool!"

Bran. But he was not in time. Kara risked a glance over her shoulder as she drew the dagger over the final inch of pattern. Bran stood in the door, with Olcas's companion, the charred man, standing beside him, a black velvet grave bag in his arms.

"No!" the banished one cried out, the word twisted by his agony as the final thread was severed, and his soul snapped completely from its anchor.

He was too late. Kara smiled, but only briefly as someone yanked her close from behind. There was only one person it could be. She watched on, her jaw tight and her face twisted in a frown, as the charred one grabbed the slumped Bran about the waist and dragged him forward. Kara cursed her stupidity as she felt the world dissolve around her, the void sucking all of them in. The banishing had worked, and Kara was in the hands of the enemy. There were three of them, all with a massive grudge.

Mór Halla had become a combat zone. Aí took in the carnage. Every surface gleamed somewhere with the ruby sheen of blood and few bodies were not dreadfully scored by claw or sword or even teeth, some severe enough to have dropped from the fight, though even those sought to strike when they could. It was like some hellish nightmare out of Dante. Sound warriors fought beside what would have been the mortally wounded, were they not in *Tír na nÓg.* Aí closed down his empathic gift behind thick shields to stave off the onslaught of pain and rage and bloodthirsty malice that saturated the air. Brandishing his sword, he darted into the fray, but that was not the answer to ending this.

For all that's sacred, he broadcast to all those near. *corral them, people, get them close together and bind them with yer magic. Stop reacting and use some strategy!*

Once everyone worked toward that one purpose, it didn't take long. There weren't many of the *Namhaid.* Nor of the *Sidhe,* actually, he now noted. Perhaps, ten of the invaders and eighteen of the *Sidhe.* Odd…were the rest of the Court unaware, off in their own little world, as usual? Or was there more going on? Disturbed by the thought, he turned his gaze back to the prisoners.

One or two *Namhaid* had vanished into the ether before they could be captured, but the rest thrashed and growled within a cell of mage energy. Now what to do with them? Aí shook his head as he wiped the enemy's blood from his blade. As long as they were contained, disposing of them was Goibhniu's problem.

Goibhniu…

Aí stopped one of the *Fianna* organizing the wounded for Miach. "Where's Goibhniu?"

"There were more o' this sort...they grabbed a few o' us. Goibhniu prevented them from disappearing as those others did, but they fled with their prisoners. Goibhniu and the rest o' the *Fianna* went after, leaving us to defend here."

"We didn't have as much luck as ye had here, though we did get our own back," the Smithgod's familiar rumble sounded at Aí's back. "The cursed beasts fled, but empty-handed." He strode forward. Aí pivoted toward him and stepped back out of his way. Goibhniu stopped just at the edge of the containment. His eyes narrowed, and he drew the sword at his side. Quick, so quick, he thrust it forward over and over until each of the *Namhaid* was pierced through the heart.

Spinning away, Goibhniu said not a word as he stalked in the direction of his forge, merely waving a hand behind him. The Namhaid, shield and all, vanished and Aí realized they'd been sent back to the mortal realm to die.

◒

Kara was fairly certain she would never again find pleasure in sweet nothings murmured by her ear.

"Time to play for real," her assailant whispered from behind her as they reappeared elsewhere, and even in the void, she could feel as Olcas drew his tongue the length of her neck and up her face.

"Not friggin' again," she grumbled as the world formed up around her once more. The dagger was still firm in her grip. The moment she felt solid, she lunged forward, twisting her shoulders to break Olcas's grip. The move brought her face to face with the one called Dubh. Up close, she could smell him. Pain and charred flesh blended with the scent of physical pleasure. Kara shuddered with disgust, then realized this close she could hear the possessed man's tortured cries with each breath Dubh took, a faint echo of what would have been screamed aloud had the host control of his own voice.

Raging at the cruelty Carmán's children were capable of, Kara brought the dagger up, blade parallel to the ground, and thrust between those prominent ribs straight into Dubh's half-cooked heart.

Shock and gratitude transformed the stranger's gaze as Dubh's spirit vanished, and his victim slid off her blade and to the ground. Without Dubh's magic to sustain it, the body turning to ash before it even landed. The next shock was hers, as to either side of her, the bodies possessed by Dubh's brothers joined his ashes on the ground. Cautiously, she turned. She was in a basement somewhere, alone. Weary to her very core, her magic barely recharged. Prepared for some sort of attack, Kara approached the bodies. Bran was alive, but catatonic, Tony...frankly, Tony looked mad...as in stark-raving, his body twitched, and his eye showed white all around when they weren't rolling into his head. But at least they were his own eyes, and she could sense nothing of Olcas within him. The difference was jarring.

Kara found she could not leave him, even if she had the energy to leave herself. She had promised to save him. And there was definitely no way she had enough energy to reach them both back to *Tír na nÓg*.

Aí? she called into the ether, desperately willing him to hear her.

For a long time, there was nothing. Reaching out to drag the grave bag into her arms, Kara slumped to the floor some distance away from the bodies, the wall supporting her.

Aí? she tried again. Something stirred in the dark surrounding her, not physically. Something other. Kara drew her thoughts back in an attempt to recharge at least some, waiting only until she could not resist the urge to try again. Her limbs felt heavy as if something sucked the life from her. Sparing the smallest bit of energy, she drew the wild magics to her and shaped them into a shield, which she settled all around her. The draining stopped, and an ominous sense of foreboding grew.

On her fifth try to reach Aí, she was loud enough he heard her.

Where are you?!

*I don't know, it's dark, and damp — * she felt foolish adding it, but in the end she did. *— and I think there's something down here that wants to eat me.*

The weight of the grave bag across her legs, slight as it was, woke a thought in Kara's mind. She did not know what was here with her or what her chances were against it. Best that she return the remains while she could. No need to risk all being lost. Shivers traveled up her spine. She ignored them. Remembering what Aí had told her about sending something to another, with her thoughts, Kara gave him a mental tap to get his attention.

Here... She thought hard at him so that her precious energy would not be wasted as she reached the grave bag out to him. From their connection, she got a sense of confusion, then awe. It was fleeting. Her attention was yanked away by the crushing wrath loosed upon her shields. It bore the faint essence of Olcas and his brothers as if whatever attacked had absorbed their freed souls.

"Shit!" She had just enough time to give a hard shove against her shields, sending the edge shooting out to cover Tony's prone body. She pulled him even closer, laying her body across his for added protection. After that, something let loose several cans of whoop-ass all around them, tearing shelves from the wall and tossing the goods stored on them about the basement with the capricious aim of a poltergeist.

Kara prayed.

When the grave bag landed in Aí's hands out of nowhere, his heart clenched. He handed it off to one of the Bean Fianna, who hurried off to safeguard the remains with those others previously lost. He then turned his senses toward Kara. If she thought there was something with her that meant her harm, he believed her, humbled that she squandered her energy to send at least this much out of harm's way…

Aí turned to the others in the room. The *Fianna* watched him closely. Most bore partially healed claw marks somewhere on their flesh. All wore the hard, intent look of battle-readiness. They'd been attacked in their own home. They and their loved ones brutalized. Their foe retreated tauntingly out of reach…That was more than enough to rally them, but to then find Gypsy Rose, an honored guest, *slain* in their very Hall, and one of their own missing…Goibhniu's warriors wanted retribution.

"I don't understand," Jacko said for yet another time. "You said this couldn't happen. How can she be dead?"

Rose. He spoke of Rose. Aí was more concerned about Kara at the moment. And yet, they needed every warrior willing and ready to fight, including the Romani. So, with extreme patience, Aí explained one more time in the hopes of bringing the focus back to Kara's rescue.

"None may die by normal means in the Land o' Youth, but yer Rose was not killed by normal means. They call Lugh's sword the god-killer. Do ye ken why?"

Jacko glowered and shook his head.

"Because any touch o' the blade, regardless o' how slight, is fatal," Aí told him. "No matter the nature of the one struck, or where, no matter the place they were standing when they caught the blow. Now, ye think ye might focus on saving the one what still can be saved?"

With a grimace, Jacko nodded. Aí knew he was there for only one reason: the possibility that he might have a chance to save his own love. Aí was not above using that.

"There is a chance Kara is not alone, but I can't be sure," he said to the room at large, though the message was aimed at the Romani. "I've tried to go to her…I've tried to bring her to me…All I've managed is to soulspeak her. Something blocks everything else, as bad as hitting an electric fence. Some o' ye have different strengths than I when it comes to this. Who will link with me? I lay the trail, and ye come in behind to force open the way…"

As they began their attempts, the chamber door flew open, slamming against the marble wall hard enough to send wood splinters to the floor. "Jacko! Aí, you must go, you all must go after her," Brid spoke with straining breath. "It's *Carmán*, Kara is facing *Carmán*, and she wants Agnieszka's babe for her host."

On the heels of her pronouncement, a flood of faelings swarmed the room. At the fore were two familiar sprites. Agnieszka's Rex and Beag Scath. There was some debate whom he claimed as his. The latter clutched Kara's violin to his chest.

"Why?"

The question was so faint Kara hardly heard it over the chaos surrounding them. She scrunched down closer over Tony, afraid her shield would give at some point.

"I know what I…I did to ya…so why? Why are ya doing this?"

Kara's breath caught in her chest. Such shame, such torment…such suffering. She almost regretted his return to lucidity. No matter how his body had been used against her, there was no way she could condemn that tormented soul.

"No."

Tony's body flinched beneath her at the sharpness of her response.

"Not *you*, Anthony DeLocosta. *You* only tried to snatch me, once, and you didn't succeed. Compared to everything else, that's nothing." Shocking even herself, she brushed her lips across his temple. "Not you. I know who hurt me and seeing you now, he hurt you even more. Don't help him keep doing it now that he's dead and gone."

"Gone?" It was the barest whisper, but she heard it, now that she knew to listen.

"Destroyed. I'd say gone for good, but there was nothing good about him." She wasn't sure Tony heard her. He just kept repeating the word, as if desperate to believe it, yet not quite able to. Kara was having some problem with that herself.

"Gone forever," she murmured against his ear, over and over, soothing him as she would a child, with the occasional light kiss against his temple and a constant, gentle caress up and down his shoulder. As he stilled beneath her, she reached her thoughts to Aí, desperate for reassurance herself, for some hope her fate would not be the same as Olcas's.

Almost immediately, the *Sidhe* caught the tendril of her thought. *Catch,* he called in a rush, sounding a bit frantic to her. She automatically reared up and away from Tony, not knowing what was being sent to her. The next instant, Quicksilver landed in her arms. She actually laughed; her smile wide, and her heart suddenly light. Maybe her hubris was showing, but she believe she could do anything as long as she had Quicksilver. Already she could feel her energy recharging.

Kara-love, ye must help us open a way. We've tried and we can't get through. His thoughts were tinged with desperation…with fear. There was a pause as if he were trying to compose himself. *Kara, 'tis…*

And things beyond her shields went even wilder until Kara had to wonder if her protections would block a falling ceiling. Tired of sitting there in the dark, waiting for the bogeyman to get them, Kara spent a bit of her newly claimed energy to light up the ceiling as if it were brushed particularly thick with foxfire.

"Oh God," Tony muttered, his tone a bit shrill. "Oh, my God! They were wrong…they were so wrong…" She almost shut it down again the moment she saw Tony's face. He sounded almost lucid, but his eyes still rolled like a frightened colt's.

Kara held the violin to the side and leaned closer, careful to keep the instrument within the shields, but out of the way of being crushed. She turned her head to bring her ear closer to Tony's lips.

"She didn't die…they thought she would die too, but they were wrong. Oh, God." Kara tried to shush him, to calm him down, but he only grew more frantic. "Carmán…Carmán's back, and they've been killed again."

Kara froze. Oh…Shit. She remembered what Arwyn had told them when they'd visited her shop in Dublin. Carmán…the goddess of black magic…unmaking *anything* by saying its name three times…mega-humungous grudge from the last time her sons had been killed in front of her. Not a good combination. And this time…it was all on Kara.

Frankly, given all of that, she was astounded her shield still held. Forcing herself as calm as she could manage, she took Quicksilver from the case and quickly tuned the instrument. *Aí wants a way open?* Kara thought. *Well…no reasonable request denied.*

She brought bow to string and began to play.

⁂

The *Bás* could not sense him, the one responsible. *Calma.* They knew his face, his flat, bone-colored eyes. They knew his scent, they would track him. The one who challenged them for prey. The one who brought down death on their young by riling the ancient enemy. The one who ordered the *Conairt* to toy with that enemy, to draw their attention away, leaving even more of the *Bás* dead upon the ground. The one they would drain dry once they could close with him. They would dart and slash and howl his end. Then, when he was in their grasp, they would whelp their young on him, and he would pay at least in part for what was destroyed. Perhaps even more. His essence was strong. Strong enough for more than one whelping at once, and no harm to the young.

Fixated on their vengeance, the *Bás* reached out their senses until a wisp of scent from their prey brushed over their tongues across the void. As one, the remaining *Conairt* launched their strike, the air and ether trembling with their yips and howls.

⁂

Kara stood now, garnering enough energy to strengthen her shields and press them higher. As music flowed from her strings, a familiar presence wrapped itself around her. Kara had never attempted to put a name to it. Now she couldn't help but recognize Danu coming to her aid. The moment Kara drew her bow across the strings, even more power began to build. She shaped it, guided it, coaxed it as she would have any audience, and in the end, a pipeline formed through the nothing. Kara murmured a thank-you as she focused on her finger work and the angle of her bow slicing across the strings. She nearly lost tune as *Namhaid* boiled through her portal.

No! Do not close it, Lhiannon. We're nearly through!

The Namhaid are here ahead of you, she warned him.

It was hard to say if they fought among themselves or if Carmán took exception to their actions. The Namhaid darted and weaved. Hissing one moment, snatching at Bran's limp form the next. They could not seem to keep their grip. And for some reason, they paid Kara no mind at all.

While they were still struggling to claim their chosen prize, Aí and the *Fianna* joined the fun. The spirit women whirled on them, attack being their preferred defense. Likewise, Carmán made her wrath known, most particularly on those who drifted too close to the far corner of the basement.

Kara did not slack her playing, but she did intentionally drop her focus on the pathway she had formed. Who knew what else might come through? That done, Kara shored up her rescuers, sharing out extra energy as had been done for her.

"Get up," she ordered Tony, nudging him with her toe. "We're in the middle of a battle. Participation is mandatory."

Surprisingly, Tony listened. He came to his feet, his fists raised and ready, glowing with mage energy. He stared at them as if they weren't his. Kara could sympathize. Though her gift had been suddenly revealed, Maggie had helped her adjust; his had been exploited by Olcas, leaving Tony with instincts but little knowledge of a gift he apparently hadn't known he had.

She nudged him to get his attention. "Over there, we need to get over there."

"Why?"

"Because *she* doesn't want us too."

They fought their way across the basement to the corner in question, Kara wielding Quicksilver—and her magic—defensively, while Tony represented quite well with his mage-powered fists. Once there, they discovered a door, freshly battered by Carmán's tantrum. Locked. And shielded. Apparently more someones didn't want anybody in there. Kara began to understand the earlier seemingly undirected violence.

A cry rose behind them followed by the smell of fresh-spilt blood. Looking over her shoulder, Kara spied her Romani friend, Jacko. A claw mark scored him from temple to hairline, and as he struggled to see, the Namhaid darted in en masse, snatching their prize and tearing their own way through the ether.

Frankly, Kara didn't care. It was one less group to fight, and she couldn't really work up any concern for Bran being taken. Yet a sense of urgency hit her. It came from what Kara thought of as Quicksilver's soul. Danu very decidedly insisted that the *Namhaid* be pursued, to the point of feeding images into Kara's brain, glimpses of how the creatures got their young and how they snatched at more and more as their numbers grew.

"Aí," Kara cried out. "The *Namhaid*! You have to go after them! If they get away, no one with a bit of magic will be safe ever again. Not the People, not the elf-kin…" As she spoke, she flashed him the images she'd just been shown. Not all of them were a shock to him. Kara reminded herself he was also Goibhniu's Hound, until recently charged with tracking down the *Namhaids'* victims.

He set his jaw and looked as if he would argue, but Danu exerted herself, swelled into a presence rivaling that of the dark goddess. With a sense of stern resolve, she wrapped her awareness around the warriors like a hen corralling her chicks. In an instant, and with a shocked expression on his face, Aí and his men were gone. Danu seemed to go with them.

Kara gulped, in awe of the power she'd carried so casually all these years. And then the realization struck her: there she and Tony were alone again, with an angry, disembodied goddess.

And they…*Kara* was responsible for the second death of her children.

"The door, Tony…think you can get it open?" With hope, it was a way out of the basement.

The look he gave her was sly, the smile sharkish. His eyes still weren't completely sane as they rolled toward where she pointed. That was the extent of his answer as he turned to the door.

"No," a voice called from near the floor. Kara looked down to find Jacko slumped there, his head slightly weaving. A disturbing amount of blood covered his face.

"Quick, help me up. I will breach the way, you and the boy start slinging that magic."

The ominous feeling returned. Like ten seconds before a lightning strike. Or pending death. Kara's sense of the brothers' spirits grew stronger. How had the evil bastards managed to linger? She reinforced the shields around her and Tony and then settled one around Jacko as well. The effort distracted her, the drain causing her to sway until she adjusted. Something slammed into her from behind, pinning her to the wall. Only quick reflexes kept her violin from being smashed. Tired of it all, Kara scowled and set her lips to whistling, seeing as playing violin was some-what out of the question right now. The magic gathered, and still, she held it until she had what she thought of as a double handful. Closing her eyes, she separated those handfuls into a million little shards, sharp and nasty, and visualized them launching upward. They sliced through Carmán's awareness like a dream, scattering her focus and disrupting the goddess's next attack.

The pressure in the room changed. Kara was free to move, but breathing was twice as difficult in the charged air. She would gladly bear it though, considering the source. Danu had returned to engage Carmán.

As Kara gathered more magic the room gave a massive shudder. Dust filled the already stale air, causing those with bodies to cough. Darting a glance toward their goal, Kara nearly laughed. Having no luck with the door, Jacko had chosen to break through the weakened wall. And then the way was clear…for all of them. Beyond the hole he'd made lay another room. Through the shattered slats, Kara spied a woman's body on a narrow table. The evil in the air surged in reaction. With a shout, Kara threw up a barrier to protect the woman, drawing upon everything she could of what the violin had to offer, in addition to her own mage energy and what she could glean from the wild magics surrounding her. She readied another attack only to find herself pressed hard against the floor, her chest crushed by nothing but air. Really heavy air. Her vision began to grey, and Kara cried out to any and all for help.

And Quicksilver began to play seemingly by herself.

Danu. Danu played her. That would take getting used to.

Grief and anger and a mother's fierceness filled the notes, and Kara felt the weight back off of her chest. Scrambling up, she found herself beside Tony and in a sense, Danu. The three of them formed a net of magic, and when her essence would have turned and fled, they cast it over Carmán, binding her tight. The glow of the magic revealed four distinct essences—three much smaller, faint and tattered in comparison to the fourth. Kara's fear that the brothers lingered was borne out. But it ended now.

Remembering Murna, the hapless *Sidhe* trapped between life and death as a living incubator for *Namhaid* young, Kara closed her eyes and started to sing in the ancient tongue to Quicksilver's melody. Each note gathered even more power to her, until her voice vibrated with the strength of it. And still, she drew the power. Almost too much for her to make her own. She let the song trail away. Breathing deep, she opened her eyes. Looking at that space where the air shimmered most thick, she narrowed her gaze and uttered one word, not three.

"*Burn.*"

And like a ball of marsh gas, the goddess of black magic and the remnants of her sons went up in flames. Kara collapsed to the ground. She would have liked to have claimed it was intentional, but her legs just would not hold her up. A good thing, though, as falling on her ass prevented her from getting a carbon facial. She looked over to find that Tony had crouched with a bit more style, not to mention conscious intent.

Jacko was nowhere in sight.

And then he was, stepping through the makeshift opening beside the still-locked door, the woman Agnieszka cradled in his arms. He flinched away from the sudden heat as the timbers overhead burned along with Carmán and her children. "We should probably get out of here."

Kara heartily agreed, only she was in no shape to reach them anywhere, and Tony didn't know how. She did reach a thought to Maggie, though, finding her still in *Tír na nÓg* with Papa and a good dozen of the *Fianna*, left behind to defend the home-front, as it were. *Please…* was all Kara could manage before exhaustion bore her down into darkness.

Chapter 23

Agnieszka woke in what could only be called a bower, the word *múscailt – awaken –* echoing in her ear. Slowly she sat up and opened her eyes, wondering at her stiffened muscles and the slight rounding of her belly, not much, but noticeably bigger than before.

Across the room, the one called Goibhniu stood at the threshold. "Please, when ye feel ready, join us." And he walked away, gently closing the door behind him.

The distinct urge to say something rude had her pursing her lips. That one had meddled in her life all too much for her to jump at his say, good manners or no. Her heart ached as she recalled a brief moment of awareness in a glade, with Goibhniu telling her to remember. Such a simple word to turn her life upside down. To make her question everything of who she was. He claimed she was one of the…the *Sidhe*. Let him think that. Agnieszka never had been one for labels.

Still, she couldn't remain here, in this bed.

Looking around the room, she noticed another bed, that one holding a young woman dead pale and covered in dust. Another woman Agnieszka didn't recognize tended her.

The sight left Agnieszka feeling empty and alone. She had had enough. Confirming her own person was free of dust or injury and rebraiding her hair, she felt marginally closer to civilized.

Time to rejoin the human race.

And she stepped out of the room. Several people waited there, half of them looking like they'd just come from battle. Again with the dust, and a bit more blood. She swept the group with her gaze. She knew two of them. Agnieszka turned to the young man who she'd first encountered at her own cottage. Back before her life went catawampus. She didn't even know his name, but of the two faces she recognized, his was the one she mistrusted the least.

"Take me home, *now*."

He stepped forward and took her arm. Her skin tingled, and her heart felt a little lighter until she frowned at him. Agnieszka was new to the sensation of magic bending reality. That didn't mean she wasn't learning to recognize it and its effects. "Home," she snapped, "and nothing more."

With a sigh, the Sidhe reached up to an ornate torc around his neck, drawing it down and holding it up in the air like a comic attempt at a circus lion's hoop. Fed up, Agnieszka nearly pulled away. Only, as she watched, the ring expanded, and beyond the rim, she saw the wreckage of her gardens and the damage to her home, Wicklow Cottage. Gasping, she swayed, and only the *Sidhe*'s grip on her arm held her upright.

"I promise, we'll fix it," he murmured. "I promise ye."

"You'll do no such thing," she told him as she yanked her arm away. Slowly, with dignity, she turned her gaze on each person, *Sidhe* or otherwise, within sight. "You'll leave me alone, the lot of you. You'll not meddle in my life. You'll not take from me the bit of comfort I've built for myself. I'll clean up that mess myself, thank you, and be glad to never lay eyes on any of you again."

The moment she said it, a groan drew her attention to what she'd missed before. She may have only recognized two among those there, but she knew a third much better by far. Only she hadn't realized until now, his face was so caked with blood from a vicious slash across his forehead. Jacko was clearly stricken at being included in her decree.

Sniffing sharply, she let it stand, though her heart ached to see how she hurt him.

It is a kindness, she told herself. Though she was touched to find him here, clearly having risked his life for hers, nothing had changed. She was old, he young in comparison. He was bold and vibrant, she timid and staid. Besides, she needed time to understand what had happened, what it meant to be…other. Didn't she? Time to decide if she'd the strength for more heartache. A perverse voice from deep inside, a selfish, annoying voice whispered in her ear: *after a lifetime of being other, a lifetime of heartache, what is a little more?*

She shut the voice down. This discovery of her nature was just one more thing to separate her from her fellow man. Literally, in fact. Where was the kindness in encouraging Jacko, knowing her elven nature would leave her as she was while he grew older, when he died?

Liar, the voice spoke again, faint and far away. *Complain no one wants you then shove them all way…disgraceful.* She laughed bitterly at that, turning her back on all of them to walk through the rabbit hole. Briefly, she glared back, stopping the young man before he could join her on English soil.

Sighing, he shook his head but honored her wish. Before the way closed, he called out to her. "My name is Aí. An ye need help o' any kind, speak it, and I'll come to ye straightway."

As her answer, she turned away. The sensation of the pathway closing made her shiver. It all went right from her thoughts when she caught sight of her gardens again. She nearly went to her knees at the devastation. Flower beds torn up, apple trees literally shredded, scratches marring the stucco walls. When she saw the claw marks on her window, she blanched. God help her…not that he hadn't already; to have come away from that unscathed…. Agnieszka rethought her decision to return here on her own, without even Rex to comfort her fears. She vaguely remembered the siege. The clawing at her window, the glimpses of women not quite normal, voracious and dangerous. Another shiver took her.

Too battered by the memory to face the results, Agnieszka carefully made her way across the dooryard to her back stoop. It was odd to stand there and not have a host of felines vying for her attention. Given the condition of her yard, she didn't want to consider the absence of the cats. Reaching up, she took down the key she kept above the jamb.

Jacko would have railed at her for that.

Agnieszka shut that thought down, turning the key and letting herself inside where only the dust evidenced her absence. Or so she'd thought, until she turned and saw an overturned chair at her kitchen table, a dark brown stain beside it that she did not care to examine closer.

It was too much. All of it was too much.

Closing the kitchen door behind her, Agnieszka headed to her room to retire. Along the way, she reached above each doorframe, and then the windows. Each time her fingertips brushed against the pennies Jacko had insisted on putting there, she relaxed a bit more. To defend her against evil, he'd said. Her cynical laugh was abrasive against her own ears.

Right now, to her, everything was evil. For a little while, she just wanted the world and all its little mysteries to go away. Determined to lose herself in the common act of preparing for bed, Agnieszka methodically went through her usual routine: Brushed her hair and rebraided it. Cleaned her face and teeth. Shed her clothes and drew a nightdress over her head, letting it fall in soft folds to her feet. It helped. Some.

Drawing down the bedspread, she slid between the sheets. Out of long habit, her hand slid beneath the pillow, her fingers entwining in silken fabric, a jarring contrast to her simple cotton pillowcase. Slowly, she drew it out. And she remembered. Everything. Cian and his love. Their brief moments in each other's arms. The horror of those memories being stripped away. The suspicions and censure from the Sisters after. Agnieszka ran a hand down her body to her rounded belly. Remembered the outrageous claims of her former doctor, and the more recent reassurance from the one called Goibhniu that it was so. She didn't know what to do. Her quiet life here was over after all. Could she stand to leave everything she knew? Yet, what choice did she have? Who would believe she was pregnant at sixty? Who would believe conception had occurred forty-four years after the act was consummated? No one. Even were she fool enough to share those details. Yet if she stayed, everyone would wonder. At the very least, she would have to leave until the child was born. The thought frightened her. Not just the thought of going into the unknown, but the fact that anywhere she went, there would be questions, speculation. The threat of reporters hoping to build a career on a miracle.

What a nightmare.

And yet, such joy. A piece of Cian to cherish. A child to love.

Family.

That realization was enough to soothe her. The wonder of it followed her into sleep, where Cian cradled her in his arms one last time.

✦

A flood of adrenaline sent Kara jerking upright. Immediately, she reached for the mage energy around her, frantic with the need to defend, only to have her vision grey out and her body sway with the deepest exhaustion she'd ever experienced.

"Shhh…lie back down, young lady," her mother's voice murmured. "Right back down… and no more of that."

Kara drew a broken breath, blinking open her eyes, which were determined to close. When she went to speak, she found she didn't have the energy. Another burst of adrenaline, much reduced from the last. More eye blinking.

"Just stop it." Mathair frowned. "You need rest."

Panic made it hard to breathe. Kara had the overwhelming feeling there was something she had to do.

It must have shown in her expression because Mathair leaned over and kissed her brow, a look of such pride on her face. "Relax," she murmured while she pressed Kara back down onto the pillow. "You've already saved the world…not to mention a Romani man, and some woman I'm told is from England. Everyone's safe. We're all in *Tír na nÓg*, and nothing important is going to happen until you've woken up. I promise."

Relief washed through Kara, stealing what little energy she'd mustered. It wasn't a dream. Olcas and his infernal family were no more. No longer driven to rise, Kara did not resist as her mother tucked the blankets firmly around her. It felt bizarrely mundane and absolutely wonderful.

"Now sleep and get your energy back, please," Mathair said. "I'm told you nearly drained yourself dry…"

Kara didn't find that hard to believe. She felt like she could sleep several days straight without even trying. With a shallow sigh all she could manage, Kara stopped fighting to keep her eyelids open. She let Mathair's light chatter sooth her as her mother kissed her brow and again straightened the blankets. "No more of that! You scared the hell out of me."

In the comfort of her mother's care, Kara drifted back to sleep.

✦

It took courage to knock on Agnieszka's door. Jacko stood there for a long time. Long enough that the *Fianna* on guard peered out at him from the distant branches of one of the remaining gnarled apple trees. Jacko grimaced and shooed her back. He wasn't at all sure of his own reception. Were Agnieszka to spot the elven warrior, Jacko knew without a doubt they'd both be sent on their way. Not that his purpose for being here wasn't enough to get him booted all on his own. She wouldn't be happy when she learned he was here at Goibhniu's bequest.

In the distance, a jaybird mocked Jacko. As well it might. He'd been standing there ten minutes already. Before he could bring himself to knock, there was a solid thud from the region of his feet. Startled, he looked down to find Rex there. The sprite glared up at him and thumped the door again. From inside the sound of brisk footsteps and muttering could be heard. Rex smirked and with a shimmy resumed the appearance of a cat, which seemed his preferred form. Jacko barely had time to look up again when Agnieszka snatched open the door.

"What the bloody hell is this?" Her eyes snapped with anger. "I've been back all of two days, and I've had more company than I've had since I moved in. Everyone from the neighbors to the Mother Superior…and your bloody *Sidhe* as well. Snooping and lurking in my orchard. And don't bother to shake your head no, I feel them. All the time, watching me…"

He hadn't been about to shake anything but now did not seem the time to argue. Jacko remained silent as Agnieszka went on.

"It's enough to send me screaming mad into the night without a lantern! For the first sixty years of my life, not a soul wanted me." —again, not true, he wanted to say—"Now that I'm done with the lot of you, I can't get anyone to leave me alone!"

Jacko winced, then looked down, lest Agnieszka see his amusement at her uncharacteristic show of temper. Her gaze must have followed his because her anger trailed away at the sight of Rex sitting at Jacko's feet. Her expression softened.

"Get in here, you infuriating man. And bring my cat while you're at it."

She needn't have added that last. Before the words were out of her mouth, the furry bugger darted in to press against her leg. She immediately bent and scooped him up. Jacko frowned. He wasn't comfortable being jealous of a cat…or what seemed like one. Rex's purrs rattled Jacko's ears, but the joy softening the shadows that clung to Agnieszka's expression almost made up for the discomfort.

"Where have you been?" she murmured as she ruffled the 'cat's' fur. That rankled a bit, but perhaps it was to Jacko's advantage. Rex held her attention, such that she did not seem to notice as Jacko moved across the threshold to stand before her. Not until his hands gently but firmly gripped her shoulders, turning her toward him.

Grumbling, Rex leapt down and out of harm's way.

Agnieszka gasped, her lips open, and Jacko's desire broke loose from where he'd caged it for so long. With his gaze, he transfixed her, leaving her no time to protest.

And then he kissed her.

Not hard. Not rough, but likewise not a gentle brushing of the lips. He kissed her like a man with intentions. When he released her, she breathed a trembling sigh as he stepped back. Jacko could empathize. He was a bit unsteady himself, experiencing a strange mix of bemusement and defiance shot through with sheer joy. She had resisted his overtures for so long, yet now her hand rose as if she would reach for him…to draw him back. Or maybe he'd wanted her touch so bad he imagined it. With his gaze, he challenged her to doubt him now. To send him away.

She couldn't doubt him anymore. Sending him away was another matter.

Jacko held his breath as Agnieszka took a step forward to close the gap again. Part of him braced for a slap, but instead, her hand came to rest on his shoulders and then moved to his forehead, where her gentle fingers traced his new scar.

"I told them to leave me that," he said, quite solemn. "At the time, it was all I had left to remember you by."

Her face twisted in an incredulous look, but he told her with his eyes he was completely sincere. With a huff, she tugged him down and brushed his lips with a second, more tentative kiss. No more than a bump of her lips against his. He could tell the experience was new and a bit frightening for her. It was a sharp reminder to him how solitary her life had been. He wanted to change that. The chance had nearly been stolen from him, as had she. The pain of that reminder rattled his breath. His arms came around in a loose embrace, and he drew her against him, his body shaking. Not with desire — though she surely felt the evidence of that well enough — but with silent sobs, his tears wetting her head. He couldn't hold it in. He'd come so close to never even seeing her again. Agnieszka tensed as his grip periodically tightened in spasms, but she didn't pull back. She just stood there holding him while he cried, until a brush of fur twining about their ankles.

Jacko looked down and met Rex's gaze. The sprite gave a little mew, twined their legs once more, then broke away to the parlor, where he perched on the sofa, watching them, his expression clearly saying, "well, come on…"

Agnieszka did pull away then, the moment broken. Jacko wanted to curse. Briefly, when she stepped back, his grip tightened before he got control of himself and forced his arms down. She smiled up at him, slight but sure, and reached for his hand. Bemusement took the forefront in Jacko's gaze when she tugged him toward the parlor.

"Let's sit, shall we?" she asked, the words a bit breathy. She looked uncertain, though he could see she tried not to.

He gave a half-smile in reply, some of the tension going out of him. "Anything you like, *camlo*."

"What?" she asked, understandably unfamiliar with the word.

His eyes crinkled as his smile came out full. "Lovely one," he answered as he gently pressed her hand with kisses. "*Camlo* is 'lovely one' in Romani. *Camlo* is you." He gazed at her with unabashed desire.

Agnieszka blushed and again drew him closer to the sofa, settling herself properly on the cushion: back straight, as she'd been long-ago taught, knees together and ankles slightly to the side.

She needn't have bothered.

Jacko sat close beside her and immediately drew her across his thighs and into his arms. The moment he had her on his lap, Rex leapt up beside them and sprawled the length of the remaining cushions.

"I need to hold you," Jacko murmured, his voice still rough with tears. "Just hold you and know you're safe. You were gone too quickly for it to sink in."

Agnieszka said nothing but did slide her arm around his waist. He closed his eyes, in awe of the sensation as she actually relaxed against him. They sat there without speaking, drawing comfort from one another well into the twilight, their hands occasionally wandering, their lips brushing, but nothing more. When true dark settled around them, he pressed his face against her neck and began to speak hushed, taut words.

"I'm sorry. I am so sorry you were left on your own, that I wasn't there to protect you." He drew a shuddering breath. "I'm sorry I almost lost you before I made you see what you mean to me." His hand came to rest on the mound of her belly. "I'm sorry this isn't mine…and never could be."

It was the first either of them mentioned her true nature….or her gravid state.

"You're barely a chick from the egg, you know…by *Sidhe* reckoning," he whispered in her ear. "By rights, I'm robbing the cradle twice over."

Agnieszka gave a startled laugh, then shivered and nestled closer against his chest. "Where do we go from here?" she asked.

Jacko groaned.

I wanted more time, he thought wistfully as he looked up at her. This close, he could see her gleaming eyes, her brilliant white hair, and little more. Jacko felt the sharp edge of guilt. He had to look away as he confessed. "I'm here for myself because I needed to see you, but I do bear a message from another…a request."

She set herself slightly back from him, her face settling in stern lines. "Spill it."

"Goibhniu says to tell you they honor your desire to remain apart, but he asks that you come take part in a ceremony. He called it the Welcoming…"

Agnieszka jerked at the mention of Goibhniu. Understandable. Aí had told Jacko how the Smithgod had separated her from her first love, Cian, and had robbed her of her memories of their time together. It had been necessary. She was meant to be hidden, separate from her race as a safeguard against another genocide. Then things had gone wrong. Jacko pushed those thoughts aside, not wanting to think of her with another, though the evidence rested beneath his hand.

"Why? Why does he want me there?" she interrupted his thoughts, practically spitting the words.

"To honor the departed…and to cleanse your child's soul."

"To cleanse my child's soul?!" Agnieszka scowled, her earlier outrage rekindled. "It isn't even born yet, it's innocent as can be."

"Now, now…" Jacko tried to sooth her. "No one is saying otherwise. The ceremony's for cleansing memories, not sins, if I understand rightly. Will you consider it, please? My friend, Brid, tells me it's important."

Her scowl deepened in confusion at his mention of Brid. "Why did they send you…why did *you* agree?"

He reached up and held her head still, the better to find her lips with his. "Because I needed to see you, and playing messenger got me here much, *much* quicker than if I came here on my own."

She shook her head in exasperation, apparently unable to argue in light of his honest confession. Extracting herself from his lap, she tried to draw Jacko to his feet. He resisted. The hurt and uncertainty in her expression was like a needle in his chest. It was a look he never wanted to see on her, let alone cause, but there was one more thing to say, and it was best said now before she had a chance to distance herself as he expected she would once the lights were on.

"Do you trust me?"

She looked wary, but she nodded slowly.

"You need to go. You need to take part in the ceremony. For you, for your child…not for any other reason."

A small frown bowed her lips. She held his gaze a moment, then looked down. It was too dark to tell if she blushed. He suspected she did. Slowly, gently, he ran his fingers up her arm, unable to resist the soft, smooth skin. "Please?"

Rather than answer, she trembled at his touch, her gaze deep and dark. This time he did not resist as she drew him to his feet. He was too busy holding his breath in hope.

"We'll talk about it in the morning," she told him and tugged him toward what he knew was her room.

Maggie leaned against the arch set in the wall, a black velvet bag cradled in her arms. Behind her lay Goibhniu's garden, before her lay the path to the meadow where the rest of the Daoine Maithé gathered for the rebirth celebration. She closed her eyes against the sight, then drew a deep breath and exhaled slowly, willing the night's peace to enter her heart. It was no simple thing to go from the somber deed of the Unraveling, just days gone by, to the ebullience of the Welcoming, a ceremony she'd witnessed but once, long, long ago.

As one with cause to both mourn and rejoice, it was particularly difficult to reconcile the two.

Warring memories fought for prominence as she clutched her lover's ashes tight: Demne's face glistening with the sheen of sweat as they shared passion; then that selfsame face spattered with his own lifeblood, pallid beneath, as he died upon her rooftop. Closing her eyes and focusing with all her will, Maggie forced away the latter memory. The murmur of others coming out from the Hall and moving past her intruded as the grim image again came to the fore. There was no evading it. It was nearly time for the *Sidhe* Host to gather beneath the stars for the Welcoming, a ceremony also of remembering and letting go. Maggie's shoulders tensed, along with her jaw. She forced herself to relax and rested her palms against her belly.

The child within was not Demne, but it was his gift to her and would bear his soul. It was not always so that the lover of the fallen gave birth to the child to come. No, the soul was drawn to the Bean…woman with the strongest bond to the one who had passed on, regardless of the nature of that bond. Maggie, however, could feel the echo of her mate's spirit—the sensation bittersweet as it faded day by day. The child would not be born until the soul was cleansed of his essence, his experiences, and then Demne would be no more than a memory. That was the main reason for the ceremony, to aid the soul along.

With a resigned sigh, Maggie breathed deep of the evening air, emptying her thoughts as best she could and letting her senses be soothed by the scents of night-blooming jasmine and rich loam from the nearby garden. She continued to breath slow, steady, and deep, willing herself to relax, until her head dropped forward and her fingers tingled. Then, with care not to dwell on it, Maggie tucked her final memory of Demne away and drew out all those that had come before, let herself feel the hope and joy and even the distrust that marked their first hours. With an exhale, she stepped on the path and joined those trekking to the meadow where they would all rejoice the coming children.

"Cliodna!" The hail rose from those already celebrating before the formal ceremony began. Two *Sidhe* bearing the insignia of Goibhniu's Hounds came forward to escort her to her place. They waited respectfully at the edge of the clearing. Maggie nearly turned and fled. As one of the blessed, she'd be made much of this night, something she was not sure she could handle.

"Would ye deny them, *leanbh*?" Smithgod rumbled at her back. The irony of being called child was not lost on her. "This is not what he would want. Where is the joy he gifted you? Was it so weak it cannot outshine the sorrow? Is it so easily cast aside?"

Tension and guilt tightened Maggie's jaw once more as she met Goibhniu's stern, but understanding gaze. She grimaced and sloughed off her tension, absorbing the serenity that overfilled the Smithgod's spirit, brushing against her as if he weren't several strides away, just coming through the verdant undergrowth sheltering the clearing.

"What can I say?" she said. "A couple centuries o' living human is hard to shake." Though she made light, neither of them was fooled. The *Daoine Maithé* bid welcome to returning souls this night, but for Cliodna and others like her who were close to those lost, this was the last farewell, formal, public, final.

"Our souls were not given such years for looking back on heartache."

"Indeed." Maggie nodded, her gaze far off and her expression considering. "I suspect my soul will need reminding once the night is done." She squared her shoulders and held out her hand, her smile ghosted by sadness, her eyes bright. "Shall we?"

Goibhniu frowned.

Maggie stared him right back, daring to capture his eye and hold it as she spoke low, so only he could hear. "I understand, I accept, and I will celebrate right along with the rest o' my blood. But expecting me not to mourn while I do so is rather dim o' ye, don't ye think?"

The Smithgod gave her a wry smile in response, his eyes soft with compassion. Without a word, he took her hand, drawing her forward into the clearing, forcing steps she'd not been able to make, no matter her blunt words.

As they left the brush, the honor guard took their place before them. With each step, faint mists swirled about their feet, clinging and climbing, only to whip away like banners on the night breeze. The promise of colors threaded the fog like unformed images…like rainbows flirting with the clouds on a moist morning, only no radiance from above teased out the tones. The deeper Maggie moved into the clearing, the denser the mists grew, until her fellow *Sidhe* waded through it, causing swirls and eddies reminiscent of surf on the shore.

Maggie drew another steadying breath. The mingled scents of night flowers, tasty delicacies, and honey wine wafting through the dusk brought a smile to her lips as she called out greetings to those who waved hello. She found comfort in those familiar faces seeded among the gathered: Urias and Miach lounged beneath a willow on the far edge of the clearing, deep in discussion; Aí wandered from cluster to cluster, chatting with those waiting, while Manannan Mac Lir—god of the sea and her former liege—held informal court beside a spring-fed pool just off-center of the clearing. All of this gave Maggie no pause. Only when she spied Kara amidst the *Sidhe Fianna*—Quicksilver angled across her back—did her step falter. The girl still looked a bit faded, as if she hadn't gained back her full strength yet, but that wasn't what shocked Maggie.

Never, as far as she knew, had a mortal been allowed to witness the Welcoming, a most sacred and private ceremony. It was something of a shock that the spirit of the glade itself had not barred one not of the Kin, no matter how great her deeds on the People's behalf or the level of fae blood in her veins. A quick glance around the clearing confirmed that no other humans were present; not Kara's parents, not the Rom, not the doctor. Even the faelings were absent. Yet, here was Kara.

Maggie wasn't sure how to feel about that. The sight of the girl was a shock, but at the same time, fitting. After Kara's part in the Unraveling and all that followed it, Maggie would have expected more reaction to her presence, but none of the *Sidhe* seemed to take note...or perhaps Kara's informal honor guard quelled any reaction, positive or negative. As if to mock Maggie's doubts, pleasant laughter rose from a group near the girl. Maggie looked to the Smithgod, her brow furrowed in confusion. There was a considering expression on his face as he noted the girl as well, then Goibhniu nodded, an encouraging smile upon his lips. He gave Maggie's fingers a gentle squeeze before releasing them. Lightly pushing her onward, he then settled upon a moss-covered boulder on the fringes of the gathering. This was not his ceremony; he would witness, not lead.

Now Maggie...her place was front and center among the...blessed. She continued on toward the cluster of seven women nearest the heart of the clearing. As she passed it, her eyes caught on an open stone cairn. The cavity would soon be filled with her black velvet bag—and those of the others—once the ceremony was complete. Her heart wailed at the stark reminder of her loss.

She tore her gaze away and anchored it on the blessed. Never in anyone's memory, or the whole of their recorded history, had there ever been so many at once. She shuddered as the thought occurred that, in truth, there should be at least twice their number waiting for her to join them. They had rescued Agnieszka from the Cursed One, and the Hounds had liberated five of the *Namhaid's* victims before their souls were consumed, but beyond that...who knew how many others had been taken, before the recent battle, during, and after? Maggie raised a quick prayer for the safe return of all those souls and then continued on.

The women before her stood tall and regal amidst the rising mists, their bodies appearing no more than silhouettes, their faces floating above the vapors, pale and glowing. Peaceful expressions betrayed none of their internal turmoil; only their eyes revealed the maelstrom of emotions, both high and low, colliding within them.

Each held a velvet bag containing the dust of those whose souls they bore.

Maggie echoed their unvoiced cries, the mournful wail of the lost heart at odds with the joyful song of the blessed womb. With a respectful bow, she stepped past the Hounds and took her place among the blessed, standing beside Agnieszka, who looked uncertain. In Maggie's wake, the cresting mists roiled in to enfold those assembled, swirling and dancing and caressing Danu's Children in a frolic that called to her mind many a display of Beag Scath's delight from their years across the Pond.

In the protection of the shrouding mists, cut off from the direct view of those watching on, the women joined in a group embrace as only kindred souls could, hearts and hands and spirits completely entwined. One arm clutched their burdens while the other draped the shoulder of the sister beside them. As they did so, all sound of chatter in the glade beyond the mists faded into silence. Tranquility engulfed them, and it was as if the Mother Goddess herself wrapped them in her arms, brushing the barest of kisses across each brow. The burden of their heartache lessened.

"Blessed Danu!" The invocation rose unbidden from every throat, echoed beyond the mists by those waiting to witness the Welcoming. Hands falling to their sides, the blessed spread to form a circle in the confines of the vapor. As one, they raised the bundles with both arms, and the mists came alive with the colors only hinted at before.

Cliodna's head fell back—the part of her that was "Maggie" had no place in this sacred round—and all sense of her sisters faded until she stood alone before the memory of her beloved.

Images of those lost formed upon the mists.

⚘

For the first time in days, Kara felt the desire to keep her eyes open. Better yet, she felt capable. Rising from her bed, she dressed with just a bit of weariness lingering to slow her down. Not understanding the urge, but glad to comply, she took out Quicksilver and slipped the strap over her head so the case hung across her back. She then went out into the public room, looking for something to eat, and perhaps someone to tell her what she missed.

There was no one there at all. But there was a bowl of fruit on the table. Kara grabbed something that resembled a purple apple but tasted like vaguely like both cherry and mango.

On impulse, she went out into the garden, figuring to spend some time in the sun. But as she neared the bench that was her goal, her feet refused to stop, carrying her along the path leading out into the greater wilderness surrounding *Mór Halla*. Kara didn't question it. She'd learned not to. Eventually, she heard chatter and laughter and followed the sound, absorbing a bit more energy with each step closer, revitalized by the merriment and occasional singing. It was the sound of celebration, though there was a solemn air about it as well, faint, but unmistakable.

When she stepped into the clearing, one she'd never been to before, she discovered what appeared to be every *Sidhe* in *Tír na nÓg* in attendance. They were more relaxed than she had ever seen them, infused with a joy that left her both shaken and smiling. A few cast her odd glances, but most did not seem to notice her, or surely they would have protested. That gave Kara the confidence to continue, moving across the glade through swirling mists to stand among the *Sidhe Fianna*. She couldn't see Maggie anywhere, but there were familiar faces all around, so Kara was comfortable enough to relax. The longer she was there, the more energized she felt until there was nothing left of her earlier weariness.

With the energy came a revival of her curiosity. She wanted to ask what was going on, only she didn't want to draw attention to her differences, so she remained quiet and watched, simply enjoying being among others, and not worrying that danger might descend upon them at any moment. At some point, Maggie would turn up. Kara could ask then.

As twilight slid to night, darkness cloaked the glade. All around them, the mists took on a magical glow. All eyes turned toward the center, drawn by the pillar of vapor now suddenly residing there. Kara gasped at the sight. It was both solid and ethereal all at once. Broad and high, it reached toward the heavens, billowing and swirling, yet never losing cohesion.

The witnesses moved forward until they clustered in a tight circle about the cloud, several yards out from the surface, but pressed close together. They stood there, still silent until suddenly all heads lifted as one and eyes locked forward. Like a movie, images began to form, only nothing as mundane as that, for even with the "magic" at their disposal, Hollywood could never have managed such a thing as Kara saw.

The echoes of a lifetime took shape, then faded one after another.

"*Neasa...*" the crowd murmured, including Kara, though she didn't even know the *Sidhe* whose face was most upon the vapor. Around the central image, smaller, fainter glimpses appeared, flashing in and out, some almost identical, but for subtle shifts Kara almost didn't notice, as if seen from another perspective, through the filter of another set of eyes. Each glimpse of that long life bore with it feelings, some intense and gripping, others warm and gentle. Though none were as sharp as those felt first hand, the sensation was unsettling.

With every memory shared, the essence that was Neasa faded until all but gone. Kara was left trembling, oddly bereft. Though she'd never met her, this woman was no longer a stranger.

Things stilled a moment and only the faintest of colors danced upon the column with no forms shaped by them. Then, another name was whispered, and another. The name Cian was familiar, his face less so, though Kara knew he'd fallen in her defense. The order of memories appeared jumbled, though in most cases, the final image was the ending of their lives. That part was most difficult to bear.

When Murna's name was spoken, Kara found herself both fearful and fascinated by this woman she had known only after death. Each set of memories formed up. Some pleasant. Some not. Though raking breaths heaved her chest and her eyes stung, Kara watched, growing tenser with each display. It was a jolt to her when, in the final image, she recognized herself from a jumble of perspectives as she cleansed the Temple and freed Murna's soul.

The quiet serenity of the ritual was disrupted as all turned to look on her. It was difficult to read their expressions. To be truthful, she didn't want to. Kara would have fled the sudden regard, only to discover her friends gathered around her, shoring her up. Though she hadn't realized, their presence was a comfort.

To her right, Miach watched her closely, his expression concerned.

"What…what was that?" she asked in hushed tones, staving off tears. Even to her own ears, she sounded strained. "What just happened?"

The Welcoming, lhiannon, he answered her in her thoughts, using a word she now knew meant "sweetheart." * 'Tis as much about farewells as greetings.*

Like that tells me anything, she thought back with annoyance, a little uncomfortable with the endearment and still not completely used to soul-speaking…or cryptic responses.

The healer's eyes briefly danced with silent laughter. *Our souls must be cleansed before they can return. Left to themselves, this takes longer, so…the Welcoming, where all Kin gather to help the souls lost to shed the memories of a life now past, speeding them on to the one yet to come.*

So…each image…. Her mind balked at continuing with such a fantastical concept.

Miach smiled. *…a memory of the lost from someone watching on. As each point is remembered, the soul strips it away.*

The concept was so foreign to her, but the premise itself made sense, as Miach explained it. Deep within, Kara experienced a feeling of rightness. Now that she understood, she was less shaken by the experience, even her unexpected part in it. She smiled her thanks.

Before she could ask anything more, the crowd shifted again and then went taut. They seemed different this time, more reverent.

"Demne…" they whispered, and Kara's head whipped around, her eyes widening and her body trembling anew. Again she shuddered. She now knew where Maggie was.

Kara had not known Demne long, but he too had died for her, on the roof of Maggie's pawnshop, standing with the other *Sidhe* to safeguard her from Olcas. After Murna, she was not sure she could bear what was to come. The memories of a long life abruptly ended…the image of his death. Beside her, to either side, her friends reached their arms around her and shored her up as they bid farewell and welcome to their friend. She trembled and wanted to pull away, to flee. At her back, there was sudden warmth, and her ears strained for the almost heard notes of a violin as a familiar presence slid between her and dread.

It was like watching fragments of a movie…the bits left on the cutting room floor scooped up and patched together any which way. Other than recognizing Demne, most of them meant nothing to Kara, but every so often, a flash of something familiar kicked her in the gut. She drew a sharp breath and felt the world fade around her upon recognizing memories of her own projected for all to see. Demne handing her a cup of restorative tea after Tony's first attempt at abducting her…the time he drove her and Papa home when she'd first learned magic and he'd explained to her what iron truly meant to the *Sidhe*, and how they came to bear their young. There was a flash of him behind the wheel of Mathair's car, face fierce and ready for battle as he rushed them all to the safety of Yesterday's Dreams, weaving the New York traffic like a pro. Very little about her time knowing Demne had been pleasant, yet as she closed her eyes against the darker memories, she still saw his smile clearly. When she opened them, she gasped again. Projected on the column of mist were rapid-fire glimpses of Demne's smiling face, his grin, his passion-filled eyes against a backdrop familiar enough that Kara glanced away blushing. The echo of Demne's joy washed over the glade and those gathered there.

Kara's shock was carried by those around her when suddenly those memories were followed by Demne as a youth, and then a child. Why this should startle anyone, she did not know until it occurred to her that Demne had born that name for much longer than most among the *Tuatha de Danaan* could claim their own. Who among them was older still? Goibhniu, perhaps? Except Kara recognized the Smithgod—much, much younger—among those ancient flashes of memory…He would not have been seen had they come from his remembering. Kara looked around, confused, somewhat uneasy at the degree of awe upon the *Sidhe* faces, though it echoed what she felt herself. When she looked back only one image remained upon the column: a babe in a mother's arms.

The company cried out, and all went to their knees.

"Sweet Danu!" Miach uttered beside Kara in a breathless voice, as he reached up and tugged her down hard enough to bruise her. Even had she not already known what was before her, Kara would have sensed that his words were not meant as an idle oath. But having grown up with Quicksilver and now knowing the soul within, she could only nod in agreement. The glade remained hushed as the final memory faded. With it, the mists dispersed, revealing the blessed…and something more.

For just a moment, nine stood within the circle, where only eight had stood before.

Goibhniu was waiting for Kara as she left the glade.

"It's more than been made clear to me that yer by nature more *Sidhe* than mortal, lass. However that may be, and whatever ye chose to do from here, we'd like to honor ye as one o' our own, make clear for all and sundry, as it were, that ye'll always have a place among us, an ye want to claim it."

Still shaken from the ceremony, Kara just stared at him, not quite comprehending.

"Aye or no?" He asked more precisely. His eyes crinkled in amusement, though the rest of his expression remained serious and dignified.

Kara blinked, then widened her eyes as she realized what he'd said. "Oh…*oh*…more than a few members of your Court are going to have kittens over that." She grinned at the thought. "Sure, I'd love to."

Goibhniu managed not to laugh aloud, though her head rattled with his soulspoken chuckles. "When the last o' this mess is sorted out, we'll have a Naming, I promise ye."

Closure

Kara lounged beneath the willows lining Goibhniu's private garden, her attention on a nearby cluster of flowers. They bobbed and dipped from time to time, and then suddenly thrashed, before falling still again, releasing a fresh waft of perfume on the air. On occasion, Beag Scath's grinning face poked through, or Kara's cat, Pixie, pounced from the shelter of the bush, pinning dust motes Kara hoped were nothing more. The blossoms and the guests both seemed undisturbed by the antics. Those watching even laughed, at points luring the little ones out with a tidbit or two. Other faelings frolicked in the garden, but only Beag Scath was bold enough to do so openly. More an aspect of his nature, than from any realization that he was the day's hero several times over. Kara had to laugh at the scamp.

This was a private celebration for Kara, her family, the *Fianna*, and of course, Goibhniu. They had shared a simple meal laid before them picnic-style, and now they spoke among themselves in a comfortable camaraderie. Missing from their number were Jacko and Agnieszka, who still stubbornly insisted on keeping separate, and Uncle Arn, who struggled with the changes in both his life and his perception of the world.

Somberly, Kara let her gaze trail over each of those that were there. Thanks to Goibhniu's healing skills, few bore scars. On the outside, anyway. But each of them had changed in some fundamental way. Mathair had gained strength and serenity, Papa, health and peace. Maggie glowed with joy for her coming child, and Aí burned for a wholly different reason. Kara took pleasure in her friend and mentor's happiness but shied away from the other. Goibhniu was Goibhniu, and though she could not be certain, she thought she saw a lessening of his heartache. It was the best that could be expected. Nothing could completely wipe away a child's betrayal of a parent.

Though unspoken, this was also to be farewell. Urias was going back to New York to resume his duties there, as were several other of the *Sidhe*, and the mortals presumably were returning as well. Kara had not decided what she would do.

"Are ya sure they're gone?"

Kara jumped at the sudden question. Uncle Arn stood in the archway leading away from the garden, out to the wilder aspects of *Tír na nÓg*.

Arn stared intently at Goibhniu as he asked again, "Are they definitely gone?"

With a solemn expression on his face, Goibhniu turned to answer. "Carmán and her spawn? Yes…The *Namhaid*? We hope so, and we've done our best to make it so, but I cannot in good conscience guarantee. My Hounds went hunting them and killed what they could find, but the creatures are blasted good at hiding. We'll all o' us have to remain vigilant for any sign they're about, rebuilding their numbers."

A tic pulsed in Arn's jaw, and his scowl deepened. "That Earl Gerard that Patrick told me about, these are the types of things he'll come to fight, right?"

Goibhniu nodded.

Arn's expression sharpened, his eyes overflowing with determination. "I'm not going back." As if to punctuate his statement, Arn thrust his jaw forward, daring any to deny him.

Papa came to his feet, Mathair with him. For once, it was her father who seemed distraught, at a loss for how to make things right, while her mother's expression was anything but shocked. Gently she slid her arm around Papa, who seemed unaware he needed the support.

"But, Arn…"

Her father's best friend silenced him with a tormented look.

"I'm no longer a healer. My heart's too broken, my hands too bloody. The only things I claimed as my own in life were my calling as a doctor and my Lynn. Now all of that is gone, and I have no purpose." His voice cracked on that last. He ignored it as he raised his hands and splayed his twelve fingers wide, turning back toward Goibhniu as he did so. "But if you'll have me, I'll gladly be a part of the cure for a different ill. I'll be your Miller's Son." His eyes held the ghost of his former passion. "What are the words for that in your language?"

"Mac Muilleoir," Goibhniu answered.

"Then that's what you should all call me, 'cause Arnold Barnert's dead."

Everything about his demeanor supported the oath he spoke with those words.

In response, there was a sound in the air like steel being unsheathed, followed by a flash of bright light. When both faded, Grandda stood in the midst of them resplendent in garments befitting of a proud old clan. Murmurs rose among the *Fianna*, drowning out three mortal gasps.

Arn gathered his composure quicker than either of her parents. Mathair looked drawn and pale, Papa stricken. Arn merely stood straight and proud as Grandda crossed the hall to stand before him.

"I, Conall O'Keefe, steward to Gerald, the Wizard Earl, accept Mac Muilleoir's pledge to service, in proxy to my laird."

He reached out and laid his hand on Arn's shoulder. In another flash, they both were gone.

"Well…there went our reason for going back," Papa said in a quiet voice as Mathair leaned her head against his chest in clear support, agreement in her expression.

When all was said and done, only Urias made the journey back to America. For now, at least. Kara had been surprised when Goibhniu asked her to take the Sidhe back. She suspected it was his way of pushing her to settle her mind. To choose his world or hers. As if those were the only options. At the same time, it was absolutely no surprise when Aí announced he was going with her.

An annoyance, but not a surprise.

She had to admit, Goibhniu was right, though. She'd needed to come home, at least once, to acknowledge what she would give up to follow some other path.

It was now dawn over New York City, vibrant and Technicolor; a sunrise in shades only a major megacity could boast, as the sun's rays refracted through the haze of pollution. They'd dropped Urias off at his east-side loft, and now Kara stood on the edge of a rooftop above Lincoln Center, Aí at her side. Both of them looked down at Alice Tully Hall, on whose stages Kara had performed countless times during her study at Julliard, where much of the woman she had become was shaped, if not precisely as her instructors had expected.

"How it must ache to have been so close, to nearly grasp yer dreams, yet having to turn from them."

The compassion in Aí's gaze forced Kara to look within and confront the truth buried in the depths of her heart. Who knew what was in store for her? The last few weeks had been harrowing, to say the least. Still, she knew her current course was more fitting to who she was than the path she'd been groomed to follow. She looked down on those venerated halls and sighed.

"I have no idea if it's the same in your world, or peculiar to mine, but there are two types of dreams we cling to," she told him as her eyes drifted upward to where she would have seen the endless stars, if not for the constant city lights. "There are those we nurture deep in our hearts, with roots so intertwined with what we are as a person that to betray that dream is to deny our own soul." Here Kara met his eye, one side of her mouth lifting wryly. "Then there's the type that we look out at from love-dazzled eyes and pull around us like a sweater we dutifully put on when we're told we should, never questioning if it will stifle us or leave us cold. It's sad…sometimes it is so hard to tell if it's your dream, or just a dream others have for you."

"What o' the difference then?" Aí asked. She couldn't tell if he were truly interested, or just sensed she needed to talk, to figure it out for herself so she could decide where life was taking her.

Kara thought hard about how to explain. Most humans couldn't even tell the difference between the two; otherwise they wouldn't be so tormented as a race. "One leaves you incomplete until you achieve it; the other is a constant drain on your soul even when you have it in your grasp."

"An' if 'tis the latter?"

"God bless you if you ever manage to find your true self again."

They sat quietly. Kara could almost see the rapid dance of Aí's thoughts as he integrated this new concept into his image of the human race. Let him puzzle over mankind as if it were a specimen in a jar, she could only be glad that he hadn't questioned of which type her own dreams had been. And yet, she found herself telling him anyway.

"Life used to be so simple…" Kara remained silent a moment, her amber eyes aglow as she looked out over the city. So much like herself. A hodgepodge of mingled elements. Familiar, yet filled with the unknown. "Only a few weeks ago, all I wanted was to play, to rest Quicksilver beneath my chin and set everything to music. Other than Papa's health, my biggest worry was how to pay the bills. Now…I have no idea what I want now, what life holds for me…"

Aí offered her a melancholy smile. "Welcome to my reality. Everyone's, for that matter. Did ye not ken… life's what happens when yer busy making plans?" His wry comment startled a laugh from her. It was brief, then she sobered.

"I don't fit here anymore," she said, startled by the dawning realization. "New York is not enough for me." She turned to look at her friend and felt her excitement tempered by the hope kindling in his gaze. "I wasn't really that upset to leave to begin with, so what would be accomplished by coming back?"

"So…ye'll come with me?"

Kara's heart ached. It was clear what he wanted. Aí had made no secret of where he'd like things to go between them, but that too was not right for her, at least not now, when she barely knew herself, let alone her heart. The awkward moment grew, and she watched his hope dim. After the conversation they'd just had, there was only one answer she could give. She would be traveling with him to *Tír na nÓg*, but that was only a transition, not her final destination. The smile she offered him was steeped in sorrow. "Not the way you hope. I'm sorry. Tell me it's cliché, but too much has happened for me to say yes or no to anything between us. Too much has changed. I have to figure out what that means to me before I make a pledge to you or anyone. I won't risk the wrong choice by being hasty. Bitterness takes a lot less time than forever to ripen."

His lips made an attempt at a smile. "Mine or yers?"

Before she had time to wonder if it was wise, she placed a hand on his arm. "Does it matter which?"

"More than it should," he admitted. "Bitterness is a familiar burden. I would gladly chance my own rather than say farewell to another love."

She gave him a hard stare foreign to her face only weeks before. "Too bad. Give me time or say goodbye, because I won't."

Aí flinched, and his jaw worked soundlessly a moment. Then he let out a breath that might have been half of a bittersweet laugh. For a moment, his head dropped, then he glanced up and away, eyes traversing the city as if looking for something that would sway her. He sighed and took a step back. "Where will ye go?"

Kara let her own gaze roam as she considered his question. It wasn't the city she saw before her, though, but a pair of deep brown eyes in a face that once had shot her through with terror. She had made good on her promise to Rose, technically, but Tony was still a prisoner to guilt and fear and half a dozen other corrosive emotions stemming from his time as Olcas's host. She knew the bite of those relentless feelings, how they damaged and shackled a person inside. Though he was no longer possessed, Kara knew the truth. He was as much a captive now as before Carmán's children were banished. Could she help him? Would he let her, or would he shun her attempt?

Did it matter? Either way, she would take the Rom up on their offer. More than honor, compassion would not allow her to do otherwise. She knew his demons, how to root them out, how to fight them. When he was ready, she would be also.

"I don't know…everywhere, I suspect," she finally answered with a little laugh, her voice already far off, even to herself. Phantom strains of "Free Bird" teased her ears. She smiled. Despite the heavy weight of her thoughts, she felt the first currents of pleasant excitement she'd experienced in quite some time. Worlds she'd never expected had opened to her. Old joys resurrected, new ones to be learned. Her heart raced at the thought of the literal road ahead of her. But first, she still had some obligations left to fulfill.

And yet another ceremony, one which she featured prominently. The Naming. It was time to let the Tuatha de Danaan that Anu's soul had finally returned in Kara herself, though she doubted her announcement would be well received by all.

When Aí reached for the torc around his neck to open a gate to take them home, she drew his hand away. He looked puzzled but did not object as she linked her fingers with his.

"Let's take the long way home," she said to him. Aí smiled.

Kara didn't know how Maggie had summoned the clouds when she'd taken them all to *Tír na nÓg*, but instinct was a soft voice whispering in her ear. Kara listened. Humming beneath her breath, she summoned a ribbon of magic, offering the end to the aerie ones hovering in eager anticipation nearby. The faelings went into a frenzy. Whether at the sudden influx of power or at the opportunity to do her a service, Kara could not say, though she suspected both. In short order, a plush white cloud hovered at the edge of the roof.

"Next stop, *Tír na nÓg*." She climbed aboard, tugging Aí after her.

EPILOGUE

It was the day of the Naming, as perfect as was to be expected Underhill, and yet it transcended any other Maggie could recall. The foes were vanquished, the souls of those stolen had been reclaimed, and today—though some would call her impure...waterkin—Kara was to be declared of the *Daoine Maithé*.

There was a sense of anticipation threading every breath, and some urge had Maggie wanting to dart a gaze around in search of what set this simple ceremony apart from the Namings that had come before. She restrained herself. Between the garb of the Court and the efforts of the faelings to fill the place with blossoms, the Hall was awash with beauty, sweet perfumes, and—mostly—a gentle, joyous murmur.

There was some dissent, but it was not voiced.

As sponsor, Maggie stood to one side of the dais with Beag Scath entwined about her neck. She kept a restraining hand upon him as they waited for the ceremony to begin. The *Fianna* were arrayed at her back as an honor guard.

The attention of the Court came back to the dais as Goibhniu stood from where he waited with the other *Sidhe* rulers. He moved to the center of the dais, the Great Wall rising in glory behind him, all traces of corruption banished, all souls once more linked in the eternal cycle.

It was a gratifying sight.

Waving Kara forward, he explained the purpose of the ritual about to take place. "When the People are o' an age to mingle with the world, they choose the name they will share with it," Goibhniu told her. "For ye, Kara, 'tis different. The name ye show the world was given ye, now ye must claim for yerself the private name by which ye will be known among the Kin. Have ye chosen?"

"I have," the girl responded, the words strong and serene.

"By what name shall the People ken ye?"

"I am Anu."

Though Kara spoke softly, Maggie had no doubt all those present heard her response.

The Hall went dead silent...still...tense. There were two names from their past that were never used. The first, Danu, for the Great Mother yet lived...and even if she hadn't, it would have been the ultimate conceit. The other, Anu. None had borne that name since the death of the savior. To even think of using either was the closest thing the *Sidhe* had to sacrilege.

Despite all that had transpired, some had objected to this Naming. They now surged forward, their outrage a palpable, roiling mass. Maggie stepped toward Kara, protectively, coming between her and the Court.

"Ye must choose another, *leanbh*," Maggie spoke as she placed her free hand on Kara's shoulder. "None may bear that name."

Slowly the girl turned, drawing Maggie's gaze as if with a glamour or compulsion. Somewhere along their journey, the softness of youth had fallen away, along with the rough edges of inexperience. In their place were the graceful lines of immortal strength and a dreadful knowing. Maggie gasped, and of its own accord, her left hand rose to brush Kara's hair away from her face, leaving the girl completely open to perusal.

"No, Cliodna," Kara answered with solemn precision. "I *am* Anu."

Maggie wasn't sure which overwhelmed her more: that this was the first ever Kara had called her by her true name, or that the girl's declaration rang with echoing truth. Sliding a nervous look toward the Smithgod, Maggie tried again, keeping her tone reasonable. "Ye do not understand, love, 'tis not possible."

With an admonishing tilt to her head, Kara pointed to the Great Wall where the very center flared, then faded as high on the Wall, on the other end of the spiral, a new pattern took shape. She quirked a weary smile and asked: "Since when has that stopped either one of us?"

That response startled a laugh out of Goibhniu and no few others among those witnessing the ceremony. Maggie barely noticed, her attention captured by the truth she could not deny. She was so shocked she lost her grip on the sprite, who promptly climbed to Kara's shoulder.

"Mother Goddess! How can this be?" Maggie asked, not really expecting an answer.

Even if she cared to, she could not deny what she saw when she met Kara's gaze. Maggie had to search hard for the young, uncertain Kara that had once walked into Yesterday's Dreams.

What she found was only a memory. That which stood before her was a woman, wholly *Sidhe*. A part of Maggie mourned the loss, particularly when the deep amber pools of Kara's eyes flashed, and she drew herself up full and proud. The reaction was familiar in this Court. Irrefutable. Regal and confident and knowing. Some would call it arrogant. And yet, swirling around the weightiness of that immortal soul was a sparkle, undeniable and fresh. Maggie felt contentment come over her. Kara was not changed, her humanity not lost; she had merely discovered unplumbed depths of self none of them had suspected went so deep.

As if there had been no question, no doubt, Goibhniu smiled, a satisfied gleam in his eyes. "Turn and be recognized, Anu o' the Daoine Maithé," he told her.

There were gasps of outrage—quickly quelled—and not a few stunned expressions as Kara stepped from behind the shield of Maggie's body. Beag Scath lounged across the woman's shoulders, from one side to the other, draped artfully in Anu's fiery red tresses. One minuscule hand snaked out and flipped the Court the bird and half a dozen other rude gestures Maggie hadn't any idea he'd known. The gestures were very clearly aimed at deserving parties…by the set of their features, members of the Court most ready to protest. As those expressions soured further, it was clear the message wasn't missed…or appreciated. Any protests were silenced by stern glowers from the rulers on the dais. Beag Scath chortled and withdrew into the mass of hair until he was all but unseen, reaching out only his hand to tug a curl or toss another gesture. When he peeked out from the curls in back to wink at her, Maggie nearly lost it, fighting to smother a laugh as the pair walked to the edge of the dais and stopped. And yet even the sprite's antics were insufficient to distract her from this momentous occasion.

This is going to turn the Courts on their ears, she thought with unexpected glee. *And about time too, before we molder under the complacency was weighing most o' us down.*

Briefly, Kar…*Anu*, glanced back, the barest glimmer of uncertainty in her gaze. Maggie nodded in encouragement and smiled, offering no further protest as the newly named Anu turned to scan the Court. Stepping back into her place by the *Fianna*, Maggie waited to hear what she would say.

"Some of you do not care for me. Do not approve of me. Do not believe I belong among you." Each word had a bite backed by hard-won strength. "Some of you are outraged at my choice." Pausing a moment, Kara swept a now-calm gaze over the Court. "So be it. But know, you, I do not particularly care. I am Anu, and this is my place. I am not she whose name I rightly take, any more than you are the one whose soul became you, but she has been a long time in returning to the *Daoine Maithé* and however you feel about the matter, she deserves for her name to live again in more than memory, even as her soul does."

And with that, the ceremony was most certainly done.

With a respectful bow in the direction of Goibhniu and the other rulers of the *Sidhe* Lands, Anu left the dais and, with eternal grace, strode from the Hall. Waiting for her at the arch was the Romani woman, Sveta, and Maggie relaxed as she realized her friend had found her balance, her place.

When cries of "Anu!" were raised, Maggie knew the *Daoine Maithé* had likewise grown through adversity.

Tony DeLocosta was no longer a boy. He'd never been an angel.

He was a man, a scarred and broken man. A prisoner within himself. No amount of magic could heal a victim's soul overnight.

Kara knew this intimately.

Tony had not even begun to recover from his ordeal, in many ways much worse than anything Kara had suffered at Olcas's hand. He would need help. Loved ones surrounding him, familiar, everyday tasks to distract him, someone who knew the path out of the darkness to show him the way. Someone who understood the silences, the brooding, the bleak hopelessness, the sudden lashing out...

And after all that, he'd need someone to teach him, for Tony was also mage born.

Right now, all he had was her. That wasn't working out well for either of them. While she had walked his path and understood, she also fed his shame.

She still slept in Sveta's vardo but had taken to traveling in Tony's wagon when the caravan hit the road. It had been almost a week. They barely spoke. Hell, Tony would scarcely even acknowledge her or anyone else. When she did manage to catch his eye, his gaze swam with guilt and quickly darted away.

Kara watched him now from the front of the wagon. He perched on the back ledge, one long leg dangling outside the window, the other knee bent, with his foot flat on the ledge. Months ago, she had watched another Rom sit thus, confident but alert, balanced; Tony sat in a fog, carelessly, as if he didn't care about—or likely even perceive—the potential for injury...or worse.

Or did he tempt death?

Kara closed her eyes briefly against that thought. At one time, she would have gladly helped him find it. Even now, her emotions twisted and swirled like a tempest within her, clashing with reason. Though she knew that Olcas had controlled his hand, hatred lingered in her heart for Tony's face, which she could not separate from the memories of her torture and subsequent curse. The face Olcas had doomed her to see on every man she'd looked on *after*—and feel his touch—until Rose had broken the spell. And yet, Kara felt compassion for Tony's warm brown eyes—different from Olcas's cold, icy blue—which she'd yet to see steeped in anything except confusion or torment. Somehow, despite all that, beyond any comprehension, a seed of friendship had taken root. Both New Yorkers, both victims of the same evil force. Both freed yet still fighting demons. It pained her to think of Tony wishing for death...passively seeking it, even.

While Kara wasn't completely comfortable with this Romani man, she would not condemn him for deeds she knew were not his. Perhaps she could not heal him, but she could show him the way out of the deep dark hole swallowing him up. And then, she would be free to follow wherever her heart led.

Rising from the bench where she'd been staring out a side window, Kara reached into the cupboard for Quicksilver. The latch *snick*ed as she closed and secured the door. Tony did not even tense, let alone look back in reaction to the sound. Keeping her motions relaxed and easy, Kara made her way to his side, nudging his perched leg into the wagon under the pretext of joining him on the ledge. She kept both legs planted on the floor and canted her body so that she faced her companion. Firmly settled, she removed the violin from its case. Her soul brushed briefly against its other half but did not engage the essence of the goddess Danu. Kara tuned Quicksilver and brought the violin into position beneath her chin. She laid bow to strings and let the music and magic loose on the breeze, not guiding either, but letting them flow freely from tune to familiar tune as a spiritual balm. Though he did not acknowledge her presence…did not, in fact, even bring his eyes off the road scrolling out beneath the wagon's wheels…Tony subtly relaxed, his foot tapping softly in rhythm to her song.

And thus, with the smallest step, their shared journey to healing began.

GLOSSARY

Anu: In Celtic lore, an alternate name for the goddess Danu, from whom the *Tuatha de Danaan* took their name. The names are used interchangeably throughout the mythology, though there is some debate as to whether these were one and the same goddess, or two separate ones. In the author's fabricated legend of Danu's time before arriving in Ireland, Anu is not a variant on the name Danu but a person in her own right, Danu's older twin. For the purpose of this fiction Anu sacrifices herself to allow Danu to escape the clutches of the Namhaid, the enemy. In reverence Danu uses both names after the crossing to Ireland, ensuring that her beloved sister will ever be remembered (thus explaining the presence of both names in the actual Celtic mythology and Irish place-names). In the author's created mythology to allow her sister to escape the *Namhaid,* Anu uses magic and her own soul to create the lesser fae creatures of the world. Because of this her soul was not lost when she was taken by the *Namhaid,* but it also could not return to the *Daoine Maithé* after her death because only her body died. As the faelings died, parts of her soul gathered and were ultimately channeled into a human birth through Danu's intervention to preserve the babe, which would have been lost, and to bring Anu back into the world. The child born, Kara O'Keefe, is a melding of both human and *Sidhe,* but without the drawbacks of being a Halfling. Through Anu's soul, she is linked to the faelings and the portion of the soul they still possess.

Ard Namhaid: a combination of the Irish Gaelic words for High (Ard) and enemy (*Namhaid*). These are a fictitious caste of a race created by the author to explain several key points in Celtic myth of which no details are known. The Ard are all male and dominate the *Namhaid.* In appearance, they are similar to the *Namhaid Conairt* (the female of the species), with a fine, velvety white pelt and dagger-like teeth in a blood-red mouth, however, their hair and eyes are deepest black, whereas the females' hair and eyes are red. Also, though their hands are likewise clawed, they are nowhere as pronounced as those of the *Namhaid Conairt. (See also Bás; Namhaid Conairt.)*

Ar Carmán…Scrios…Tógail…Díoltas…: Irish Gaelic for "For Carmán…Havoc… Destruction…Revenge." For the purpose of this story, the battle cry of Carmán's children.

Ard Ri: Irish Gaelic for "High King."

Bás: Irish Gaelic for Death. In the author's created mythology, this is the name the *Namhaid,* the ancient enemy race of the *Sidhe,* have for themselves. In *Tomorrow's Memories,* they are given the name *Namhaid* na Tuatha by Goibhniu, which translates to Enemy of the People.

Beag Scath: A combination of the Irish Gaelic words meaning Little (beag) and Shadow (scath). The name Maggie gave the sprite that became emotionally attached to her long ago in Eire.

Bean Fianna: For the purpose of this story, the women warriors of the *Sidhe Fianna.*

Bean Sidhe: translating into woman of the hills, the *Bean Sidhe,* or banshee, is a faerie harbinger of death. Appearing as a woman in a green dress and grey cloak, with eyes fiery red from weeping, she is seen scrubbing bloody garments in a stream, or heard wailing outside a household where a family member is doomed to die. If the *Bean Sidhe* is caught, she must relinquish the name of the doomed. When multiple *Bean Sidhe* wail together they are heralding the death of a great or holy person. Cliodna, the goddess of beauty, is *Bean Sidhe* to the Clan O'Keefe.

Brian Boru: (960-1014) The last High King, or *Ard Ri,* of Ireland. He defended Ireland against the attacks of the Vikings and ended that race's hopes of ever taking the island.

Camlo: Romani for "lovely one."

Carmán: An Athenian goddess (possibly rooted in the Greek goddess Demeter) who, with her three sons: Calma (Valiant), Dubh (Black), and Olcas (Evil), terrorized early Ireland. They were eventually defeated by the *Tuatha de Danaan.* She was bound in chains and her three sons destroyed. It is said Carmán died of grief. Carmán is also portrayed as a goddess of black magick, destroying anything by chanting a spell three times. (There are several different accountings of the names of the goddess's sons, but for the purpose of this series the author has chosen to adhere to those names listed in the first accounting of this legend that was encountered during the research phase.)

The Cosaint: Irish Gaelic for safeguard. A legend of the author's creation, developed to support her extrapolation of why the *Sidhe* are called *Tuatha de Danaan* (The Children of Danu). The *Cosaint* is a *Sidhe* woman hidden at birth so that not even she knows what she is. Raised as a human, she is meant to be a safeguard against the *Sidhe* race being destroyed without a means of the souls returning to the earth, as nearly happened in the author's fabricated tale when Danu herself was the last of her kind and had to hide from the *Namhaid*.

Cúchulainn (the Hound of Culann): One of the most famous heroes in Irish mythology. Originally called Sétanta, Cúchulainn got his name from defending himself and slaying the hound that defended the fortress of Culann, after which he vowed to defend the fortress himself until a new hound could be found and trained, thus becoming known as the Hound of Culann. Though his achievements are many, he is chiefly known for his single-handed defense of Ulster during the war of the Táin.

Cuimhnigh: Irish Gaelic for "remember". For the purpose of this story Goibhniu, the Smithgod, has used this word, along with a touch at three key points on the *Cosaint's* person, to release the hidden memories of her true nature.

Curragh of Kildare: The place where Earl Gerald is said to ride his horse around every seven years. To this day the region is known for the horse racing that takes place there.

Danu: In Irish Celtic mythology, the goddess from whom the *Tuatha de Danaan* took their name; for the purpose of this story, the birth mother of every *Sidhe* born in Ireland. The sole survivor of a concerted attack on the *Sidhe* in their homelands, she alone remained to give birth to the *Sidhe* souls returning for their next incarnation.

Daoine Maithé: Irish Gaelic for "Good People", one of the names by which the *Sidhe* are called. In the author's created mythology, this is also the name by which the *Sidhe* originally called themselves, before coming to Ireland and becoming the *Tuatha de Danaan*.

Dearmad: Irish Gaelic for "forget."

Díoltas: Irish Gaelic for "Revenge". In the author's created mythology this is also the name of a muse who inspires and instigates revenge, a minion of Calma.

Eire: The original name for Ireland.

Elf-kin: the author's term for those of mixed *Sidhe* and human parentage, the non-derogatory term for waterkin.

Falias, Finias, Gorias, and Murias: Four great cities said to be the former home of the *Tuatha de Danaan,* before they arrived in Ireland. Nothing more specific is mentioned of their original homeland. Each city contained a magical artifact that the *Tuatha de Danaan* carried with them to Ireland.

Faelings: a term encompassing the "lesser" fae of mythology. In the author's usage it represents the more wild, natural fae such as the pixies, sprites, etc. Also called by the author the kin-cousins to denote that they are related to the Sidhe, but not of them. These are Anu's Children, created and sent out in the world to muddy the trail so that Danu could escape from the *Namhaid.*

Fear Fianna: For the purpose of this story, the men warriors of the *Sidhe Fianna.*

Fianna: In Ireland's far past these were the warriors who were the royal bodyguard for the *Ard Ri,* the High King. (*See also, Sidhe Fianna*)

Fionn Mac Cumhail (Finn Mac Cool): One of the most celebrated heroes in Irish myth. Born Demna, he gained the name of Fionn (the Fair One) when he burnt his finger on the flesh of the Salmon of Knowledge, which he was cooking for his master. Sucking his thumb to cool it, he obtained wisdom from the magical fish. He went on to become leader of the *Fianna,* the royal bodyguard. His wife was the goddess Sadb, who was originally transformed into a fawn by a spurned Druid, who eventually whisks away and transforms her back into a fawn again while she is pregnant with Fionn's son. Fionn never found his wife, but his son, whom he named Oisín (fawn), eventually was discovered and came to be with him.

Fledh Ghoibhnenn: The Otherworld feast held by the Smithgod Goibhniu. Any mortal to take part in the feast and the drink served becomes immortal.

Garda Faoi Rún: A combination of the Irish Gaelic words Garda (guard) and Faoi Rún (in secret). The name given to the sprite answering to Aí, left with Agnieszka to look over her until she could be brought to safety. Also called Rex by Agnieszka.

Geal leanbh: Irish Gaelic for "cherished child."

Geal leannán: Irish Gaelic for "cherished lover."

Gearoidh Iarla (Earl Gerard): A great man of the Fitzgeralds, he had a rath (fortress) at Mullaghmast. He was known for standing against injustice and for his abilities to transform himself into any form. It is said that he and his warriors now sleep in a long cavern under the Rath of Mullaghmast. Every seven years the Earl rides around the Curragh of Kildare on a white steed with silver-shod hooves. At a time when those hooves are worn thin as a cat's ear, the miller's son with six fingers to each hand will blow his trumpet to wake the warriors and *Gearoidh Iarla* will return to the land of the living. He will defend Ireland against their enemies, and reign as Ireland's king for two-score years, or seventy times seven, depending on the account.

The Gentry: One of the names given to the *Sidhe* by the common folk so that they could be referred to without invoking their name or drawing their uncomfortable attention.

Glamory: A spell to make whatever the caster wishes — himself, an object, or another person — appear other than it really is.

Goibhniu the Smith: An Irish/Celtic blacksmith god. Son of the goddess Danu. He manufactures swords that always strike true, and he possesses the mead (ale) of eternal life. He is also considered the god of healing due to the role of iron in Celtic life and the magical properties it is said to have. Goibhniu presides over an Otherworld feast (*Fledh Ghoibhnenn*) where any mortal to take part becomes immortal; exempt from common death and disease. In some accounts, this is attributed to the food, and in most others it is attributed to the ale or mead given to drink at the Feast.

Gorgio: In England, the term the Romani use for non-Romani folk.

Grimoires: ancient, mystical texts, usually full of dark occult knowledge. These texts contain the spells and references that represent painstaking research and experimentation, often of the dark arts, though the term has come to imply any book of spells, be they Black or White magic.

Hounds (Celtic): well respected by royalty and warriors. Symbols of honor. The name was assumed as a title of loyalty and courage. They were the traditional guardians of roads and crossroads, protecting and guiding lost souls to the Otherworld. For the purpose of this story, a reference to Aí Goibhniu's messenger and Hound. He is sent to safeguard the *Cosaint*s in *Tomorrow's Memories,* and to rescue the souls of the *Namhaid*'s victims in *Today's Promise.* He is not the only one sent out on these tasks.

If Thine Eye: Mark 9:47 (King James Edition) — "And if thine eye offends thee, pluck it out: it is better for thee to enter into the kingdom of God with one eye, than having two eyes to be cast into hell fire."

Leanbh: Irish Gaelic for "child."

Leprechaun: In Irish Celtic Mythology a diminutive member of the fairy folk known for making shoes, but only one at a time, never in pairs.

Lhiannon: Irish Gaelic for "Sweetheart."

Mamó: Irish Gaelic for "Grandma."

Manannan Mac Lir: Ruler of *Tír Tairnigiri* (the Land of Promise). A shape-changer, he is depicted with a mantle and helmet of invisibility (or flames), and an unfailing sword. He was also attributed with bringing fertility and prosperity and was associated with the cauldron of regeneration.

Mathair: Irish Gaelic for "Mother."

The Miller's Son: It is said in the legend of Gearoidh Iarla, that the miller's son, who will be born with six fingers on each hand, will blow his trumpet and wake those who sleep beneath the Rath of Mullaghmast.

Múscailt: Irish Gaelic for "awaken." The trigger word to cancel the spell keeping Agnieszka asleep.

Namhaid: Irish Gaelic for "enemy." A fictitious race created by the author, they are the reason why the people who would come to be known as the *Sidhe* flee their original homes in Falias, Finias, Gorias, and Murias. The Enemy slays all but one of the *Sidhe*, a young elf named Danu. She escapes and flees to Ireland, there to bear her children, who from that day forward are known by the name *Tuatha de Danaan*, or the Children (People) of Danu. In Tomorrow's Memories, Goibhniu calls them by the name *Namhaid* na Tuatha, which translates to Enemy of the People.

The Namhaid Conairt: a combination of the Irish Gaelic words for "enemy" (*Namhaid*) and "pack" (Conairt). As created by the author, these are the hunter caste of the *Namhaid* (or the *Bás*, as they call themselves) responsible for hunting down the elves and either capturing or killing them. They are all female, with a fine, velvety white pelt and flowing deep, red hair. Their eyes are likewise red, and their teeth like dainty daggers in their blood-red mouths. Each hand is clawed with dagger-like nails, while those on the feet are blunted from running and capable of gouging, not slicing. The Conairt do not eat when they are breeding and they do not bear their own young. When they mate, the sperm and eggs are stored in a sack at the base of the spine. Once a suitable host is found, the eggs are extruded through a barb that extends like a retractable tail from the female. Jabbed into the body of the victim, the eggs are seated in the abdomen. The individual so implanted is for all intents and purposes dead as a chemical injected with the sack inhibits the thought centers of the brain, allowing only the autonomous impulses to operate, and those only barely.

Olcas: Irish Gaelic for "evil." This is also the name of one of the three sons of the Athenian goddess Carmán.

Pixie: In Irish Celtic Mythology, a cheerful and mischievous fairy that adores music and dancing.

Pucá (Pooka): in Irish Celtic mythology, a fey creature that leads travelers astray and performed other mischievous deeds. By some accounts, it appears in the likeness of a fierce black steed that will pull the unwary onto his back run away with them through river and fen, not shaking them off until the grey of dawn.

Rath: A fortress or earthwork, usually circular, surrounding a chieftain's house. This has also come to mean the hills where the *Tuatha de Danaan* retreated beneath after their defeat by the Milesians.

Rath o' Mullaghmast: The hill beneath which Gearoidh Iarla (Earl Gerald) is said to sleep. This is where legend says the miller's son will blow his trumpet.

Redcap: in Irish Celtic mythology, a fairy known by his red hat and bloodthirsty ways.

The Rom, The Romani: These are the nomadic gypsies most common in Europe but found in one form or another all around the world. They are known occasionally to settle, though they do not lose their Romani ways.

The Royal Ulster Constabulary (RUC): the police force in Northern Ireland. Originally over 90% Protestant, this has been a major focus of reform.

Scrios: Irish Gaelic for "Havoc," in the author's created mythology this is also the name of a muse that instigates and inspires havoc. A minion of Calma.

Selkie: In Irish Celtic mythology, a creature of seal-like appearance that, when it sheds its pelt, assumes the likeness of a human. It is said that if anyone captures the shed pelt and hides it away, the selkie will remain with them forever as their mate, but should the selkie find the hidden skin, it will return once more to the sea.

The Sidhe: Pronounced "shee," the Fair Folk, Otherworldly beings that came to live in Ireland in the time before it was invaded by the Milesians. After their defeat, they were banished underground, living in mounds, also called *Sidhe.* They were said to be very long-lived, if not immortal, and possessing of mystical powers. (*See also,* Daoine Maithé, The Gentry, *Tuatha de Danaan*)

The Sidhe Fianna: The author's created mythology for the purpose of this book. First seen in *Tomorrow's Memories,* a group of warriors selected by Goibhniu the Smithgod to combat the assaults being perpetrated against the *Sidhe* in this series. There are two groups of the *Sidhe Fianna:* the *Bean Fianna,* or warrior women, and the *Fear Fianna,* the warrior men.

Sowlth/Somhlth: In Irish Celtic mythology, a supernatural being without shape. Refers — for this series only — to Carmán's sons, who, for the author's purposes, were not destroyed but merely disembodied.

Sprite: Spirit faerie. Very creative, sprites are often depicted as muses, artists, and poets. They are some of the most creative fairies and may even decide to bond with a human or *Sidhe* and stay with them their whole lives.

Tír na mBan: The Land of Women/Land of the Maidens. Part of the Irish Celtic Otherworld, the land ruled by Balor of the Fomorian giants.

Tír na nÓg: The Land of Youth. Part of the Irish Celtic Otherworld, this is where Goibhniu presides over the *Fledh Ghoibhnenn.*

Tír Tairnigiri: The Land of Promise. Part of the Irish Celtic Otherworld, this is where Manannan Mac Lir, the major sea-god, held his seat of power.

Tógail: Irish Gaelic for "Destruction." In the author's created mythology, this is also the name of a muse that instigates and inspires destruction. A minion of Calma.

Tuatha de Danaan: The Children of Danu, also translated in other texts as the People of Danu, another name for the *Sidhe,* said to be blessed by the goddess Danu, also called Anu or Danaa. The alternate, more common spelling is *Tuatha de Danann,* but as the version used was the first one the author encountered in her research, that is the one that appears in this series.

Mar aon ó thús, mar aon go deo: Irish Gaelic an idiom meaning "As one from the beginning, as one forever." (A big thank you to Mary Kinsella for this phrasing and translation.)

The Unraveling: In the author's created mythology, this is a ritual by which the *Sidhe* banish one of their own for crimes too heinous to ignore. To all effects, they never existed and their soul, should they die, will never be reborn as a member of the *Sidhe* race. The banished one's soul is literally cut away from the racial collective. This collective has a visual representation in the form of a massive, interlocking knotwork design on the Great Wall, located in Goibhniu's Court in *Tír na nÓg.* Using a ritual dagger, each living *Sidhe* must trace the knotwork pattern representing the banished one's life. When all have done so the soul's connection is severed. This also means the individual will no longer be able to enter the *Sidhe* Lands.

Waterkin: a term originating with the author to describe those of mixed blood, with both a *Sidhe* and human parent. It is originally a condescending term referring to the fact that the *Sidhe* blood has been diluted…watered down, thus less than the original, though repeated use has reduced it to merely an identifier. The more friendly term is elf-kin.

The Welcoming: In the author's created mythology, this is a ritual that is performed when one of the *Tuatha de Danaan* is pregnant. The *Sidhe* have a finite number of souls. Those souls are reborn as their decedents (this is extrapolated from elements of actual Celtic beliefs on reincarnation). Before a child is born the soul must first strip away the memories of the former life. Through the ritual, the *Sidhe* who knew the individual who has passed help the soul shed its memories. All gather in a special glade. Those pregnant with the returning souls gather at the center of the glade and magical mists form a column around them. As they share the memories they have of the deceased, which appear on the column, the watching crowd shares theirs as well and the memory is released by the soul. While a soul will be reborn without this assistance, the time it takes would be longer without this mass purging.

Sources

PRINT RESOURCES

- Ellis, Peter Berresford, *A Dictionary of Irish Mythology*. (Santa Barbara, CA: ABC-CLIO, Inc, 1987.)
- *Ireland: The Complete Guide and Road Atlas*, 7th ed. (Guilford, CT: The Globe Pequot Press, 2002.)
- Kelly, Sean and Rosemary Rogers, *Saint Preserve Us!* (New York: Random House, 1993.)
- Mac Mathúna, Séamus and Ailbhe Ó Curráin, *Collins Gem: Irish Dictionary*. (New York: HarperCollins Publishers, 1995).
- Rolleston, T. W., *Celtic Myths and Legends*. (Mineola, NY: Dover, 1990.)
- Tong, Diane, *Gypsy Folk Tales*. (New York: MJF Books, 1989.)
- Yeats, W. B., *Irish Fairy & Folk Tales*. (New York: Barnes & Noble Books, 1993.)

INTERNET RESOURCES

Celtic Myth
- http://www.alia.ie/tirnanog/myth1.html
- http://www.livingmyths.com/Celticmyth.htm
- http://www.celticattic.com/olde_world/myths/fairy.htm
- http://www.ladywoods.org/roots4.htm
- http://www.seanachaidh.com/godcelt.html
- http://magickwell.20m.com/danu.htm
- http://www.danann.org/library/herb/cup2.html
- http://joellessacredgrove.com/Celtic/deitiesg-h-i.html
- http://www.deoxy.org/h_mounds.htm

Romani
- http://www.romani.org/
- http://www.christusrex.org/www2/gypsies.net/
- http://www.herts.ac.uk/UHPress/Gypsies.html

Miscellaneous
* http://www.peevish.co.uk/slang/search.htm

About the Author

Award-winning author and editor Danielle Ackley-McPhail has worked both sides of the publishing industry for longer than she cares to admit. In 2014 she joined forces with husband Mike McPhail and friend Greg Schauer to form her own publishing house, eSpec Books.

Her published works include six novels, *Yesterday's Dreams, Tomorrow's Memories, Today's Promise, The Halfling's Court, The Redcaps' Queen*, and *Baba Ali and the Clockwork Djinn*, written with Day Al-Mohamed. She is also the author of the solo collections *Eternal Wanderings, A Legacy of Stars, Consigned to the Sea, Flash in the Can, Transcendence, Between Darkness and Light*, and the non-fiction writers' guide, *The Literary Handyman*, and is the senior editor of the *Bad-Ass Faeries* anthology series, *Gaslight & Grimm, Side of Good/Side of Evil, After Punk*, and *In an Iron Cage*. Her short stories are included in numerous other anthologies and collections.

In addition to her literary acclaim, she crafts and sells original costume horns under the moniker The Hornie Lady, and homemade flavor-infused candied ginger under the brand of Ginger KICK! at literary conventions, on commission, and wholesale.

Danielle lives in New Jersey with husband and fellow writer, Mike McPhail, and three extremely spoiled cats. To learn more about her work, visit www.*Sidhenadaire*.com or www.especbooks.com.

9 781942 990598